Praise for the Kate Bu

"A pulse-pounding Amish thriller (really!) that's all too relevant to our time."

—*Kirkus Reviews* (starred review) on *Outsider*

"[A] fast-paced, suspense-building ride, showing the character development and sensitivity to the Amish culture that mark Castillo's masterful crime fiction."

—*Booklist* (starred review) on *Outsider*

"Bestseller Castillo's suspenseful twelfth Kate Burkholder mystery . . . Castillo presents a loving, realistic portrait of Amish life. Readers will hope Kate has a long career."

—*Publishers Weekly* on *Outsider*

"Swiftly paced . . . Castillo again captures Kate's empathic understanding of Amish culture and Deitsch, and adds atmosphere with falling-down, peeling-paint, rural settings. If they haven't already, readers looking for a fierce-female-fronted procedural should check out Castillo's bestselling series from the get-go."

—*Booklist* on *Shamed*

"The tension mounts [to] a gripping conclusion . . . another violent, fascinating story."

—*Library Journal* on *Shamed*

"Electrifying . . . more than one twist propels the plot to its dramatic conclusion . . . a morally complex tale."

—*Publishers Weekly* on *Shamed*

"A captivating story by a gifted storyteller."

—*The Washington BookReview* on *A Gathering of Secrets*

"An atmospheric thriller about fear, revenge, and the dark side of Amish life . . . Linda Castillo is a true master of suspenseful police procedurals."
—*Bustle* on *A Gathering of Secrets*

"Magnetic."
—*People* on *A Gathering of Secrets*

"Exquisitely plotted . . . a standout in a stellar series."
—Associated Press on *A Gathering of Secrets*

"Castillo weaves the particularities of the Amish mindset into a complex mystery that will leave you crying with pity or seething with rage."
—*Kirkus Reviews* (starred review) on *Down a Dark Road*

"Thrilling . . . Castillo skillfully sets each scene, compelling readers to fear the raging stream, sense the tension in a room."
—*Publishers Weekly* on *Down a Dark Road*

"A first-rate and very unusual thriller; Castillo builds suspense brilliantly, using both the snowbound setting and the difficulty of working as an undercover Amish woman to great advantage."
—*Booklist* on *Among the Wicked*

"[An] incisive and affecting series."
—*Richmond Times-Dispatch* on *Among the Wicked*

"Murder in Amish country has a certain added frisson, and Castillo's the master of the genre."
—*People* on *The Dead Will Tell*

ALSO BY LINDA CASTILLO

Sworn to Silence

Pray for Silence

Breaking Silence

Gone Missing

Her Last Breath

The Dead Will Tell

After the Storm

Among the Wicked

Down a Dark Road

A Gathering of Secrets

Shamed

A Simple Murder (Story Collection)

OUTSIDER

A KATE BURKHOLDER NOVEL

Linda Castillo

MINOTAUR
BOOKS
NEW YORK

Published in the United States by Minotaur Books, an imprint of St. Martin's Publishing Group

www.minotaurbooks.com

Designed by Omar Chapa

The Library of Congress has cataloged the hardcover edition as follows:

Names: Castillo, Linda, author.
Title: Outsider / Linda Castillo.
Description: First edition. | New York: Minotaur Books, 2020. |
Series: A Kate Burkholder novel; 12
Identifiers: LCCN 2020009587 | ISBN 9781250142894 (hardcover) |
ISBN 9781250780782 (signed edition) | ISBN 9781250142917 (ebook)
Subjects: LCSH: Burkholder, Kate (Fictitious character)—Fiction. |
Women police chiefs—Fiction. | Amish—Fiction. | BISAC: FICTION /
Mystery & Detective / Police Procedural. | GSAFD: Mystery fiction. |
Suspense fiction.
Classification: LCC PS3603.A8758 O88 2020 | DDC 813/.6—dc23
LC record available at https://lccn.loc.gov/2020009587

ISBN 978-1-250-79629-5 (trade paperback)

First Minotaur Books Trade Paperback Edition: 2021

10 9 8 7 6 5 4 3 2 1

With every book, I learn something new about the Amish culture—the traditions, the religion, the history of the Anabaptists, and the challenges they face. My respect and admiration for them grow with every book. This one is dedicated to you—all of the Amish who've taken the time talk to me, have lunch with me, or invited me into your homes. Thank you for helping me better understand your ways, giving me a deeper perspective and a peek into your lives.

ACKNOWLEDGMENTS

Outsider is the twelfth book in the Kate Burkholder Amish mystery series. I like to think that after so many books I've gotten pretty good at what I do, but the process never gets any easier. I'm incredibly lucky to have so many dedicated people to support me along the way. I owe a heartfelt thank-you to my wonderfully talented and insightful editor, Charles Spicer. You are the best, Charlie, and I think the world of you. I'd also like to thank my amazing agent, Nancy Yost, who is always there with her ever-smart advice and guidance. You make me smile (even when I shouldn't). With this book in particular, I also owe a special thank-you to Jennifer Enderlin, for your creative ideas, your faith in the story and characters—and me. Extending a huge thank-you to my publicist, Sarah Melnyk. You are the best of the best, Sarah! You're always there for me, always ready for a new adventure, and you make it so much fun. Cheers! I'd also like to thank the rest of my publishing family at Minotaur Books: Sally Richardson. Andrew Martin. Kerry Nordling. Paul Hochman. Allison Ziegler. Kelley Ragland. Sarah Grill. David Rotstein. Marta Ficke. Martin Quinn. Joseph Brosnan. Lisa Davis. I'm seriously lucky to have all of you so squarely in my corner.

AUTHOR'S NOTE

I took much literary license when depicting some of the law enforcement agencies in the novel. The Columbus Division of Police is a top-notch agency administered by consummate professionals who are very good at what they do. I embellished liberally to get the story right. All mischaracterizations are fictional. Any procedural errors are mine.

OUTSIDER

PROLOGUE

She'd always known they would come for her. She knew when they did that it would be violent and fast and happen in the dead of night. Despite all the training, the mental and physical preparation, she'd also known that when the time came, she wouldn't be ready.

She wasn't sure what woke her. Some barely discernible noise outside the front door. The scuff of a boot against a concrete step. The clunk of a car door as it was quietly closed. The crunch of snow beneath a leather sole. Or maybe it was that change in the air, like the energy of a static charge an instant before a lightning strike.

She rolled from her bed, senses clicking into place. Her feet hit the floor an instant before the front door burst inward. She smacked her hand down on the night table, snatched up the Sig Sauer P320 Nitron, seventeen plus one of lifesaving lead. In the living room, a dozen feet thudded against the hardwood floor.

A cacophony of shouted voices rang out. "Police Department! Get on the floor! Hands above your head! Do it now!"

Two strides and she was across the room. She slammed her bedroom door shut, slapped the lock into place. Spinning, she yanked her jacket off a chair back; she jammed one arm into the sleeve, covered her head and shoulders, and sprinted to the window. Without slowing, she bent low and dove. An instant of resistance as she went through. The sound of snapping wood and shattering glass. The pain of a dozen razor cuts.

The ground rushed up, plowed into her shoulder. Breath knocked from her lungs. Snow on her face, down her collar, in her mouth. Spitting, she barrel-rolled and scrambled to her feet, kept moving. Keeping low, every sense honed on her surroundings. She stuck to The Plan, the one she'd lived a thousand times in the last days, and she sprinted to the hedge that grew along the chain-link fence. Around her, snow floated down from a starless sky. A glance over her shoulder told her there were vehicles parked on the street, no lights. Typical no-knock warrant. Or was it?

She was midway to the alley at the back of her property when she spotted a silhouette in the side yard, thirty feet away, moving toward her fast, equipment jingling. "Halt! Police Department! Stop!"

In an instant she noticed a hundred details. The big man dressed in black. POLICE emblazoned on his jacket. The nine-millimeter Beretta leveled at her, center mass.

"Show me your hands! Get on the ground!" Crouched in a shooter's stance, he motioned with his left hand. "On the ground! Now! Get down!"

She swung toward him, raised the Sig. Simultaneously, recognition kicked. He was a rookie. Young. A good kid. She murmured his name, felt the knowledge of the decision she was about to make cut her and go deep. "Don't," she whispered.

His weapon flashed and the round slammed into her shoulder. Impact like a baseball bat, the momentum spinning her. Pain zinged, a red-hot poker shoved through bone marrow from clavicle to biceps. An animalistic sound tore from her throat as she went down on one knee.

Get up. Get up. Get up.

Out of the corner of her eye she saw him step back, lower his weapon. He went still, looked at her for a too-long beat. "Drop the weapon! Get on the ground! For God's sake, it's over." Then he was shouting into his lapel mike.

She launched herself to her feet, flew across the remaining stretch of yard, her feet not seeming to touch the ground. A volley of shots thundered as she vaulted the chain-link fence, pain snarling through her body. All the while she imagined a bullet slamming into her back.

Then she was in the alley. No police lights. No movement as she darted across the narrow span of asphalt. Heart pumping pure adrenaline, she hurdled the fence, entered her neighbor's backyard, stumbled to the garage door. She twisted the knob, flung the door open, lurched inside, slammed it behind her. Breaths hissing through clenched teeth, she rushed to the truck, yanked open the door, and threw herself onto the seat, trying desperately to ignore the pain screaming in her shoulder, the knowledge that she was badly injured, and the little voice telling her The Plan wasn't going to work.

Her hands shook as she fished out the key, stabbed it into the ignition, turned it. She jammed the vehicle into reverse, stomped the gas pedal. The pickup truck shot backward. A tremendous *crunch!* sounded as the bumper and bed tore the garage door from its track. The metal folded over the tailgate and was pushed into the alley, crushed beneath her rear tires.

She cut the steering wheel hard. Red lights in her rearview mirror. Twisting in the seat, she raised the Sig and fired six rounds through the rear window. A thousand capillaries spread through the glass. The smell of gunpowder in the air. Ears ringing from the blasts. Ramming the truck into drive, she punched the gas. No headlights. Moving fast. Too fast. She sideswiped a garbage can, sent it tumbling, overcorrected. The truck fishtailed and she nearly lost it, regained control in time to make the turn. On the street, she cranked the speedometer to eighty, blew the stop sign at the corner, kept going.

For the span of several seconds, she was an animal, mindless and terrified, hunted by a predator that had scented her blood. The only sound was the hiss of her breath. The pound of a heart racing out of control. The hum of panic in her veins. The knowledge that there was no going back. Her entire body shook violently. Her brain misfiring. Fear shrieking because she didn't know how seriously she was hurt. Because she knew this wasn't over. That this nightmare she'd been anticipating for weeks now was, in fact, just beginning.

At James Road she hit a curb, backed the speedometer down to just above the speed limit, forced herself to calm down, kept her eyes on the rearview mirror. No one knew about the truck. All she had to do was stay calm and get the hell out of the city. For God's sake, it had seemed like a good idea when she'd conceived it.

As the adrenaline ebbed, the pain augmented. Her shoulder throbbed with every beat of her heart. Looking away from the road, she risked a glance at it. Blood had soaked through her shirt, into her coat—which still wasn't on properly—red droplets spattering onto the seat at her hip. The sight of so much blood piled another layer of fear atop a hundred others. Nothing broken—she could still move her arm—but it was bad, potentially life-threatening if she didn't get to a hospital. But she knew emergency room personnel were required by law to report all gunshot wounds to law enforcement. For now, she had no choice but to keep going.

Eyes on the rearview mirror, she made a right at Broad Street and headed east, praying she didn't run into a cop. Even if they didn't have her plate number or a description of the vehicle, she'd have a tough time explaining the bullet holes in her rear windshield, not to mention the blood.

By the time she hit the outskirts of Columbus, the snow was coming down in earnest. The wind had picked up, driving it sideways, and she could see the whisper of it across the surface of the road in front of her. Soon, it would be sticking. As much as she didn't relish the thought of slick roads, especially with an injured shoulder, she knew it might work to her advantage. If the state highway patrol was busy with accidents, they'd have less time to look for her. The problem was they weren't the only ones looking. The state police were the least of her problems. They weren't the ones who would cuff her, walk her into a cornfield, and put a bullet in her head. She needed help, but who could she trust?

Twice she'd picked up her cell phone to make the call. Twice she'd dropped it back onto the console. The realization that there was no one, that at the age of thirty-five she'd cultivated so few meaningful relationships during her lifetime that there wasn't a soul on this earth that she could call upon, made her unbearably sad.

Against all odds, The Plan had worked; it had gotten her out the door and into her vehicle. How ludicrous was it that she didn't have a destination in mind? Or maybe she simply hadn't believed she was going to survive long enough to need one.

She took Broad Street past Reynoldsburg and the Pataskala area and then turned north onto a lesser county road. The snowfall was heavy enough to obscure visibility by the time she hit the outskirts of Newark. The bleeding showed no sign of abating. As the miles inched past, it formed a sickening pool on the seat at her hip. There was no pulsing or spray, which meant there was no catastrophic vascular damage. Still, the pain and trauma were making her nauseous and light-headed.

By the time she hit Ohio State Route 16 East, her heart was racing and she was shivering beneath her coat. Her hands were shaking and wet on the steering wheel. To make matters worse, visibility had dwindled to just a few feet and she inched along at an excruciatingly slow pace. Three hours had passed since she'd fled her house. Early on, she'd made good time and managed to put over fifty miles between her and her pursuers. In the last hour, conditions had deteriorated; she'd encountered a total of two motorists and a single snowplow. The pavement was no longer visible and she'd fallen to using mailboxes, the occasional fence line, and the trees and telephone poles on either side just to stay on the road.

It wasn't until she passed the sign for Holmes County that she thought of her old friend. A lot of years had passed since they'd spoken. There was some baggage between them—and probably a little bit of hurt. But if there was anyone in the world she could count on, it was Kate. . . .

As she drove through another band of heavy snow, even the poles disappeared from view. It didn't look like a plow had made it down this particular stretch; the snow was several inches deep now and there wasn't a single tire mark. Slowing to a crawl, she drove blind, squinting into the whiteout, struggling to find the road. If the situation hadn't been so dire, the irony of it would have sent her into hysterical laughter. That was how they would find her—bloodied and clutching the steering wheel and laughing like a hyena.

The truck wasn't equipped with four-wheel drive, but the tires were good and holding their own. The tank had been full, and there was still half a tank left. Enough to get her where she needed to go. All she had to do was stay on the road and not get stuck.

She idled over a small bridge, reached down to turn up the defroster. The tree came out of nowhere, a black beast rushing out of the maelstrom like an apparition. She yanked the wheel right, but she wasn't fast enough. Steel clanged. The impact threw her against her shoulder harness. The front end buckled; the hood flew up. The airbag punched her chest hard enough to daze.

Cursing, she disentangled herself from the airbag, wincing when her shoulder cramped. The truck sat at a severe angle, nose down, bumper against the tree. The engine had died. The headlights illuminated a geyser of steam shooting into the air.

Struggling for calm, she jammed the shifter into park. If she could get the truck started, she might be able to wire the hood shut and be on her way. She twisted the key.

Nothing.

"Come on," she whispered. "Come on. *Come on.*"

She gave it a moment and tried again, pumping the gas this time, but the vehicle refused to start.

Closing her eyes, she set her forehead against the steering wheel. "Fate, you are a son of a bitch."

The raised hood caught wind and rattled, spindly branches scraping against the surface. Pulling out her phone, she checked the battery. Plenty of juice, but no bars. . . .

The laugh that tore from her throat sounded manic in the silence of the cab.

She had two choices. She could leave the relative shelter of the vehicle and find help. Some farmer with a tractor who could pull her truck from the ditch so she could be on her way. Or she could stay put and wait for dawn, which was hours away, help that might not come—or the local sheriff, who would likely ask a lot of questions she didn't want to answer.

As far as she was concerned it was a no-brainer.

Unfastening the seat belt, she shoved open the door and stepped into the driving snow.

CHAPTER 1

The sleigh was an old thing. It had belonged to his *grosseldre,* who'd passed it down to his *datt,* who'd given it to him when he married nine years ago. Since, it had been used for everything from hauling hay, milk cans, and maple syrup buckets to carrying the sick calf that had been rejected by its *mamm* two springs ago. Last fall, Adam had replaced the runners, which cost him a pretty penny. Christmas three years ago, one of the shafts had broken, so he'd replaced both. There was still work to be done on the old contraption; the seat needed patching—or replacing—but the old *shlay* was functional enough that he and the children could get out and have some fun before the weather turned.

As he led Big Jimmy from his stall, Adam Lengacher tried not to think about how much his life had changed in the last two years. Nothing had been the same since his wife, Leah, died. All of their lives had changed—and not for the better. It was as if the heart of the house had been sucked out and they were left grappling, trying to fill some infinite space with something that had never been theirs to begin with.

His Amish brethren had rallied in the days and weeks afterward, as they always did in times of tragedy. Some of the women still brought covered dishes and, in summer, vegetables from their gardens for him and the children. Bishop Troyer always made time to spend a few extra minutes with him after worship. Some of the older women had even begun their matchmaking shenanigans.

The thought made him shake his head—and smile. Life went on, he thought, as it should. The children had adjusted. Adam was comforted by the knowledge that when the time came, he would be with Leah again for all of eternity. Still, he missed her. He spent too much time thinking of her, too much time remembering, and wishing his children still had a *mamm.* He never talked about it, but he still hurt, too.

In the aisle, he lined up the old draft horse, lifted the shafts, and backed the animal up to the sleigh. He was in the process of buckling the leather straps when his son Samuel ran into the barn.

"Datt! I can help!"

Adam tried not to smile as he rose to his full height, walked around to the horse's head, and fastened the throat latch. His oldest child was the picture of his *mamm,* with her exuberant personality and her gift of chatter.

"Did you finish eating your pancakes?" he asked.

"*Ja.*"

"You take all the eggs to the house?"

"The brown ones, too. Annie broke one."

A whinny from the stall told them their other draft horse, a mare they'd named Jenny, was already missing her partner.

"We won't keep him too long, Jenny!" Sammy called out to the horse.

"*Vo sinn die shveshtahs?*" Adam asked. Where are your sisters?

"Putting on their coats. Lizzie says her shoes are too tight."

Adam nodded. What did he know about girls or their shoes? Nothing, he realized, a list that seemed to grow with every passing day. "Why don't you lead Big Jimmy out of the barn?"

The boy squealed in delight as he took the leather line in his small hand and addressed the horse. "*Kumma autseid, ald boo.*" Come outside, old boy.

Adam watched boy and horse for a moment. Sammy was just eight years old and already trying hard to be a man. It was the one thing Adam *could* do, the one thing he was good at, teaching his son what it meant to be Amish, to live a humble life and submit to God. His two daughters—Lizzie, who was barely seven, and Annie, who was five—were another story altogether; Adam didn't have a clue how to raise girls.

He had a lot to be thankful for. His children were healthy and happy; they kept his heart filled. The farm kept his hands busy and earned him a decent living. As Bishop Troyer had told him that first terrible week: *The Lord is close to the brokenhearted and saves those who are crushed in spirit.*

Adam had just closed the barn door when his daughters ran down the sidewalk, their dresses swishing about their legs. They were bundled up with scarves and gloves, black winter bonnets covering their heads. This morning, they would surely need the afghan Leah had knitted to cover up with if they got cold.

"Samuel, help your sisters into the *shlay,*" Adam said.

As the children boarded, Adam looked around, assessing the weather. It had snowed most of the night, and it was still falling at a good clip. The wind had formed an enormous drift on the south side of the barn. Not too bad yet, but he knew there was another round of snow coming. By tonight, the temperature was supposed to drop into the single digits. The wind was going to pick up, too. According to his neighbor, Mr. Yoder, there was a blizzard on the way.

When the children were loaded—the girls in the backseat and Sammy next to him—Adam climbed in and picked up the lines. "*Kumma druff!*" he said to the horse. Come on there!

Big Jimmy might be a tad overweight and a smidgen past his prime, but he loved the cold and snow and this morning he came to life. Raising his head and tail, the animal pranced through snow that reached nearly to his knees, and within minutes the sled zoomed along the fence line on the north side of the property.

"Look at Jimmy go!" cried Annie, motioning toward the horse.

The sight of the old gelding warmed Adam's heart. "I think he's showing off."

"We're going to have to give him extra oats when we get home!" declared Lizzie.

"If Jimmy eats any more oats, we're going to have to pull *him* in the sleigh," Adam told her.

At the sound of the children's laughter and the jangle of the harness, the bracing air against his face, Adam felt some of the weight on his shoulders lift. He took the sleigh north through the cornfield, the tops of the cut stalks nearly obscured by a foot or so of snow. The trees and branches sparkled white. As they passed by the woods, he pointed out the ten-point buck standing at the edge of the field. He showed them the flock of geese huddled on the icy pond where the water had long since frozen over. The beauty of the Ohio countryside never ceased to boost his spirits, especially this morning with the falling snow and the sound of his children's laughter in his ears.

On the north side of the property, he turned right at the fence line and headed east toward Painters Creek. It was too cold for them to stay out long. Everyone had dressed warmly, but the wind cut right through the layers. Already his fingers and face burned with cold. Now that they'd moved past the tree line, he noticed the dark clouds moving in from the northwest. He'd take the sleigh to the county road and then cut south and go back toward the house. Maybe have some hot chocolate before afternoon chores, feeding the cows and hogs.

They'd only traveled another hundred yards when Adam noticed the hump of a vehicle in the ditch. The paint glinting through the layer of snow. It was an unusual sight on this stretch of back road. There weren't many farms out this way and almost all of his neighbors were Amish. As they neared the vehicle, he slowed the horse to a walk.

"What's that?" came Annie's voice from the back of the sleigh.

"Looks like an *Englischer* car," said Sammy.

"Maybe they got stuck in the snow," Lizzie suggested.

"Whoa." Adam stopped the sleigh and looked around.

For a moment the only sounds came from the puff of Jimmy's breaths, the caw of a crow in the woods to the east, and the clack of tree branches blowing in the wind.

"You think there's someone inside, Datt?" asked Sammy.

"Only one way to find out." Securing the lines, Adam climbed down from the sleigh and started toward the vehicle.

"*Ich will's sana!*" Sammy started to climb down. I want to see it.

"Stay with your sisters," Adam told his son.

From thirty feet away, he discerned that the vehicle was actually a pickup truck, covered with snow, nose-down in the ditch, the bumper against a big hedge-apple tree. The impact had buckled the hood, causing it to become unlatched. Evidently, the driver hadn't been able to see due to the heavy snow last night and must have run off the road. From his vantage point, Adam couldn't tell if there was anyone inside. He waded through deep snow in the ditch and made his way around to the driver's side. Surprise rippled through him when he saw that the door stood open a few inches. Snow had blown onto the seat and floor. Bending, he looked inside.

The airbag had deployed. A crack split the front windshield, but the glass was still intact. His gut tightened at the sight of the blood. There was a lot of it. *Too much,* a little voice whispered. Adam didn't know anything about cars or trucks, but he didn't think the impact would have been violent enough to warrant so much blood. What on earth had happened here?

Adam leaned into the vehicle for a closer look, but there was nothing else of interest. Straightening, he looked around. Any tracks left behind had long since been filled in. Where had the driver gone?

He walked to the rear of the truck. A tinge of apprehension tickled the back of his neck at the sight of the bullet holes in the rear window. Six holes connected by a mapwork of white cracks.

"Datt? Is someone in there?"

He startled at the sound of his son's voice. Turning, he saw the boy come up behind him, hip-deep in snow, craning his neck to see into the vehicle.

"Go back to the sleigh, Sammy."

But the boy had already spotted the blood. "Oh." His thin little brows drew together. "He's hurt, Datt, and needs help. Maybe we should look for him."

The boy was right, of course. Helping those in need was the Amish way. Still, the bullet holes gave Adam pause. How had they gotten there and why?

"Let's go back to the sleigh," he told his son.

Side by side, they struggled through the ditch. Adam kept his eye out for tracks as they walked, but there were none. Either someone had come by and picked up the injured driver or he'd walked away and found help.

"Who is it, Datt?" asked Annie.

"No one there," he told her.

"Are we going to look for him?" Lizzie asked.

"We'll look around a bit," he said.

Sammy lowered his voice, as if to avoid worrying his sisters. "Do you think he's hurt, Datt?"

"*Fleicht,*" he said. Maybe.

Adam set his hand on his son's head. Such a sweet boy, so helpful and caring. But Adam didn't like seeing those bullet holes. He sure didn't like seeing all that blood. Even so, if someone was hurt, finding them and helping them was the right thing to do.

"I'm going to look around," he told the children. "I want you to stay close to the sleigh. Call out if you see anything. If we don't find anyone here, we'll ride down to the freezer shanty over on Ithaca Road and use the phone."

"The Freezer" was a metal building containing a dozen or so freezers the Amish rented to store vegetables and meat. It had a community toilet, a hitching post, and a phone.

Adam lifted his youngest daughter from the sleigh and looked around. The fence that ran alongside the road was a jumble of bent posts and sagging barbed wire. On the other side of the road, the woods grew thick all the way to Painters Creek.

"Be careful, children," he said as he started along the fence line. "Stay together and watch out for deep drifts or else I'll have to dig you out, too."

His words were met with a spate of giggles as they started toward the road.

Adam traversed the ditch and followed the fence. Fifty feet ahead, there was a knoll with a smattering of saplings and a place where blackberries flourished in late summer. He'd only gone twenty feet when he saw the scrap of fabric hanging from the barbed wire. Farther, a disturbance in the snow. At first, he thought maybe a deer had been hit and run into the ditch to die. But as he drew closer, he spotted the black leather of a boot. Blue denim.

He broke into a lurching run. "Hello? Is someone there? Are you hurt?"

From ten feet away he recognized the silhouette of a woman. Dark hair. A black leather coat and boots. Blue jeans.

Adam reached her and knelt. She was lying on her side, her head and shoulder against a fence post. Her legs were pulled up nearly to her chest, as if she'd been trying to stay warm. Brownish-black hair stuck out from beneath a purple knit hat, covering much of her face. Her clothes were caked with snow. Adam brushed the hair away and was shocked when he found it frozen stiff. He saw blue-tinged lips set into a face that was deathly pale. She wore a scarf at the collar of her coat. A single leather glove on her right hand. The other was bare and covered with blood. Her skin was cold to the touch and for a terrible moment he thought she was dead. Frozen to death.

Shaken by the thought, he worked off one of his gloves, set his fingers against the back of her neck, beneath her hat and hair. Warm, he realized. Still alive.

Relieved, he looked around. The closest house was his own. The Yoder farm was another mile down the road. The snow was coming down so hard he couldn't even see the roof of their barn. They were Amish and didn't have a phone, anyway. The closest Amish pay phone was at the freezer shanty, which was in the opposite direction.

He craned his neck right, spotted Lizzie and Annie using sticks to play tic-tac-toe in the snow. Sammy had made his way twenty yards ahead, checking the area along the fence.

The woman moaned. Adam turned back to her to see her twist. She raised her head and squinted at him. She was staring at his hat, her eyes wide. Her face was a mask of confusion and pain. "Get the fuck away from me," she slurred.

He didn't know what to say to that. He was trying to help her. Was she confused? He'd seen it happen, like the time he'd been hunting and his cousin fell through the ice. By the time they arrived home, his cousin hadn't even been able to speak.

"Don't be afraid." Raising his hands, he sat back on his haunches. "I'm going to help you."

"Back off." She raised her left hand as if to fend him off. "I mean it."

"You were in an accident," he told her. "You're bleeding. You need a doctor."

"No doctor." She tried to scoot backward, as if to put some distance between them, but ended up flopping sideways. Her face hit the snow. There were ice crystals on her skin. A smear of blood on her cheek. Propping herself up on one elbow, she reached beneath her coat with her right hand and pulled out a pistol.

"Keep your fucking distance," she hissed. "Stay back."

Adam lurched away, raised his hands. "I have children."

She raised her other hand, fingers blue with cold and covered with blood. She looked at it as if she wasn't sure it was hers, wiped her face. "Who are you?"

"Adam . . . Lengacher."

She blinked at him. "Where am I?"

"Painters Mill."

Out of the corner of his eye, he ascertained the location of his children. They were ten yards away, near the fence. Too close. If this woman was *narrisch*—crazy—and fired that gun, there would be no protecting them.

Adam scooched back another foot, kept his hands raised. "I'm leaving. Just stay calm and we'll go. Okay?"

"It's a *lady*."

His heart gave a single hard thud at the sound of his son's voice.

He hadn't heard him approach. He twisted around fast and made eye contact with him. "*Gay zu da shlay, Samuel. Nau.*" Go to the sleigh. Now.

The boy's eyes widened at his *datt*'s tone. He took a step back. "What's wrong?"

"*Gay,*" he said. "*Nau.*" Go. Now.

The boy walked backward, frightened. Adam turned back to the woman. She was looking at Sammy. Gripping the pistol as if it were her lifeline. Dear God, what had he stumbled upon?

Before he could ponder the question, the hand holding the pistol collapsed as if she no longer had the strength to keep her arm outstretched. The gun slid from her palm. Her body went slack and she settled more deeply into the snow. She stared at him for a moment and then closed her eyes.

"I'm spent," she rasped.

Adam wasn't sure how to respond. The one thing he did know was that he didn't want her reaching for that gun again. Moving closer, he picked it up. The steel was cold in his palm, wet from the snow, bits of ice on the muzzle. Not a revolver. He was no stranger to rifles; he'd been a hunter since he was thirteen years old. He had a .22 and an old muzzle-loader at home. This was . . . something else. What was she doing with a gun? Was it for protection? Was she a trustworthy individual? A criminal? If he helped her would he bring danger into his home?

Keeping the weapon out of sight from the children, Adam turned it over in his hand. It took him a moment, but he figured out how to release the magazine that held the ammunition. He dropped the clip into his coat pocket. He pulled back the slide, checked the chamber, dumped the single bullet into the snow. He put the weapon in another coat pocket.

"I guess I'm at your mercy now, huh?" the woman whispered.

Adam got to his feet. A glance over his shoulder told him all three children were sitting in the sleigh, their faces turned his way, expressions curious and worried. Around him the day no longer seemed magical. The snow no longer a gentle thing, but a threat. The wind had picked up, driving the falling snow sideways. Even the horse was hunched against the cold and wind.

He looked down at the woman. She lay still, unmoving, her eyes closed, as if she'd given up. Already a thin veil of snow clung to the newly exposed area of her clothes, her hair. If he left her here, she would freeze to death—or become buried if the sheriff's deputies couldn't get to her quickly.

She shifted as if in pain, made a sound that might have been a word. Keeping his distance, Adam knelt. "Do you want me to help you?" he asked.

She didn't open her eyes. Her lips barely moved when she spoke. "Get Kate Burkholder," she ground out. "I'm a cop. Get her."

Adam knew the name. He'd known Katie Burkholder most of his life. How did this stranger know her? This was not the time to question her. She was injured and weak. He looked at his children. "Make a place for her on the backseat!" he called out. "We're taking her home."

"*Ja!*" Sammy said.

Adam looked at the woman. "Can you walk?"

She shifted, winced, her left leg flailing and then going still. "I don't know. Give me a minute."

He didn't think a minute would help. In fact, if she didn't get out of the cold soon, she'd likely fall to unconsciousness and die.

"I'll help you." Not giving himself time to debate further, he bent to her, plunged his hands into the snow beneath her, and scooped her into his arms. She was small, smelled of cold air and some sweet English-woman scent.

"Sammy!" he said. "Take the lines. We're going home."

The woman's head lolled; she was dead weight in his arms. Concern for her niggled at the back of his mind when he saw blood on her coat. He felt the warmth of it run across his wrist as he trudged through deep snow.

"An *Englischer,*" Sammy said as Adam approached the sleigh.

"*Ja,*" he replied.

"Is she frozen?" the boy asked.

"Hurt. And weak from the cold."

"Who is it, Datt?" came Lizzie's voice.

"I don't know," he told her. "Must have gotten lost in the storm. Someone's probably worried about her, though, don't you think?"

"Her *mamm* probably," Lizzie said. "They always worry."

"Annie, get the afghan so we can cover her up. Quickly now."

"Datt, she's bleeding!" Sammy pointed, alarm ringing in his voice, his little hands gripping the leather lines.

"She must have hurt herself in the wreck is all," Adam told him. "Come on now. Girls, move to the front seat. Give her some room."

Lizzie and Annie scrambled into the front. Adam stepped into the sleigh and set the woman on the rear bench seat, trying to ignore the smear of blood on the leather. The seat wasn't long enough for her to stretch out, so he bent her legs at the knee.

"Hand me that afghan," he said.

Annie thrust the throw at him. "She looks cold."

"I think she's been out here awhile," he said. "Too long."

"Is she going to die?" Lizzie asked.

Since losing their mother, the children had become aware of death and all its shadowy facets. Adam did his best to answer their questions. They knew death was part of the life cycle. They knew that when people died, they went to heaven to spend all of eternity with God. But they also knew that death had taken their *mamm* from them and she wouldn't be coming back.

"That's up to God now, isn't it?" Adam draped the afghan over the woman, tucking it beneath her. "We will help her as best we can. The rest is up to Him."

He worked off his coat and draped it over the woman. Under different circumstances, he would have taken the lines and asked one of the children to stay with her. In light of the gun and her rough language, he didn't want them getting too close to her.

Kneeling on the floor between the front seatback and the rear seat, he set his hand on his son's shoulder.

"Let's go," he said.

CHAPTER 2

When you've been a cop for any length of time, you learn to appreciate the mundane. In a town the size of Painters Mill, Ohio, population 5,300—a third of whom are Amish—mundane is a criterion we can pretty much count on. Except, of course, when Mother Nature drops a foot of snow and everyone decides they need to get to work on time anyway. Such is the life of a small-town chief of police.

I'm standing next to my city-issue Explorer on the shoulder of Township Road 18, a mile or so out of Painters Mill. Around me, heavy snow slants down at a nearly horizontal angle. The wind is kicking to about thirty knots, and visibility has dwindled to less than an eighth of a mile. If the weatherman is correct, things are going to get worse before they get better.

The vintage Mercedes went through the wood fence, busting all four rails along with two posts, the tires digging deep trenches through the ditch, and now sits at a cockeyed angle in the pasture. A dozen or so of Levi Hochstetler's black angus cattle decided the car was a lot more interesting than the pile of hay up by the barn, and came down to investigate. Two of the animals are already poking around the opening in the fence.

"I was on my way to the shop and came over that hill." The driver,

Joe Neely, the owner of the wrecked Mercedes and Mocha Joe's—a nice little upscale coffeehouse in town—motions to the road behind him. "Must have hit a slick spot, because I went into a spin. Next thing I know I'm in that pasture."

I nod, saying nothing, but I have a feeling there's a little more to the story than he's letting on—like maybe he was in a hurry and driving too fast for the road conditions. I keep the theory to myself. I've met Joe several times in the year since he opened Mocha Joe's; I make it a point to get to know all the merchants and shopkeepers in town. He never hesitates to offer up free coffee to me and my officers—the sheriff's department, too. He's a decent fellow, a family man, and I'm confident he'll make things right with the homeowner.

"Are you injured, Mr. Neely?" I ask. "Do you need an ambulance? Get yourself checked out?"

"Oh, heck no, Chief Burkholder. I'm fine. Just . . ." He looks at his car and sighs. "I sure do like that car. She might be vintage, but she's my first Mercedes. Bought her the day I opened the shop and had a crush on her ever since."

"Going to need a new headlight," I tell him. "Maybe get that quarter panel replaced. You want me to get you a wrecker?"

"I sure would appreciate that."

Tilting my head, I speak into my lapel mike, trying not to notice when snow sneaks down my collar. "Ten-fifty-one," I say, requesting a wrecker and giving the general location.

"Ten-four," comes my first-shift dispatcher's voice over the radio. Lois Monroe is in her mid-fifties, with a big laugh and a temperament as prickly as her hair. She might be our resident "mom," but I've seen her put more than one tough customer in his place. "Ricky's Towing is running behind this morning, Chief. Says they've been getting calls for a couple of hours now. Gonna be a while."

"Try Jonny Ray."

"Roger that."

This is the fourth fender bender I've responded to this morning and it's not yet nine A.M., a sure sign that the first day of the week is going to live up to its name.

I'm in the process of setting out flares when I hear tires crunch through snow. I look up to see Rupert "Glock" Maddox's cruiser roll up and stop behind my Explorer, lights flashing. He's my usual first-shift officer, an experienced cop and former military man, and as always, I'm glad to see him.

"Need a hand, Chief?"

I drop the final flare and look up to see him approach. Not for the first time I wonder how he always manages to show up just when I need him. "If you wait here for the wrecker," I tell him, "I'll let Hochstetler know he needs to pen those cows up in the barn until he can get some wire on this fence."

Glock breaks open an additional flare and drops it on the centerline. "Definitely don't need cows running around with slick roads and low visibility."

I'm midway to the Explorer when my cell vibrates against my hip. I glance down to see DISPATCH on the display and pick up. "You're keeping us busy this morning, Lois."

"I just took a call from Adam Lengacher, Chief. He says he was out for a sleigh ride with his kids and found a woman lying in the field. Evidently, she wrecked sometime during the night, left her vehicle to find help, and lost her way."

Squinting against the snow blowing into my face, I reach the Explorer and yank open the door. "How badly is she injured?"

"He isn't sure."

"Check to see if ambulances are running. See if they can pick her up and take her to Pomerene Hospital. Do you know where the accident occurred?"

"Township Road 36."

"Call County," I say, referring to the Holmes County Sheriff's Department. "Tell them we're jammed up here, will you?"

"That's exactly what I was going to do, Chief, but Adam told me the woman asked for you."

The statement gives me pause. "Does this mystery woman have a name?"

"He didn't think to ask."

I sigh, wondering who she is and why she would ask for me. "All right," I tell her. "Cancel County. Let me get things tied up here and I'll head out that way."

I end the call, think about going back out into the snow, but instead I call Glock. He's standing on the shoulder with Joe, talking and looking in the general direction of the wayward Mercedes. I see him pluck his cell from a compartment on his belt.

"I've got to take a call out at the Lengacher farm," I tell him. "Can you let Hochstetler know he needs to pen those cows until he can get that fence repaired?"

He looks at me, phone to his ear, and grins. "You got it, Chief. Be careful out there."

I've known Adam Lengacher since I was eight years old. I was friends with his sister for a time. Their *datt* ran a hog operation, butchered livestock for meat on the side, had a smokehouse for venison, and a reputation for making good German-style sausage. For a couple of summers, while the men cut meat and smoked their pipes, the three of us would coo over the piglets and play hide-and-seek in the cornfield next to their house. Those carefree days didn't last and we lost touch as we entered our teen years. Adam married and started a family. I fell out of favor with my Amish brethren and eventually left the fold, trading Painters Mill for the big-city lights of Columbus.

I've seen him around town a few times since I've been chief, just to wave or smile or say hello. The last time I spoke to him was at his wife's funeral, two years ago, and then it was only to offer my condolences.

He lives with his three children on a lesser-used township road that's more gravel than asphalt a few miles out of Painters Mill. I pass a snowplow on the way, but I know they won't be clearing the secondary roads much longer. As I creep along TR 36, my tires bumping over ever-growing drifts, powdered snow blowing in my rearview mirror, the severity of the weather situation hits home. I've not received official word that emergency services are grounded, but there's no way an ambulance is going to venture into rural areas and risk getting stuck.

The road is virtually invisible, not only due to low visibility, but because the roadway and shoulder are obscured by a foot of snow. Worse, the wind has picked up and the drifts are growing exponentially. In a few more hours, the east-west roads will be impassable. If the injured motorist Adam stumbled upon turns out to have a medical emergency and she's able to travel, I'll likely have to transport her to Pomerene Hospital myself.

Jamming the Explorer into four-wheel drive, I turn into the lane of the Lengacher farm. Despite the severity of the weather, I can't help but notice the beauty of the snow against the old farmhouse and the eighty-foot-tall pine trees in the side yard. White four-rail fences line both sides of the long driveway. I climb a low rise, and a big red bank barn looms into view. The barn door stands open. An antique-looking sleigh is parked just inside. Two Amish girls bundled in coats and wearing winter bonnets lead a fat dapple-gray draft horse deeper into the interior.

I park as close to the house as I can manage, kill the engine, and pull my hood over my head. Wind and snow pummel me as I take the walkway around to the front door and knock. The door swings open and I find myself looking at a boy of about eight with yellow-blond hair and eyes the color of a blue jay. He's wearing a brown coat and a flat-brimmed hat, and he's in his stocking feet, his big toe sticking out of a hole.

"Hi." I smile, look past him. "Is your *datt* home?"

"*Ja.*" The boy cocks his head. "Are you the police?"

"Yes, but you can call me Katie."

"Datt said to bring you back." Reaching out, the boy takes my hand. "Come on. We found a girl. An *autseidah.*" Outsider. "She's hurt so we put her on the cot in Mamm's sewing room."

His hand is small, roughened with calluses, and cold in mine as he leads me through the door and into a dimly lit living room. The smells of woodsmoke and a house well lived in float on the heated air. I see a ragtag sofa piled with crocheted pillows, a handcrafted coffee table, a macramé wall covering. A propane floor lamp hisses at me from the corner.

"I'm eight, but I'm going to be nine next month." The boy prattles as he leads me through the living room. "My sisters are putting Jimmy away."

"Jimmy must be that big plow horse I saw when I pulled in," I say.

"He's fat but he still likes to pull the sleigh." He doesn't miss a beat as we enter a narrow hall. "Annie likes him because he's got a pink nose."

He takes me down the hall and stops outside a doorway. The room beyond is a small area, about ten feet square, with a single window, a workbench set against a wall, and an antique Singer sewing machine that looks like it hasn't been used in some time.

Adam Lengacher stands just inside, looking at me. He's tall and blond with a rangy build and the blue eyes he passed down to his son.

He still wears his heavy coat, dark trousers that are wet around the hem, and boots that left a trail of watery prints.

"Hi, Adam," I say.

"Katie."

Remembrance flickers in his eyes. The hint of a smile on a mouth that doesn't seem to quite remember how to do it. Even after all these years, I still see the boy he once was. The one who could talk a blue moon. The one I'd locked in the corn crib until he cried. . . .

"I hear you have an injured motorist on your hands," I say.

"Found her when we were out for a sleigh ride. Looks like she wrecked out. I think she's hurt. There's blood."

"We thought she was dead," the boy says with a tad too much enthusiasm, "but Datt said she was just cold."

Adam addresses his son. "*Hohla die shveshtahs. Fazayla eena zu kumma inseid.*" Fetch your sisters. Tell them to come inside.

Giving me a lingering look, the boy leaves us, his stocking feet echoing as he runs down the hall.

I start toward the cot, but Adam stops me. "*Sie katt en bix,* Katie." She had a gun. "*Sie gedroit mich mitt es.*" She threatened me with it.

"Where's the gun?" I ask in *Deitsch.*

Frowning, he reaches into his coat pocket and produces a Sig Sauer P320. It's a nine-millimeter. Polymer grip.

"Where's the clip?" I ask.

He reaches into his other pocket and pulls it out. It's a typical magazine that holds seventeen rounds. I take the weapon, check the chamber, find it empty, drop it into my own coat pocket, the clip in the other.

"Did she say anything?" I ask.

"Not much."

"Did she give you her name?" I'll run her through LEADS to check for a record or an active warrant.

He shakes his head. "She was in and out. Delirious from the cold, I think."

I'm ruminating the presence of the gun and the fact that he brought her here in spite of it. Another cop might have questioned his judgment, especially with three young children in tow. But having been born and raised Amish, I understand the mind-set. You don't leave anyone, including an outsider, to the elements, especially if they're hurt.

My eyes move past Adam to the woman on the cot. She's bundled in a tattered quilt that's pulled halfway over her face, damp hair sticking to her cheek. Even from several feet away, I see her shivering violently, which is a good sign if she's hypothermic. Wet leather boots on the floor beneath the cot. A sopping coat hung on a chair back, water dripping. A smear of blood mars the wood plank floor next to the cot.

"Stay here," I say to Adam, and start toward the woman. "Ma'am?" I begin. "I'm a police officer. I need to see your—"

The woman lifts her head and looks at me. The slap of recognition stops me in my tracks, cuts my words short. I haven't seen Gina Colorosa in ten years. Once upon a time we'd been friends. We attended the police academy together. Graduated from the same class. We shared an apartment. Shared a hell of a lot more than that—all the trials and tribulations of young women finding their place in the world. If it hadn't been for Gina, I probably wouldn't have found my way into law enforcement.

"Damn. Kate Burkholder. Took you long enough to get here."

Her voice is rougher than I remember. Weak despite the echo of the old attitude I used to admire back when I was too young, too naive, to know better. I don't know what to say to her. Or how to feel. I can't stop looking at her. I can't believe she's here in Painters Mill. That we didn't part on good terms adds an uncomfortable dimension to all of it.

Her entire body quakes beneath the quilt. Her teeth chatter uncontrollably. Her complexion is shockingly pale, her lips tinged with blue. Her hair is wet. My EMT training kicks in. I look at Adam. "We need blankets. A dry towel. And hot tea, if you have it."

Nodding, he leaves the room.

"Get me . . . electric blanket," she says.

"How long were you out in the cold?" I ask.

"Not sure. A few hours. Too damn long."

"You're hypothermic. I'll get you warmed up and then we need to get you to the hospital."

"No . . . hospital," she says between bursts of shivering.

I look down at the smear of blood on the floor. "You're bleeding. Were you injured in the crash? How badly are you hurt?" In the back of my mind I acknowledge the possibility that if she's seriously hypothermic, she may not know or remember. Confusion is a common manifestation of hypothermia.

"Airbag got me in the face, gave me a bloody nose," she says. "That's all. I'm fine."

Something in the way she's looking at me gives me pause, gives credence to the odd sense that something isn't quite right with all this.

"We've got serious weather on the way," I tell her. "Ambulances won't be running long. I can get you to the hospital, but we need to leave now. I suggest you take me up on the offer because we may not be able to get out later."

"Kate, I'm fine." When I don't respond, she musters a weak grin. "For God's sake . . . I just . . . need to warm up."

I turn to see Adam standing at the door, several folded blankets and a ratty bath towel in his arms. "The girls are making hot tea," he tells me, his eyes flicking to Gina.

"Good. Thanks." I take the blankets. As I drape them over Gina,

I try not to notice the way her arms and legs are shaking beneath the quilt. The unsettling blue hue of her lips. The way she keeps clenching her teeth to keep them from chattering.

"Hair's wet," I tell her. "We need to get you dry. Are your clothes dry?"

"They're . . . fine."

"Can you sit up?"

"Yep." Face contorting as if she's in pain, she manages and reaches for the towel. "I can do it."

I let her, trying not to notice the paleness of her hand, that she's weak and doing her damnedest to pretend otherwise.

While she scrubs her hair dry with the towel, I tuck the blankets beneath her legs and layer yet another over her. "So what happened?" I ask. "What are you doing here?"

"I didn't know we were in for this kind of weather. It was dark and snowing like crazy. I couldn't see. Ran off the damn road and hit a tree."

"Airbags deployed?"

"I told you they did."

I nod. "Where were you headed?"

She hands me the towel. "To see you."

"A heads-up would have been nice."

"Yeah, well, hindsight."

We stare at each other a full minute, minds working, neither of us speaking. "Are you still with Columbus Division of Police?" I ask.

"Last time I checked."

"What the hell does that mean?"

The old wiliness flickers in her eyes. "Where's my gun?"

"You mean the gun you pointed at the unarmed Amish man who was with his children and trying to help you?"

"That would be the one." Sighing, she sinks back into the mattress.

"Look, I'm sorry. I barely remember. I mean, I was in and out by that point. I'd been in the snow a long time." She shrugs. "I didn't know who he was or what he was up to."

A quiet alarm starts to simmer at the back of my brain. Not a clanging bell warning me of impending danger, but a more subtle hum that stirs when someone's not being up front. I'm well versed in the symptoms of hypothermia. I've seen a dozen cases in the years I've been a cop. The hunter that fell through the ice on Painters Creek a couple years ago. The kid who plunged through the ice on Miller's Pond last winter. Confusion is common. Is that the case here? Or is there something else going on?

"Why didn't you call me?" I ask.

"It was sort of a last-minute decision."

"Why is that?"

"Let's just say it was unplanned."

A youngster's voice in the hall draws my attention. I turn to see Adam taking a mug from a girl of about seven. She's curious, her inquisitive eyes probing the mysterious *Englischer* woman. Her *datt* is on to her and he's quick to send her on her way.

"Go to the root cellar and get a couple jars of sausage for supper," he tells her. "Beets, too. Have Annie help you."

"Okay." She cranes her neck for a final peek and then turns and leaves.

Adam brings the mug into the room, passes it to Gina. "Tea," he tells her. "It's hot."

"Thank you." She wriggles to a sitting position, accepts the mug, and gives him a contrite look. "I'm sorry about what happened out there," she says. "I mean, with the gun. I'm a police officer, and I didn't know what your intentions were. I'm sorry if I frightened you and your children."

He nods.

She blows on the tea and sips. "My name's Gina, by the way."

"Adam Lengacher," he says. "You're warming up?"

"Yes. Finally. Thank you."

He looks at me, not quite comfortable with all this. "I tossed more wood on the stove."

The window rattles with a sudden gust wind. Gina startles so violently tea sloshes over the rim of the cup. "Shit," she hisses, glancing down at the spill. "Sorry."

Out of the corner of my eye I see Adam glance my way. Grabbing the towel, I move to her and blot the spill. "You expecting someone?" I say under my breath.

"Not yet."

I stop blotting and meet her gaze. "So what aren't you telling me, Gina?"

Her laugh is short-lived. "Still have that suspicious mind, don't you?"

"I guess that's why I'm a cop," I tell her. "I've got a pretty decent built-in lie detector. You'd be wise to remember that."

Outside, the wind howls, hurling snow against the window, the panes trembling beneath the force.

"I'm in trouble," she whispers.

"What kind of trouble?" I ask.

Her gaze flicks to Adam and back to me, telling me she doesn't want to discuss it in front of him. "It's bad."

Realizing she's asking for some privacy, the Amish man clears his throat. "I've got to drop hay for the cattle," he tells us. "I won't be long."

When he's gone, I go to the door and close it. Pulling the chair from the sewing table, I drag it to the cot and settle into it. When I run out of things to do, I look at Gina. "I think you'd better start talking."

CHAPTER 3

Trust is an elusive thing when you're a cop. When I was younger, trust and friendship were instantaneous and uncomplicated. Life was straightforward, not yet cluttered with baggage. I could close my eyes and charge forward, my heart overflowing with conviction, any risks be damned. It was one of many things Gina Colorosa and I had been good at. Maybe a little too good, because a couple of times both of us paid a price for having that kind of blind faith when we shouldn't have.

I'm older now and not as foolish—or so I like to believe. I wonder where the last ten years have led Gina. Has she become as cautious as me or is she still the reckless dynamo I'd once admired?

"I got involved in something." She picks up the tea, grips it with both hands, and drinks. "I'm in deep, Kate. I handled it badly. I did some things I shouldn't have done."

"Maybe you ought to start at the beginning and tell me everything."

She nods. "I'm with the vice unit now. Have been for almost five years. It was a big promotion. More money. More prestige." She laughs. "Bad hours."

I'm familiar with the vice unit. Back when I was a rookie, it was a small but esteemed division of the Columbus Division of Police. It falls under the umbrella of the Narcotics Bureau and handles prostitution, alcohol, narcotics, and gambling. A lot of young cops clamored to be part of it, especially the adrenaline junkies. The unit saw a lot of action, serving warrants, setting up stings, even partaking in some undercover work.

Gina continues. "The first year was great. Satisfying work. Exciting. I got to know the guys in the unit. We were tight, you know, like a brotherhood or something. We made a lot of busts, took out some very bad guys, did some good. A few years ago, I started seeing and hearing things I didn't like."

"Like what?"

"For example, in the course of a bust I saw two patrol officers steal cash from a known pimp," she tells me. "On another occasion, a prostitute I arrested told me that in the course of an arrest, one of the male cops let her go in exchange for sex." She shrugs. "At first, I thought they were isolated incidents. A cop stepping over the line, taking advantage of his position. But I kept hearing things."

"What did you do?" I ask.

She hesitates, looks everywhere but into my eyes. "Not enough."

Knowing there's more to all of this than she's telling me, I rise and stalk to the window, look out at the whiteout conditions beyond. "You looked the other way."

"Pretty much. I made some bad choices."

"*Bad choices*? What is that, Gina? Secret code for your letting a bunch of dirty cops continue being dirty cops?"

When she doesn't respond, I get a sinking sensation in the pit of my stomach. I turn to face her, the old anger stirring in my gut. "Even before I left the department, you weren't exactly on the straight and narrow."

"It's a hell of a lot more complicated now, Kate. I was odd man out. There were a lot of dynamics to the situation. A lot of pressure—"

"Pressure? Are you kidding me?" I stalk over to her, jam my finger a few inches from her face. "What did you do?"

Shame flashes in her eyes, but is quickly replaced by attitude. "Nothing. I let it happen. I'm not proud of it. I screwed up. I got caught up in it. Kate, you have to understand . . . they made it far too easy to look the other way and that was by design. That's how they operate."

Needing a moment to process what I'm hearing—and the repercussions of it—I remove my parka, hang it on back of the chair, and sit. "Why are you here, Gina? What do you want from me?"

She laughs as if genuinely amused, and for a moment she looks like the fun-loving, errant young woman I'd known a lifetime ago. The one with a raucous laugh and a sense of humor that was invariably inappropriate. The one who could make me laugh even when I knew I shouldn't.

"For God's sake, you haven't even heard the bad news yet," she says.

I stare at her, saying nothing, bracing because I know she's going to tell me something I don't want to hear. Something that's going to bring an element into the situation that will fundamentally change a relationship I'd once held dear.

"The things I saw—the things I heard about after the fact—were just the tip of the iceberg." She sits up, intensity flaring in her expression. "I'm talking widespread corruption. The whole unit. Falsifying affidavits for search warrants. We're talking no-knock warrants served in the middle of the night with SWAT on scene, so they can go in and make good on a threat or take what they want."

I let the words settle, try to digest them, make sense of them so I can decide how to handle this, but the revelations sit in my stomach like a plateful of bad food. I'm sickened by the thought of an institution I believe in—an institution I'd once been part of—being desecrated. Worse, a monstrous doubt that Gina isn't telling the whole truth has taken up residence in the forefront of my mind.

"What are we talking about here?" I ask. "Money? What?"

"Over the last three or four years?" She shrugs. "I'd say hundreds of thousands of dollars. Titles to vehicles. Boats. Jewelry. Motor homes. Tickets to sporting events. Sex in exchange for a get-out-of-jail card."

When she looks down at her hands, they're shaking. "That's not the worst of it."

It's the first honest reaction she's shown, and I find myself bracing for what comes next.

"Last month," she says, "two people were killed in the course of a no-knock warrant. Happened in Franklinton. A couple. It's been on the news."

A memory licks at the back of my brain. "What happened?"

"One of the detectives wrote up a phony affidavit based on the word of a confidential informant by the name of Eddie Cysco. They got the warrant and went in, middle of the night no-knock. Vice unit raided the wrong house. The homeowner was armed—legally—and all hell broke loose. Everyone started shooting. The couple was shot to pieces. The vice unit covered it up. They planted drugs and no one was ever the wiser."

"Were you there?"

"I was parked on the street. I heard it unfold. Saw the aftermath." When she raises her gaze to mine, her eyes are haunted. "The Garners were good people. They worked. Led stable lives. Sandra Garner was six months pregnant. Looking forward to her first baby. Kate, I read the coroner's report. Tox was negative. She'd been shot eighteen times."

The words strike a blow, but I deflect it, look away. "Do you have proof of any of this?"

"I was working on it." She sighs. "Until they came after me, anyway." She raises a determined gaze to mine. "Here's what I know: The real target couple—the couple whose house never got raided—had been told by the vice unit to stop selling heroin. Evidently, they were interfering with another dealer who'd been given preferential treatment by the unit."

"How do you know?"

"I know because the informant they used to get the warrant is Eddie Cysco, *my* CI." She taps her chest with her palm. "I recruited him. Two years ago. I brought him in. Groomed him. Got to know him. When I asked him about the raid, he denied knowing either couple. He has no connection to them and no reason to lie."

She sniffs a runny nose, runs her sleeve across her face. "The affidavit was bogus. The warrant was bogus. The cops covered it up and rewrote history. They murdered two innocent people, ruined their reputations. That was the end of it for me. I had to get out."

"What did you do?"

"I took everything I had to Deputy Chief Frank Monaghan," she tells me. "I gave him names. Dates. Amounts. He seemed extremely concerned, supportive of me, and said he would look into it. Keep everything confidential. He asked me to lay low for a few days." She looks toward the window, where snow and wind pound the glass. "I should have known it was too easy." She meets my gaze. "I guess that brings us to the bad-news part of all this."

The dread in my gut augments to something darker. I rub a hand over my face, shoring up, knowing she's about to throw something terrible my way.

"I knew there would be consequences if they found out I'd turned on them," she tells me. "I knew they'd find a way to protect themselves. Destroy my reputation. My career. Or kill me."

A shudder moves through her, but she doesn't seem to notice. "I had no idea how it would go down. Best-case scenario, they'd threaten me, tell me to keep my mouth shut. Get me to resign. Worst case, I'd the get the 'shot in the line of duty' treatment. Some convenient friendly-fire incident. In the end, it came in the form of a no-knock warrant last night."

Wind hammers the window as she outlines in horrific detail the SWAT team descending on her house in Columbus at three o'clock this morning. "They thought they were going to catch me unaware, but I was ready for them. I had the pickup truck parked across the alley in my neighbor's garage."

I listen, my heart pounding. My hands and feet are cold and yet I'm sweating beneath my uniform shirt. "Was anyone hurt?"

"I don't know. There was a lot of chaos. It happened fast."

"What was the warrant for?"

"I don't know." Her eyes burn into mine. "Whatever the charge, it's trumped up."

I stare at her, a plethora of emotions boiling in my chest. Disbelief that she could become involved in something so reprehensible. Once upon a time, Gina was an idealistic young cop who would no more partake in corruption than cut her own throat. I feel betrayed, too. I'd once looked up to her, loved her like a sister, and trusted her with my life.

"What do you want from me?" I ask, trying not to notice the tightness in my throat.

"I need your help," she says. "I can't do this on my own."

"Do what exactly?"

"Stop them. Save what's left of my reputation. My life. Kate, I know this puts you in a precarious position, but you're the only person I can trust."

But can I trust you?

I don't pose the question, but it hovers on the tip of my tongue. Doubt is the source of the turmoil in my chest. "If you're wanted, if there's an active warrant, I can't aid and abet you. You know that."

"I'm not asking you to put your career on the line. I wouldn't do that. But I need some time to make this right." When I say nothing, she adds, "Kate, I wasn't supposed to survive that raid."

The words hang, damning and unfathomable. The silence is punctuated by the crash of wind against the house, snow pattering the window, and the hiss of our elevated breathing.

After a moment, Gina leans over to set the empty mug on the table at the head of the cot. Her flannel shirt gapes and I notice the blood coming through the turtleneck beneath it just below her left shoulder. It's bright red and wet and it's sure as hell not from some sham nosebleed caused by the airbag.

"When were you going to tell me about the gunshot wound?" I ask.

Giving me a withering look, she settles back onto the cot and pulls the blankets up to her chin. "What are you going to do? Take me to the hospital? Turn me in?"

A thread of worry goes through me as she pulls back the blankets and I take in the full extent of the bleeding. A red-black stain that's soaked her shirt all the way to the hem at her hip. "How bad is it?" I ask.

"I don't know. Haven't had a chance to look. Hurts like a son of a bitch."

"There's no way around your seeing a doctor, Gina."

"You know I can't do that."

"Let's get something straight right off the bat. You are not in charge and you are not calling the shots. Do you understand?"

She looks away, seems to sag more deeply into the mattress. For the first time, she looks defeated, as if she's come to the realization that she's fighting a battle that can't be won.

I fish my cell from my pocket, glance down at the screen, drop it back in. Everything we've discussed spirals in my brain. Allegations of police corruption. A voluntary confession that she was part of it. All of it punctuated by the fact that I haven't seen or spoken to her in ten years.

The most pressing issue, however, is the gunshot wound. Unlike the way those kinds of injuries are depicted on TV and in movies, even a flesh wound can become life-threatening without immediate treatment.

I think about my significant other, John Tomasetti—who's an agent with the Ohio Bureau of Criminal Investigation—and another layer of dread settles over me. I'm hesitant to involve him at this juncture, at least until I have more information and a better handle on what happened last night in Columbus. I won't be able to put off calling him much longer.

"Gina, do you have proof of any of this?" I ask.

"I have some audio. On my cell. It's not great. It's not enough. But it's a start." She gestures toward her coat, hanging on a chair back. "If you want me to play it—"

I shake my head. "We need to get that bullet wound looked at first. Let me make a call." I'm thinking about Tomasetti as I pull the notebook and pen from my pocket. "I need to know who is involved. I need names. All of them."

"Damon Bertrand. Nick Galloway. Half a dozen patrol cops in the unit. I don't have all their names."

An uneasy familiarity curdles inside me as I jot the names on the pad. Damon Bertrand was a patrol officer when I was a rookie. I didn't know him well, but he was a solid cop, a few years older, well thought of, and on his way up. Nick Galloway was a patrol officer and also had a stellar reputation.

I look up from the pad. "Who else?"

She grimaces. "Ken Mercer."

The floor shifts beneath me and for an instant it feels as if the gale outside has ripped the house from its foundation and spun it. When I resigned from the Columbus Division of Police, Ken Mercer had just made detective. He was a few years older. Ambitious. Charismatic. Everyone knew he would move up. He and I worked together a dozen times. We were friends. We were more than friends for a short time. He's the one and only cop I slept with in the ten years I was with the department.

"In case you haven't kept up with things, Bertrand and Mercer are detectives with the Narcotics Bureau. Galloway is a sergeant in the Patrol North Subdivision. Frank Monaghan is deputy chief."

Deputy chief is one of the highest positions in the Columbus Division of Police, just below chief.

"They are the heart of this," Gina says firmly. "They're tight-knit and if you cross them, they will find a way to take you out."

I get to my feet, look down at her, and sigh. Gina Colorosa was always larger than life. Back in the day, I'd looked up to her. She was ambitious and unafraid. Flawed and unapologetic. I'd wanted to please her. Be like her. Now I look at her and I see woman who betrayed not only herself, but the institution we loved, and the laws we'd sworn to uphold.

I think about Adam Lengacher and his children. Though I haven't yet decided how much I believe of her story or what I'm going to do about it, I'm struck by the possibility that someone—law enforcement or some other unsavory individuals—is looking for Gina.

"Does anyone know you're here?" I ask.

She shakes her head. "I wasn't exactly sure where I was going until I ran out of options."

"When's the last time you used your cell phone?" I ask.

"I was still in Columbus." She frowns at me. "Don't worry. It's a burner. No one knows about it."

"I'm going to make some calls. See what I can find out about that warrant." I send a nod to the bloodstain on her shirt. "We need to take care of that gunshot wound."

She looks away, saying nothing.

I stare at her a moment. She looks wiped out. Pale. Shivering again. Somehow diminished. Not just physically, but in ways that make me think less of her.

Realizing I have nothing left to say to her, I leave the room.

CHAPTER 4

I find Adam at the kitchen table, drinking coffee, still wearing his barn coat, the shoulders of which are wet with melted snow. Lizzie and Annie are at the sink—Annie standing on a wood crate in order to reach—washing dishes. Sammy is nowhere in sight, but I hear him talking from the mudroom.

"Datt! The snow is almost up to the windows!" the boy calls out.

"It's just a drift from the wind." Adam smiles at me as he responds to his son. "Bring in the rest of that wood from the shed, Sammy, and stack it in the corner by the stove."

The boy appears at the doorway, hair sticking to a sweaty forehead despite the chill. His eyes flick from his *datt* to me and back. Little Mr. Social. "Maybe I should go to the barn and see if Suzy had her calf."

"Not now, son. Just the wood. We'll check on Suzy later."

Grinning, the boy spins and runs back to the mudroom.

The door slams and Adam rises, takes off his coat, and hangs it on the chair back. "How is she?" he asks me.

"She needs a doctor." I let my eyes slide to the two girls at the sink. "Do you have a minute?"

He motions toward the living room. I head that way, taking him past the stairs, to the window at the front of the room, out of earshot of the children. Outside, wind and snow batter the pine tree standing guard in the front yard. We watch the storm for a moment.

"How badly is she hurt?" he asks.

"She's been shot. I don't know how bad it is."

His eyes widen. "An accident?"

"No. Adam, there are some things going on you need to be aware of."

He nods, his gaze steady on mine. "All right."

"You know Gina is a police officer."

"Yes."

"She's involved in . . . a troubling situation. I'm trying to get to the bottom of it," I tell him. "Since she's here in your home with you and your children, I thought you should be aware. If you want me to find another place for her to stay until we can get things straightened out, I'll do it."

He stares at me a moment, his mind working over everything that's been said. "She is badly hurt?"

I nod. "You're under no obligation to get involved."

"The Amish do not close their doors to anyone in need, Katie. It's not our way. 'The Lord sustains them on their sickbed and restores them from their bed of illness.'"

I nod, trying not to feel too much, for him, for the community I left behind. "Psalm Forty-one."

"You remember."

"Of course I do."

He's still staring at me, gauging, trying to read between lines he isn't quite sure how to interpret. "This woman," he says. "Is she dangerous?"

"No," I tell him. But even as I say the word I know the situation isn't quite that straightforward.

"What are you going to do about her injury?" he asks.

I shake my head, hating that I've placed him in the middle of this.

That I've let myself be drawn into a situation that could bring my own ethics into question. "I need to get her to the hospital." I glance out the window and laugh. "The problem is I'm not sure I can make it all the way to Millersburg."

Grimacing, he looks out the window, where the snow is piled on the sill, sticking to the panes, nearly obscuring the view. "Joe Weaver was here the day last summer when Amos Yoder cut off his finger with the pneumatic saw. Joe isn't a doctor, but he knows about medicine."

I've never met Joe Weaver, but I'm familiar with his story. Years ago, when he was on *Rumspringa,* instead of partaking in the usual antics young Amish men get caught up in—smoking and drinking and staying out late—Joe got a job and went back to school, against the wishes of his Swartzentruber parents, and earned his GED. He loved animals and wanted to become a veterinarian. Without the support of his Amish brethren, Joe took a job with a vet, saved his money, and—against all odds—attended The College of Wooster for two years. All the while, he was under tremendous pressure from the Amish community to join the church and marry. Higher education is considered worldly and frowned upon by the elders, one of several tenets I disagree with. The situation made such a stir, the *Times-Record* interviewed him and ran a front-page piece. In the end, Joe gave up his dream of becoming a veterinarian, but he's well versed in animal medicine, and the Amish travel for miles to bring their sick or injured pets and livestock to his small clinic outside Painters Mill.

"He knows about English medicine, Katie. He treated Big Jimmy for colic last summer, stitched up my bull when he got tangled in barbed wire. Joe knows what he's doing."

The thought of a would-be veterinarian administering medical treatment to a human being, especially for something as serious as a gunshot wound, makes me second-guess the whole idea of not attempting the drive to Millersburg. I think about other options, like asking Doc Coblentz—the coroner, local pediatrician, and friend—to drive over. But I nix the idea; any such request by me would place him in a compromising situation. That's not taking the inclement weather into consideration.

"Do you think Joe would be agreeable to treating someone he doesn't know?" I ask. "For a gunshot wound?"

"He is Amish, Katie. If someone is hurt, he will help, no questions asked."

No questions asked.

The words hover in the air between us, like a curse whispered in the presence of the bishop. My cop sensibilities struggle with my conscience and the knowledge that I could be making a mistake that, once put into play, won't be easily undone or corrected.

I'm rarely apprehensive about talking to my significant other, John Tomasetti. He's the one person in this world I trust implicitly, the one person I can count on no matter the circumstance, the one who will not judge me too harshly if I screw up. He's a critical thinker, sees the world from a broad perspective, but he also possesses the puissance to speak his mind even when it's something I don't want to hear. At the moment, I need to know if he's heard any whisperings about corruption inside the Columbus Division of Police. Or maybe I just need someone to talk me out of taking that first, dangerous step down the wrong path.

I make the call as I creep along on the township road, the Explorer buffeted by wind, tires bumping over drifts deep enough to scrape the undercarriage. Visibility is down to just a few feet in areas where the snow is blowing sideways. My palms are sweaty inside my leather gloves despite the coldness of the steering wheel.

He picks up on the first ring, his voice easy, relaxed. "I fired up the John Deere and cleared our lane half an hour ago," he tells me. "Unfortunately, it's drifted over again."

"I think you're going to need a bigger tractor," I say.

"How bad are things in Painters Mill?"

"We've had a few fender benders. Wrecker service is busy. Glock's on duty. School sent the kids home a couple hours ago."

"Any chance you can call it a day?" he asks. "I thought we might build a fire. Make a pot of chili. Watch a movie."

I can tell by his tone he's already realized I won't be coming home anytime soon. While most people grumble about getting snowed in and having to hunker down inside their homes, this is the kind of weather that keeps those of us in law enforcement out on the street.

"Tomasetti, I'm not exactly sure how to explain what's going on, so I'm just going to put it out there."

"That sounds ominous."

Taking a deep breath, I tell him everything I know about Gina Colorosa.

"I saw something come over the hot sheet this morning," he says. "It was Columbus, so I didn't look too hard." The tempo of his voice changes, telling me he's walking toward our home office to log in to his computer.

"I ran her name," I tell him. "There's an active warrant and a BOLO. I don't have the details."

"Let me take a look. Are you with Colorosa now?"

"I'm on my way to Joe Weaver's place."

"Dare I ask."

I close my eyes briefly. "She's been shot. Joe Weaver isn't exactly a veterinarian, but he's had some medical training."

"Isn't that kind of like getting on a plane knowing the person in the cockpit has had a couple hours of flight instruction?"

"If you have a better idea . . ."

A too-long silence and then he says, "I don't have to tell you what you're getting involved in is a bad idea, do I?"

"I'm aware."

The tap of computer keys sounds on the other end of the line. The curse that follows tells me the news isn't good. "There's an open arrest warrant for Colorosa."

"What's it for?"

Keys click over the line. "All I can tell you from what I'm seeing here is that she was under investigation. The rest of it is sealed."

"That's unusual, isn't it?"

"Yes, it is," he says slowly.

For the span of several heartbeats the only sounds are the wind pummeling my vehicle, the tap of snow against the windshield, and the occasional bark of my police radio.

I tell him about the couple killed in the course of the no-knock warrant. "She's given me names. She claims to have dates and amounts. And an audio recording that may or may not be helpful."

"Kate, you need to stop what you're doing, while you still can. Turn around. Take her to Pomerene. I'll meet you there, and we'll get this figured out."

"Tomasetti, what if she's telling the truth? She believes she wasn't supposed to survive the raid last night." Even as I speak the words, I realize how improbable they sound. As if I'm too involved to see the situation clearly and listening to my emotions instead of my common sense.

"That's an extremely serious allegation, Kate. If she's going to come forward, she'd better have something to back it up."

The line hisses between us, reminding me of the distance that's both literal and figurative. "Have you heard anything? Rumors? Gossip?"

You're grasping at straws, Kate, a little voice whispers in my ear.

"Columbus doesn't fall in my region, but I can make some calls. You got any names for me?"

I recite them from memory. "There are others, too. Street cops. Patrol mostly. She claims to have taken all of this to Frank Monaghan. He's deputy chief now, over the Investigative Subdivision."

The silence stretches, expanding into a high-wire tension that wasn't there before.

"I know who he is," Tomasetti says after a moment.

Something in his voice sends a prickly sensation across the back of my neck. "You know him?"

A brief hesitation and then, "I know of him."

"What does that mean?"

"That means I can't talk about it."

I'm ever cognizant that there are certain topics that, due to his position with BCI, Tomasetti isn't at liberty to discuss. I would never ask him to cross that line. I'm okay with those kinds of boundaries and I've no problem honoring them. Though Painters Mill falls within his region, confidentiality has never been an issue. Until now.

"Tomasetti, what am I supposed to do with that?"

A too-long beat of silence ensues and then he makes a sound of frustration. "Let me look into a couple of things."

"And in the interim?"

"See if you can get that damn pseudo-vet out there to look at her gunshot wound."

I start to say something else, but he hangs up on me.

• • •

What should have been a ten-minute drive ends up taking nearly an hour. By the time I make the turn into the lane of Joe Weaver's "clinic" I'm sweating beneath my coat. I can't stop thinking about my exchange with Tomasetti. The mention of Frank Monaghan changed the tone of our conversation and added a tension that wasn't there before. All of it gives credence to Gina's claim that not everything is as it should be within the Columbus Division of Police.

I power the Explorer through a series of drifts, fishtail sideways as I roll up to the hangar-size Quonset hut. Joe Weaver comes to the door as I tromp through deep snow. I reach a small, covered porch and he ushers me inside.

"There is an emergency?" He looks past me to the Explorer, wondering if I've got a sick dog or cat lying on the front seat in need of treatment. If only the situation were that simple.

"No emergency," I tell him as I stomp snow from my boots.

He's wearing insulated coveralls that are unzipped enough that I can see the front of his blue work shirt and suspenders. He's in what I guess to be his late thirties, with longish brown hair and the typical beard of a married Amish man.

The Quonset hut is warm and smells of hay and molasses with the tang of woodsmoke from a potbellied stove in the corner. The sound of the wind and the pop of burning wood fill the silence as Joe pushes the door closed.

"I was just over at Adam Lengacher's place," I begin.

"Everything okay over there?" he asks, still trying to figure out why I'm here.

The last thing I want to do is involve someone in a situation that could have moral or legal implications. But with emergency services shut down and the weather deteriorating by the minute, I've run out of options. I've seen enough gunshot wounds to know that even if Gina's injury is minor, if left untreated it could become life-threatening.

"Joe, I've got an unusual situation and I need your help."

Concern suffuses his expression. "Of course. What is it?"

Leaving out details he's better off not knowing—not to keep him in the dark, but to protect him from any problems that might arise—I lay out the basics of Gina's situation. "She's a police officer and she's involved in—" I grapple for the right words. "—a sensitive situation. There was an incident last night. Joe, she's been shot."

His eyes narrow. "How bad is it?"

"All I know is that it's a shoulder wound. There's some bleeding, but it's not profuse. I think she was probably hypothermic when Adam found her."

"How long ago was she shot?"

"Ten hours, give or take."

"Is the bullet still inside her?"

"I don't know," I say.

"Gunshot wounds are very serious, Chief Burkholder."

"I know. Joe, I'd never ask you to become involved in a situation like this if there was another way. But emergency services aren't running because of the storm. And I don't believe I can get her to the hospital myself."

He gazes at me intently. In the depths of his eyes, I see the bloom of knowledge. "Doctors are required by law to report those kinds of wounds."

"Yes."

"I'm not a doctor."

I nod. "You are not obligated to help."

"She is a criminal?" he asks.

"She's a police officer," I say. "But she . . . made some bad choices and now she's wanted by the police. I'm trying to help her do the right thing."

His eyes slide to the window, where wind-driven snow assaults the glass. "If infection sets in, she will have a serious problem."

I nod. "If you decide to help . . . Joe, there will likely be an investigation. A lot of questions. I want you to know that going in."

He stares at me, his expression troubled. For a moment, I think he's going to refuse. A choice I will not hold against him. Instead, he gives a single, decisive nod. "Let me get my bag."

CHAPTER 5

The drive back to the Lengacher farm is a harrowing ordeal. Drifts reaching as high as the bumper bog down the Explorer several times, but I manage to bust through and keep going. If current weather conditions continue, roads will likely become impassable overnight—a reality that sends a thread of anxiety through my midsection. If Gina's gunshot wound is life-threatening, we'll be left to deal with it without a doctor, because the window for me to get her to the hospital in Millersburg has closed.

I drive up the lane too fast, the Explorer bucking over massive drifts, snow exploding over the hood. Beside me, Joe Weaver clutches the door handle. "You've done this before, no?"

"A time or two." The rear tires fishtail when I make the turn toward the house. "Wouldn't have made it without the four-wheel drive and chains."

The Amish man grins. "And then Adam would have to get Big Jimmy to pull you out."

"Right."

I park as close to the house as I can manage and throw open my door. Joe does the same. Wind lashes us as we trudge to the back porch. Snow pelts my face like a sandblaster as I yank open the door.

Adam meets us in the mudroom. "I was starting to get worried."

"She's a good driver, no?" Winking at me, Joe extends his hand, and the two men shake.

Adam tips his head, his eyes falling to the bag at Joe's side. "That she is."

"How is Gina?" I ask.

"Sleeping."

The two men exchange looks, their expressions thoughtful and uneasy. Adam motions toward the kitchen. "This way," he says.

We don't take the time to remove our coats or boots. Adam leads us through the kitchen, where the two girls are sitting at the table, playing a game of checkers, curious eyes tracking us.

Sammy joins us in the living room. "Annie made Gina another cup of tea but she fell asleep and it got cold," he proclaims. "Should we wake her so she can drink some tea, Datt?"

Adam sets his hand on the boy's head as we enter the hall that will take us to the sewing room. "Not now."

We find Gina lying on the cot, the quilts pulled up over her shoulders, watching us, her expression wary. Her gaze flicks from me to Adam to Joe Weaver and finally to the bag at his side. "Who are you?"

"Joe Weaver."

She eyes the bag. "You a doctor?"

"No, ma'am," Joe says.

"Looks like a medical bag."

Joe stares at her, not sure how to respond. Adam's gaze moves from Gina to me. He shifts his weight from one foot to the other.

"He's . . . got some medical training," I tell her. "He's going to treat that gunshot wound before infection sets in."

Using her uninjured arm, she pushes herself to a sitting position, propping her back against the wall at the head of the cot. "So if he's not a doctor, what the hell is he?"

"He's your best bet," I tell her.

"I'm an animal practitioner," Joe offers.

Before anyone can add anything, Gina laughs. It's a slightly manic sound in the silence of the room, with the wind and snow battering the window. The two men exchange another look, not sure how to react, likely wondering if she's not only on the outs with the law, but insane, too.

Under different circumstances I might've joined her. But I don't. That she would laugh in the face of two men who've offered their help, perhaps at the risk of legal repercussions or their standing in their community, ticks me off.

"A simple thank-you would be a good way to get things rolling," I tell her.

"Sorry, it's just that . . ." Choking back laughter that isn't entirely born of humor and contains a distinct edge of desperation, she sobers. "I'm a little out of my element here."

"In case you haven't noticed, all of us are out of our elements." I look at Joe. "What do you need to get started?"

"I have everything I need right here." He pats the bag.

I go to Gina. "He's going to need to take a look at that shoulder."

"All right." Grimacing, she nods at Joe. "Thank you."

The Amish man steps forward, looks around for a place to set his bag. I spot an old-fashioned rack of TV trays against the wall, pull one out, and unfold it for him.

Joe nods. "*Danki.*"

Adam sets his hand on his son's shoulder. "Ah . . . we probably ought to go break ice for the cattle."

"And check on Suzy to see if she had her calf," Sammy adds, but he doesn't take his eyes off of Gina.

I make eye contact with Adam. "Thank you."

Giving us a final nod, the Amish man guides his son from the room. I close the door behind them, fold my arms at my chest, and lean against it. From her place on the cot, Gina watches as Joe opens the medical bag and sets a roll of wrapped gauze, a large plastic syringe, and a bottle of Betadine solution on a small tray.

"Have you ever treated a gunshot wound?" she asks.

Joe continues his work, disinfecting his hands and pulling on a pair of disposable gloves. "Two years ago, one of Mark Miller's buggy horses was shot in the withers. An accident, you know. A stray bullet from a hunter, probably. It was deer season."

"The horse survived?" she asks.

"No," he says, deadpan.

At her stricken expression, Joe glances at me over his shoulder and grins. "The horse was fine. Got him out of work for a few weeks."

I've always had an appreciation for Amish humor and I smile back at him.

"How are you feeling overall?" he asks Gina.

Her gaze flicks to mine. "Is that a serious question?"

A hint of a smile whispers across his features. "Any sweating? Sensations of heat? Throbbing at the site of the wound?"

"Some throbbing," she responds. "It's getting worse. No heat."

Joe finishes readying his tools, uncaps a digital thermometer, slides a cover onto the tip, and passes it to Gina. "Under your tongue. No speaking for twenty seconds."

Frowning as if she's not quite sure if he's messing with her, she eyes the thermometer, then does as she's told.

When the thermometer beeps, Gina removes it from her mouth and hands it to Joe. He squints at the reading. "No fever. That's a good sign." He tips his head at me and clears his throat.

Realizing he's not comfortable asking her to remove her shirt, I leave my place at the door and go to Gina. "You're going to have to slip that shirt off your shoulder."

"Right." Using her uninjured arm, she sets to work unbuttoning her shirt.

Seeing that she's having difficulty, I go to her, kneel next to the cot. I finish the last of the buttons. She's wearing a turtleneck beneath the flannel shirt, so I roll it up at the hem and stretch it out at the armpit. Wincing in pain, she maneuvers her arm out of the sleeve.

"*Schmatze,*" Joe murmurs, which is *Deitsh* for "be in pain."

"*Miah sinn glikk see is net yoosa fluch-vadda,*" I say. We're lucky she's not cursing.

"*Net alsnoch,*" he says. Not yet.

"I can't defend myself unless you insult me in English," Gina grumbles as the damaged flesh looms into view.

Gunshot wounds are hideous things. I've seen several in the years I've been a cop, both accidental and intentional, inflicted by everything from a .22 to a shotgun. I've suffered a gunshot wound myself. Though mine wasn't life-threatening and I received prompt medical care, it was a traumatic experience, not just physically but psychologically.

Like most cops, I'm an emergency medical technician. I've read enough to know that the main elements that affect tissue damage are caliber, velocity, and distance. Luck, of course, has a lot to do with it, too. Noting the location of this particular wound—which is an inch or so into the muscular part of her shoulder—I suspect Gina is one of the luckiest people walking around.

The wound itself is about the size of a pencil eraser and round in shape. The surrounding flesh is the color of eggplant, swollen, and covered with dried blood.

"If you could lower that." Joe indicates her bloodstained bra strap.

I slide the narrow strip of lace off her shoulder.

"Glad I wore my good bra," Gina murmurs.

Rising, I step away to give Joe better light and room to work. I watch as he swabs the entire shoulder, front and back, with a sterile gauze saturated with the Betadine solution. He uses a fresh gauze to pat it dry. Once the area is clean, the full impact of the wound looms large.

"Are you able to remove the slug?" I ask.

"There is no slug," he tells me. "The bullet passed through." The Amish man indicates the hole I noticed initially. "It entered here. Exited in the back."

I hadn't noticed the second wound. Craning my neck, I spot the quarter-size, slightly jagged cavity on the back side of her shoulder. "The bullet passed through cleanly," I say. "That's good, right?"

"Passed through, yes." He makes a sound with his tongue. "Cleanly . . . probably not. You see, the bullet picks up bits of clothing and other debris as it enters, and forces it into the wound."

"She'll need antibiotics?" I ask.

"And I'll need to flush the wound," he tells me.

"I'd appreciate it if you two would stop talking about me as if I'm not here," Gina grumbles.

Joe reaches into his bag and produces a sealed sandwich baggie filled with a couple of dozen large oval-shaped pills. "One tablet every twelve hours until they're gone."

"They look like horse pills," Gina says.

"They are," Joe says. "But they are good for people, too, I think. Eight hundred milligrams of sulfamethoxazole and trimethoprim."

I take the bag and set it on the sewing table.

"I need to flush the wound now." He looks at Gina and frowns. "Going to hurt, probably."

"Of course it is," she mutters.

"I'll make it quick." He picks up the syringe. "The good news is that the bullet didn't hit bone or the joint. You are very lucky."

Paper rattles as he unwraps the syringe and attaches a length of clear irrigation tubing to the needle hub.

Gina eyes the device with suspicion. "Please tell me you're not going to stick that thing in my shoulder."

"I'm going to fill the syringe with sterile saline solution, insert the irrigation tube into the wound, and flush away any foreign particles."

"For God's sake." Raising her uninjured arm, she lowers her head and presses her fingers against the bridge of her nose.

"That same God was watching over you when this happened," Joe says as he eases the plunger from the syringe, filling the barrel with the clear solution. He looks at me. "I think she'd be wise to remember that."

I've got to hand it to Gina; she handles the procedure well. Over the next half hour, Joe flushes both wounds, front and back. It's a messy, painful procedure. He then stitches the larger exit wound, leaving a drain tube in place. Finally, both wounds are bandaged. Throughout, Gina doesn't utter a sound. Her expression remains impassive. If it weren't for the sheen of sweat on her forehead, the damp hair at the back of her neck, I wouldn't have been able to tell she was in pain. By the time Joe fashions the makeshift sling for her, she's begun to shiver.

"Any special instructions?" I ask.

"Start those antibiotics now. Stay warm. Get some extra sleep. Drink a lot of water."

"Drink a lot of something," she says on a sigh.

I go to Gina and help her ease the turtleneck over her shoulder. "You did good," I say.

Shrugging, the Amish man tilts his head to make eye contact with Gina and smiles. "She was nearly as good a patient as that horse."

CHAPTER 6

They met in the parking lot of the diner in Franklinton. The food was an atrocity for the most part, made edible only by the concentration of fat and a generous amount of salt. The clientele was dodgy—par for the course in this part of Columbus—but mostly kept to themselves. The owner, a Ukrainian guy who had several aliases and could never quite explain where he came from or how long he'd been here, appreciated it when the cops came by for lunch or dinner or stopped in for coffee. Their presence, he said, kept the riffraff away. The waitresses felt safer walking to their cars or the bus stop at closing time. The sight of a city-issue Crown Vic with all the trimmings warded off even the most determined homeless who liked to sleep out by the dumpster at the back of the building. According to the owner's wife, Mila, thanks to Columbus's finest, the place hadn't been robbed for going on two years now.

Damon Bertrand had been coming to this little hole in the wall the entirety of his career, which would span thirty years this month. During that time, the ownership of the diner had changed hands eight times. The name had changed at least six times. Once, the place had closed for two weeks without explanation and without so much as a sign on the door. In the course of a welfare check, the police discovered the owner's body in the kitchen. He'd hanged himself with an electrical cord attached to the deep fryer.

Despite the seediness of the neighborhood and the dubious nature of the establishment and its patrons—or maybe because of those things—Bertrand would continue to frequent the diner. A bottomless cup of coffee was hot and bitter and free of charge if you had a badge. The pancake-and-scrambled-eggs breakfast was decent enough—mainly because even the most inept cook couldn't screw up bacon. He thought maybe it was the one thing he'd miss when he retired.

The big silver Suburban rolled up next to his unmarked Crown Vic, headlights on, wipers waging a losing war against the snow. He watched the driver leave the cab, pull up his collar against the cold, and trot across the space between their vehicles. The door swung open, a swirl of snow blowing in.

"Hell of a day to be out." Ken Mercer shook snow from his coat, his expression sour, as he slid onto the passenger seat.

"Welcome to Ohio in January," Bertrand muttered.

"Yeah, well, one of these days I'm going to move to fucking Miami."

The two men sat in silence for a moment, giving the rise of tension a moment to settle. Bertrand had known Ken Mercer for going on sixteen years now. He was a good guy, a good cop, and had recently been promoted to detective in the Narcotics Bureau. A husband and father of four, he coached Little League in the summer, counseled inner-city kids every other Saturday, and took part in the Division of Police fundraiser for juvenile cancer every Christmas. But Mercer also had a fondness for nice clothes, a small herd of kids to put through college, and a wife whose tastes he couldn't afford. At just forty-two years of age, he'd already been with the department for twenty years. Like Bertrand, he was a lifer.

They'd ridden together back when Mercer was a rookie. They were like-minded and had bonded the way cops do. For years, they'd enjoyed weekend barbecues with spouses and kids, Friday-night beers at the cop bar over on Sullivant, and the occasional weekend at the fishing cabin on Lake Erie. It was the kind of relationship that suited Bertrand to a T. Simple. Beneficial. And easy to walk away from when you were through. He figured they had another year or two, until he retired, anyway.

Cursing beneath his breath, Mercer reached down and turned up the heat. "You get a line on Colorosa?"

"I got nothing and it wasn't for lack of trying." Bertrand looked at his passenger and frowned. "Last night was an epic fail."

Mercer shrugged. "That raid was textbook. We—"

"Colorosa isn't some dumb-shit drug dealer."

"She knew we were coming."

"No one talked to her, if that's what you're suggesting." Bertrand made the statement with conviction, but he wasn't sure he believed it. Truth be told, he wasn't sure who he could trust these days. "How'd we miss the pickup truck?"

Mercer sighed. "She must have figured we'd come for her. She was ready for us. Had a plan."

"You search the place?"

"We tore that place apart. The house. The yard. Garage. We even searched the neighbor's place. It wasn't there."

"She's got it with her." The thought made Bertrand frown. "Now we have people sniffing around things we don't want sniffed. We need to find her. Get this cleaned up. No loose ends."

"Blood we found at the scene hers?"

"Not back from the lab yet."

"If she's hit and goes to a hospital or clinic, we'll know about it," Mercer said.

"Maybe." Bertrand knew the situation would not be that simple. Not with Colorosa involved. She was street smart, tough as nails, and a survivor. "We got all our ducks in a row on this end?"

Mercer nodded. "We've got a shitload of dirt on her. I'm talking hard evidence that'll stand up in court, if it gets that far. All the items entered into evidence in the course of the warrant last night. Assistant DA says it's a slam dunk. Colorosa is going down and she's not coming back up."

"Not quietly. That bitch hasn't done anything quietly since she learned to talk."

"All we have to do is find her," Mercer said. "Make the arrest. If she starts talking—and I suspect she will—there's not a soul on this earth who's going to believe a word comes out of her mouth."

Bertrand glanced toward the diner. Through the steamed-up, snow-caked windows, he spotted his favorite waitress, a red-haired beauty, standing at the counter, taking someone's order. "Colorosa got any family?" he asked.

"Not that we know of," Mercer said. "We're checking known associates."

"Cell phone records?" Bertrand asked.

"Warrant should come through any time." He looked at his watch and frowned. "Once we get that, if we can triangulate to the nearest tower where it last pinged, we'll know which direction she went."

Bertrand was still thinking about known associates. "What about cops? She tight with anyone?"

"We're looking at that, too. But you know Colorosa. She's kind of a loner. Never got too close to anyone."

Bertrand glanced toward the diner, watched the waitress hustle away from the table, and he thought about the night he'd met the pretty redhead four years ago. It was raining and cold and he offered to drive her home. On the drive, he'd learned she was from the Ukraine, too. She was young and pretty with big crooked teeth and eyes that had likely seen more than their share of trouble. When he'd asked about her citizenship, she'd admitted she was way past her visa and then she'd proceeded to give him a blow job right there in the parking lot of her apartment complex. He didn't even have to ask.

"The longer Colorosa is on the street, the more likely this is to come back to bite us," Bertrand said. "That can't happen. Do you understand?"

"We'll get her," Mercer assured him.

"We have a good thing going, Ken. We trusted her and she turned on us. Stabbed us in the back. I don't want that bitch screwing it up for the rest of us."

Mercer hit Bertrand with a red-eyed glare. "I said we got it covered."

Bertrand looked away, turned his attention back to the diner, trying to catch a glimpse of the redhead through the fogged-up windows.

"Keep me posted, will you?" he said.

Without another word, Ken Mercer swung open the door, and stepped into the swirling snow.

CHAPTER 7

I leave Gina sleeping and take Joe Weaver back to his farm. Road conditions have worsened exponentially in the three hours since I picked him up. Twice, I have to take evasive action to circumvent drifts too high to pass through. I zip up the lane too fast, knowing if I stop I'll get stuck. Finally, I roll up to the Quonset hut and park in a partially cleared area just off the front door.

I know even before I pull out my wallet that the Amish man won't accept payment; I try anyway. I've only got two twenties on me, which isn't enough for his time and the antibiotics, and I shove the bills at him as he reaches for the door handle.

"For your expenses and time," I say.

He raises his hands and shakes his head. "Your money is no good here, Chief Burkholder."

"For the medication then."

He smiles as if amused by my persistence and shakes his head. "Your friend is going to be all right. What I did today will tide her over until she can get to a hospital. But I wouldn't delay that too long."

He starts to open the door, but I stop him. "Joe, you know you can't talk to anyone about this, right?"

"I talk to my cats, mostly. I've got five of them, you know. Feral, or so they think. Unlike most of my human friends, they never repeat a word."

I grin, liking him. "Thank you."

"I hope your friend finds peace."

"Me, too."

Hesitating, he looks around. "I will wait until you get turned around, Chief Burkholder. If you get stuck, I have a shovel inside and a frisky Dutch colt in that little barn out back."

I thank him again and then he's gone.

The Explorer bogs down twice while I'm turning around. Taking it easy on the accelerator, thankful for the tire chains, I rock back and forth and manage to free up my wheels both times. Then I'm flying down the lane and making the turn back onto the township road. I come upon a farmer on a massive John Deere tractor, lights flashing. I'm nearly on top of him before I realize he's clearing the road. He's traveling in reverse with a snowblower attachment hitched to the rear, auger spinning, the chute propelling snow thirty feet downwind.

I flash my lights and raise my hand in greeting as I pass. He waves back, a shared moment between two motorists who might've been the last souls on earth. The rest of the trip to the Lengacher farm is uneventful. I'm midway to the house when a four-foot-high drift slams into my bumper hard enough to throw me against my seat belt. Snow cascades over the windshield, and the Explorer lurches to an abrupt stop.

"Shit," I mutter as I unfasten my safety belt.

I sit there a moment, thinking about pulling out the collapsible shovel I keep in the back. But I know any attempt to dig out of such a mountainous drift with the wind kicking would be a fruitless endeavor. From where I'm sitting, I can see that the snow is as high as the headlights. It's coming down fast and already blowing across the hood. Even if I manage to dig out of this particular drift, chances are there's another one waiting a few yards ahead. I've no choice but to hoof it to the house and hope I can free up the Explorer once the weather breaks.

Throwing up the hood of my parka, I open the door and step into the maelstrom. Wind and snow pummel me as I start in the general direction of the house. It crosses my mind that my vehicle is now blocking the lane, but there's nothing I can do about it, so I keep going.

I'm no stranger to snow. I've lived in Ohio my entire life. When I was a kid it was a magical thing, despite the fact that my family faced many hardships caring for the livestock and keeping the farm up and running. Even so, I couldn't wait for that first big snowfall—the more, the better. As an adult—and a cop—I'm invariably out in inclement weather, helping motorists or handling fender benders. While snow can be a stunning phenomenon, it makes life plenty difficult. A blizzard like this one is dangerous.

Wind thrashes me as I tromp through drifts as high as my hips. Some areas have been scoured by the wind so much that I can see gravel. Snow stings my eyes and sweeps down my collar. Visibility is down to a few feet. I'm close to the house, but I can't see it. I can barely make out the fence on either side of the driveway, which is just a few feet away.

By the time I reach the steps of the front porch, my coat and trousers are caked with snow. My face is wet and burning with cold. I cross the porch and knock. The door swings open and I find myself looking at young Sammy. His eyes widen at the sight of me. "Katie! You look like a snowman!" he exclaims as he ushers me inside.

I enter the living room to see Adam standing in the hall, head cocked, expression concerned as he takes my measure. "Is everything all right?"

"I got stuck in your lane." I push the hood off my head. "I'm pretty much blocking it."

"I don't think we're going to be taking the buggy out any time soon. We have a rear gate for the sleigh if we need to get out."

"Datt, now we can put the harness on Jimmy and he can pull her out, like he did Mr. Besecker last winter." Sammy looks up at me. "Wait till you see how strong he is, Katie. Jimmy may be old and fat and sometimes he's lazy, but he's the strongest horse in the world."

A smile drifts across Adam's expression, but he doesn't let it reach his lips. He shifts his gaze to mine. "Samuel is right. Once this snow lets up, we can pull you out if you'd like."

My gaze travels to the front window. The storm is so ferocious I can no longer see the tree off the porch. As chief of police in the midst of a blizzard, there are a dozen things I should be doing. This is the kind of weather that brings with it an onslaught of emergencies. Undoubtedly some of my officers won't be able to make it in for their shift. But having just been outside and knowing conditions are only going to get worse, I accept the reality that I'm not going anywhere for the time being.

"I might just take you up on that," I say. "How's our patient?"

"Sleeping." I see him looking at my coat, which is still encrusted with snow. "Would you like to dry your coat by the stove?"

"That'd be great," I say, unzipping it, wiping my boots on the rug.

"Samuel, take Katie's coat to the mudroom where the stove is, hang it on back of the chair to dry like we do."

I work the coat from my shoulders and hand it to the boy. "*Danki.*"

Flashing a shy grin, the boy takes the coat and starts toward the kitchen.

I turn my attention to Adam. "I'm sorry to intrude on you and your family like this," I tell him as I brush the remaining snow from my trousers. "I think we're officially snowed in."

He sends a pointed look to the window, where snow has piled up against the panes. "I'm glad we found your friend when we did."

I know he means it and with all sincerity. Still, his willingness to help doesn't alleviate my concern that I've asked too much of him. Or that I may have involved him and his family in something I shouldn't have.

While Adam clangs dishes around in the kitchen, I call Tomasetti from my place on the sofa. "Were you able to find anything on Gina Colorosa?" I ask.

"I'm waiting for a couple of callbacks," he tells me. "The most interesting thing I've discovered so far is that no one wants to talk about it."

"What does that mean?"

"If I were to guess, I'd venture to say there may be some kind of ongoing investigation. She was on active duty, so I'd say it was likely a covert operation."

"Any idea what she's being investigated for?"

"From what I've been able to piece together, Colorosa is suspected of engaging in some kind of corrupt activity. I don't know the details yet or who else is involved."

"What about the warrant? Any idea what it was for?"

"All I know is that a judge signed off on it. Since she's a police officer and was likely armed, the vice unit did a no-knock at three A.M. this morning. Investigators were looking for evidence showing any pattern of corrupt activity, money or property, any tampering with government records, witnesses, or obstructing official business."

I close my eyes, try to digest the enormity of the information, weigh it against everything Gina has told me so far. "Did they find anything?"

"All I know is that they confiscated her laptop. Notebooks. Two handguns. A prepaid cell. And four thousand dollars in cash."

A thread of disappointment goes through me. "Most people don't have that kind of cash lying around."

"It gets worse. Yesterday, a CI by the name of Eddie Cysco was gunned down," he tells me, using the cop-speak term for 'confidential informant.' "The scene is still active and there's not much information coming out. But I understand he's got some connection to Colorosa."

The name reverberates in my head. "Gina mentioned Cysco," I tell him. "He was the CI the vice unit used to obtain a warrant for the no-knock in which Louis and Sandra Garner were killed." I lay out the circumstances. "According to Gina, anyway."

"I heard about that raid," he tells me. "The department took some flak."

"Timing of Cysco's death is interesting," I say. "Did they get the shooter?"

He sighs unhappily. "This isn't official, but Colorosa is a person of interest. They're doing ballistics testing now on the handgun confiscated at her home."

For a moment I'm so dumbstruck I can't speak. The urge to defend her rises in my chest, but I quickly bank it. The truth of the matter is I have my doubts about Gina. But murder? Is it possible she's done something unthinkable? That she's lying to me about all of it, and I'm harboring not only a dirty cop, but a cold-blooded killer?

"Tomasetti, I can't believe she would do that," I say quietly. "Unless it was self-defense."

"If the lab matches her weapon to Cysco, it's over for Colorosa."

But my thoughts have already jumped to everything Gina told me. "If we are, indeed, dealing with corruption, someone could have planted the gun found at her house."

"Combined with everything else, Cysco's death is a damning scenario for her."

We fall silent, our thoughts buzzing through the airwaves between us. "Which agencies are involved in the investigation?" I ask.

The ensuing silence hangs heavy.

"You can't tell me," I say.

"I can't tell you because I don't know."

"Tomasetti, I thought you knew everything."

The laugh that follows is short-lived. "Look, we both know that when a cop is under investigation for something as serious as this, multiple agencies will likely get involved and they're going to do their damnedest to keep it under wraps."

"BCI?" I ask.

"And/or the FBI."

"That's why no one wants to talk about it."

"Franklin County is out of my region. I've had to call in some favors just to get what little I've told you."

"So this could get . . . precarious. I mean, for you."

"It already is."

Silence hisses over the line and then he asks, "Kate, do you trust Colorosa?"

"I used to," I tell him. "I trusted her with my life."

"That doesn't answer my question."

"I don't think she shot that CI," I whisper, hating the echo of uncertainty in my voice.

"Where are you?" he asks.

"Adam Lengacher's place." I tell him about the Explorer getting stuck in the lane. "I can't get out."

"What's the address?"

"I don't think you're going to be able to make the drive. The roads are nearly impassable."

"I'll make it."

Groaning, I give him the address. "Tomasetti, I could be wrong about Gina. I mean, we were friends. But I've been around long enough to know . . . people change."

"Don't sell yourself short. You've got pretty good instincts."

Now it's my turn to laugh. "Maybe not when it comes to her. We were close once."

"Look, even if she's not been completely straight with you, we've uncovered enough to conclude there's something else going on at the Columbus Division of Police. Let's keep digging. See where it takes us."

"You realize we're basically harboring a fugitive from justice."

"Let me worry about that." He sighs. "Look, I'm on my way. Do me a favor and don't tell Colorosa about Cysco. Let's see how she handles some asshole from BCI coming in and dumping a load of bad news in her lap."

CHAPTER 8

I'm standing at the front window, watching snow pile up on the sill, trying not to worry about Tomasetti making the drive, when I hear the whine of an engine. At first, I think the sound is Adam using some piece of equipment—a generator or snowblower—but then I catch a glimpse of a headlight and realize there's a vehicle coming up the lane.

I'm wondering how the driver got past my Explorer when I see that it's not a car or truck, but a snowmobile. A moment later a figure emerges from the white wall of snow. A man clad in a safety-orange and black snowsuit and helmet. I recognize the way he moves and feel a smile emerge as I open the door.

"You look like a well-dressed abominable snowman," I say as Tomasetti takes the steps to the porch.

"That's what all the lady Bumbles tell me." Grinning at his usage of the cartoon character's name, he unfastens the helmet and slips it from his head. "Been a long time since I drove a snow machine. Just about took out a mailbox on the corner."

"Mailbox would have bested you." I step back and he comes through the door.

"You underestimate the thickness of my skull." Tomasetti enters the living room and works off his gloves.

The insulated suit is encrusted with snow. He looks down at his boots, at the snow that's fallen onto the braided rug.

"There's a mudroom," I tell him.

"Lead the way."

He follows me through the living room and kitchen and into a narrow space where half a dozen pairs of boots line the wall. Above, hooks set into the wall hold coats and scarves.

"There's a woodstove in the corner." I motion toward the old potbellied stove. "You can hang up that suit and it should dry pretty fast."

He unzips the suit, steps out of it, and hangs it on the hook nearest the stove. I take in the sight of him as he toes off the boots. Faded jeans. Henley waffle-weave shirt covered with a flannel shirt. Dark, direct gaze already on mine.

"Where's Colorosa?" he asks.

"Sleeping." I motion toward the kitchen. "Have a seat. Adam made coffee. I'll go get her."

I enter the darkened sewing room to find Gina sleeping soundly. In light of her injured shoulder, the last thing I want to do is wake her, but I don't have a choice.

"Gina." I go to her, set my hand on her arm, and shake her gently. "Hey."

She startles abruptly, springs to a sitting position, cries out in pain, and falls back onto the cot. "You scared the shit out of me," she snaps.

"Get dressed. We need to talk."

She stares at me, her breathing elevated; then she nods. I watch as she gingerly rolls from the cot and sits up. She's wearing the same turtleneck and jeans. Dark hair a tangled mass about her shoulders. Socks on her feet, boots tucked beneath the cot.

I look around, spot the flannel shirt she'd been wearing on the back of a chair, and hand it to her. "It's cold."

"Tell me something I don't already know." She slips it on slowly, wincing with each movement of her shoulder. "How long was I out?"

"A couple of hours. How are you feeling?"

"Like a snowplow ran over me."

Before leaving, Joe Weaver fashioned a homemade sling for her arm. She reaches for it, fumbles to get it over her head, so I cross to her and help her slip her arm into it.

"Amish vet knows his stuff. I don't think I thanked him, after."

"I did," I tell her.

She reaches for the knitted beanie on the table, pulls it onto her head. Jams her feet into her boots. "This house," she says. "These people. Their clothes. I feel as if I've stepped into a time warp."

"In some ways, you have." I think about it a moment. "I don't want them involved in this. The only reason you're here now is because I can't get you anywhere else at the moment."

She nods. "As long as I don't have to wear a damn bonnet, the Pilgrims and I will get along just fine."

She follows me down the hall and into the kitchen. Tomasetti is standing at the sink, looking out the window. He turns when we enter the room, his expression impassive.

Gina eyes him suspiciously as she crosses to him, shakes his hand. "You must be John Tomasetti."

Introductions are made and then she asks, "Kate filled you in?"

"She relayed to me the story you told her," he returns evenly.

Moving with the sluggishness of a centenarian, she goes to the table, pulls out a chair, and gingerly lowers herself into it. Her face is pasty and pale, her lips are dry, her hands are not quite steady.

The three of us are alone in the house. Adam and the children went to the barn twenty minutes ago to check on a cow that's about to calve. A single propane floor lamp in the corner casts minimal light, so I go to it and crank up the mantle. The room brightens marginally. I pour coffee into two mugs, hand one to Gina, and take the chair adjacent to her.

Facing us, Tomasetti leans against the counter, his eyes on Gina, and crosses his arms. "You know there's a warrant out for your arrest."

"I figured that out when they busted down my door at three A.M." Using her left hand, she sips coffee. "So, what's the warrant for?"

Tomasetti doesn't respond, doesn't look away from her. "You've got one chance to tell me what led up to this," he tells her. "This is it. I need the truth. All of it. Do you understand?"

"I want immunity," she says.

He laughs nastily. "You're asking the wrong person."

"I need some kind of guarantee."

"You're not going to get it from me," he says with heat. "We're all you've got. We are your best hope. At this point, I'd say we're your only hope." He glances at his watch. "If you'd rather take your chances with the Holmes County Sheriff's Department, I will accommodate you. I will put you on that snowmobile and take you myself. Right now. Are we clear?"

She slants me a where-the-hell-did-you-find-this-guy glower, then looks down at the tabletop. Over the next minutes, she relays the same story she told me earlier.

He pulls out a small notebook. "I need names."

"Damon Bertrand. Ken Mercer. They're part of the vice unit. Frank Monaghan is—"

"I know who he is." He scribbles on the pad. "Tell me about the vice unit."

"It's an elite group. The men I mentioned are its golden boys. They're making a lot of busts. Good busts. Getting recognized. Riding high. Making the unit—and the department—look good. They get a lot of kudos from the brass. The media loves them. They're heroes. Untouchable." She shakes her head. "Even before I came on board there were rumors."

"What rumors?"

"That there are a few bad eggs in the unit. That we have patrol cops and detectives shaking down drug dealers and pimps and anyone else they have something on. We're talking money. Property. Cars. Boats. Sex. You name it. I know a couple of cops were under investigation a while back, but it never went anywhere and the higher-ups didn't seem to be too worried about it."

"How do you know they were under investigation?" Tomasetti asks.

"Rumor mostly. Internal Affairs was asking a lot of questions."

"Did IA talk to you?"

"No."

"How involved are you?"

Her eyes skitter away from his. Not for the first time I get that scratchy sensation on the back of my neck. *Something there,* a little voice whispers in my ear, and with every beat of silence that follows, I can practically hear the nails being driven into her proverbial coffin.

When she doesn't respond, I say her name. "Answer the question." *What didn't you tell me?*

"I screwed up," she snaps. "I . . . took some cash. I looked the other way while other cops did the same thing—and worse."

Tomasetti makes a sound of disgust. I feel that same sentiment burning in my chest. Tension slices the air between us. For the span of several minutes no one speaks.

She played you, that little voice whispers, but I slam the door on it, shut it up.

Gina rakes the fingers of her uninjured hand through her hair. "First time, it happened during a bust. Team went in with a warrant.

It was dicey. A lot of adrenaline. There was a bunch of cash laid out on the kitchen table. Thousands of dollars. All of it unaccounted for. Instead of logging it into evidence, the cops divvied it up."

"Who?"

"Bertrand and Mercer."

"Did you report it?"

Her mouth tightens. "No."

"How much did you take?"

"A couple thousand."

"Tell me how they operate."

"They're tight-knit. Gung-ho. Known for pushing boundaries and getting things done. In the years since the unit was created, they'd cultivated relationships with the prostitutes and drug users, pimps, small-time dealers. They used those relationships to go after the big dogs, the traffickers, the high-volume guys. Once they got those relationships in place and the pecking order figured out, they started shaking down the guys with money."

"So, they were extorting drug dealers." It's not a question.

"They extort any criminal who has something they want."

Tomasetti stares hard at her. "And you're willing to testify against them."

"For immunity."

He humphs. "Why turn on them now when you're receiving a piece of the pie?"

"Look," she says with heat. "I got that money shoved into my hand. Yeah, I took it. But I got sucked into this. They wanted me to commit and they wouldn't take no for an answer. Once I did, I was in. They told me to keep my mouth shut and I did."

"Answer the question, Gina," I say quietly.

She doesn't look at me. "Like I told Kate, they went too far. Lying on affidavits. Getting bullshit warrants from judges." She tells him about the couple that was killed. "I wanted no part of it after that."

"Noble of you," Tomasetti says. "Or maybe you realized the ship was going down and you figured you'd save your own neck."

Temper flares in her eyes. "I'm here because I'm trying to do the right thing. I can't do it on my own. If you're not up to helping me out, say the word."

"It's interesting that the day an arrest warrant is issued for you you decide to come clean," he says.

"That warrant is some fantasyland bullshit." She sets her hand on the table, starts to rise, ends up wincing in pain. "If they'd gotten their hands on me, I wouldn't have survived."

Tomasetti stares at her, unmoved. "Is that why you murdered Eddie Cysco? Because they used his name on the warrant?"

Gina lurches to her feet, her eyes darting from Tomasetti to me and back. "*What?* Eddie Cysco? That's not possible. I just talked to him. A couple days ago. What the hell are you talking about?"

"You are a suspect," he tells her. "The weapon they confiscated from your residence is being tested. If ballistics match, you are going down for murder and a slew of other charges, and there isn't a soul on this earth who can save you."

"I did not kill Eddie Cysco!" Something akin to panic flashes in her eyes.

"So you say," he mutters.

Visibly struggling for calm, she divides her attention between the two of us. "Cysco was part of this. He was the source named on the affidavit that got Louis and Sandra Garner killed. For God's sake, he was proof that someone inside the unit lied on that affidavit, that two innocent people were killed, and that the unit covered it up."

Tomasetti stares at her, saying nothing.

Gina continues. "Eddie Cysco had no knowledge of that couple. No connection whatsoever. He didn't know them. Had never been to their residence. The unit needed probable cause for that warrant, so they used him."

Gripping the side of the table with her uninjured hand, she sinks back into the chair, seeming to work through the possibilities. "They knew he was my snitch. In terms of that bogus warrant and his connection to me, he was a loose end. They didn't trust him to keep his mouth shut, so they killed him."

"Tell me about Cysco," Tomasetti says.

"He was a lowlife." Gina makes the statement without malice. "He was a small-time dealer. A junkie. Estranged from his family." Eyes burning with conviction, she looks at Tomasetti. "No one's going to ask questions when someone like that turns up dead."

"Why did they turn on you when, evidently, you were content to take the cash and keep your mouth shut," he asks.

"After the Garner fiasco, I made the mistake of letting them know I wanted out. They stopped trusting me. At some point they decided I was a liability."

His mouth twists. "Because you had a sudden attack of conscience?"

She glares at him, saying nothing.

"You said you had an audio recording," I say.

Reaching into her jeans pocket, she pulls out a smartphone. The screen is cracked, but it doesn't look too damaged to function. She swipes through several pages, taps a button, and holds the phone out to me.

I take it, tap the play icon. The video is little more than a collage of monochrome shadows. The audio is scratchy and faint. A female voice.

"What the hell happened to Louis and Sandra Garner?" Gina's voice. Angry. Distraught.

"You pull a gun on a cop, you get shot." Male voice. Familiar. *"That's the way it works."*

"I heard that's not how it went down."

"No one gives a damn what you heard. Those fuckers were armed. We confiscated four ounces of heroin. It was a good bust. We did what we had to do."

"People are asking questions about that warrant."

"It'll die down."

Something unintelligible and then, *"People are asking questions about you, too, Gina."*

"You mean Bertrand?"

"I mean everyone. They're saying you can't be trusted. Is that true? Do I need to be worried about you?"

The sound of her laugh has an unpleasant edge. *"Maybe I ought to be worried about you."*

Rustling in the background sounds and then, *"Keep it up and you'll go the way of the Garners. You got that?"*

The clip ends abruptly. I play it again, turn up the volume, run it a third time, trying to make out the garbled words, but no luck.

"That could be interpreted a number of ways," I say.

"Bullshit," she hisses. "I mentioned Bertrand and he responded. You recognize the voice?"

I nod. "Nick Galloway."

"In case you're not reading between the lines, he threatened me."

Tomasetti pulls out his cell. "I'm sending you my number. See if you can forward that recording to me," he says.

"What about my guarantee?"

"There isn't one." He clocks her with a hostile look. "Send it. Now."

"I'm not going to let you railroad me." Tossing him a drop-dead glower, she taps the screen with her index finger. "I want immunity and I want it in writ—"

She cuts the word short when we hear the back door slam. The kitchen window shudders with the change in pressure. Boots sound on the floor. The rustle of coats being hung. The chatter of children speaking in *Deitsch*. Adam Lengacher appears in the doorway, takes in the sight of us sitting at the table, the lingering tension in the air. Not for the first time, I feel as if we're intruding, as if we've brought something profane into his home, a toxin his family shouldn't be exposed to.

I introduce the two men and they shake hands.

"You're a police?" Adam asks.

"With the State of Ohio," Tomasetti tells him.

Adam's eyes flick to Gina, the sling strapped over her shoulder. "You're feeling better?"

She nods. "I'll be sure to thank Joe next time I see him."

"Suzy had her baby calf!" Sammy interjects. The boy's cheeks are blushed with pink. He's got bits of hay in his hair, more stuck on a face that's wet with melting snow.

"He's cold, but he's going to be okay," Lizzie tells us.

"We put them in the warmest stall and put down extra straw." This from Annie.

"Datt said we might have to bring him in the house," Sammy adds.

"What about the *misht*?" Annie asks, using the *Deitsch* word for manure.

Grinning, Sammy pokes her shoulder. "You have to pick it up."

"No!" the girl squeals, but she's on to his prank.

The sight of the children's banter warms me, reminds me of an era of my own life when things were simpler and a lot more innocent.

"I'm glad mama cow and her *kalb* are okay," I tell them.

"He's black with one white ear and one black one," Lizzie tells me.

"We're going to name him Lucy," the youngest girl puts in.

Sammy snickers. "But he's a boy!"

Lizzie puts her hand on her little sister's shoulder. "We're going to call him Leroy, not Lucy."

Adam brings his hands together. "Sammy, I think there might be some snow on the front porch that needs shoveling."

The boy grins, suddenly shy, and he slinks past us into the living room.

"Lizzie and Annie, this is a good day to beat rugs. Upstairs and down. Go on now. Hang them just outside the door. Use that old broom."

Joining hands, the two girls leave the kitchen.

An awkward silence ensues when the children are gone. The sense that we've overstayed our welcome sits like a brick in the pit of my stomach. I don't like that this man and his family have been dragged into the situation with Gina. But I don't know how to remedy it. Other than loading Gina onto the snowmobile and transporting her to the farm where Tomasetti and I live in Wooster—or the police station in Painters Mill—there is no viable solution. At least not until the storm abates.

Gina breaks the silence. "Adam, I don't know how to thank you for everything you've done. You saved my life. You opened your home to me."

"You were lost and cold and hurt," he tells her.

"The circumstances were questionable," she admits, "and yet you stepped in anyway. Thank you."

"The only time to look down on your neighbor is when you're bending over to help them." His gaze moves to the sling. "Joe is a good doctor, no?"

"Best animal doctor I've ever been to." She grins and, in that instant, looks like the woman I knew all those years ago. The one who was anxious to make her mark. The young police officer who would never compromise her ethics. Once again, I'm reminded of the seriousness of the charges against her and the possibility that I'm too personally involved to see the situation clearly.

"Where's your vehicle?" Tomasetti asks her.

"I'm not sure. It was dark and snowing like crazy. I had no idea where I was." Gina looks at Adam and raises her brows.

The Amish man nods. "A couple of miles north on Township Road 36. It's in the ditch. Twenty feet off the road."

"Sheriff's department finds an abandoned vehicle and they'll call in the plate." Tomasetti slants a look at Gina. "What's the plate going to tell them?"

"That it belongs to a man by the name of Phillip Rifkin from Westerville."

Tomasetti sighs. "You thought of everything, didn't you?"

"Everything except this storm," she returns evenly.

"There's not much traffic out that way," I point out. "Sheriff's department is likely operating on a skeleton crew due to the storm. That's not to mention the roads are impassable. I don't think anyone is going to be patrolling the secondary roads until the storm lets up."

Gina startles when the wind rattles the kitchen window. She recovers quickly, sends me a tense look. "I know this is a bad situation." Her eyes move from me to Tomasetti. "All I ask is that you look into the things I've told you. When the time comes, I'll do everything in my power to back it up."

She turns her attention to Adam. "I know my presence has disrupted your home. I know the circumstances must be confusing and upsetting for your children, and I'm sorry for that."

"The Amish do not turn away anyone in need. You are welcome to stay until the storm passes. Both of you." He says the words with earnestness, but when he looks at me, I see hesitation, and I know the part of him that is bound by Amish norms is at war with the part of him that is a father.

Nodding, he re-zips his coat. "I'm going to give Samuel a hand."

When he's gone, Tomasetti addresses Gina. "You know you're a fugitive."

She looks down at the tabletop. "Yeah, I got that," she says dryly.

He moves away from the counter and looks down at her. "If you've lied about any of this, I will make it my mission in life to bury you. Are we clear?"

"Crystal," she says.

I walk Tomasetti to the front door. He's back in the snowsuit, the helmet at his side, looking as troubled as I feel. Neither of us is thinking about the weather anymore.

"What do you think?" I ask.

"I think this is a clusterfuck." He grimaces. "The only reason she's not in the county jail right now is because I know there's some kind of ongoing investigation involving the vice unit."

"Do you think she's telling the truth?" I ask.

He takes his time answering. "I believe the scenario she laid out is plausible. Whether we're getting the whole story . . ." He shrugs. "Her assertion that there were questions about the warrant in which the Garners were killed is correct, by the way. Most judges won't sign off on a warrant based on the word of a CI. I need to call in some favors, apply some pressure if I can. If this investigation is being led by another agency, my getting anything concrete is going to be tough."

"How do you feel about the audio recording?"

"I think it could be interpreted a number of different ways. Useful for the time being. If this moves forward, it could garner some interest. Likely inadmissible if this thing ever goes to court. Bottom line, it's not enough."

From where we're standing, I can hear young Sammy on the porch outside chatting with his *datt,* his shovel scraping across the wood planks. The heavy curtains are parted slightly, and I can see him running the shovel across the floor, pitching the snow over the rail. It's more play than work, but then that's the Amish way.

"Where do we go from here?" I ask.

"I'll see what else I can find out or verify." Sighing, he turns to me, his expression grim. "Kate, you know I have to talk to my superiors about this."

Of course I knew that would be the case. Cops don't harbor fugitives from the law—even if said fugitive is a cop with a story to tell. Still, a sense of unease moves through me, because involving BCI will invariably complicate an already complicated—and delicate—situation.

"I'll start with Denny McNinch," he says, referring to the special agent supervisor, his boss.

McNinch and Tomasetti have a complex relationship and they've had their differences in the years they've worked together. Both men have strong personalities and no compunction about speaking their minds, even when their opinions differ. They've weathered difficult times; McNinch has seen Tomasetti at his worst—and most vulnerable—namely in the months after a career criminal murdered Tomasetti's wife and two little girls eight years ago. But McNinch is as much politician as he is cop. He was fair while Tomasetti worked through his losses—defending him even when his work suffered—but McNinch has a reputation for protecting himself first and foremost.

"I have no idea how this is going to play out." He tilts his head, lowers his voice. "I'm usually pretty good at getting a handle on someone. I couldn't get a read on Colorosa."

"She's always had a good poker face."

"Maybe a little too good," he says. "Can she be trusted?"

It's the million-dollar question. A complex and deeply personal one that's hounded me since the moment I laid eyes on her. A question I can no longer avoid. The years I spent with her, the friendship we shared, flashes unbidden in my mind's eye. All of it is tempered by the things I know about her now, the things I would have done differently, the way our friendship ended, and I realize that my uncertainty is an answer unto itself.

"I don't think we're getting the whole story," I say after a moment.

"I guess that's a good enough answer for now." He reaches for my hand and squeezes it. "Do me a favor and watch your back, will you?"

I try to smile, but my lips don't quite manage. "Tomasetti, I don't believe she's a danger to me or anyone else."

He holds my gaze, saying nothing. The silence between us is nearly as loud as the storm outside.

CHAPTER 9

Downtown Columbus looked like some postapocalyptic wasteland when Ken Mercer pulled into the lot on North Ludlow and parked. Usually, at this time of day the lot was full. With the storm bearing down and a blizzard warning in effect, a dedicated few had shown up for work. The smart ones had already gone home. He sat for a few minutes, engine running, using the time to check email and texts on his cell, the din of the wipers and the scratch of his police radio filling the silence. Mostly, he thought about Gina Colorosa.

He'd always known she was a wild card. She was fun-loving and unpredictable with just enough kink to keep the hook sunk in deep. Yes, she was a good-looking woman—in a carnival-gypsy sort of way, anyway. But there was so much more to her, and every single element appealed to him in ways he didn't quite have a handle on. She was a magnet for trouble, an adrenaline junkie, and she considered danger the greatest aphrodisiac of all time. She was loyal when it suited her, a fighter when cornered, and had the sex drive of a feral cat. It was a combination Mercer couldn't resist despite his best efforts, and for over two years now he hadn't been able to get enough.

The first time he'd been with her was after hours—in the men's room at Police Substation 19, down on Sullivant. The next time had been in the back seat of his cruiser when they'd both been on duty and yards away from an active crime scene. Once, she'd had the audacity to show up at his house. Had he done the right thing and told her to hit the road? He could no more have done that than he could slit his own throat. Gina Colorosa was not conducive to his doing the right thing. And so while his wife put the finishing touches on her chicken piccata, he'd sneaked out to the detached garage, bent Colorosa over the hood of the Corvette he was restoring, and fucked her until neither of them could see straight.

Not for the first time, he worried that he was in too deep. For nearly three years, he'd jeopardized his job. His marriage. His family. His reputation. For what? Sex? The knowledge that he'd gotten away with something he shouldn't have?

He hadn't been with her for almost a month now. It felt like a lifetime. He hadn't much cared for her putting him off. He tried to convince himself he didn't give a damn. That he was immune to emotional attachments. He sure as hell wasn't the needy type. He was married, for God's sake; he actually *liked* his wife. No, Ken Mercer didn't get sucked into anything he didn't want to get sucked into. Yet here he was, parked behind the Columbus Division of Police headquarters with a hard-on, wondering if he still had Gina's throw-down number in his phone or if she'd pick up if he called. . . .

Cursing beneath his breath, Mercer shifted in the seat and glanced out the window. Beyond, the snow was coming down so hard he couldn't see the building across the street. Bertrand didn't know he'd been sleeping with Colorosa. No one did. Mercer intended to keep it that way. The last thing he needed was Bertrand wondering about his loyalties—something he didn't want to examine too closely himself.

The question he faced now was how to best handle the situation.

Bertrand was on the warpath. He wanted Colorosa drawn and quartered, the sooner the better. In all honestly Mercer did, too. He didn't want her spilling secrets. He sure as hell didn't want his wife to know he'd been sleeping around. The problem was he knew more than he was letting on. Not only about Colorosa, but where she might be heading. The key, he decided, was to use that knowledge to his benefit without letting on he'd known all along.

He was reaching for his cell to check messages again when Bertrand's Subaru Outback rolled up beside him. Hitting the door locks, he waited for the other man to join him.

"Sorry I'm late," Bertrand said as he slid onto the passenger seat. "Fuckin' snow."

"Yeah, well, I got a pot of chili waiting for me at home so make it quick. You said it was important."

"I heard from the lab. They matched the blood found in the alley. It's Colorosa's."

"So we winged her."

"Looks that way."

Mercer thought about that, didn't let himself acknowledge the fact that it left a sour taste in his mouth. "What else?"

"Her cell phone provider—one of them, anyway—came through. We're looking to identify every number, incoming and outgoing, in the last six weeks."

The sour taste went bitter. "Might help," Mercer said.

"Get this," Bertrand said. "The last ping they got was on a tower in Fallsbury Township in Licking County."

"Licking County?" Assuming a puzzled countenance, Mercer scratched his head. "There's not much out that way."

"We doubled down on known associates. She's got a brother in Dayton, which is west. He says he hasn't seen her in a couple of years.

I got someone on the way to talk to him in person. No other family that we know of."

Mercer looked out the window, watched a woman with a grocery cart full of bags and aluminum cans disappear into the alley at the back of the lot. He thought about Gina. He thought about known associates and the other name that came to mind. Another woman he'd been quite fond of once upon a time.

"My guess is she reached Interstate 70 eastbound," Mercer said.

"The interstate is too far south to hit a tower in Fallsbury Township." Bertrand shook his head. "Why the hell is she heading east, which is basically out in the middle of nowhere?"

Mercer said nothing, but his mind whirred with possibilities. If he'd learned anything during his years in law enforcement, it was how to find someone. Not only did he have a plethora of resources at his fingertips, but he was good at getting inside people's heads.

"Look," he said, "if Colorosa has a gunshot wound—even if it's minor—she'll likely be trying to get herself to a hospital or doctor. Or else she's looking for a safe place to lay low."

"We're checking hospitals and clinics in Licking County," Bertrand said. "Contiguous counties, too. There's a hospital in Coshocton." He scrubbed a hand across his chin, thinking. "What else is out that way?"

"There's a good-size hospital in Millersburg," Mercer said carefully.

"What county is that?" Bertrand asked.

"Holmes," he said, watching the other man for a reaction. "Does she have family out that way?"

"Not that we found."

"She might be trying to get out of the state. Pittsburgh?"

"There's no way she could get that far in this weather."

The two men fell silent, their minds working over the dynamics of what they knew.

"That fucking Colorosa has nine lives," Bertrand muttered, brows knit, thinking. "What about men? She never met one she didn't like. Any boyfriends? Old or new?"

Mercer swallowed, surprised by the hot spike of annoyance. "Not that I know of."

"She tight with anyone else? Cops?"

"I don't think she had many friends. But I'll dig around, see what I can find."

Bertrand looked at the clock on the dash. "She's been gone fourteen hours. We need to find her before this situation turns into something we can't fix. That bitch starts making noise to the wrong people and our lives are going to get complicated. We need to pull out all the stops."

Feeling confined, Mercer lowered the window an inch, tried not to notice the flakes blowing in. "Let's take a look at possible routes she might've taken. See what's out that way."

Bertrand nodded. "Maybe we can get our hands on CCTV from DOT or security cameras." The detective shrugged. "If she stopped for gas."

"Or a pharmacy." Mercer looked out the window and heaved a sigh. "Damn snow isn't helping. Let's give it twenty-four hours. See what pops."

Bertrand shot him a sideways look. "Twenty-four hours?" The laugh that followed held a distinctly unpleasant note. "If we don't get a line on her by morning, we've got to move. You game, buddy?"

Mercer met his gaze, held it. "I'm game."

"Good." Bertrand reached for the door handle. "Enjoy your chili," he said, and left the vehicle.

CHAPTER 10

I find Gina at the kitchen table, staring down at a mug of coffee in front of her. Adam and the children have gone to the barn, ostensibly to ogle the newborn calf. More than likely he's avoiding us—or doing his best to shield his kids from Gina's not-quite-child-appropriate language.

She looks up when I enter and offers a halfhearted smile. "So this is how you grew up, huh?"

I go to the old-fashioned percolator on the stove, grab a mug, and pour. "In a farmhouse," I say. "Just like this one."

"How do they do it?" she asks. "I mean, live without electricity and a phone?" She shudders. "Not to mention heat."

"They manage." I take the chair across from her and set my mug on the table. "It's not so hard when that's all you've ever known."

She chortles. "I guess that explains why you were in such a fired-up hurry to leave."

Gina is one of the few people I told about what happened when I was fourteen years old. She knows about Daniel Lapp, the boy who raped me when I was too young to even comprehend that such things existed in my safe and protected world. I lost my sense of belonging that summer. Though I remained Amish and lived with my parents for another four years, I felt as if I'd been abandoned not only by my family, but by the community that had once been the center of my world. I became an outsider those last years, as if I'd been cast adrift by some rogue wave that washed away the foundation upon which my life was built.

Gina knows that my parents swept the incident under the proverbial rug, and that their lack of support was one of the reasons I left. She also knows there's more to the story than I've told her. To her credit she never asked, she didn't judge me, and never broached the subject again.

The thing she *did* do, this most unlikely of individuals, was help me pull myself together and build a new foundation. She gave back to me something that had been stolen. Something precious that had been missing for so long I didn't even realize it was gone.

"Who would've thought an eighteen-year-old Amish girl could leave the only place she's ever known and not only make a new start in the big bad city, but become a cop?" She gives me that trademark smile again. The crooked one that's impish and bold.

"Not me," I tell her.

"Do you remember the day we met?"

"I remember that diner."

"Nasty."

"Food was good."

"If you like fries with your grease."

We stare at each other and for an instant we're those girls again. Gina was confident, brash, and utterly certain that she was going to take the world by storm. All she needed was her big break and by God she was going to make it happen, if only by the sheer force of her will. I was lost, light-years out of my element, missing the only life I'd ever known—my parents, my siblings, my Amish identity—and I was equally certain that same world was going to tear me apart piece by piece.

"That dress you were wearing," she murmurs. "I figured you were in some kind of weird sex cult or something."

"Your waitress uniform wasn't much better."

"God, I hated those uniforms. Pink polyester with all the trimmings."

I'd left Painters Mill just a few days before meeting her. I was living in my junker of a car and I was down to my last forty dollars. I had no idea where my next meal would come from. I didn't have a place to sleep. Gina was working as a server at a diner near downtown. I stopped in late one evening for food and maybe some confirmation that I wasn't the last person left on earth. She waited on me. Gave me free coffee. A day-old piece of cherry pie. She made me laugh. At the end of her shift, she sat in the booth with me and we ended up drinking a pot of coffee and talking for three hours.

She was a woman with a plan and the kinds of dreams I'd never conceived. The young Kate Burkholder I'd been was captivated. I saw her brashness as confidence. Her certainty as determination. I was astounded by all the things she was going to do with her life, and I had absolutely no doubt she would succeed, no matter what stood in her way.

At some point she recognized my predicament. I was hoarding the last of my cash. When she realized I didn't have anywhere to go, she invited me to spend the night at her little one-bedroom apartment "as long as you aren't an ax murderer and promise not to steal me blind." I was horrified that she could envision such things. My shock only made her laugh. When I told her I needed a job, she talked to her manager and somehow managed to convince him I would be a perfect addition to his waitstaff even though I had zilch in terms of experience. Gina was persuasive, and when we walked out of the diner at midnight, I had a matching ugly uniform of my own and my first-ever English friend. More importantly, for the first time in four years I thought I just might have a chance for a future that didn't include the expectation of marriage and children before I was ready, or submitting to rules I didn't always agree with.

One night at her apartment turned into two, and in the following weeks, I took a crash course into how not to be Amish, courtesy of Gina Colorosa. When she found out I'd only gone to school through the eighth grade, she got me signed up to earn my GED. I continued working at the diner. She landed a job answering phones at a police substation in a bad neighborhood a few blocks from the apartment. The stories she told when she came home were the most exciting I'd ever heard. We'd sit on the living room floor, watching TV, smoking cigarettes, and drinking Heineken. During those late-night sessions, I realized there was a great big world out there and I desperately wanted to be part of it.

"I'm going to be a cop," she'd proclaimed.

The thought made me laugh, something I did a lot of since meeting her. It sounded as far-fetched as taking a spaceship to another planet. She was too young—*a woman*—and a rule breaker who didn't have much respect for any kind of authority. But Gina had a knack for making the impossible sound like a cakewalk, and with great flourish she pulled out the brochure from the local community college. "All we have to do is get our criminal justice degrees. We're so poor, we won't even have to pay tuition. Look here, Kate, they have night classes. Weekends, too. Obviously, we'll have to keep working." She grinned. "The only problem is that to make time for all this, we'll have to cut back on our drinking."

It was the funniest thing I'd ever heard. We'd laughed until we cried, and in the weeks that followed, that college brochure became so wrinkled and creased that by the time we were enrolled, the print was illegible.

Now, a lifetime of experience later, sipping coffee and listening to the storm rage outside, we look at each other and all of those memories boil in the backs of our brains.

After a moment, she laughs. "Do you remember the time I got pulled over in your Mustang for not dimming my bright headlights when I passed that frickin' cop?" she asks.

"You were a terrible driver and the recipient of more than one ticket."

"Which I couldn't afford." She chuckles. "There I was, in the pouring rain, down on my knees, in the dark looking for that stupid dimmer switch on the floorboard, telling him 'I know it's here somewhere.'"

I grin. "The dimmer switch was on the turn signal."

"That cop thought I was an idiot."

"You were."

She grins and the simple artlessness of it goes deep into me, stirring that small place where trust is absolute, every word is believed, and your friends never break your heart.

"So what happened?" I ask. "After I left Columbus?"

"I was a good cop for a while. Not perfect. I gained some experience. Paid a few dues." She lifts her uninjured shoulder and lets it drop. "Not everyone in the department was as idealistic as you," she says. "The years, the things you experience, change you. I guess I got cynical. Fell in with the wrong kind of cops."

The truth is that I'd seen that part of her even before I left. Gina had started down a road I didn't want to travel. She was drinking too much. Going to cop bars every night after work. I'd started to hear stories about her sleeping around. About the rules being bent. Procedure not being followed and later lied about. There were whispered stories about our counterparts and some of them had begun to include her name.

"How long has the vice unit been on the take?" I ask, hating the words, the dirty feel of them as they come out of my mouth.

Gina takes the question in stride. "Too long. Years."

"That's a pretty damning answer," I say.

"It started out the way bad things usually do. Small scale. You know, innocent things like concert tickets in exchange for not writing a speeding ticket. It didn't stay small scale. The unit would do a raid and bust some scumbag. Said scumbag had a ton of cash laid out on a table. A kilo of cocaine. Cash never made it to evidence. I rationalized that he hadn't exactly earned the money. He wasn't going to be needing it where he was going, right?" Her gaze sweeps to mine. In the depths of her eyes I see shame. Regret. Most of all, I see what I can only describe as . . . grief.

"I thought: Why not me?" she whispers. "Why should some dregs of the earth get all that cash and not me?"

The back door bangs, startling us from our reverie. Gina sets down her cup. I'm getting to my feet when I hear the pound of footsteps. An instant later Sammy appears at the door. He's breathing hard, his face red and speckled with bits of hay, snow stuck to his coat.

"Datt's bringing in the baby calf!" he exclaims. "The mama cow doesn't like him and she won't let him drink any milk. I'm going to sleep with him tonight!"

The boy darts back into the mudroom. Beyond, I hear the girls and Adam enter, moving around.

Gina looks at me. "Seriously?"

"I'd say Sammy's a little too wound up to be kidding."

Leaving my coffee, I walk to the doorway and peer into the mudroom. Adam stands just inside the back door, a tiny black calf in his arms, both of them covered with snow. Next to him, Lizzie holds a two-gallon galvanized nipple bucket at her side. Sammy wrestles with a bag of milk replacer that's nearly as big as he is. Annie can't seem to keep her hands off the calf. Everyone is staring at it. The little animal is sweet-faced, shivering with cold, and not quite strong enough to struggle against the arms holding it.

"Looks like you have your hands full," I say to Adam.

"Literally," Gina murmurs.

The Amish man raises his gaze to mine. "*Sei mamm verlosse eem.*" His mother orphaned him. Kneeling, he sets the calf on the floor. The tiny animal wobbles and then collapses to its knees.

"He's hungry, Datt!" Sammy exclaims. "Can I feed him the bottle?"

Adam sets his hand on the animal's back, brushing snow from its coat, and addresses Lizzie. "Warm some water on the stove. Not too hot, just warm."

"*Ja.*" Nodding excitedly, the girl ducks past me and trots toward the sink.

"Sammy, get that bale of straw and break it open," Adam tells his son. "Get it spread out on the floor. Annie, get the door for your brother."

The little girl opens the door and Sammy charges into the swirling wall of white. Annie mans the door, ignoring the snow blowing in. When her brother hefts the bale to the jamb, she reaches for a string, not helping much but trying, and the two children wrestle the bale into the mudroom.

Gina and I stand at the doorway, watching the chaos unfold.

"What could possibly go wrong?" she murmurs.

As the children mill about, chattering as they prepare the mudroom for the calf's overnight stay, the uneasiness of the last hours melts away. This is Amish life, I think. It's not perfect, but simple and straightforward, and for the first time in a long time, I miss it.

I enter the mudroom and look down at the calf. "*Er is schnuck,*" I say. He's cute.

Adam gets to his feet. "Likely full of *kedreck.*" Cow dung. But he smiles.

I've always had a soft spot for animals, especially the babies. Growing up, I saw dozens come into the world—horses, goats, hogs, cattle, even chicks—and I spent many a winter morning mucking stalls, hauling water, and dropping hay. I was never fond of chores, but caring for the animals was the one task I never complained about.

"What's not to love about that face?" Gina says. "It's like having a giant puppy."

Adam tilts his head at her. "You can pet him if you like."

After a brief hesitation, she approaches the calf. Gingerly, she goes to one knee, reaches out with her uninjured arm, and runs her hand across the animal's face and back. "How old is he?"

"A few hours," Adam tells her.

"What happened to the mother cow?" she asks.

"She hasn't decided if she likes him just yet," he replies. "Had the same problem with her last year. She'll come around. But with this cold, I wanted to make sure this little guy stayed warm tonight and got enough to eat."

"Is he going to make it?" she asks.

"If we can get some milk into him," Adam tells her.

I kneel next to Gina. I don't even realize I'm going to touch the calf until my hand makes contact with its face. I run my fingertips over the fur between its eyes and along its jaw, trailing a finger over a wet nose. A soft coat that is still damp from birth. Warm to the touch despite the cold.

A noise from the kitchen doorway draws my attention. I glance over to see Annie and Lizzie hauling the galvanized nipple bucket into the mudroom. "Is this enough water, Datt?" Lizzie asks.

"It's warm," Annie adds helpfully. "Not hot."

"I think that's just right," Adam tells them. "Annie, go fetch that big wooden spoon of your *mamm*'s."

He looks at me. "Can you keep an eye on the calf for a moment?"

"I think I can handle him."

He gets to his feet and takes the bucket from Lizzie. "Sammy, bring me a scoop of that milk replacer."

The boy grabs the bag and drags it across the floor toward his father, tearing at the tape along the top as he goes. "I got it, Datt."

The man looks over his shoulder at his son and laughs. "I think the bag is getting the better of you. Grab that measuring cup out of there and fill it up."

Annie trots into the mudroom, wood spoon in hand, and passes it to her *datt.*

Sammy jams the plastic measuring cup into the bag of milk replacer, scoops out a heaping mound, and carries it to his father. I watch as Adam dumps powder into the pail of water, then stirs the muddle with the spoon.

I read somewhere that our sense of smell is one of the most powerful memory triggers. The creamy-sweet redolence of the milk replacer fills the air of the mudroom, taking me back to a hundred winter mornings in which my *datt* and I would feed the calf or calves, and a time when I had no concept of all the intricacies of the world around me. Life was simple, regimented, filled with work and as much play I could get away with. As I watch the children tend to the calf, their faces filled with wonder and the anticipation of keeping the animal here overnight, I feel the loss of that innocence and the empty place it left behind.

Lifting the pail, Adam casts a look at me. "Do you remember how to do this?"

"Some things you never forget." I use my finger to check the temperature of the milk-replacer mixture and find it tepid, so I take the bucket from him. He kneels next to the calf and, supporting its body with his legs, he cups its head between his hands and gently upends its snout. I move in close with the bucket, sliding the nipple between the animal's lips. At first the calf has no interest. He's weak and cold and missing his mama. I persist, letting some of the milk replacer dribble out the side of his mouth and onto his chin. After a few minutes, the calf rouses. Instinct kicks in. Nudging the bucket, he begins to suckle.

"He's drinking!" Sammy exclaims.

"Of course he is," Adam replies without looking away.

The nipple apparatus clanks with every draw of milk, a sound that adds to my sense of nostalgia. It's a messy ordeal; milk oozes from the sides of the calf's mouth and drips onto the floor. As he settles in to eat, his eyes roll back and he begins to suckle with gusto.

Gina can't seem to take her eyes off the calf. "I don't believe I've ever seen anything so sweet," she murmurs.

Adam glances up from the animal and smiles at her. "For the Amish, God is manifest in a closeness to nature, caring for the land and animals," he tells her.

It doesn't elude me that Adam is giving Gina as much attention as he's giving the calf.

"Well, he may be cute," she says, "but I'm not giving up my room for him."

Adam laughs outright, then turns his attention to the children. "Spread the rest of that straw on the floor. I think things are going to get messy in here tonight."

Gina looks at the calf as if he's suddenly not quite so cute. "Oh. He's going to—"

"Yeah," I say.

Adam and I catch each other's gazes and his eyes slide to Gina. "You want to feed him?"

"Ah . . . you know, I'm good."

But I'm already shifting aside, nudging the pail into the hand of her uninjured arm. "Tilt it slightly," I tell her. "Like this. Make sure the nipple is at the right angle. I'll help you."

"Hold my beer and watch this," she mutters as she takes hold of the bucket.

The calf nudges the pail, and she hefts a laugh. "Wow. He's a hungry little squirt."

"You're a natural," Adam tells her.

"Look at him go," she whispers.

"His name's Leroy," Sammy reminds us as he kicks straw around, spreading it.

"I dated a Leroy once," Gina murmurs. "He wasn't nearly as cute as this little guy."

That's when I notice that everyone's watching the calf—except for Adam. His eyes are on Gina.

CHAPTER 11

A few minutes later, while the children are helping Adam set up a cot for Sammy in the mudroom, so the boy can "keep an eye on the calf" overnight, Gina and I stand in the living room at the front window, looking out at the storm.

"So what's the story on Adam?" she asks.

"I've known him since I was a kid. We lost touch when I left. He's a good guy."

"I haven't seen a wife."

"She died." I look at her, wondering about her curiosity. "They used a midwife here at the house and there was some kind of medical emergency during childbirth."

"Did the kid . . ."

I shake my head. "A baby boy. He didn't make it."

"That's a tough break," she says. "Losing two people in one day. How long ago did she die?"

"A couple years," I reply, remembering the funeral, a stone-faced Adam, and the utter silence of the children as they'd clung to him and watched their *mamm* laid to rest for all of eternity.

"The Amish believe in life beyond death," I tell her. "That's a comfort when you lose someone."

"I've never been big on the whole faith thing."

I offer her a half smile. "If you were Amish I suspect you'd get excommunicated pretty quickly."

She laughs. "You know, Kate, for an Amish dude, Adam's a nice-looking guy. Is he—"

"He's off-limits," I say before she can finish.

She stares at me, weighing my response. "Well, damn, Burkholder, it's not like I'm going to jump his bones or something."

When I say nothing, she moves closer to the window, parts the covering, and peers outside. "For what it's worth, I don't do that anymore."

"He's from a different world than we are," I tell her. "He's religious. There are a lot of rules. People making judgments. That's all I'm going to say about it."

"Forget I asked." Sighing, she looks out at the snow. "Any idea how much longer this damn storm is going to last?"

"I checked the weather app on my cell a couple hours ago. It's supposed to let up tomorrow."

"If someone finds that truck, it won't take them long to find me."

"We'll get to it as soon as we can. Pull you out of the ditch and bring it back here. As it is now, we don't even know when the roads will be passable."

At the mention of the coming day, the weight of the situation we face settles over me, as dark and cold as the storm outside. "We're going to have to make some decisions," I tell her. "Figure out how to handle this. Do you have an attorney?"

She shakes her head. "Never needed one."

"You do now. A good one."

Giving a final look at the whiteout conditions, she drops the window covering and faces me. "They're going to bury me, Kate. They're going to frame me for murdering Eddie Cysco. They're going to produce or manipulate evidence to back up whatever story they decide to push and they're going to make it convincing. They won't stop there. They're going to pile everything they can on me."

I stare at her, part of me believing her and wanting to help. Another part resists the urge to shake her, shout at her, tell her she never should have compromised herself or gotten involved with cops she knew were corrupt.

"You haven't exactly helped your cause," I tell her.

"If I could take back what I did, I would." With a dry laugh, she says, "We both know you don't get a do-over." She blows out a sound of anguish. "Jesus Christ, the thought of jail time gives me the shudders."

Even if she manages to garner immunity in exchange for information or testimony, she will never be fully exonerated. She'll never work as a cop again. The stain of her past deeds will follow her the rest of her life.

"I suspect in the coming days, the investigators at BCI will want to talk to you," I tell her. "If the FBI is involved, they'll want to talk to you, too."

"Yeah, well, they're going to have to make me some kind of deal," she says. "Maybe I ought to just run."

We fall silent, the words zinging, all the things that could happen in the coming days playing in my head like some movie trailer and a story that doesn't have a happy ending.

"Your credibility is a problem," I tell her.

"What's really scary is that these cops have the power to lay a dozen more crimes on me. Crimes that I had nothing to do with. Things they themselves did. They have access to everything. The ability to manipulate evidence. Intimidate people. You name it."

I think about that a moment. "Is there someone you trust who might come forward or corroborate any of this?"

"I've been racking my brain." Her laugh is a humorless sound fraught with hopelessness. "Pretty sad when you can count the number of people you trust on one hand."

I wait.

"There's a patrol cop," she says. "He's a decent guy. Has a family. I don't know him well, but we've talked. I don't know how involved he is. But I do know he's privy to some of what's going on. I got the impression he doesn't approve of what he's been seeing. He's a rookie. Doesn't want to screw up his career."

"Does Mr. Decent Guy have a name?"

"Jack Tyson."

"Why didn't you tell Tomasetti about him?"

"Tyson is a long shot." She offers a crooked smile. "Now that I've had sufficient time to entertain the notion that this is the end of my life as I know it, I realized if there was ever a good time for desperate measures this is it."

Pulling out my cell, I add the name to my notes. "I'll let Tomasetti know."

She tightens her mouth, her gaze holding mine. "Kate, I don't know if he'll talk. Even if he does, I don't know if he'll tell the truth. I have no idea how much he knows."

"If he's the best witness you've got, we don't have a choice but to approach him."

A dark heart sees the things that an honest one is blinded to by the nature of its own goodness.

I was fifteen years old the first time I heard those words. They were uttered by my *datt,* who was less philosophical than my *mamm* and rarely offered up the kind of admonition that didn't involve the denial of a meal or, when I was younger, a couple of smacks with a switch. In this particular instance, I'd accused an Amish friend of stealing a tube of lipstick from me—an item I shouldn't have had in my possession to begin with. My *datt* believed that I had seen in her what I myself was guilty of.

I didn't like hearing those words, but I understood them and I knew he was right because I'd shoplifted that lipstick from the pharmacy just a week before. I never forgot the adage—or the way it worked on my fifteen-year-old conscience.

No cop ever wants to believe that their fellow officers are capable of breaking the same laws they've been sworn to uphold. That a member of the law enforcement community would stain the reputation of all cops is an affront. What Gina became involved in offends me. It grates against everything I believe about the institution to which I've devoted my life. Yet here I am, putting my own reputation at risk to help her. What does that say about me?

At five P.M., Gina and I share dinner with Adam and the children. The food is a uniquely Amish compilation of home-cured ham, fried potatoes, and canned beets. The children are curious about their English visitors. They're too well behaved to ask all the questions I see on their faces. But their eyes are watchful, their ears wide open.

The routine of being in an Amish home—the sights and smells, the chores, the reciting of the Prayer before Meal—is achingly familiar. It's not that I want to be Amish again. I made the decision to leave a long time ago and it was the right one for me. Still, being here brings with it a certain nostalgia, makes me miss the closeness I'd once shared with my family.

Gina's presence adds yet another facet to the mix. She was a big part of my past, our relationship a time of rapid growth and profound change. Looking back, I can't help but acknowledge the sense of things lost there, too.

At nine P.M. Adam and Lizzie come into the living room and offer me a pillow and two blankets—along with a place on the sofa—for the night. By ten o'clock the house is quiet and dark, the only sounds coming from the creak of the rafters, and the wind tearing around the windows, a beast trying to find its way inside. Adam has retired to his bedroom upstairs. Gina has been in the sewing room for about an hour. Alone in the living room, snuggled beneath the blankets on the sofa, I call the station only to find out from my dispatcher, Mona, that Painters Mill has lost power.

"The manager at Quality Implement told me there was a run on generators," she says. "This afternoon they were down to writing rain checks."

Quality Implement is the local farm store, a fixture in the community, and the only retailer that carries generators and woodstoves and the like. The next-closest retailer is in Millersburg, which is an impossible drive.

"Call Harry Morgan first thing in the morning and see if he'll set up a temporary shelter at the VFW Hall," I tell her. Harry is a Vietnam War vet who manages the VFW Hall in Painters Mill. When disaster strikes the community, whether it's a tornado or flood or winter storm, Harry can always be counted on to jump in and lend a hand. Two years ago, he opened up the VFW Hall to victims of the tornado that plowed through Painters Mill, setting out dozens of sleeping cots and blankets, opening the restroom for showers, and recruiting some of the best cooks in the county for hot meals—and a little bit of love.

"If people don't have heat, they're going to need a warm place to sleep and something to eat until the power is back on, especially if they're elderly or have young children."

"Will do, Chief. If I'm not mistaken, I think Harry has the cots and blankets left from that blizzard three years ago."

"Call the Holmes-Wayne Electric Co-op and get an update on when the power will be restored."

"I'm waiting for a callback now."

"Who's on patrol tonight?"

"T.J.," she tells me.

"Make sure he's got tire chains and a winch. Tell him not to take any chances. If he gets stuck, no one will be able to reach him for a while."

"You got it."

"Mona?"

"Yeah, Chief?"

"If you can't get home in the morning, I can ask Tomasetti to take you. He's got a snowmobile."

"I thought I might bed down in the cell downstairs," she says, referring to the single jail cell in the basement. "Just in case Lois or Jodie can't make it in."

A thread of warmth stirs in my chest. Not for the first time, I'm pleased I promoted Mona to patrol officer, a position she's been transitioning to for weeks now, and will take on full time as soon as I can find a replacement. I'm thankful to have such a dedicated team of officers working for me. "Thank you. Let me know if you need anything."

I call Tomasetti next. "Electricity is out at the farm," he says by way of greeting. "I've got the generator going and built a fire. So far so good."

I think about the farm where we live and try not to acknowledge the swirl of homesickness. The old house is drafty and creaky, and though we've put a tremendous amount of work into it, it's an ongoing project. Even so, it's homey and warm, and the six acres upon which it sits are as stunningly beautiful in the snow as they are at the height of summer.

"Good thing you cut all that wood last weekend," I say.

"My rotator cuff is still thanking me." He pauses. "You guys without power there?"

"Um . . . no idea."

He laughs. "I suspect the Amish will fare a hell of a lot better than the rest of us when the apocalypse comes."

"Any news on Colorosa?" I ask.

"I talked to a few cops I know in Columbus." He pauses. "Kate, I'm hearing some things about her."

"Like what?"

"She's got a few marks against her. She's been disciplined several times. A couple years ago, some cash went missing in the course of a bust. Three thousand dollars. Colorosa was part of the chain of custody. Evidently, someone pointed a finger at her. There was an inquiry. Nothing was ever proven, and no formal charges were ever filed, but the money wasn't recovered and was never accounted for."

Disappointment moves through me. I close my eyes, trying not to let the news shake my already tenuous faith in Gina. "I've got a name for you." I tell him about Jack Tyson. "Gina seems to think he may be willing to come forward."

"I'll see what I can find out about him."

"Did ballistics come back on the weapon that was confiscated at Gina's house the night of the raid?" I ask.

"The lab isn't exactly lightning fast to begin with, but this storm has slowed everything down to a crawl," he tells me. "People can't get to work. Like everyone else, the lab is operating on a skeleton crew."

"Anything on the vice unit?" I ask.

"I'm not getting much. Either there's nothing there, or they keep their secrets well guarded. I did speak to a guy I used to work with in Cleveland; he was a sergeant with the Columbus Division of Police.

Retired now. Off the record, he says the vice unit has had an integrity problem for years."

"Anything specific?"

"He either didn't know or wouldn't say."

"Interesting that he wanted to keep it off the record."

"Retired or not, no one in law enforcement wants to point a finger at another agency unless he's damn sure he's right." He pauses. "Look, if the roads are open, I'm going to try to get out and make the drive to Columbus tomorrow. I set up a meeting with Denny. Closed door. If there's an investigation and BCI is involved in any capacity, he'll know about it."

"Weather app says the storm will end in the morning."

"True. But there's a narrow window. Polar vortex is supposed to arrive by afternoon."

I groan. "Tomasetti, you're a fount of good news, aren't you?"

"DOT says I-71 will be open tomorrow. One lane, but the plows will be out in full force throughout the night and working on all major thoroughfares. If I can make it to the interstate without getting blocked by a wreck or a stuck vehicle, I should be able to reach Columbus."

"If it's not too much trouble would you be careful?" I say.

"I'll wear my superhero suit."

"You don't have a superhero suit."

"That you know of."

I'm feeling more optimistic when I end the call a few minutes later. My cell battery is low and, of course, there's no electricity in the house, so I make a mental note to charge it in the Explorer come morning. I'm about to turn off the propane lamp and call it a night when I hear the shuffle of feet against the floor. I look up to see Gina emerge from the hall. She's got a blanket wrapped around her shoulders. Hair smushed on one side. Stocking feet. Her face is devoid of makeup, but somehow it only makes her look prettier.

Careful not to jar her injured shoulder, she settles into the chair across from me. "What the hell do people do around here at night without electricity?"

"Read. Sleep." I shrug. "Talk to each other."

"That's a scary thought." She hefts a cynical laugh. "If memory serves me, insomnia was one of the things we had in common."

Leaving the lamp burning, I settle back onto the sofa and tug the blankets over my legs. "Doesn't help that we have a lot on our minds."

For a moment we listen to the wind rattle a loose pane of glass in the front window and the thump of something that's been torn loose outside.

"House smells like . . . frickin' cows," she says quietly.

I smile. "Sammy's sleeping in the mudroom with that calf."

Her expression softens. "He *is* cute. I mean, Sammy. For a kid. I'm not usually a fan of, you know, little people."

"I recall your aversion to children," I say lightly.

She turns thoughtful. After a moment, she chuckles. "Do you remember that first big call we took over on Avondale?"

I'm not in the mood for a jaunt down memory lane. There's too much history between us and not all of it is good. Still, it would be disingenuous of me not to admit there was fun, too.

I nod, let the memories rush over me. "The home-invasion call."

"We'd been on the job for what? Six months?"

"One of the rare times we got to work together."

"We were dying to see some action, make that first big arrest. Make a name for ourselves."

"We definitely made a name for ourselves."

"Not the kind we had in mind." Gina chortles. "I'll never forget the way that dude looked, running down the alley, buck naked, trying to pull up pants that were two sizes too small. One leg in, one leg out."

"Some things can't be unseen."

She throws her head back and gives a raucous laugh. "Our big home-invasion arrest turned out to be a husband walking into his house with no idea his loving wife was upstairs doing the wild thing with another dude."

"In his haste to get out of the house, Romeo grabbed *her* clothes instead of his own, and jumped out of the upstairs window."

"Thinking there's an intruder, the genius husband called 911."

"His wife couldn't exactly tell him what she'd been up to, so she let him report it as a home invasion."

"Colorosa and Burkholder to the rescue."

"Talk about a couple of geniuses," I say. "Took us a while to straighten that one out."

"First time I had to cuff a naked guy."

We look at each other, grinning, and for a moment we're partners again, best friends with no emotional baggage between us, no experience, and just enough youth that we're not afraid to charge into our lives no holds barred.

"The detectives made fun of us for months," I mutter.

"Called us the Naked Squad."

"Title justifiably earned."

Caught up in the memory, we look at each other and break into laughter. The release of tension that follows is palpable. But we're older now, more than a little cynical, and we quickly fall silent, lost in the thoughts and memories compressing the space between us. We listen to the whistle of wind, the quiet patter of snow against the glass, trying not to acknowledge that the silence isn't quite comfortable.

Gina turns her gaze on mine. "Those were the best days of my life."

"We had some good times," I concur.

"I didn't appreciate it."

"Young people never do. That's part of youth."

She nods, her expression sober. "Did you hear from Ken Mercer after you left?"

The muscles between my shoulders go taut at the mention of Mercer. I'd worked with him dozens of times in the years I was with the Columbus Division of Police. He was older. An experienced cop. A mentor. We were friends first and then lovers. We were only together a handful of times. But it was a handful of times too many.

"Never heard from him," I say.

She tilts her head, her eyes probing mine, looking for something I'd prefer she not see. Like maybe she isn't the only one who's not proud of certain elements of her past. "He was crazy about you," she says quietly. "Talked about you months after you left."

"He was also a liar and a cheat."

A smile plays at the corners of her mouth. "A *charming* liar and cheat. Not to mention good looking."

I say nothing, holding her gaze. She stares back as if I'm some human contradiction that must be made to make sense. "Did you tell Tomasetti about him?"

"There's nothing to tell. Mercer is ancient history and got filed under Mistake." I shrug, trying to look nonchalant, not quite sure I'm succeeding. "It never came up."

Her look turns knowing and one side of her mouth curves. "You were crazy about him, too."

"I was twenty-four years old."

"Youth and hormones can be a potent mix."

"And I think that's the end of this particular conversation," I say, keeping my voice amicable.

"Okay." When she speaks again, her voice is wistful. "We never talked about what happened. I mean, between us. When you left. We should have. I've always regretted that we didn't."

"I don't think our discussing it would have changed anything," I tell her. "Once you started down the wrong road, there was no stopping you."

"You knew and yet you never told anyone. Why is that?"

You were my best friend. I loved you like a sister. I didn't want to ruin your life. I don't say the words aloud, but at the time all of them were true.

I study her face, the steady gaze and set mouth, and I wonder how honest she's been with me. In the weeks before I left Columbus, I'd been faced with the biggest decision of my career. I spent months trying to move on, trying to forget about what she'd done, what I knew about her, and how I handled it. To this day I'm not certain I made the right choice.

It was the one and only time I looked the other way in the face of police wrongdoing. I kept what I knew—what I'd seen—to myself, and I didn't tell a soul. Not because I approved, but because I'd known the truth would destroy her. It's one of the reasons I left the Columbus Division of Police.

"I never thanked you for that," she says.

"I'd prefer if you didn't."

She nods. "If it's any consolation, Kate, the circumstances weren't exactly black-and-white."

"Do not try to convince me that what you did was all right," I say. "It wasn't. Not then. Not now."

The words hover in the air between us. A thousand more clog my throat, but I don't dare say them aloud.

She breaks eye contact, then forces her gaze back to mine. "I didn't realize what I was getting into. The depth of it. The *wrongness.* I didn't know there would be no going back."

It had been the beginning of the end of our relationship. A friendship that had been genuine and deep and untainted.

When I say nothing, she looks away, but not before I see the shame peek out from beneath the attitude and bravado. "If I could go back and change it, I would," she whispers.

"Too late," I say. "For a lot of things, the least of which is regret."

"I fucked up my career. My life. Just about every relationship I've ever had. I'm sorry."

I stare at her, trying to gauge her sincerity, wanting to believe her. Wanting to see just a glimpse of the woman I used to admire. The idealistic cop I'd spent so much time trying to emulate. It hurts knowing that part of her was quashed by something overbearing and dark, that it may no longer exist. That it may never have existed at all.

"You'd better get some sleep," I tell her.

"Yeah." Pulling the blanket more closely about her shoulders, she rises and leaves the room.

CHAPTER 12

I'm standing in the kitchen, nursing my first cup of coffee, and trying not to ponder the possibility of being stranded on this farm for a second day. It's not quite daylight outside. The snow has slowed, but the wind continues to batter the house and surrounding trees. The three Lengacher children are sitting at the table, chattering and eating sausage and toast, when the rat-tat-tat-tat of gunshots sounds outside. Four of them in quick succession. Nearby. Too close for comfort.

Gina rushes into the kitchen, her eyes darting to the window, to me, back to the window. "Did you hear that? Where did it come from?"

"The woods along the creek probably," I say.

"Hunters?" She can't seem to stop looking toward the window. "Sounded close."

I get to my feet. "Deer season ended two weeks ago."

I take in her agitation and it occurs to me she doesn't realize that shooting in the woods isn't all that unusual in rural areas. She's a city girl, after all. Not a nervous Nellie—and she's sure as hell not afraid of guns—but in light of the circumstances and her having recently sustained a gunshot wound, a certain level of jumpiness is understandable. That someone would be out shooting in such extreme weather gives me pause.

Gina strides to the window, parts the curtains, and peers outside. Unbeknownst to her, the window doesn't face Painters Creek. "Maybe we ought to check it out."

I'm aware that the children have stopped eating, forks suspended in midair, and they're watching their English visitor with a mix of curiosity and uneasy amusement. I understand the source of Gina's fear; she's afraid someone from Columbus has come looking for her. The thought puts a prickly sensation on the back of my neck.

"Mr. Swisherking got a big ten-point buck last month." Sammy spreads apple butter on his toast and takes a bite, then chews as he speaks. "He brought us over some jerky, and I got to keep the antlers. Do you want to see them?"

I look at the boy and smile. "Where's your *datt*?"

"He took Leroy to the barn," he says, referring to the calf.

"I'm going to take a stroll down to the creek to make sure no one's hunting down there out of season," I say easily.

"Can I go, too?" The boy rises quickly, stuffing the toast into his mouth and looking a little too excited by the prospect of a trip to the creek to nab a poacher.

"No." I soften the word with a smile and look at Annie and Lizzie. "Stay here with your sisters and finish your breakfast."

I start toward the mudroom. Someone has already mucked after the calf, but the small room reeks of manure and milk replacer.

Gina follows me, watching her step, hovering as I open the cabinet and grab my .38 and holster from a high shelf. "I'm going with you," she says.

"That's not necessary." At home, I always keep my sidearm handy. Since I'm a guest in someone else's home—someone with young children—I've kept the .38 and speed loader with extra rounds out of sight and out of reach. Most Amish kids are well versed on gun safety.

Many Amish men hunt; rifles or muzzle-loaders are common in just about every household. Not so with a handgun, so I've done my part to quell any curiosity.

I turn to see that Gina's already struggling into her coat, one sleeve draped over the sling and her injured arm. "I need my gun," she says.

I laugh as I reach into my pocket, grab the loose cartridges lying next to the speed loader, and drop them one by one into the cylinder. "I don't have to remind you there's a warrant for your arrest, do I?"

"I'm a cop," she snaps.

"Look, it's not all that uncommon for people to go shooting in the woods." I shrug into the holster, buckle it.

"Yeah, well, I don't like it."

"Are you expecting anyone in particular?"

"Maybe someone decided their life would be a hell of a lot simpler if I wasn't around to point a finger."

Snagging my parka off a hook, I work it on, stomp my feet into boots, and quickly lace them. "And now they're in the woods, shooting trees?" I scoff. "Does anyone know where you are?"

"No, but how hard would it be for someone to remember you and I used to be friends?"

Considering, I pull out my cell and I hit the number for Dispatch.

Mona answers on the first ring. "You're up early—"

"Who's on duty this morning?" I ask.

"Glock," she replies, all business now that she's realized I didn't call to chat. "He's the only one who could get out of his driveway."

"I'm at the Lengacher place. Someone's shooting in the woods by Painters Creek. I'm going to check it out. Can you send him down to the bridge?"

"Ten-four."

I drop the phone into my pocket; then I'm through the mudroom and out the door. It's not yet fully light as I take the steps two at a time and start toward the yard facing the woods. I glance left toward the barn. The door stands open. Adam's nowhere in sight. Gina tracks me, moving at a steady clip, staying close. For an instant I'm reminded of all the times we did this very thing, back when we were rookies.

The wind cuts through my coat and sneaks down my collar as I jog across the side yard, muscle through a drift that reaches to midthigh. I hear Gina behind me, cursing, her injured shoulder hampering her. I don't look back, keep going.

I'm familiar with the area. Painters Creek is two hundred yards away. A greenbelt runs along both sides of the waterway, old-growth trees tangled with the winter skeletons of wild blackberry, saplings, and brush. The deer congregate along the creek, using the trees for cover, grazing the twigs and undergrowth, and feeding on the hickory nuts that have broken open. It's a long greenbelt and a favorite place for hunters looking to bag a buck. Of course, they're only allowed to hunt during the season and must get the express permission of the landowner.

I reach the rail fence at the side yard, climb over it, and stumble through another drift. Then I'm in the pasture, where the snow is only a foot or so deep, jogging toward the tree line ahead.

Gina has fallen behind. I hear her struggling over the fence as I cross the pasture. Several cattle look up from their round bale of hay as I pass. The trees ahead are a wall of charcoal and white rising sixty feet into the sky. Three more shots echo off the treetops, and I pick up the pace. The meager light falls away as I enter the forest. It's hushed within the shroud of trees, as if the woods are holding their breath. I stop a few yards in, listening, trying to get my bearings and figure out where the shots came from. I can hear the tinkle of water where it runs swift over rock and hasn't yet frozen. I glance over my shoulder to see Gina approach, breathless and on alert.

"Where did it come from?" she whispers.

Another shot rings out, the sound echoing among the treetops. "North." I point ahead and slightly to my left.

We veer that way, our coats rustling, snow squeaking beneath our feet. I stick to the thickest part of the forest, using the underbrush for cover. I don't know who's out here or what they're shooting at. Chances are it's some guy with cabin fever who just wanted to get outside, away from the wife and kids, and give the rifle he got for Christmas a go. Or a farmer who caught a coyote trying to get at his chickens and tracked it here. Or maybe some unscrupulous hunter is out looking to poach a deer. The problem with those theories is that the deep snow and near-zero temperature are tremendous hardships even for the most hardy individual.

I work my way east and north until I reach the creek. It's frozen solid. Some of the ice has been scoured by wind. To my left I hear water trickling over rock where the stream narrows. I don't have my lapel mike clipped in, so I pull it out of my pocket, fumble with it before speaking.

"Ten-forty-three-B," I say quietly, using the code for shots fired, likely by hunters. "Glock, what's your twenty?"

"TR 36 and the bridge. Nothing here, Chief. No vehicle. No tracks."

I glance toward the south, but the bridge is too far, the trees too thick for me to get a visual. "I'm half a mile to your north on the west side of the creek."

"Any sign of a vehicle?"

"Negative, but there's a pullover by the bridge farther north." I address Dispatch. "Mona, notify County. Ten-forty-three-B."

"Roger that."

I'm pocketing my radio when another shot rings out, so close I instinctively duck. "Shit."

"There."

I glance over my shoulder to see Gina standing twenty feet away, pointing. I swivel, eyes seeking. Sure enough, through the trees, on the other side of the creek, I see movement. Adult male wearing camo. Moving fast.

I run north along the bank of the creek, speaking into my lapel mike. "I got eyes on him. Subject is male. Wearing camo. Running northbound, toward Dogleg Road."

"Ten-seven-six." The voice of a county deputy cracks over the radio.

I'm aware of Gina slightly ahead and running parallel with me, struggling through snow. I've only traveled a few yards when I lose sight of camo guy.

The last thing I want to do is get my feet wet. The water temperature hovers at the freezing mark this time of year. It doesn't take long for frostbite to set in. My boots are waterproof, but they're not tall enough to keep my feet completely dry.

I scramble down the bank of a feeder creek, my boots sliding. I glance right, across the water, catch another glimpse of movement. "Shit." I muscle through a drift, pause at the water's edge, and start across. The water reaches my knees; it's swift, unseen rocks making it difficult to maintain my footing. The cold penetrates fast, burns my skin. I've lost sight of Gina, but I hear her coming down the bank a few yards away. I rush through the water, stumbling over rocks, slip on ice on the other side and clamber up the bank.

"Police Department!" I call out. "Halt! Police!"

I stop, breaths puffing out in front of me, and listen. The rush of water over the rocks seems inordinately loud. I hear Gina tromping through snow on the other side of the creek. The call of a hawk above. I keep moving, going north toward Dogleg Road, hit my lapel mike.

"Glock, what's your twenty?"

"North a hundred yards from TR 36. I got tracks."

"I had eyes on him. He's running. Heading north. I'm north of you."

"Roger that." He's breathing heavily, telling me he's running, too.

I break into a run, zigzagging through trees, eyes ahead and on the ground, looking for tracks. Where the hell is he?

I'm nearly to Dogleg Road when I get my first good look at him. He's a large man. Camo coveralls and jacket. Long stride. Running full out.

I pour on the speed. "Painters Mill Police! Stop!"

I speak into my lapel mike. "County, what's your twenty?"

"County Road 4."

Too far away to help.

I traverse a deep ditch, lose sight of the man, nearly lose my footing at the base, climb up the other side, plunging my gloved hands into the snow to steady myself. The road looms into view. I burst from the trees.

"Burkholder!"

I spin toward the sound of my name to see Gina running full out, thirty feet away, parallel with me. The creek has curved, putting her closer to the man we're pursuing. She points with her uninjured arm. "There!"

I follow her point and catch a glimpse of camo through the trees. Thirty yards ahead and to my left. "Police Department!" I launch myself into a run, plunge into deep snow, nearly go down, right myself just as I come out of a drift.

Gina and I are running straight north. Ten yards apart. She's having a difficult time because of the sling and her injured arm, but moving at a decent clip.

I hear her shout something at the running man. For the first time I spot the rifle he's carrying, one hand on the stock, the other clutching the barrel. Relief skitters through me when he makes no move to raise it. He tosses a look over his shoulder, not slowing down.

He disappears into a thicket of trees. I've no longer got eyes on Gina. "Dammit," I pant, run headlong into another drift, stumble on something buried in the snow, and go down hard. My face plows into snow. In my eyes. My mouth.

"Stop!" comes Gina's voice, ahead and to my left. "I'm a police officer! Get on the ground!"

Spitting, I scramble to my feet, follow the sound of her voice. I round a fallen log and a bramble of blackberry. I'm nearly to the road when I spot Gina. She's standing over a man the size of a bear. He's lying facedown in the snow, arms and legs spread. I watch her pick up the rifle with her uninjured hand and toss it aside. She kneels, sets her knee against his back.

"Do not move," I hear her say.

A few yards away, a blue pickup truck with big tires and a camper shell covering the bed sits parked on the shoulder.

I reach them, taking in the scene. I'm so out of breath I can barely speak into my radio. "Ten-twenty-six." I pant the words, using the code for detaining subject—expedite.

I look at Gina. She's mussed and covered with snow, cheeks red, breaths puffing out in front of her. Looking far too satisfied with herself, she grins when my eyes meet hers and mouths, "Got him."

Shaking my head, I walk to where the man is lying on the ground. He's huffing, his entire body heaving with each breath. He raises his head and looks at me as I approach. "I didn't do anything wrong," he says.

I get my first good look at his face, and I recognize him. I busted him on a DUI last year. He wasn't very nice about it and I ended up having to call Skid for assistance.

"What are you shooting at?" I ask, noticing that the door of the camper shell is open.

"Saw a coyote," he tells me.

Because of coyote overpopulation in Ohio, the animals can be hunted legally year-round, unlike game animals such as deer, which can only be hunted during a narrow window.

"Do you have permission from the landowner?" I ask.

Shaking his head, he looks away. "Didn't know I needed it."

"Are you armed?" I ask. "You got another gun on you?"

"Just the rifle," he says.

"You can sit up," I tell him. "I need to see your driver's license."

"I didn't do anything wrong." He rolls over, sits up, digs out his driver's license, and hands it to me. "This is a bunch of shit," he mutters.

Ignoring him, I look at the ID. Bruce Winslow. Painters Mill address. Thirty-eight years old. "You have your hunting license on you?"

He looks down at the ground, shakes his head.

"Is that your truck?" I ask, motioning toward the pickup.

"Last time I checked."

"Do not move," I tell him.

I walk to the truck. I do not have the right to search any vehicle without the owner's permission or a warrant. That doesn't mean I can't look through the open door at the rear to see what's inside. The sight of the deer carcass laid out on a blue tarp, a big buck with a nice rack of antlers, shoved hurriedly onto the bed, makes me shake my head.

"Big coyote." I turn to him and frown.

"Aw, man. Come on."

"Deer season ended two weeks ago."

"I got my dates mixed up is all. Give me a break, will you?"

"He was shoving that carcass into the truck when I caught him."

Gina comes up beside me, looks at the dead deer, and lowers her voice. "For a fat guy, he runs pretty damn good."

I don't succumb to the smile tugging at my mouth. Instead, I tilt my head and speak into my radio. "Mona, I need a wildlife officer."

"Ten-four," comes her reply.

I give her my approximate location as well as the man's name and license number. "Expedite."

I'm standing next to the truck when Glock emerges from the trees. Unlike the rest of us, he's barely out of breath and moves through the snow with the ease of an athlete out for a morning jog. I see him taking in the scene, eyeing the man sitting on the ground. His eyes widen slightly at the sight of Gina. He sends a questioning look my way.

I address Winslow. "Stay put." Then I look at Gina. "Keep an eye on him, will you?"

She gives me a mock salute.

I cross to Glock, who's looking around the truck a short distance away. "You're a sight for sore eyes," I tell him.

"I get that a lot." He punctuates the statement with a grin.

I tell him as much as I can about Gina. "She's a cop. Columbus Division of Police. Tomasetti is involved. I can't get into the details."

"Okay." His eyes narrow, but he nods. "Everything going to be okay, Chief?"

I think about the question a moment before answering. "I have no idea."

CHAPTER 13

It wasn't yet eight A.M. and for the first time in months Damon Bertrand sat down for breakfast with his wife and their two adult children. By all rights, the "kids" should have started their careers and been living on their own by now. His son graduated from Ohio State a year ago, but had yet to land a job with which he could support himself. His daughter would graduate in the fall and spent more time partying on High Street than studying. When he was his son's age, Damon had been working patrol on the graveyard shift, was married, and had a kid on the way. Not for the first time he wondered where he and Doreen had gone wrong.

Usually by this time of day, he'd already swung by the diner for coffee and landed at his desk at the Division of Police building downtown. This morning, due to the inclement weather, he'd decided to wait until the plows cleared the streets.

In spite of his children's lack of ambition, he generally enjoyed spending time with his family. This morning, he was distracted. He couldn't focus, couldn't relax. The situation with Colorosa had eaten at him through the night and he'd spent most of the last eight hours either tossing and turning or in the guestroom channel surfing and trying to come up with a plan.

He was two years away from retirement. He'd reached a point in his life where he had a lot to lose. The last thing he needed was some turncoat cop destroying everything he'd ever worked for. Things like the pension that would see him and Doreen through their golden years. The love and respect of his family. That nice little condo they'd just bought down in Florida. His future. Maybe even his freedom. He would not let Colorosa or anyone else screw things up for him.

Damon had done what he could. He'd planted the seeds, gotten his hands as dirty as he dared. Still, he didn't know how this was going to play out. If he'd been smarter, he would have cut ties with Colorosa a long time ago. He would have cut her off. Gotten her fired. Now, all he wanted was for her to be gone.

The one thing life had taught him was that while you couldn't undo mistakes that had already been made, if you had the right tools, you *could* change history—and that was exactly what he'd done. Would it be enough?

At nine A.M. he left his wife in the kitchen and went to his small office off the foyer. He logged in to the Division of Police computer system and checked email. He brooded. He stewed. Most of all, he worried. He was in the process of finishing up a report for an upcoming court appearance when the call he'd been waiting for came in on his cell.

"You find her?" he asked without preamble.

"No, but I got a lead," Ken Mercer said.

Rising from his desk chair, Bertrand crossed to the French doors that separated his office from the foyer and closed them. "For God's sake, it had better be good," he said, settling back behind his desk.

"There was a cop she used to be tight with, back when she was a rookie. They lived together for a while. You remember a young cop by the name of Kate Burkholder?"

"Vaguely. She was religious or something."

"Yeah, the original odd couple, right? Burkholder left the department ten years ago. I started digging around and found out she took a job as chief in a small town about an hour and a half east of here."

Bertrand thought of the last ping from Colorosa's phone. At the time they hadn't been able to figure out where she'd been headed. He sat up straighter. "A fucking chief of police?"

"I pulled up what I could find on Burkholder. She's had a couple of high-profile cases in the last few years. That's how I found her. She's in Painters Mill, Damon. Holmes County."

"I've been through there. A lot of Amish out that way." He sighed unhappily. "That would explain that last ping on Colorosa's cell."

"Burkholder's from that area."

"What else do you know about her?"

Papers crinkled on the other end of the line. "It's a small department. Podunk town. From what I can tell she's kept her nose clean."

"If she hung out with Colorosa for any length of time, she's probably not that clean." He rubbed the stubble on his chin, thinking. "Did Burkholder leave the department on good terms? Is there anything on her record we can use against her if we need some leverage?"

"I checked. Her record's good."

"Do you think Colorosa's in Painters Mill?"

"I think it's the best lead we've got."

Bertrand let the news settle. A dozen scenarios played in his head. None of them ended well.

"This isn't exactly good news," he said.

"We're going to have to deal with it. It's all we've got."

"We need to find out if she's there."

The two men went silent, the phone line whispering dark possibilities. "What kind of police chief takes in a fugitive and doesn't notify the appropriate law enforcement agency?" Bertrand said.

"Good question."

"That fucking Colorosa is spilling her guts."

"The big question is whether Burkholder is listening."

The loose ends that had tormented Bertrand most of the night unraveled a little more, sharp strands settling around his neck like a garrote. He looked around, felt the walls of his office closing in. "I never trusted that bitch. She wasn't one of us. We never should have brought her in."

"Hindsight," Mercer mutters.

"A fucking chief of police." Leaning forward, feeling as if he needed air and light, Bertrand opened the blinds, looked out at the snow beyond. "This is a worst-case scenario."

"Look, if there's a silver lining to any of this, it's that Painters Mill isn't exactly on the map. Small town usually means small-town mentality. I say we get a warrant and go pick her up. We've got enough dirt on her to put her away for a long time."

Bertrand didn't think it was going to be that simple. What had Colorosa told Burkholder? Who else had she talked to? What had she said? Had she named names?

Mercer wasn't finished. "Look, Colorosa might be talking to some small-town police chief, but she has zero credibility, especially now that she's been implicated in the murder of Eddie Cysco."

Bertrand closed his eyes, wishing he'd handled the situation differently. Wishing he'd tied off that loose end the moment it frayed. "I'll take care of the warrant."

The beat of silence that followed told a dark and eloquent story.

One he'd heard a hundred times in the last twenty years. One he didn't want to partake in again. This time, he didn't have a choice.

"Roads are open," Mercer said. "For now. But we got weather on the way, buddy."

"In that case, we'd better move," Bertrand said. "I'll pick you up downtown as soon as we can get out. Pack an overnight bag."

CHAPTER 14

I graduated from the police academy and became a police officer when I was twenty-one years old. I'd been living in Columbus for three years, earned my GED, a criminal justice degree from the community college—and a whole new sense of my non-Amish self. For the first time in my life, I had accomplished something. I was going to actually be the person I wanted to be, and I charged into my new life with the gusto of a kid plunging off the high dive and wanting to do it again. I was free and I had been transformed. No longer was I the awkward and self-conscious Katie Burkholder. I had become Kate Burkholder, a woman with an important job and an exciting future.

I'd seen my family just once since leaving Painters Mill, and though my life was full and I'd made a slew of new friends, I was secretly lonely. I didn't talk about it, didn't tell a soul, in fact. But I missed my family with a desperation I'd never known. Though I was doing exactly what I wanted to do, fulfilling dreams that had seemed out of reach for so long, my parents and two siblings were still the center of my universe.

Some days I felt as if the world was spinning too fast, not always in the right direction, and no matter how hard I tried, I'd never be able to keep up. Late at night, when I was sleepless and reflective, the loneliness a bottomless ache, I acknowledged that I had failed my parents. I was afraid I'd never see my brother, Jacob, or my sister, Sarah, ever again. I'd committed a serious transgression in the eyes of the Lord, and there was no question in my mind He had abandoned me. While those dark moments were usually pretty short-lived, they were part of the Kate Burkholder I had become.

Because Gina and I were rookies with no seniority, we were assigned the graveyard shift, which runs from midnight to eight A.M. I worked in the Patrol North Subdivision, Zone 1, which basically covered the north part of the city. Gina was assigned the Patrol South Subdivision, Zone 5, which encompassed the central part of the city, including the downtown area. Graveyard shift was tough, not only because of the odd hours and resultant sleep deprivation, but because it was also a busy shift in terms of calls and incidents, especially after the drinking establishments close. While there were fewer people on the street overnight, the ones who were awake during those wee hours were oftentimes up to no good.

After a few tumultuous and stressful months of settling into our new routines and getting a feel for police work, Gina and I started meeting for breakfast on occasion, taking an hour or so to wind down before calling it a day and heading back to the apartment to sleep. One rainy spring morning, we met for coffee at an all-night diner called The Spoon, which was located in the zone Gina patrolled. As usual we were tired, glad to be off duty, and still in uniform.

I wore that uniform with a great sense of pride in those early days; I still do. But back then, it was a big deal. When I walked into a public place and felt the eyes on me, my chest swelled. That morning was no different.

The Spoon was like a dozen other flagging mom-and-pop diners in the downtown area. It had changed hands several times over the years, never quite reclaiming the grace or success of its heyday. The redbrick building was built in the 1920s and wore every decade like a scar. The interior was narrow with dirty windows facing the street, red Naugahyde booths replete with the occasional bulge of stuffing, and a Formica-topped bar that ran the length of the room. The aromas of frying bacon, coffee, and toast caressed my senses with the promise of comfort food and the company of a friend who'd become more like a sister in the last three years.

I felt the eyes on me as I made my way toward the rear booth where Gina and I usually sat. I smiled at the uniform-clad waitress, who all but snarled back. I was used to that, too, and I'd learned to take it in stride. I found Gina sitting at our booth, coffee cup and saucer in front of her. She looked up as I approached. I took in the mussed hair, the stain on the sleeve of her uniform, a red scrape on her chin, and the frazzled persona.

"Rough night?" I ask.

"Nothing an omelet and toast won't cure. I'm starving."

I slid into the booth opposite her and set my hat on the seat next to me. "You involved in that hit-skip over in Franklinton?"

"That guy ran like a damn cheetah and then proceeded to maul me."

I told her about an unusual traffic stop involving chickens and a house cat, a situation that turned out to be more humorous than serious. But this morning, Gina didn't laugh. She seemed agitated, looking around with impatience, giving me only a fraction of her attention.

"You're distracted," I said.

"Waitress is slow."

"Probably just busy."

"Yeah, well, she can be busy on someone else's time," she told me. "I gotta get back to work."

"You working a double?" I asked, trying not to let my disappointment show.

"I've only got about twenty minutes."

It wasn't unusual for us to put in extra hours or even a double shift for the overtime pay. I was in the process of checking messages on my cell when the waitress hustled up to our table, pad in hand. The name tag fastened to the collar of her uniform told us her name was Cheryl.

"You girls ready to order?" she asked.

"Cheese omelet and toast," Gina told her.

I ordered pancakes. "And coffee."

"You got it." Her hand flew across her order pad. "You can pay at the register when you're ready." The waitress motioned absently toward a small electronic register.

Gina passed her the menu she'd been looking at. The waitress started to take it, but Gina didn't relinquish it and the two women made eye contact. "Cops who get free food have faster response times."

I spat out a laugh before realizing the smile on Gina's face wasn't sincere. The waitress wasn't smiling, either. I nudged Gina with my boot beneath the table, but she didn't look at me, didn't take her eyes off the waitress.

"Just kidding," Gina said after a moment.

The waitress's eyes swept from Gina to me and back to Gina. "Your food'll be out in just a minute."

When I asked Gina about the incident later, she said she'd been kidding. The comment was some ongoing joke between her and the waitress. That was the first time she lied to me, but it wasn't the last.

After Gina left for her shift, I went to pay for our meals. The young hostess at the cash register told me my money was no good at The Spoon. "All cops get their meals for free here," she said.

CHAPTER 15

The snow stops at noon. Sunshine slashes down between cumulus clouds the color of a bruise, reflecting off the snow with an intensity that blinds. The outside world has been transformed. Everything glitters with the brilliance of a diamond sheen. Drifts are piled six feet high in places. The north wind scours the surface, moving layers of undulating crystal sand. It's a stunning scene, but with the windchill hovering somewhere around thirty below, I don't think the sun is going to do much in terms of melting.

Kids making lunch is not a silent ordeal, even when said children are Amish. I'm restless from being cooped up, and cold because the three wood and propane stoves are ill equipped to heat a farmhouse this size. I'm also tired, because I spent most of the night sleepless, trying to work through a situation that simply doesn't have a good resolution no matter how many times I rearrange all the pieces. My past relationship with Gina, both good and bad, is ever present, all of it tainted by the knowledge that she is guilty of serious wrongdoing—and I face a slew of difficult decisions in the coming days.

I'm curled on the sofa, cell in one hand, a cup of coffee in the other when I become aware of a presence. I look up to see Sammy standing a few feet away, watching me tap the screen as if it's the most fascinating thing he's ever witnessed.

"*Guder nammidaag,*" I tell him. Good afternoon.

"What are you doing, Chief Katie?"

"Checking my email."

He makes a face that tells me he's never heard the term before. "You mean there's a letter in your phone?"

"Lots of them."

"Can I see?"

"No." I soften the blow with a smile.

He grins back. He's got a smear of peanut butter at the corner of his mouth. Bread crumbs on the front of his shirt. Cheeks chapped from being out in the cold. In that moment he looks so much like Adam when he was a youngster, I feel a little piece of my heart melt.

"Datt says Jimmy and Jenny can pull your car out of the ditch today. Gina's, too. But we have to hurry because it's going to snow again."

Energized by the thought of freeing up the Explorer, I put my phone away. "Where's your *datt*?"

"Him and Gina went to the barn."

The statement takes me aback. Earlier, I saw Adam go outside to check on the calf. I didn't, however, notice Gina leaving. I'd assumed she was in the sewing room. How is it that she slipped out the door unnoticed? And what the hell is she doing in the barn with Adam?

"In that case, I think I'll go help them," I tell Sammy.

"I can help, too. I can get Jimmy and Jenny ready to pull out the cars."

"How about you finish your lunch first?"

"Okay, but I'm going to eat fast."

I walk with him to the kitchen and then I continue on to the mudroom, slip into my parka and boots, and head outside. I'm met with air so cold it sucks the breath from my lungs. Wind burns my cheeks and reaches down my collar like an icy hand. The sun reflecting off the snow is blinding. Flipping up my hood, I pull my sunglasses from a zippered pocket and head toward the barn.

The sliding door stands open. A thin layer of snow covers the dirt floor, having blown in. Shoving my sunglasses onto my crown, I step inside. I'm greeted by the smells of horses and hay and the earthy essences of a well-used barn. A dapple-gray draft horse stands cross-tied in the aisle to my left, looking at me. A second horse still wearing its quilted winter coat is tied outside its stall and whinnies. The stairs to the loft are on my right. A raised wood-plank floor is straight ahead, where a dozen or so bags of feed are stacked against the wall. Outside, the wind whips at a loose shingle, clanging it against the roof.

I go to the gelding, run my hand over his topline. "You must be Jimmy."

The animal nuzzles me, not because he's lovable, but because he's likely looking for a carrot or apple.

"Hello?" I call out. "Adam?" I walk toward the raised floor at the rear of the barn, looking around as I go. "Gina?"

A quiver of worry goes through me when I don't get a response. I'm ever aware of the events that have taken place in Columbus. I know better than to write off the possibility that someone might come looking for her. Cops are a resourceful bunch with an arsenal of people-finding tools at their fingertips, not to mention the experience to get it done. It wouldn't take much for one of them to remember that Gina and I had once been friends.

Someone like Ken Mercer, a little voice whispers.

A sound to my left startles me. I spin, my hand hovering over the place where my .38 would have been had I thought to bring it.

Surprise flits through me at the sight of Gina and Adam clattering down the steps. They're laughing. I discern Gina's raucous laugh, vivacious, a little too loud. Single file because the steps are narrow, Gina in the lead, Adam right on her heels. Hands joined between them.

At the base of the stairs, she stops and spins to him, raising her uninjured hand as if to fend him off. "I told you I'd beat you!"

"You cheated."

He moves in close, eyes alight, his attention riveted to her. It's a response that has nothing to do with Amish or English, but the age-old dynamics inherent between male and female.

It's such an unexpected and improbable sight, it takes my brain a moment to process. I've interrupted a private moment. Decorum tells me to make a quick exit and forget it. But I know Gina. More importantly, I know Adam. I know what he's been through, that he's vulnerable in a way that won't be taken into consideration by her, and I know nothing good can come from their getting too close.

"Looks like the snow has finally stopped," I say.

She startles, her gaze flying to mine. Adam lurches away from her, his hand dropping away from hers. His smile evaporates. An emotion akin to guilt flashes in his eyes and is quickly followed by embarrassment.

The Amish can no more be lumped together than any other group of people, but certain norms prevail. Mature Amish men are generally well behaved. Married men are aware of appearances, especially with regard to how they will be seen by the Amish community. I've no doubt Adam embodies that inherent propriety and good manners. He's a single father with young children to raise, a farm to manage, and a reputation to uphold. All of that said, he's also a man who's been alone for long time.

Gina, on the other hand, operates with a devil-may-care attitude. She's a rule breaker and never hesitates to speak her mind, the louder, the better—even when she's wrong. She's engaging, fiercely loyal, and passionate about everything she does. When I discern the reckless half smile on her face, I know Adam doesn't stand a chance.

"I hear you might be able to pull a couple of vehicles out of the snow," I say.

Adam takes another step away from Gina. His eyes don't quite meet mine as he moves past me and approaches the gelding in the aisle. For the first time I notice the leather pulling collar in his hand.

"We've got a small window of good weather," he says. "I thought we might put it to use. Get the cars out while we can."

"Can I help?" I ask. I'm aware of Gina holding her ground at the base of the stairs, watching us, but I don't look at her. "It's been a while, but I remember my way around a horse and harness."

He slants a look at me, but his eyes don't hold mine. "I've got it."

I watch him unbuckle the gelding's halter and then reposition it around the horse's neck; then he slides the pulling collar over its head.

I approach Gina. "You must be feeling better."

"Don't look at me like that," she mutters. "We were just goofing around. Blowing off steam after being cooped up."

"I didn't ask." I try to gauge her sincerity, but I'm annoyed because she's unaffected and unapologetic. In typical Gina fashion, she has no understanding of the repercussions of her actions.

"I'll fill you in on a few things later," I say quietly.

"I can't wait." She whispers the words beneath her breath, then turns away and walks to the door.

Adam goes to where the mare stands tied in the aisle. I watch as he unbuckles the belly strap of the winter blanket, pulls it over the animal's head, and drapes it over the stall door. Untying the horse, he leads her to the open area where the gelding waits and ties the mare next to him.

I go to the mare and run my hand over her shoulder. She jigs left, tossing her head. "They're restless."

"They've been cooped up in their stalls too long," Adam says. "Ready for some fresh air and heavy pulling, I think."

He still won't look at me or meet my gaze. "I haven't used Jenny for heavy pulling in a while," he says as he drapes the leather harness over the mare's head and proceeds to buckle the straps.

"Think they can do it?" I ask, though I know from experience Percheron drafts are capable of pulling thousands of pounds. My *datt* owned a team of four when I was a kid, and I've seen them pull a plow through fields and wagons loaded ten feet high with hay.

"They've pulled heavier." He loops the near leather line around the O ring of the bit, buckles it, and runs the line through the terret at the collar. "I checked both vehicles earlier," he tells me. "Yours doesn't look too bad. Hers might prove to be a little more difficult." He doesn't say Gina's name. "But I think we can get them out."

He runs his hand over the gelding's rump. When his gaze finally meets mine, I see self-recrimination and shame in his eyes. I don't know what to say to him or how to assuage his discomfort.

"Katie, about what you saw—"

I raise my hand. "You don't owe me an explanation."

He tightens his mouth, looks away, then turns his gaze back to mine. "It was my doing. Not hers."

Half a dozen responses dangle on my tongue. I want to caution him about Gina and her charms. Let him know that his attractive and fun-loving visitor has a talent for sucking the unsuspecting into her life. But Adam is a grown man. He knows his mind. And this is likely none of my business.

"You're a gentleman, Adam." I run my fingers through the horse's mane. "Gina is . . . complicated."

He nods, thoughtful. "In that case, I'll just finish harnessing the horses and we'll get those vehicles pulled from the snow."

Fifteen minutes later, both horses are harnessed. The children have emerged from the house, bundled in coats and scarves and hats. The harnesses jingle as Adam leads the team of horses toward my Explorer. An uncharacteristically subdued Gina falls into step beside me.

The wind pelts us with drifting snow as we make our way down the lane. We find the Explorer partially buried in a drift.

"A few more inches of snow and we might not have found it," Adam says as he brings the horses to a halt.

I motion toward the western horizon. "If those clouds are any indication, we're here just in time."

Beside me, Gina groans.

Hitting the fob, I slog through three feet of snow to the rear and pull the nylon tug strap from my equipment box. I've hauled enough vehicles from ditches to know it's going to entail my tunneling through the snow beneath the vehicle to secure the tug-strap hook to the frame. Grabbing the folding shovel from the rear, I close the hatch, make my way around to the front, and jam the shovel into snow.

Gina stands back, shivering. "Sorry, Chief, but I'm not going to be much help with this loused-up arm."

"I'll dig!" Sammy exclaims. "I'm good at building snow tunnels. I built an igloo once."

The boy's eagerness makes me laugh. "I think your *datt* is going to need your help with those horses."

While Sammy stomps over to where Adam is turning the team

around, Annie and Lizzie begin to scoop snow into their mittened hands and engage in an impromptu snowball fight.

At the front of the Explorer, I stab the shovel into snow and then toss the snow into the ditch. After a few minutes I settle into a rhythm. Jam. Withdraw. Toss.

Sammy and his father chat as they send the horses into a side pass and then back them to the front of the Explorer. The horses are frisky due to the cold, tossing their heads, snorting, and shifting restlessly. When the animals are in place, Adam calls his son over to hold them, then approaches me and usurps the shovel.

"This is going to take all day at the rate you're going," he says with a smile.

"I won't take that personally." Smiling, I relinquish the shovel.

I stand back and watch as he digs a pseudo-tunnel beneath the front bumper, tossing the snow out behind him. When he's finished, I position the tug line on the ground between the vehicle and team of horses. Taking the hook end, I get down on my belly and scrabble beneath the Explorer. Upon reaching the frame, I loop the nylon strap around the frame, hook it, and back out.

Adam stands behind the two horses, holding the lines, looking back at me. Sammy stands at the animals' heads, watching. I'm covered with snow and freezing cold. Quickly, I slide into the Explorer, start the engine, and shift the transmission into neutral. I roll down the window. "Ready!"

Adam faces forward, snaps the lines gently against the horses' rumps. "*Kumma druff!*" he says to them. Come on there!

Sammy tugs the lead lines. "Pull, Big Jimmy! Come on, Jenny! You can do it. Pull!"

The horses surge forward, pushing against their collars, haunches bunched. The tug line jerks taut. The horses strain against the weight, veering left and then right as their might meets resistance, breaths puffing from flared nostrils in great white clouds. The Explorer shifts. The vehicle lists at a slight angle, so I turn the wheel slightly so that the tires follow the direction of the horses.

"*Kumma druff!*" Adam says.

"Look at Big Jimmy go!" Lizzie exclaims.

Bearing witness to these magnificent animals pulling a nearly five-thousand-pound vehicle from several feet of snow is an awe-inspiring sight. Hooves slipping and sliding and digging in, heads down, the horses drag the vehicle several feet. I put the Explorer into four-wheel drive, touch the gas pedal. The vehicle slides sideways and moves forward until it's out of the drift, and finally sitting in the lane.

"Whoa." Adam stops the horses, and backs them up a couple of feet. The tension on the tug strap relaxes.

Even Gina is in awe. "Wrecker service, Amish style," she murmurs. "That is seriously badass."

"Don't underestimate the old ways," Adam says.

I park the Explorer in a wind-scoured area of the driveway and let the engine purr. Getting out, I go to the horses and run my hands over their thick winter coats. "Nicely done."

"I have no idea where I left the truck," Gina tells me. "That night is a blur."

For the first time Adam looks at her. "I know where it is. Not too far."

Adam and Sammy lead the team of horses up the lane. With Gina, the two girls, and me bringing up the rear, we pass through a gate near the barn, and then we're in an open field heading toward the back of the property.

"The children and I took the sleigh this way that morning." Adam gestures to the fence line that parallels the township road. "The truck is just ahead. There's a gate."

The sleigh tracks have long since been erased by the wind and covered with snow, so we follow the fence line to the rear of the property. Sure enough, the bed of an older F-150 pickup truck protrudes from the snow at a cockeyed angle. The hood is completely buried, an ancient bois d'arc tree jutting from a massive drift about where the bumper is located.

As I approach the vehicle, the first thing I notice is the half dozen bullet holes in the rear windshield. I struggle through hip-deep snow. The driver's-side door is slightly open and buried up to the window.

"Going to have to pull this one out backward," Adam says.

"That'll work." I unfold my shovel. Using it for balance, I make my way to the driver's-side door and dig. When Annie comes up behind me with an offer to help, I grab a palmful of snow, form a snowball, and toss it onto the top of her winter bonnet.

The girl squeals in delight. As I dig to free up the door, Gina and Adam join the fun and before long everyone is throwing snow at everyone else. That the kids are having fun seems to make the work easier, and makes me forget that my feet and hands ache with cold. I'm relieved the children haven't noticed the bullet holes, which would surely generate questions no one will quite know how to answer. I work as quickly as I can, sweating beneath my coat now. Within minutes, I'm able to open the door.

I slide behind the wheel, trying not to notice the blood frozen on the seat. I turn the key, but the engine doesn't make a sound. "It's dead."

Gina pushes her way through snow, the sling hampering her balance. "I tried starting it after I hit the tree, but it was dead right after the accident."

"Maybe the impact caused the battery to shift and become disconnected," I say.

There are a half a dozen things we could check, but it's too cold to take the time. The windchill is nearly unbearable. At the moment, our priority is to haul the truck out of the ditch and get it back to the farm so it's out of sight, and the children can get inside to warm up.

Grabbing my shovel, I go to the rear of the truck and quickly tunnel beneath the bumper. While Gina holds the shovel, I get down on my belly and attach the tug strap to the frame.

Adam and Sammy position the horses while I go back to the driver's-side door and slide behind the wheel. Ignition on, I shift the truck into neutral. "All right!" I call out to Adam.

The horses surge forward and within minutes the truck sits on the road. I get out, remove the tug strap from the rear frame, and move it to the front undercarriage. The hood has become unlatched at some point, likely upon impact with the tree, but there's no way to secure it. I brush away the excess snow, shove the hood down as much as I can so I can see, and I get back behind the wheel.

"Let's go!" I call out.

Adam and Sammy lead the horses along the fence, struggling through knee-deep snow, the truck bumping along behind them. At the wheel, I steer around the deeper drifts, keeping the wheels aligned with the track of the horses.

The driver's-side window is down, and as we head back to the house, Lizzie and Annie chatter. Adam and Sammy stay ahead with the horses, keeping the tug strap taut. Gina sits in the passenger seat next to me, making the occasional comment, but she's mostly quiet. Her commentary isn't quite up to her usual standards, her brash front replaced by something I can't quite identify. Though we're wholly alone, on a back road that's unreachable by all accounts, I've noticed her looking around, her eyes scanning the tree line to the east, the township road ahead. She's wearing sunglasses, but they don't conceal the uneasiness I see on her face.

She's no shrinking violet in the face of danger. She's coolheaded and an adrenaline junkie to boot. Today, she's not simply uneasy, but scared. Once again, I wonder if she's told me the whole truth. If she's hiding something I need to know.

There's a certain cadence to an Amish home. Voices and life and activity. There's a set routine. Chores that must be done. A house to be managed. Animals to be cared for. A farm to run. And for the children, fun to be had at every opportunity.

I find myself falling into the routine with an ease that surprises me. While Adam and Sammy muck stalls and feed the livestock, Annie and Lizzie and I clean the mudroom, where the calf made quite a mess, and take a mop to the floor. Even Gina pitches in and tackles the scouring of the sinks and toilets. It's the first time I've ever seen her clean and I was her roommate for over five years.

It's late afternoon by the time Gina and I are alone. The girls have gone to the bedroom they share to read. Adam and Sammy are in the barn, bringing straw down from the loft. I find Gina standing at the sink in the kitchen, looking out the window, a glass of water in her hand. Outside, flurries float down from a sky the color of concrete.

"You were awfully jumpy today when we were towing your truck back to the farm," I say without preamble.

Humphing, she dumps the water in the sink and proceeds to wash the glass. "Seeing the bullet holes in the back window gave me the damn willies."

"Is that all?"

She sets down the glass and gives me her full attention. "You got something on your mind, Kate?"

"I'm wondering if you've told me the whole story. Or if there's something else I need to know."

Rolling her eyes at me, she laughs. "For God's sake, you're rocking that cop paranoia again."

"I guess that's one of the things that makes me good at what I do."

When she doesn't respond, I go to the counter, pull two mugs from the cupboard, and pour coffee into them. "Tomasetti and I are trying to help you. Your keeping secrets isn't going to cut it."

"I know." She walks to the table and sinks into a chair, silent, and stares down at the cup in her hands. "For God's sake."

I wait.

"Bertrand and Mercer think I took some cash," she says after a moment.

"Why do they think that?"

"Because eighty thousand dollars disappeared." She shrugs. "I was at the scene. Some drug dealer had a bunch of hundred-dollar bills stashed in a safe. There were five of us. They were going to divvy it up, but the cash disappeared. I got blamed."

I take the chair across from her and slide one of the cups toward her. "Did you take it?"

She humphs. "If I'd taken that kind of cash, you can bet your ass I would not be here."

I say nothing.

She reaches for the cup, but doesn't drink, sets it back down, agitated. "So, yeah, I'm worried. These guys have a lot to lose, Kate. I know what they're capable of. I have a pretty good idea of how far they'll go to protect themselves."

"What exactly are you talking about?" I ask.

She laughs, but not before I see the apprehension peek out from beneath the mask she's so good at keeping in place. "Let me put it this way: If they come here with a warrant and place me under arrest, I will not survive the ordeal. I will be dead inside of twenty-four hours."

A chill plows across the backs of my shoulders. I don't want to believe sworn police officers, men who've devoted their lives to the department, are capable of murdering one of their own to protect themselves. I hate it that I'm now open to the possibility.

"Veteran detectives don't go around killing people," I say. "They sure as hell don't go around killing cops. Not without bringing down the wrath of those of us who walk the straight and narrow."

She snorts, but this time her bravado falters. "Oh, they'll make it look perfectly legitimate. They'll make it believable. Cover all their bases and no one will be the wiser. And they will come out of it looking like heroes."

It's a disturbing scenario. For a moment, I don't know what to say. I'm not sure what to think. No LEO wants to believe career cops are involved in a level of corruption that includes extortion and murder. Complicating all of it is the kernel of mistrust I've felt for Gina since the moment I laid eyes on her, lying on that cot.

"They are cold-blooded sons of bitches," she whispers. "I've seen it. Firsthand." She sends me an acrid look. "They're thieves, rapists, and worse."

I nod, not sure I want to hear what she's going to say next, knowing I don't have a choice. "So tell me what you know."

Closing her eyes tightly, as if to erase something branded into her mind's eye, she shakes her head. "It happened during a raid. Bertrand and Mercer arrested a young woman, barely out of her teens. She was pretty. Tough talking. Cussing them. Covered with tats. They cuffed her, put her in their vehicle, and they left the scene. I was busy, working evidence or whatever. I didn't think too much about it until her mother reported her missing four days later."

"What happened?"

"No one ever saw her again."

"You think Bertrand and Mercer . . ." I struggle with the word pulsing at the back of my brain. "You think they murdered her?"

"There was never a body." She shrugs. "She was a prostitute. High-risk profession, right? Hey, shit happens. Those kinds of women disappear all the time. Aside from her mom, she didn't have any family. No one who cared about her. Who's going to point a finger at a couple of career detectives?"

"Did you ask either of them about it?" I ask.

"They claim they never took her into custody. Every cop there backed them up." She raises her gaze to mine, and in that instant, I barely recognize her through the cloud of emotions roiling just beneath the surface. "I never turned my back to Mercer or Bertrand again."

I pull out my notebook. "Does this girl have a name?"

"Tammi Guyer."

I write it down. "Why didn't you mention this before?"

"Because I don't have any proof. No offense, Kate, but you haven't exactly been receptive to some of the things I've told you."

I say nothing as I tuck the notebook back into my pocket. But I'm keenly aware of the chill at the base of my spine. Not for the first time, I think about Adam and the children. And I realize the one thing I am utterly certain of is that I don't want them involved in any of this.

CHAPTER 16

Tomasetti arrives a little later in the afternoon. I meet him at the front door, pleased to see him and hoping for news as I invite him inside. I've been stuck out here for a couple of days now and, phone calls and one short visit aside, I've missed him.

"Did anyone ever tell you you look good in that snowsuit?" I ask.

I know the instant he takes off the helmet that he's got news and it isn't good.

"Where's Colorosa?" he asks.

"I'm right here."

We turn to see Gina standing in the doorway between the kitchen and living room, her eyes skating from me to Tomasetti. She's taken note of his expression, too, and detected the tension coming off him.

"What's going on?" she asks.

"Jack Tyson is dead," he tells us.

It takes my mind a moment to recall the name. Tyson is the young patrol officer Gina thought might come forward to corroborate her story.

"*What?*" I'm aware of her taking a step back, her hand going to her chest, her expression stricken. "My God. Jack?" She utters the words as if she thinks Tomasetti is lying to her, playing some cruel joke. "But . . . how? When did it happen?"

"Early this morning," Tomasetti says. "He was on duty. Sitting in his cruiser. Three A.M. Someone ambushed him. Came up behind him. Shot him six times through the driver's-side window."

Gina utters a nasty curse, bends slightly, then slaps her palm against the doorjamb. "Jack. Jesus."

"Did they get the shooter?" I ask Tomasetti.

He shakes his head. "No."

Gina strides into the living room, visibly shaken, her expression distraught. "Of course they didn't. For God's sake, think about the timing." She smacks her hand against the jamb again. A turbulent mix of anger and shock pours off her, echoes in her voice. "I talked to Jack just a few days ago. He was thinking about getting involved. To help me. He was going to—"

"I was supposed to meet him tomorrow." Tomasetti cuts her off, unsympathetic.

"Did anyone else know about the meeting?" I ask.

"Not unless Tyson told someone." He looks at me. "I don't think he'd do that. When I talked to him, he wasn't even comfortable talking on the cell. I got the impression he wanted to keep all of this private."

He looks at Gina. "How close were you to Tyson?"

"We were friends," she says. "Went out for beers a couple times. I didn't know him well. But I liked him. He was a good guy."

"How involved was he in all of this?"

"As far as I know, he wasn't. But he'd seen some things over the last year or so."

"Like what?" Tomasetti asks.

"We never got that far."

"How far *did* you get?" I ask.

"We talked about Bertrand and Mercer for the first time a few days before they came for me. He said he hated what was going on.

He's the one who told me they were looking at me. I owe him for that. We talked about . . . getting some kind of proof. Taking it to someone we trusted."

She stops speaking, divides her attention between me and Tomasetti. "Someone found out he talked to me. That's why they killed him."

Tomasetti scowls at her. "Who?"

"I gave you the names. Bertrand. Mercer. Half a dozen other guys in the unit. Or else they got some hired guns to do their dirty work for them. Take your pick."

She raises both hands and sets her fingers against her temples as if everything that's been said is too much to absorb. "Tyson was one of the good guys. He's got a wife. Kids. He was only thirty-two years old. I can't believe those sons of bitches killed him."

She moves closer to Tomasetti, her uninjured hand clenched, and lowers her voice. "They need to be stopped. If you're not up to the task, say the word." She puts a finger a few inches from his face, her voice dropping into a whisper. "And I'll do it myself."

Tomasetti all but rolls his eyes. He doesn't relinquish ground. "Calm down," he tells her.

"Don't tell me to fucking calm down," she snaps.

I hear movement in the kitchen and look past her. Lizzie and Annie stand in the doorway, watching us, their eyes wide, mouths agape. It's as if they're frozen in place, unable to tear their eyes away from the drama unfolding before them.

Sending Gina a warning look, I start toward the children. "Girls, would you mind going to the cellar and grabbing a couple jars of green beans for tonight?"

The words seem to snap Gina from her fugue of anger. Glancing at the children, she strides to the sofa and drops onto it. She leans forward, places her elbows on her knees, and stares down at the floor.

Lizzie nods, her eyes flicking past me toward Gina. More interesting things going on here, but she's too well behaved to linger.

"I thought we might make my famous green beans and ham hock tonight," I say. "Go on now."

Taking a final look at Gina, the girls retreat to the kitchen. As they clamber down the steps to the cellar, I go back to the living room. No one has spoken. Tomasetti stands next to the front window, looking out at the snow. Gina is still sitting on the sofa, elbows on her knees, her eyes on the floor.

Tomasetti addresses me. "I didn't make my meeting with Denny," he tells me, referring to his superior at BCI. "Even with tire chains, I couldn't reach the interstate. We chatted on the phone, but he wouldn't give me much. All I can tell you is that BCI is looking at this. If the FBI isn't involved already, they will be soon."

Gina raises her gaze to Tomasetti. "You know what's going to happen next, right? The fine men and women of the vice unit are going to 'find' the person responsible for gunning down Jack Tyson. That suspect will not survive the arrest. The evidence against him will be overwhelming. The ensuing investigation will be short and the case will be closed and forgotten."

Thinly veiled fury boils in the depths of her eyes. It's tightly controlled at the moment. But I know Gina; I've seen that iron fist of control unravel. She's not the kind of person to forgive and forget. She holds on to those volatile emotions. When she unleashes them, look out.

Tomasetti returns her stare, silent, giving her nothing in terms of response.

"Where does this leave us?" I ask.

He shrugs. "We let BCI and the FBI do their jobs," he tells me. "I'll talk to Denny when I can make it to Columbus. Keep digging around on my end."

I turn my attention to Gina. "You mentioned you and Tyson were trying to come up with evidence of wrongdoing that you could take to someone you trust. You have the audio recording—"

"We knew it wasn't enough."

"Is it possible he had something else in his possession that might help us?"

"I don't know," she says. "We just didn't get that far."

"Cell phone?" I press. "Computer? Is there someone he may have entrusted it with?"

"I'm the only one he trusted," she says. "Last time I talked to him we were still trying to put all of this together. Kate, if someone from the vice unit was at the scene when Jack was killed, they probably already have his cell phone. Probably whatever was in his locker, too."

Tomasetti steps in. "BCI will have someone at scene."

Gina turns a hollow-eyed look on him. "There's no way they got there fast enough. Even if Bertrand or Mercer hired some thug to do the murder, you know someone from the vice unit got there first and took what they wanted."

Silence ensues, everything that's been said settling uncomfortably.

After a few minutes, Tomasetti turns to me. "I see you got the Explorer out."

I tell him about Adam using the draft horses to pull our vehicles from the snow. "We parked Gina's F-150 in the barn. Out of sight."

He nods. "Electricity is still out at the farm. Utility company says they should have things up and running inside of twenty-four hours. Linemen are having a tough time getting out," he says. "You want the bad news?"

I groan.

"There's another round of snow and wind in the forecast for tonight."

Gina makes a sound of disgust. “Tell me something I don’t already know.”

He lifts his lip in a poor imitation of a smile. “You guys all set here as far as supplies?”

I smile. “Adam’s only got a few hundred jars of canned vegetables and meats,” I say dryly. “I think he’s going to try to get out and cut some wood tomorrow.”

“Sounds like the Amish are faring a lot better than the rest of us,” he says.

I don’t mention that this kind of extreme weather makes caring for livestock exponentially more difficult. That the Amish have to deal with frozen drinking water and frozen pipes just like everyone else, only without the added benefit of electricity.

“You have time for a cup of coffee?” I ask.

“I’m going to head home. Get on the phone. See what else I can find out about Tyson.”

“Keep me posted, will you?”

He leans in for a kiss, then motions with his eyes toward Gina. “Keep an eye on her.”

His cell phone pinged at the stroke of midnight and vibrated across the polished wood surface of the night table next to the bed. Ken Mercer rolled away from his sleeping wife, reached for it, and squinted at the display. Though the number was unfamiliar, his heart quickened. How very like her to call at the witching hour. . . .

Rising, he cast a final look at his wife’s form and went through the door, closing it behind him. “Yeah,” he said in a sleep-roughened voice.

“Took you long enough,” came the female voice on the other end. “I didn’t catch you in the middle of something, did I?”

Regardless of her words—whether they were cutting or kind or somewhere in between—the sound of her voice always had the same effect. It put him on edge. Aroused him in ways that weren't quite sexual. Made him feel like the man he hadn't been for a long time.

"Where the hell are you?" he whispered. "I've been out of my fucking mind. Why didn't you call? I thought they'd . . ." His voice breaks. "For God's sake, I thought the next call I got was going to be about someone finding your body in a goddamn field."

"I'm fine," she said, unaffected. "Safe."

"They said you were hit. There was blood at the scene."

"I got it taken care of. I'm okay."

His breathing was elevated. He was wide awake now. Senses humming an uneven refrain. As always, she had his undivided attention. "I was afraid to call you. Even on the burner."

"You're the only one who has the number. What do you think I am, a rookie?"

No, he didn't think that. Not by a long shot. She hadn't been a rookie for a very long time. "Where are you?" he asked. Trying not to sound too anxious. Too needy. Not wanting her to know just how desperate he'd been to hear from her.

"You know I can't tell you," she said. "Plausible deniability, remember? You never know when someone is going to be looking at *your* cell phone records."

He sighed. "Look, all hell is breaking loose here. There's an APB out for you. They IDed the truck you were using and you're fucking Al Capone. Monaghan is shitting bricks, and everyone and their uncle is looking for you."

"They can look all they want. They won't find me." Despite the situation, confidence and arrogance rang in her voice. With any other woman, those traits would have been brash and unappealing. Not this woman. She wore both of those traits like a second skin that was as taut and polished as her own.

"What happened to Jack Tyson?" she asked.

"I don't know." He closed his eyes. "I couldn't believe it when I heard."

Even now, after everything that had transpired between them, he didn't like lying to her. The feeling wasn't reciprocal; lying was second nature to her. She was good at it and enjoyed the game—often at his expense. He'd learned to accept it, look past it, embrace it even. Some things were more important than the truth.

"Did they kill him?" she asked.

"No way. Tyson was solid. Everyone trusted him." Another lie, but such was the nature of their relationship. "Could have been a gang hit."

"I don't like the timing."

"Welcome to the club," he said. "I don't like any of this."

Silence sizzled over the miles between them. His need for her stirred low in his gut.

"They think you took the money," he said after a moment.

She laughed. Of course, she would laugh. Not only did she have a penchant for lying, but she had no problem courting danger. Such a volatile combination. He wondered if she knew just how much danger she'd stepped into this time.

"Maybe I did," she said.

"I guess that means you've been a bad girl."

"That's exactly why you can't get enough of me," she whispered. "That's why you're standing in the hall outside your bedroom door with a raging hard-on. That's why you're going to leave your wife and spend the rest of your life trying to live up to my expectations. Isn't it?"

He steeled himself against the truth of it, the tinge of cruelty in her voice. "Is it in a safe place?" he asked.

"Very safe," she said, and then her voice went soft. "I miss you, too, by the way."

"I can't wait to get my hands on you," he said, hating it that his voice betrayed him, revealing the urgency that had his heart racing. The desperation that had his gut tied in knots. Not for the first time he lamented his weakness, the fact that he could no more control any of it than he could his need for his next breath. God knows he'd tried . . .

"Can you get away?" she asked. "Can we meet?"

"You know things are too hot," he said. "We need to let things quiet down, babes. A few days."

"I'm not sure I can wait that long."

"We'll have to make up for lost time."

The silence that followed pricked at his nerves, making them tingle until his hands shook and his armpits dampened with sweat.

"You know they're not going to let us walk away from this," she said.

"So we'll run. The money'll get us where we need to go."

"Is there anything I can do?" she asked, finally in a softer voice that promised all the things he craved from her. All the things that, until now, had seemed so out of reach.

"Stay put and lay low," he said.

"I'm not very good at laying low."

"They haven't found you yet so just keep doing what you're doing."

"Let me know when you're ready, and I'll be there. You can count on me."

"How do I reach you?" he asked.

"You won't," she said. "I'll call you."

"I love you, baby." He closed his eyes, thought he could smell her scent, feel the warmth of her breath against his face. "Don't worry about anything. I'll take care of—"

The line went dead.

CHAPTER 17

Dawn arrives cold and gray, with snow flurries and a north wind that hammers the house like a fist. It's not as bitterly cold today, and I'm desperately hoping the six inches of snow the weatherman predicted is an overestimation. Tomasetti needs to make the drive to Columbus. It can't be put off any longer.

I'm at the sink, washing the last of our breakfast dishes. Gina sits at the kitchen table, staring at the coffee cup in front of her, brooding. She doesn't look like she got much sleep, didn't take the time to brush her hair, which is a mess. Earlier, Annie and Lizzie helped me put sausage and green beans to simmer on the stove. I did my best to engage the girls, but they seem wary of Gina and me this morning, especially Lizzie, who's older. I suspect their standoffishness may be due to the things they overheard yesterday. I make a mental note to talk to Gina about her language later.

I've just placed the last saucer in the cabinet when Lizzie comes through the door with a box of checkers. "Sammy likes to play Settlers of Catan, but we're too little," she announces as she sets up the game on the kitchen table.

"Mamm used to play checkers with us sometimes," Annie says.

"She's with God now." Concentrating, Lizzie removes the chips and sets them next to the board. "She went with our little brother, Levi. One of these days we're going to go, too, and I'll get to meet Levi. Maybe even hold him."

"He didn't get to be born," Annie explains.

"*Sis Gottes wille.*" Lizzie pats her little sister's hand. It's God's will.

I'm aware that Gina has looked up from her coffee to stare at them. I stare, too, somehow guilty, taken aback by the depth of their innocence, the unblemished sweetness, their faith, and I wonder how long it's been since I appreciated the fact that such things exist in this world.

After a moment, Gina rubs her hands together, looks from girl to girl. "I should warn you I play a mean game of checkers."

"What she means," I tell the girls, tossing Gina a reproachful look, "is that she's good at checkers and she'd like to challenge you to a game."

A knock on the door startles us. Gina gets to her feet, looking around. "You expecting someone?"

"I'll go check." Lizzie scoots back her chair, but I set my hand on her shoulder.

"I have a better idea," I say easily. "Why don't you girls get your checkers set up and I'll get it."

Gina looks at me. "Where are Adam and Sammy?"

"Breaking ice for the livestock," I say. "Stay here."

Quickly, I go to the mudroom, grab my .38 from the top shelf of the cabinet, and walk back to the living room. I check the cylinder, shove the weapon into my waistband at the small of my back, and go to the front window. Surprise ripples through me at the sight of the two Amish women. They're bundled in winter capes and black winter bonnets, standing on the porch, their backs turned to the blowing snow. Both are holding casserole dishes that are covered with tinfoil.

I open the door. "*Guder mariye.*" Good morning.

The woman to my left is a tad past middle age and heavyset, with round cheeks and wire-rimmed glasses. The younger woman is about twenty-five, with big brown eyes and a flawless complexion that's blushed with cold. I've met her a couple of times over the years. Her name is Ruthie Fisher and she works at The Carriage Stop in Painters Mill, which is one of several shops that cater to tourists visiting Amish Country.

The women look flummoxed by my presence, so I open the door wider and make an effort to appear welcoming. "*Kumma inseid.*" Come inside. I look past them to see a sleigh, the horse tethered to a hitching post, a heavy winter coat draped over its back and buckled at its chest to cut the wind and keep it dry.

The women enter. Both are cognizant of tracking snow and take a moment to wipe their shoes and shake snow from their coats.

I introduce myself and look at the younger woman. "You're Ruthie Fisher?"

"*Ja,*" she says. "Chief Burkholder?"

"We met at the shop last fall." Nodding, I smile. "You have the best caramel popcorn in town."

The compliment earns me a reciprocal smile. "We've got jalapeño now, too."

"Next time." I turn my attention to the older woman. I've met her at some point, too; Painters Mill is a small town, after all, and I interact with many citizens regularly. But I don't recall where and I don't remember her name.

"I'm Martha Stoltzfus." She looks past me, toward the kitchen. "We brought food for Adam and the children. With all the snow, I thought he'd appreciate some grub."

"*Hinkelbottboi,*" the young woman tells me, using the *Deitsch* word for chicken potpie.

"*Shtengel,* too," Martha adds. Rhubarb.

"Adam's in the pasture, breaking ice," I tell them. "Would you like me to get him for you?"

Both sets of eyes move past me. Surprise and bewilderment overtake their expressions. I turn to see Gina and Lizzie standing at the kitchen doorway, and something sinks in my chest.

Familiar with the women and delighted by their presence, Lizzie approaches, smiling. "Mrs. Stoltzfus." She goes to the woman, hugs her, and does the same with the younger woman. "Hi, Ruthie."

"I thought you'd be outside making a snowman." The older woman says the words with a brightness that doesn't quite mask her thinly veiled disapproval at finding not only me but an *Englisch* woman in Adam Lengacher's home.

"We might get to go to the creek later to skate if Datt needs to cut wood," the girl says.

"Well, I hope so!" Ruthie puts in.

Annie runs to the women and hugs are exchanged. "Do you want to come with us, Ruthie?" she asks. "You can wear Mamm's skates."

"Not today." Ruthie passes the casserole to the girl, runs her hand over the girl's *kapp,* but her attention is honed on the mysterious English woman who has yet to speak.

Gina stands in the kitchen doorway looking a little too comfortable in snug blue jeans, a turtleneck, a flannel shirt, and a homemade sling. Her dark hair is mussed, giving her a slightly disheveled countenance. The stocking feet speak of a woman who's made herself at home. She stares back at the two Amish women as if they've entered without an invitation. Etiquette dictates I introduce them. Of course, I can't. The fewer people who know Gina's here, the better.

With my eyes I urge Gina back to the kitchen. Amusement drifts across her features as she slinks away, out of sight. Turning, I take a breath and address the women. "Adam is going to want to thank you personally for the lovely food. If you'd like to sit down and warm up, I'll get him for you."

The two women exchange looks, and for the first time it occurs to me the delivery of food isn't the only reason for their being here. Ruthie, after all, is a pretty, single Amish woman; Adam is an eligible bachelor in need of a wife and a mother for his children. Enough time has passed since the death of his wife that it's appropriate, expected even, for him to partake in the courting process and remarry. If my assessment is correct, Martha has taken on the role of, if not matchmaker, then facilitator. Of course, they didn't expect to find me, let alone an attractive and mysterious *Englischer* woman, making ourselves at home in Adam Lengacher's kitchen.

"We didn't know Adam had company," Ruthie says.

Martha purses her lips. "I didn't catch her name."

"She's an old friend." I start toward the kitchen and back door. "I'll get Adam."

"Oh, Lord no," Ruthie says. "It's too cold out there, Chief Burkholder."

"Probably time for Sammy to come in and warm up, anyway." Martha's reply comes at precisely the same time as Ruthie's.

I notice the women eyeing the blanket I left folded on the sofa, stacked atop a single pillow. My cell phone on the coffee table. *Oh boy.*

"My police vehicle got stuck in the snow," I tell them.

"Of course it did," Martha says, but her earlier friendliness has cooled to just above freezing.

Lizzie tugs gently on the woman's sleeve. "*Witt du kaffi,* Mrs. Stoltzfus?" Do you want coffee? "Gina taught me how to make it. She likes hers strong because it puts hair on her chest."

The girl starts toward the kitchen, but Martha reaches out quickly and sets her hand on the girl's shoulder. "That's okay, Lizzie. We'll be going now." She offers the casserole to the girl. "Now all of you have a nice *hinkelbottboi* for *sobbah.*" Chicken potpie for supper.

"And *shtengel boi* for your sweet tooth!" Ruthie adds the comment with a cheerfulness that doesn't quite mask her disappointment.

Hospitality and friendliness are keystones of the Amish social order. Good manners are instilled at a young age. Though I haven't been Amish for a long time, old habits die hard. The last thing I want to do is send these women on their way after they've driven several miles in the cold and snow to deliver food. On the other hand, I know from experience that some of the Amish have a propensity for gossip. And I know that the longer they're here, the more their curiosity about the attractive, dark-haired English woman will grow.

"I'll let Adam and Sammy know you were here," I tell them. "They'll appreciate the food very much."

"You do that." Martha gives me a long, assessing look. "*Hochmut,*" she mutters.

It's the *Deitsh* term for a prideful person. I know it all too well; more than one Amish person has used it while referring to me.

Ruthie doesn't quite meet my gaze as she starts toward the door. I reach for the knob and open it for them. I want to say something that will explain my lack of manners, but there are no words that will make them understand and the opportunity is lost.

"Thank you for coming," I say as they pass through the door.

The two women step onto the porch and cross to the steps without speaking.

I'm standing at the front door, watching them pull off the horse's blanket and then climb into the sleigh, when Gina comes up behind me. We stand at the door and watch them pull away. "If I didn't know better, I'd say they don't like you much," she murmurs beneath her breath.

"That's not it," I tell her. "I was . . . rude."

She shrugs, her expression puzzled. "You were nice to them."

I slant her a look. "Even Amish life gets complicated sometimes, Gina."

"Complicated with electricity, I can handle. Complicated in the damn dark? No thanks."

CHAPTER 18

Ken Mercer was not in a good mood. Holmes County was normally a little over an hour's drive from Columbus. Because of the hazardous road conditions and a slew of accidents they encountered along the way, the trip had taken nearly three hours, despite the deep-snow prowess of Bertrand's Subaru Outback. The plows had deposited ten feet of snow on both sides of the highway, which had been narrowed to a single lane in places. With the wind cranking to thirty knots, snow continued to drift across the tops of the peaks, giving the road a bizarre, tunnel-like countenance. Weather aside, he was ready to put this unpleasant task behind him as quickly and discreetly as possible.

They arrived in Painters Mill proper with a band of snow that lent the town a quaint, storybook ambience. Most of the businesses along Main Street had opened despite the inclement weather. A bakery. A couple of tourist shops. Nice little coffeehouse. An old man wearing insulated coveralls operated a snowblower outside an old-fashioned barbershop.

"Fucking Mayberry," Mercer said beneath his breath as they crept down the street.

"Yep." Bertrand stared out the window, sour faced and sullen. "They took care of Tyson last night. Clean hit. Ambush."

Mercer nodded, felt his mood darkening even more. "Hated to do that. He was young."

"Couldn't be helped. He was tight with Colorosa." Bertrand growled. "Should've chosen his company a little more carefully."

Mercer was relieved he hadn't been involved. Two thugs had owed Bertrand a favor. He'd called in the marker, and they'd gotten it done without either of them having to get their hands bloody. It disgusted Mercer that a man's life—*a cop's life*—could be bought and sold so cheaply.

"Did you check with tow companies to see if any of them towed the truck Colorosa was driving?" Bertrand asked.

"There are two, and neither has towed a tan Ford F-150. No one remembers seeing a woman matching her description. As far as we know it's stuck in a snowdrift somewhere."

"She's being careful." Bertrand looked out the window, made a halfhearted effort not to snarl. "What else we got?"

"There's one motel in town. Half a dozen B and Bs. We'll check them all while we're here."

"What about Burkholder?" Bertrand said.

What about her indeed? Mercer had spent most of last night thinking about her. Remembering things he was probably better off not recalling. Ten years ago, Kate Burkholder had been an idealistic young cop with a reputation for doing things by the book. She was pretty in a girl-next-door kind of way, religious and trying not to show it, and ready to dive into a world she wasn't quite ready for.

In some ways, Kate had been more of a challenge than Colorosa. Not because she was a player, but because she was young and inexperienced. The first time he'd taken her to bed, he'd half expected her to be a virgin. To his surprise, she wasn't. He'd slept with half a dozen women since, but he'd never forgotten Kate.

Realizing Bertrand was still waiting for an answer, he shook off the memory and set his mind on the business at hand. "She lives on a farm up in Wooster. Became chief here in Painters Mill shortly after leaving Columbus. Three full-time officers. Two part-timers. No marks against her." He shrugged. "That's about it."

"I can't see a chief of police taking in a fugitive," Bertrand muttered. "Not without notifying someone."

Mercer shrugged. "They were tight back in the day."

"Or maybe Colorosa is talking and Burkholder is listening."

"Maybe."

"You call the hospital in Millersburg?"

"Clinics, too. No sign of her. No gunshot wounds treated recently."

Bertrand nodded. "We need to pull out all the stops on Colorosa."

"Everything's in the works." Mercer turned down the heat, knowing that the sweat he'd broken beneath his coat had nothing to do with the temperature.

"Let's check the motel first."

CHAPTER 19

We're on our third game of checkers when I hear the mudroom door slam. The scuffle of boots sounds on the floor as Adam and Sammy come in from outside. As usual, the boy is talking excitedly, unfazed by the cold or that they spent the last hour using a heavy pickax to pound through several inches of pond ice so the cattle in the pasture can drink.

The boy rushes into the kitchen. His cheeks glow red. Black felt hat cocked back. Blond hair stuck to a sweaty forehead. Knitted scarf wrapped crookedly around his neck. "Katie, we have to get wood now. Datt says we're going to take a load over to Amos Yoder. He said we can go ice skating after we get the wood chopped!"

Lizzie and Annie exchange looks and get to their feet, telling me the announcement is being taken very seriously. "Can we come, too, Datt?" asks Lizzie.

Adam steps through the doorway and takes in the scene. Beneath the stoic expression, I see his eyes soften at the sight of Gina and me sitting with the girls.

He addresses his daughter. "Do you think those skinny little arms of yours can swing the ax?" he asks.

Lizzie squeals. "Mine can!"

Annie breaks into laughter. "My muscles are big, too, Datt."

"In that case, let's go chop some wood," he tells them. "I think Mr. Yoder is going to appreciate it."

"I'll get the snow shovel!" Sammy exclaims.

"Samuel, I think you should put a couple pieces of wood in the stove and get yourself warmed up first."

Looking deflated because he's been relegated to warming up, Sammy lowers his head and trudges toward the mudroom.

Annie goes to him, sets her hand on his arm. "Don't worry, Sammy, I'll get the wood chip and your skates."

Gina gives them a puzzled look. "Wood chip?"

"The hockey puck," I clarify.

"I thought the Amish were nonviolent," Gina says.

The children toss her puzzled looks.

"Last time I went to a hockey game, there was more punching than playing," she explains.

Sammy looks at his father. "They fight?"

Adam ruffles the boy's hair. "Just for show," he tells his son.

I look at Gina. "You'd better bring some extra padding just in case."

Half an hour later, the five of us are bundled up and walking a narrow trail through the woods east of the house, boots crunching through deep snow. The greenbelt runs parallel with Painters Creek. In summer, the area is lush with old-growth trees and thick with brush, blackberry and raspberry. Today, it's a monochrome world of gray-black trunks and tangled skeletal brush, all of it laden with snow.

The girls walk slightly ahead. They're clad in black capes, knitted scarves and mittens, and winter bonnets. Their plain white leather skates are tied together and hanging at their sides. Sammy wears a black winter coat, a scarf, and a ski cap to keep his ears warm. He's forged ahead, his skates draped over his shoulder. He's dragging an old-fashioned sled behind him. A bundle of kindling and split logs rides the sleigh, telling me Adam's planning to build a fire so the children—and the rest of us—can warm our hands and feet.

At the rear, Gina, Adam, and I tromp through knee-deep snow. It's bitterly cold, the wind bearing a bite that nips at the bare skin of our faces. Adam carries a snow shovel for clearing the ice and a large ax for cutting wood. I lug the pickax he'll use to test the thickness of the ice.

Around us, the woods are stunningly beautiful and hushed, as if the world we've entered is holding its breath in anticipation of our arrival. Several inches of snow have collected on the tree branches, weighing down the boughs of the firs. With every gust of wind, flurries shower down. In the distance, the woeful call of a bald eagle adds another layer of enchantment to an already magical moment.

The girls stop and look up, listening. Sammy slows, raising his eyes to the treetops. The eagle calls out again, a long, shrill call that's part mournful, part alarm.

"You hear that?" Adam says quietly.

"*Awdlah,*" Sammy whispers. Eagle.

"Looking for a mouse," Lizzie whispers.

We start walking again, cognizant of our surroundings. "Weatherman is calling for more snow tonight," I say to no one in particular. "A couple of inches."

"Just what we need." Adam slants a look toward Gina. "You're getting your problems worked out?"

"We're getting to the bottom of it," she says.

The two of them hold gazes for a beat too long. Interest flashes in Adam's eyes, its intensity matching the I-dare-you glint in Gina's. Annoyed, I shake my head. "Another day or two and we'll be out of your hair," I tell him.

Neither of them has anything to say about that.

I spoke with Tomasetti earlier. He left before dawn to make his meeting with Denny McNinch in Columbus. He encountered some problems on the rural roads, but once he reached the interstate, it was clear sailing, though only one lane was open. If the lull in the weather holds, I suspect by tomorrow Gina and I will be driving to Columbus, where she'll be interviewed by detectives with the Franklin County Sheriff's Department, someone from the district attorney's office, and, likely, BCI. At some point, she'll be arrested and booked into the county jail. Tomasetti and I will have some explaining to do. It's not going to be pleasant for any of us.

The creek is a wide body of water, about forty feet across here in the lowest part of the floodplain. The surface is frozen solid, covered with snow, and scoured by the wind in places. To my left, where the creek narrows, I hear the rush of water beneath the ice as it runs fast over rock. On the opposite side of the creek, the trunk of a long-dead tree juts from the bank, reaching several feet into the air. In the summertime, it's likely the perfect place for somersaults and diving. A fifty-gallon drum that's been cut in half lies on its side several feet from the bank. Someone has shot holes in the base, and the rim is covered with soot, telling me it's been used to burn kindling and wood for warming cold hands and feet.

"There's too much snow on the ice for good skating." Adam steps onto the surface of the creek, assessing the strength of the ice. He hands the snow shovel to his son. "Clear an area there in the middle so I can test it," he says. "It's been plenty cold, but always good to check."

Gina and I stand on the bank and watch as he and Sammy walk carefully to the center of the ice. The snow gives them enough traction that they can walk without slipping. Putting his weight into the effort—all seventy pounds of him—Sammy clears an area with the shovel.

"It's kind of bumpy," the boy says, "but we can still skate, I think."

Using the shovel, he uncovers a small area, exposing the surface. Adam kneels and begins to pound through the ice with the pickax. The sounds of the shovel and chopping echo off the treetops, sending a flock of crows flying. The girls have brushed snow from a log on the bank and remove their shoes, slip their feet into their skates, and begin to lace up.

The sight of the creek, the anticipation of the skate—or an impromptu hockey game—is a scene from my own childhood. We had a pond on our farm and I grew up skating in winter. Instead of a fifty-gallon drum, we usually built a fire on the bank. I vividly recall rushing through chores so my siblings, Jacob and Sarah, and I could steal away for a couple of hours of skating. Usually, it was just us; Mamm and Datt rarely accompanied us or watched us play. Jacob, who was the oldest and most responsible, always checked the thickness of the ice before any of us were allowed to skate. The one time Datt went with us, I got into trouble for playing too aggressively. I suspect he knew his daughter was competitive. He didn't understand my drive to be the fastest or to win the game, sometimes at the expense of the other kids. Looking back, I wonder if he knew my competitive streak would cause problems later.

"I think it's thick enough," Adam proclaims.

From their place on the log, Lizzie and Annie bring their hands together. "Hurry up and clear the ice, Sammy!" Lizzie says.

The boy pushes the shovel through the snow, huffing and puffing against the weight of it, his face red from the cold and the strain of his chore. He works in a straight line, piling the snow on the bank. Within minutes, he's cleared a three-foot-wide swath that's about twenty feet long. It's not exactly a skating rink, but large enough that the kids will have fun.

Adam dumps the kindling from the sled next to the fire drum, and pulls the sled to a good-size fallen tree a dozen or so yards into the forest. He begins to chop branches from the trunk, the sound of the ax echoing off the treetops.

I look at Gina. "Want to help me build a fire?"

She slants me a look. "You know how to do that?"

I roll my eyes. "Stand back and learn, city slicker."

With her arm in the sling, she's unable to offer much in the way of help, but she manages to toss some kindling into a pile next to the drum. Since she won't be moving around much, she'll likely be the first to get cold. I empty snow from the drum, drag it closer to the lacing log, and set to work building a fire. The kindling and logs are nice and dry. Adam remembered to bring a section of *The Budget* newspaper and a pad of matches. Within minutes, the fire is hissing and popping, the pungent tang of smoke filling the air.

Despite the wind and cold, it's a pleasant scene. While the children skate and Adam chops wood, Gina brushes snow from the lacing log and sits, her legs propped out in front of her.

"I used to think the Amish were backward," she says. "Religious fanatics." She shrugs. "They're not. They just . . ."

"Live at a different pace." I sit down next to her.

She nods, thoughtful. "Looking at the mess I've made of my life, it doesn't seem so bad. You know, simple living. Having a family."

I toss another log into the drum. "It's a tough life sometimes," I say. "A lot of work. A lot of rules. But it's a good life, too."

She leans forward, puts the elbow of her uninjured arm on her knee. "Maybe they're the ones who got it right, and the rest of us are . . . fucked up."

"Even Amish life can get complicated," I tell her.

"I never understood or appreciated what you left behind. How different your life had been before you came to Columbus." She laughs.

"I was on a mission to rescue you from some weird religious cult. I get it now."

I look at her, surprised by her pensiveness, and pleased that she's able to appreciate the Amish lifestyle, because I know there are many people who don't.

"For an Amish girl, I was pretty good at guzzling Jack Daniel's," I tell her.

She tosses her head back and laughs. "That *did* throw me off."

She's watching the children, her mind working. Snow has begun to fall. Lush, wet flakes floating down from a sky the color of ash. Aside from the sound of the ax and the chatter of the children, the forest is tranquil.

"We did all right," I say after a moment.

"You did," she whispers. "Me?" She shrugs. "Maybe I never was that idealistic young cop I always fancied myself."

"It's not too late to turn things around."

"It feels like it's too late."

"We do the best we can, Gina. That's all we can do. That's all anyone can do."

"That's the thing, Kate. I haven't done my best for a long time. I lost my way. I lost . . . myself. Participated in something I detest. Became part of a problem I swore I'd fix. I didn't care about right or wrong, and now I've screwed up my life."

"This is your chance to make it right," I tell her. "Undo some of the things you did. The things you let happen. Start over."

"My career is done. I'll never work in law enforcement again. For God's sake, I'll be lucky not to end up in prison."

I sidestep the "end up in prison" comment, and focus on the future. "With your experience, there are other things you can do. Corporate security. Private detective. Lecturing."

"Wait tables at the local greasy spoon," she mutters. "Make license plates." After a moment, she turns her gaze on me. "Prison is a tough place for a cop. I'm scared."

The urge to bolster her is powerful. But this isn't the time for false reassurances. I know her too well to say something we both would know isn't true.

When I say nothing, the brash façade ever present on her face flickers, and I catch a glimpse of the tangle of emotions beneath the surface: regret, the fear of the unknown, the knowledge that whatever fate doles out in the coming days and weeks won't be easy and she will likely deserve it.

Gina Colorosa is not a reflective person. She's always lived her life by the seat of her pants, never anticipating consequences, the past—and the future—be damned. Now, it seems that that not-a-care-in-the-world attitude has finally caught up with her.

After a moment, she smiles. "So are you going to marry that nice-looking BCI guy?"

I think about it a moment. "Probably."

"Sweating him a little?"

"Sweating myself a little."

She arches a brow. "You've always been skittish when it comes to men."

"Taking my time is all. It's a big step."

"So says a woman who left her entire life behind at the age of eighteen and hooked up with me." Contemplative, she shakes her head. "I hate to state the obvious, but what you've got . . . it seems like a good thing."

"It is."

"You're not getting any younger."

"Thank you for pointing that out."

"Maybe you ought to stop overthinking it and just do what makes you happy."

I'm mulling the advice when the tempo of the children's voices changes. A yelp draws my attention. I see Lizzie and Annie holding hands, facing each other, skating in a circle. Then I spot Sammy. Head and shoulders sticking out of the ice next to the tree trunk. At first, I think he's down on his knees, playing. Then I notice his arms outstretched, the distress on his face, hands clawing at the ice.

"Sammy!" I jump to my feet. "*Adam!*"

Next to me, Gina stands. "Girls, get off the ice! Come here!"

A dozen things register at once. The girls standing too close to their fallen brother. A shout from Adam. Heavy footfalls from the direction of where he was chopping wood. Then I'm on my feet, running to the creek, skidding down the bank, sliding on trampled snow.

"Get a branch!" I hit the ice, slide, nearly go down, but my foot lands on snow, grips, and I manage to stay on my feet.

I reach the girls, grab their arms, pull them back. "Go to the lacing log! I'll get him."

I hear Gina behind me. "I got them."

To my left, I hear Adam say something. I glance that way, see him step onto the ice, start across it, eyes fastened to his son. "Grab the edge of the ice!" he shouts to his son. "Hold on!"

I don't know how deep the water is. I can tell Sammy isn't standing. His head is bobbing, his arms are splashing; there's shock and panic on his face. This is likely a deep hole, over his head. If there's a current, he could be sucked beneath the ice and the situation will become deadly serious.

"Datt!" the boy shouts.

I stop four feet away from him. The ice is gray where water has washed over the surface. "Stay calm," I tell him. "Grab the edge of the ice like your *datt* said. We'll get you."

His face is anything but calm. His mouth trembles. Water on his face. Skin pale and blue, cheeks blushed red.

I hear movement behind me, see Gina running across the ice, a big branch in her hand. "Take it!" She tosses the branch to me.

I catch it, drop to my belly, spread my legs. The branch is too small. Not substantial enough to pull seventy pounds of panicked boy from the water. But it's all I've got, so I shove the branch at him. "Grab the stick," I say. "I'll pull you out."

The boy looks at me. Panic in his eyes. Teeth chattering. Face wet, water dripping over cheeks that have lost their color.

I hear movement next to me, glance over to see Adam slide to his belly, wriggle next to me. "Grab the branch." His voice is calm, laser focus in his eyes. "Grab on, son. I'll pull you out."

"It's . . . c-cold," the boy says, teeth chattering.

Adam inches closer. "Both hands now. Grab it. Quickly, son."

The boy raises his arm, but it's shaking violently. He reaches for the branch, but his sleeve is soaked and heavy and he misses. His gloves are wet, hindering him, and his coat is waterlogged.

"Datt," he squeaks.

"Grab it." Adam says the words equably, but I see strain and alarm on his face. "God is with you. Stay calm."

Bracing one arm on the ice to keep himself from being pulled down by the weight of his coat and skates, the boy tries again. His hand breaks through some of the small branches, fingers clutching and ineffectual.

"Both hands," I tell him.

Sammy lets go of the ice and lunges, tries to grab the branch with both hands. But the branch crumples, his glove catching and sliding off. His hand smacks the water. His shoulders sink. Water washes over his face. His head goes under.

"*Mein Gott.*" Adam slithers closer. Too close. The ice gives beneath his elbows. Water rushes over the surface, soaking his coat. He doesn't seem to notice the shock of cold or the danger of his position.

"Here!"

Gina's voice. Behind me. I look over my shoulder, see the sturdy branch in her hand. Quickly, she drops to her knees, then dives onto her belly and slides toward the boy. She's closer to him than Adam or I, coming at him from the opposite side. Gray water washes into her coat, but she pays it no heed. Clenching her teeth, she sweeps the branch across the ice with such force that it nearly strikes the boy, but she stops it just in time.

"Grab it!" she shouts. "I got you! Grab on."

The boy's head breaks the surface. He's sputtering and choking, beginning to cry. He lifts his hand to grab it, but the waterlogged glove weighs down his arm.

"Shake off your glove!" I shout. "Grab the stick!"

The boy slings off the remaining glove, makes a wild grab for the length of wood, gets it on the second try. Small blue fingers cling to the branch. Adam scrambles closer to Gina. The ice groans beneath their weight. He's shoulder-to-shoulder with her and takes the stick from her.

"Hold on tight!" Adam gets to his knees, wriggles backward, pulling. "I've got you, son. Hold on. Don't let go."

At first the ice crumbles beneath the boy's weight, his body acting as an icebreaker. Adam continues to pull and finally the ice holds. The boy's shoulders, hips, and finally his legs emerge until he's face-down on the ice.

Adam scrambles to his feet, bends, and scoops up his son, wraps his arms around the boy. "I've got you," he says. "I've got you."

I sidle away from the hole on my hands and knees. Still on her belly, soaking wet, Gina scoots away from the hole in the ice, using only one elbow due to her injury. When I'm a safe distance away, I get to my feet. Watching her, realizing she risked going through the ice herself to save a little boy she barely knows, I'm moved. The punch of emotion that follows surprises me. That's the thing about Gina. She's loyal to a fault and sometimes it's all or nothing. It's one of the reasons I loved her.

Bending, I offer my hand to her. She takes it, her glove dripping. She winces as I pull her to her feet. For the span of several heartbeats, we stare at each other, breathing hard. When her face lights up with a grin I can't help but return it.

"Don't get cocky," I tell her.

"Wouldn't dream of it."

Turning away from her, I work off my coat and follow Adam. The Amish man carries his son to the bank, water dripping, the droplets turning the snow gray. Gina walks beside Adam, her hand on the boy's forehead, making eye contact with him, talking softly.

Annie and Lizzie huddle next to the lacing stump, watching. Annie has begun to cry. Lizzie looks on, frightened.

The three of us reach the bank at about the same time.

"Get that wet coat off him," Gina tells Adam.

Next to the fire, Adam drops to his knees, lays the boy on the ground. With shaking hands, he struggles to remove his son's sopping coat. All the while murmuring gentle words in *Deitsch,* letting Sammy know he's going to be all right.

The sound of Sammy's cries shakes me. Sweet Sammy, whose voice never ceases to fill the empty spaces around us. His body shakes violently. His legs and arms vibrate against the ground as if gripped by a palsy.

"It . . . b-burns, Datt," he says.

Gina goes to her knees beside them, her coat already off. Once the boy is free of his coat, she thrusts hers at Adam. "Put it on him."

Adam drapes her coat over the boy's wet shirt and suspenders. "You're going to be all right," he says tightly.

"We need to get him to the house," I tell Adam. "Get him dry."

"*Ja*." Nodding, the Amish man scoops the boy into his arms and breaks into a lumbering run toward the house.

Both girls have begun to cry, so I go to them, put my hand on Annie's shoulder and give it a squeeze. "He's going to be okay," I tell them. "He's just cold. Come on. We're going to need to get inside, too, so we can put some more wood in the stove."

CHAPTER 20

Damon Bertrand detested wholesome little towns with their steepled churches and bow-tie merchants. He'd grown up in a town just like it—less the Amish and tourists—where farming was the mainstay, the cows outnumbered the people, and the best job a man could hope for—if he wasn't a farmer, anyway—was shift work down at the auto-parts factory in the next town. The day he left for college he swore he'd never go back.

There was one motel in Painters Mill and it was a dump replete with 1980s décor, a breakfast buffet with a commercial-size waffle iron that was invariably surrounded by kids, and carpeting that smelled of sweaty feet and dog piss. He and Mercer had checked in upon their arrival and then headed to town.

Not for the first time since they had embarked on this most unpleasant of tasks, he found himself thinking about retirement. Florida was looking better by the minute. With or without his wife. His kids were practically grown and had become strangers to him in the last few years. He doubted they'd miss him. Who was he kidding? They probably wouldn't even realize he was gone. No, he thought darkly, as they idled down Main Street, there wasn't a single person, place, or thing he'd miss about Ohio.

Bertrand fingered the steering wheel and looked out at the bleak winter landscape. The one good thing about a small town was that it would be easier to find someone. Folks were friendly, helpful, and unsuspecting. And Colorosa was the kind of woman people remembered. Not because she was beautiful or flashy or some nonsense like that. No, Gina Colorosa was memorable because she possessed a larger-than-life personality, a big laugh, and she never shied away from the limelight. Women generally hated her. Men loved her, maybe a little too much. Gina just loved Gina; she looked out for number one—and fuck the lot of them.

The sun had made a short-lived appearance earlier, but a bank of clouds roiled on the northern horizon. According to the weather service, the area was in for another round of snow this afternoon. Hopefully, he and Mercer would get a line on Colorosa quickly. If she'd stopped for gas or gone into a pharmacy for first-aid supplies, or stopped for food—surely someone would remember.

As challenging as finding her might prove to be, it wasn't the most difficult task they faced. Making contact with her in just the right way was going to require finesse. She wasn't some dumb criminal or rookie cop. Not by a long shot. Gina Colorosa was wise to the ways of the world, as street savvy as any hustler, and a survivor—with nine lives to boot. She was unpredictable. When the time came, she wouldn't go down easy.

During the long hours on the road, Bertrand had considered several approaches. Initially, he figured once he and Mercer made contact, they'd convince her that they had covered her misdeeds, assure her they'd taken care of her problems back in Columbus. In fact, they'd arrested some schmuck for the crime of which she'd been accused. All she had to do was return with them so they could divvy up the eighty thousand she'd stolen from them, and she could resume her life just like before. It would likely be a hard sell. But sometimes people heard what they wanted to hear, especially when they were desperate. Even smart people. If Colorosa saw an easy out, she might jump at it.

The biggest problem they faced was that she'd met up with Burkholder, spilled her guts—and Burkholder believed enough to look into it, or pass the information along to some other agency, like BCI or FBI. If that was the case, he and Mercer could still go the official route: drop in on Burkholder, present the warrant, and demand custody. He might have to touch base with the Holmes County Sheriff's Department beforehand and ask for "assistance," since he and Mercer were out of their jurisdiction. Still, it could be done—and it could still work.

One question continued to nag. If Colorosa was with Burkholder, why hadn't the chief been in contact with the Columbus Division of Police? Even if Colorosa had convinced her old friend that she'd been framed and corruption ran amok inside the department, Burkholder should have acted in some official capacity. If she had, he would've heard. Was it possible Burkholder wasn't as squeaky clean as everyone thought and was aiding and abetting a fugitive? Or had she been in contact with another agency, and he and Mercer simply hadn't heard? Bertrand didn't see how the latter was possible with the number of serious crimes they'd piled on Colorosa. Still, the thought put a steel rod of fear right through the marrow of his spine. If Burkholder had sparked an investigation and involved another law enforcement agency, the situation would go from bad to a clusterfuck.

The more Bertrand thought about making the arrest and hauling Colorosa back to Columbus to face charges, the more the endeavor seemed like a bad idea. There were other options that didn't include the possibility of Colorosa running her mouth to anyone who might listen. The problem was, he didn't know if Mercer was ready to take this operation to the next level. Did he have the balls to do what needed to be done? Could he trust him if the shit hit the fan?

By one P.M., Bertrand and Mercer had stopped at over a dozen places, including all six B and Bs, the local greasy spoon, the pharmacy, four service stations, and the fast-food joint on the edge of town. Each time, Bertrand had produced the photo of his "sweet but troubled niece," who was "confused and self-destructive" and missing. He'd promised his sister he'd find her and bring her home. Predictably, the story garnered sympathy and cooperation. Midwesterners were a decent and gullible bunch. Everyone he'd spoken with had been virtuously concerned; they'd looked long and hard at the photo, wringing their hands because they knew what it was like to have "family problems." Most didn't ask too many questions; Midwesterners weren't nosy, and most were polite to a fault.

The problem was no one had seen her.

"We're wasting our time," Bertrand said as they drove through the parking lot of the farm store on the edge of town, looking for the tan F-150. "We're not going to find her like this."

Mercer scanned the snow-covered street as they exited and headed back toward town. "She had to have stopped for gas. There's another service station to the south, a few miles out of town. Let's try it."

"She's with Burkholder," Bertrand growled.

"We've passed the police department twice now. You volunteering to go in and ask her?"

"I'm telling you what I think."

The two men rode in silence a moment, watching a trio of women clad in down coats, knit hats, and UGG boots leave the coffee shop, yakking, to-go cups in hand.

Bertrand looked out the window, cursed beneath his breath. "This just keeps getting worse and worse."

"Look," Mercer began, "even if you're right and she's with Burkholder, Colorosa doesn't have much credibility. We've got too much dirt on her. She's going down. Why don't we just let this play out? Let her make all the wild accusations she wants."

"Eighty thousand will buy a dream team of lawyers," Bertrand grumbled. "And Colorosa can be pretty convincing. She's smart with a big mouth and balls the size of the fucking Great Lakes. If she convinces someone to look in the wrong place, things are going to get dicey for us."

Mercer shrugged. "We deny all of it. Cover our asses. We might get looked at, but the evidence we've got against her is ironclad. No one in their right mind is going to believe a word she says."

"She knows too much," Bertrand snapped. "She's got names, dates, amounts; as far as we know she's got more than that."

Mercer jerked his gaze to Bertrand's. "Like what exactly?"

"Who knows? How long has she been planning to fuck us over? She could have recorded conversations. She could have taken photos or videos."

Looking anxious now, Mercer raked his hand through his hair. "Jesus Christ."

Bertrand continued. "All I'm saying is that if some clown from BCI or a prosecutor looking to make a name for himself starts poking around, they could uncover something we didn't anticipate." He shook his head. "That bitch might go down, but we'll go with her. All the way to the bottom."

Mercer fell silent, looking worried. "Let's keep at it. Stay one more night. See what happens tomorrow."

Bertrand nodded his assent. But as far as he was concerned their mission had changed. This was no longer about simply finding Colorosa and taking her back. The question foremost in his mind was whether Mercer could be persuaded to partake in something more permanent.

His counterpart pointed to an Amish-themed shop. A sign on the window told them all Christmas decorations were seventy-five percent off. "Let's try that place."

Grumbling because he was sick of wasting his time, Bertrand pulled into the parking slot in front of the shop. It was a typical Amish Country tourist trap, with a rustic wood façade, a window display of a cozy-looking Amish home replete with handcrafted furniture, locally made stoneware, and kitchen towels that were twenty percent off and probably made in China. A handwritten sign advertised INDIAN POPCORN.

He killed the engine, and both men left the vehicle. Their shoes crunched over frozen slush and salt as they crossed the sidewalk to the front door. The bell jingled as they pushed through and went inside.

The Carriage Stop was a virtual playground of imported crap touted as "handcrafted" or "Amish made," the prices jacked up enough to cause a stroke, and out-of-towners gobbling it up like Christmas ham. The aromas of popcorn and cinnamon laced the overheated air. Their shoes thudded dully against the distressed wood floor as they made their way to the counter where a pretty young Amish woman in a drab blue dress and cardigan sweater busied herself stuffing Rockwellesque greeting cards into a display case.

Bertrand had worn his weekend parka, a John Deere cap, and khaki pants that were half a size too big. It was the kind of getup that blended in here. The kind that shouted "hapless but kindly uncle" and transformed him into the sort of man people would feel compelled to help, but wouldn't remember, even if they were asked about it later.

"Excuse me?" he said.

The woman stocking the cards turned, her brows raised, and a smile overtook her face. "Can I help you?"

She was pretty for an Amish woman, with a peaches-and-cream complexion. No makeup. No jewelry. Even though he was standing on the other side of the counter, he could smell the aroma of popcorn coming off her.

"Uh, well, I hope so." Slipping into his feckless, worried-uncle look, he fumbled with his wallet and withdrew the photo of Colorosa. "I'm looking for my niece," he said. "We're . . . uh . . . worried about her. You know, with all the bad weather." He wrung his hands. "Um . . . she's kind of . . . upset. I promised my sister I'd find her and ask her to come home." He looked around, nodding approvingly at the store. "She likes to shop, so I thought she might've stopped in. Have you seen her around?"

The woman's expression softened. She craned her neck, her eyes moving to the photo.

Hope surged in his chest when recognition flickered on her face. Her brows shot up. She beamed at him, pleased. "I saw your niece yesterday! She was at Adam Lengacher's place when we took food out there. You know, for the children."

"Adam Lengacher?" he said, putting the name to memory.

"He's a farmer. Amish, you know. Lives a few miles out of town." She cocked her head. "Is your niece from around here?"

"Naw." He tried a sheepish smile. "Do you happen to have an address for Mr. Lengacher?"

"Don't need it," she assured him. "He lives off of Township Road 36. Just take the highway past the Painters Creek Bridge. Make a left." Her brows knit. "I don't know how that road is out there with all the snow. The house is set back a ways. Big white farmhouse. Lots of pine trees. You can't miss it."

"Oh boy. My little sister is going to be so relieved. Thank you." He gives an aw-shucks shrug. "Look, this whole thing . . . it's kind of a family matter. Private, I guess. I don't want to embarrass my niece, if you know what I mean."

"I understand." She nods, sympathetic. "Sometimes these things happen."

A few minutes later they were back in the Subaru. Bertrand sat in the driver's seat, and started the engine. "She's with some Amish dude."

Mercer laughed. "You're shitting me. Who?"

Bertrand told him. "Some farmer. He's got kids."

Mercer pulled out his cell. "You want me to run his name?"

Bertrand nodded. "The more we know about him, the better."

Mercer tapped the screen. "What about Burkholder? She involved?"

"I don't know."

"So how we going to play this?"

Bertrand hesitated, wondering once again how receptive Mercer would be to scrapping their original plan, ramping it up into something a lot more effective. "The situation is fluid. Let's take a look at all the dynamics at play. Make sure we got it right. Keep our options open for the time being."

The two men exchanged looks. Ignoring the questions in the other man's eyes, Bertrand put the SUV in reverse and backed onto the street.

CHAPTER 21

I find Adam standing at the kitchen sink, a mixing bowl and an array of various bottles and containers on the counter next to him.

"How's our patient?" I ask.

He looks at me over his shoulder and grins. "Hot-water bottle helped. I think he's enjoying the attention."

"Can't blame him for that." I move to the counter and stand beside him. A ripple of concern goes through me when I recognize the items he's arranged on the counter. "Frostbite?"

"His heels look a little white." The Amish man gives me a half smile. "Frostnip more than likely."

"If I can get the Explorer out of the lane, I might be able to get him to the hospital," I say. "Say the word if you want to try."

"He's going to be fine, Katie."

I watch as he pours cooking oil into a medium-size bowl. Next comes the oil of turpentine and, lastly, a dash of ammonia. He stirs everything together with a soup spoon. "Smells familiar," I say, remembering.

I was twelve years old when my brother, Jacob, fell victim to frostbite while ice fishing at a neighbor's pond. Upon his arrival home, my *mamm* cooked up a mixture using the same ingredients and applied it to his frostbitten toes.

"It's a rite of passage for a lot of Amish boys," he says. "For Sammy, more than once."

"My *mamm* used the same remedy," I tell him.

Adam stirs the mixture, the pungent odors of the ammonia and turpentine filling the kitchen. "It's been a while. I'm not sure if I remembered all the ingredients."

"Smells right." I can't vouch for the effectiveness of the concoction, but I had it rubbed onto my fingers and toes a couple of times growing up, and I didn't suffer any ill effects.

"He's sleeping?" I ask.

"Talking more likely." He slants me an amused look. "If Gina and the girls are with him, he will not be sleeping."

"You did your fair share of talking when you were his age," I say teasingly.

Smiling, he taps the spoon on the side of the bowl, then sets the spoon in the sink. "So I've heard."

"He looks like you."

"He's got his *mamm*'s heart. Her faith."

The lightness of the moment gives way to solemnity. I want to say something to bring the smile back to his face, but the words don't come and the moment is lost.

Picking up the mixing bowl, Adam carries it through the doorway to the stairs. I refill the old-fashioned water bottle, snag a towel off the counter, and follow. At the top of the stairs I hear the boy talking animatedly, and I head toward the room at the end of the hall.

"The frost bit Datt on the heel when we went deer hunting last winter." His voice floats down the hall, making me smile. "He didn't even feel it because he's so big and strong."

I enter the room to find Lizzie and Annie sitting on the side of their older brother's bed, fascinated by the tall tale they're being told.

Adam stands just inside the doorway, holding the bowl. Gina kneels next to the bed. She's holding a stuffed animal—a faceless black-and-white cow—simulating that it's walking on Sammy's tummy. The boy is enjoying the game and giggles each time the cow decides to "buck" him with its little horns.

The sight of Gina—with her wild hair, snug blue jeans, and reckless smile—on the floor next to an indisposed Amish boy is so contradictory to everything I know about her, I pause in the doorway and take in the scene. I'm aware of Adam standing in front of me. He, too, has stopped. I don't need to see his face to know his eyes are on Gina.

The boy's face lights up at the sight of his father. "My feet aren't cold anymore, Datt."

Adam moves to the small table next to the bed and sets down the bowl. "Still have to put the *greidah-ayl* on your heels," he says, using the *Deitsch* word for ointment.

Sammy eyes the bowl with suspicion, and his smile fades.

"Take off your socks and let's have a look at those toes," Adam tells him.

The boy pulls up the blankets, revealing feet covered with well-used socks.

I cross to the bed and pass the water bottle to him. "Set this against your tummy," I tell him. "It'll help warm you up."

He grins. "*Ja*."

Gina raises her hand and holds her nose. "Those are some pretty stinky toes," she tells the boy. "Are you sure you want to save them? Maybe we ought to just cut them off and feed them to the chickens."

Annie lets out a squeal that's part delight, part horror. Sammy's mouth opens an instant before he realizes she's kidding, and the three children burst out laughing.

"Mamm always said me and Datt have the stinkiest feet in the whole house," he proclaims with no small amount of pride.

"I've no doubt," I murmur, but I'm smiling.

Adam tugs the boy's socks from feet that are still red from the cold. The heels are, indeed, pale but I don't see any telltale signs of serious frostbite. He's in the process of rubbing the unguent into the toes and heels when my cell phone vibrates.

I glance down and see Tomasetti's name pop up on the display. Excusing myself, I leave the room and duck into the hall. "Did you make your meeting with Denny?" I ask.

"Yeah," he says. "We need to talk."

I know immediately from his tone that something has changed. That it's not good. "What's going on?"

"Not on the cell. I'm on my way."

I've just taken my cell out to the Explorer to charge when I hear the snowmobile zipping up the lane. I stand in the driveway and watch as Tomasetti slides to a stop next to my vehicle and pulls off his helmet.

John Tomasetti isn't much of a hugger. He's not the sentimental type. And he's pretty good at keeping his emotions under lock and key. He doesn't quite succeed as he crosses to me and leans in for a kiss.

"Farm is kind of quiet without you around," he murmurs.

"You're not insinuating I talk too much, are you?" I ask.

"Well . . ."

I ease away from him, tilt my head for a better look, see a flicker of something that gives me pause. "Okay," I say. "Lay it on me."

"There's something else going on with Colorosa."

"Not to state the obvious, but that could be the understatement of the year."

"I drove to Columbus this morning and met with Denny," he tells me, referring to Special Agent Supervisor Denny McNinch. "I told him everything. When I brought up the possibility of police corruption in Columbus, he clammed up, wouldn't talk about it. Even when I pushed, he wouldn't confirm or deny much."

"Tomasetti, what does that mean?"

He shrugs. "If I were to venture a guess, I'd say there's another agency involved, there's an ongoing investigation, it's hot and being kept under wraps."

"Which agency?"

Another shrug. "My guess would be FBI. If we're dealing with organized corruption inside a police department, even if it's contained to a unit or involves just a few individuals, that's extremely sensitive information. No one's going to discuss it, at least not while it's ongoing."

"What did he say about Gina?" I ask. "I mean, there's an active warrant for her arrest. We can't ignore that. What are we supposed to do with her?"

He grimaces. "Officially, we don't know her exact whereabouts. Unofficially—and just between us—we need to keep her here for a few more days, if Lengacher is willing." His eyes settle on mine. "Out of sight. Safe. And quiet. My understanding is that the situation in Columbus is about to come to a head."

"If she's part of the investigation, if she has information—names, places, dates, events—that will help, why not make it official and bring her in? Depose her. *Something.*"

"I got the impression Colorosa is in way over her head. I don't believe she's the focus of the investigation."

I think about that a moment, my mind poking into places I don't want it to poke. "They're looking at another individual inside the department."

"Or individuals," he says. "Someone higher up on the food chain."

A quiver of unease moves through my gut even as all the disjointed parts of the situation fall into place. "That's the first theory I've heard that actually makes sense."

"Considering the sensitive nature of this, I can't take it any further," he tells me. "Cops are under investigation. They get wind of it and all the work that's gone into it goes up in smoke. Bottom line, we need to lay low for now."

I nod, but my head is spinning. The notion of deep-rooted corruption inside a police department I spent nearly ten years of my life in puts a queasy sensation in the pit of my stomach.

"There are so many good cops inside that department," I tell him.

"I've no doubt," he says. "We're likely dealing with a few individuals inside the vice unit. Maybe a handful of guys. And someone higher up who's letting it happen and is probably benefiting from it."

"So Gina's telling the truth." Though the confirmation of corruption is devastating, that she hasn't been lying to us settles the uneasiness that's been pricking the back of my brain since she arrived.

"Evidently, someone's gone to a lot of trouble to muck up her reputation."

"They're going after her credibility," I murmur.

"That's what I'd do," he tells me. "Destroy her reputation. Stain her character. If she points a finger, no one believes a word."

My mind forges ahead to Adam and his family. "Tomasetti, we could take Gina to the farm. Or I could check her into the motel for a few days."

"I told Denny where she was and he seemed to think it was a good place. No phone. No contact with the outside world. I know it's asking a lot of this family, that it's an inconvenience, but do you think Lengacher would agree to letting her stay here for another day or two?"

"I'll pull Adam aside and talk to him." But I'm still thinking about Gina.

He notices my hesitation. "Are you uneasy with her being here?"

"More concerned about Adam and the children. I don't want them involved."

"Gina getting on with them all right?"

I sigh. "Maybe a little too well."

Tilting his head, he arches a brow. "Seriously?"

I give his shoulder a faux punch. "I don't want her to complicate things for Adam. He's a widower. If something . . . happens, he would be judged harshly." I sigh. "The problem is, I don't know how to fix it or where to put her."

He nods, turns thoughtful. "Look, if you're not comfortable with her staying here, we can find another place. Say the word and I'll get it done."

"Do you think anyone's looking for her?" I ask.

"You mean aside from every cop in the state?" He shrugs. "We can't rule that out. But she has no connection to Lengacher. The rural roads are nearly impassable. And we're only talking about another day or two. It's your call."

"All right," I say after a moment. "I'll talk to Adam."

He nods, looking closely at me, and his expression softens. "If you're an optimist, the weather and road conditions might not be such a bad thing. Keeps the bad guys at home."

I know he's right. Still, the thought of being stuck here any longer makes me sigh. "I think I'm coming down with a serious case of cabin fever."

"Just don't go all Jack Nicholson on me. Someone is probably counting on her testimony."

I laugh. "I'll wait until she completes her civic duty."

Standing on my tiptoes, I press a kiss to his mouth. "Do me a favor and keep your snowmobile handy, will you?"

"In case you need a quick escape?"

"In case I need a quick . . . something else."

He grins. "Bet on it."

The years I was a police officer with the Columbus Division of Police were some of the most personally and professionally satisfying of my life. I loved the work. I gained a lot of experience in a short period of time. With the help of some generous mentors, I learned how to be a cop—a good one. Most importantly, I'd found my calling.

I didn't hear from my Amish family often. I missed them desperately. I thought about them every day. Sometimes I even missed the lifestyle and I worried about my relationship with God. But the despair I'd experienced so acutely early on had faded to a dull ache over the years. An ache I'd grown accustomed to and rarely acknowledged.

I was living with Gina in a nicer apartment in a better neighborhood. She was still my best friend, my confidante, and my adopted sister all rolled into one. We didn't spend as much time together as we once had. We didn't gather around the coffee table for burgers or the occasional Chinese takeout and talk for hours about our day. We didn't laugh as much. We were working a lot, putting in double shifts sometimes, and there simply wasn't time.

That's what I told myself, anyway.

I'd become adept at looking away from things I didn't want to see, especially when it came to Gina. Over the last couple of years, our friendship had become topical and sometimes strained. She was keeping company with some cops I didn't care for. She'd become brash. I still loved her, but I didn't like the person who'd emerged. The truth of the matter was she'd started down a road that could only lead to no good. But of course, I'd gotten good at rationalizing those kinds of things away.

The day I received the letter from home, I'd just completed a double shift and arrived at the apartment a little after five P.M. I'd been up all night and I was dead tired. I spotted the letter on the coffee table. My heart jumped at the sight of my sister's name. The Painters Mill address. The familiar scrawl of her handwriting. The jolt of emotion was powerful. That letter told me in no uncertain terms that I still mattered. That even though I'd mucked things up with my family, they still thought of me. They cared enough to write. They still loved me.

It was the fourth letter from Sarah in as many years. The first was to let me know she married the man who'd been courting her before I left. The second was to let me know Mamm would be attending my graduation from the police academy, which had been nothing short of a miracle. The third, to inform me she'd lost the baby she'd been carrying.

I grinned like a fool as I tore open the seal. I'd been missing them, thinking about them more often than usual. I'd been yearning for Painters Mill. The farm where I grew up and spending time outdoors. I wondered if Sarah had news. If she was *ime familye weg* again—in the family way, which was the Amish term for pregnant. I wondered if my *mamm* would finally invite me home for a visit because she'd forgiven me for my transgressions.

Dear Katie,

I hope this letter finds you well. I was hoping to hear from you after my last letter. But, of course, I know you must be busy with your new life and friends and your job as a police. You must lead such an exciting life!

Sister, I wish I could tell you everything is okay here, but it's not.

It's with a heavy heart that I must tell you Datt has cancer. He's been sick. (Of course, he didn't complain or tell anyone—you know how he is!) Then he finally went to the doctor in Wooster. I prayed it could be treated, but it's too late. The cancer has spread and he's very frail. I think it may be time for you to come home to see him. I hope you find your way.

God bless you,
Sarah

I'd barely finished reading the letter—my befuddled brain trying to digest the news—when Gina charged through the door. She was excited about something. Rushed, as usual. She didn't take the time to get a read on me.

"I got new wheels," she said as she went to the fridge and pulled out a beer.

I folded the letter and slid it back into the envelope. Datt? Cancer? The man was as strong as a bull. How could that be?

"It's badass." She prattled on, not noticing that my world had just unraveled a little. "A Camry. Practically new. Just ten thousand miles."

"Where did you get it?" I asked as I tucked the letter into the breast pocket of my uniform.

"It's part of the asset forfeiture program," she told me.

"How much did it cost?"

"Didn't cost me a thing." Grinning, she lifted the bottle to her lips and drank deeply. "Think of it as a perquisite."

"How does that work exactly?" I asked. It was not an ingenuous question; this conversation was like a dozen others we'd had as of late. The kind that didn't quite add up. The kind in which you knew there was something else going on and you weren't getting the whole story.

If I were to be perfectly honest with myself, I'd admit that I didn't *want* the whole story. I'd realized some time ago that the truth would make me think less of her. And if things came to a head, I'd have to do something about it.

"Good things come to those of us who pay our dues." At the table, she paged through the day's mail. "Or maybe I just know the right people. You really need to get out more, Kate, make some connections. I can only do so much for you. You have to show a little initiative."

From my place on the sofa, I watched her stride to the living room, toss her ever-present canvas bag onto the chair, and flop onto the loveseat opposite me. The canvas bag teetered, then tipped over, and fell to the floor. A mishmash of items spilled out—a flip phone, an iPad, a zippered case. I was only giving it half of my attention until I spotted the wad of cash. I had no idea how much or even the denominations of the bills, but the stack was half an inch thick and bound with bank wrappers.

"Shit." Muttering beneath her breath, she leaned over and began tossing the items back into the bag.

"Where did you get all that cash?" I asked.

She didn't answer. Didn't hesitate. Didn't look at me. Just continued to pick up her items—an extra clip for her Sig Sauer, her duty gloves, a notebook.

"Gina, where did you get the cash?" I repeated.

Tossing the last item into the bag, she took her seat on the loveseat, and yanked the zipper closed. "I've been working a lot. Double shifts. You do that, and there are some fringe benefits."

"Fringe benefits? Are you kidding me?" I heard the words as if someone else spoke them. The doubt in my voice. The skepticism. The anger. Gina and I had had a few disagreements over the years. This was the first time I'd demanded answers.

"Like I said, Kate, I've been working a lot. I make sure I'm at the right place at the right time."

"And someone magically gives you cash money and a car? You expect me to believe that?"

Eyes on mine, she got to her feet. Hands clenched at her sides. Eyes flashing. Combat ready. "I got this money fair and square. What right do you have to question my ethics?"

"I know where it came from, Gina."

"Since when did you become such a Goody Two-Shoes, Kate?"

Reaching into the canvas bag, she yanked out the wad of cash, shook it in my face. "All right. Tell me this. Do you think some dope dealer or hooker or pimp deserves this? Someone who's never worked a day in their entire useless life? Instead of me? Instead of us?"

I stared at the cash, the way she clenched it in her fist, and my heart began to pound. "There is no 'us,'" I tell her. "Just you."

"How many nights have we gone without sleep? How many times have we risked our lives to save someone else's ass? How many times have you feared for your own safety and had to face down someone who was violent and dangerous?"

"It's part of the job!" I shouted. "If you don't like it, quit."

"Oh, I like it just fine." Snarling at me, she flung the cash back into the canvas bag and yanked the zipper closed. "I'm not the only one, Kate. There are others. Good cops. This is the way it works in the real world and if you don't believe that you are not only naive, but a fool."

"That is not the way it works," I told her, hating it that I couldn't quite catch my breath. "Nothing in this world is free and if it is, chances are there are strings attached."

She made a bitter sound that was part laugh, part growl. "You are a holier-than-thou-art piece of work, aren't you?" Dropping the bag to the floor, she moved closer to me, jabbed her finger in my face. "You have no right to judge me. I'm the one who brought you in. I made you what you are. I got you off the street. If it wasn't for me, you'd still be waiting tables at some dump."

The fury came with such force that I was dizzy with it. I wasn't a violent person, but the urge to strike her was powerful. In that instant, I thought about my *mamm.* I thought about my sister, my *datt,* my brother, and I wondered what they would think of this callous, foulmouthed English woman. I wondered what they would think of me for being part of this, and for the first time in a long time, I felt ashamed.

I stared at her, seeing more than I wanted to see. Things I'd ignored for months because I didn't have the courage to face the truth. "I've been hearing things about your cop friends, Gina," I told her. "I've been hearing things about you, too."

"Thanks for the warning. I'll be sure to let them know." Looking at me as if I were a dog that didn't have the mental capacity to get the trick right, she picked up the canvas bag. "Me? I don't really give a damn."

I got to my feet, hating it that my legs were shaking. I got in her face anyway. "You need to return the cash."

She threw her head back and laughed. "Oh, for God's sake. What are you going to go do? Go all Amish on me?"

"If you don't return that cash, I will. You won't like the outcome."

A flicker of something I couldn't identify in her eyes. Instead of moving away, she stepped closer until her face was inches from mine. "I got the money and that car fair and square. I worked for it. I earned it. I risked my life for it. If you don't believe me, you do what you need to do. But let me tell you this, Kate. You take all of those unfounded suspicions of yours to anyone inside the department and you'll find yourself out of a job so fast your head will spin."

"If I ever see you with that kind of cash again, I will turn you in. I mean it, Gina. This is your final warning."

After a too-long moment, she stepped away from me and hefted the strap of the canvas bag onto her shoulder. As she was walking down the hall, she shot me a withering look over her shoulder and blew me a kiss.

CHAPTER 22

It's ten P.M. and I've just tossed a couple chunks of oak into the woodburning stove when I hear the backdoor slam. The children have already gone to bed; the house is quiet. Maybe a little too quiet. I'm missing Tomasetti, wishing I were at the farm, pondering how all of this with Gina is going to play out in the coming days.

The woman in question appears in the doorway between the mudroom and the kitchen, drawing me from my reverie. She's wearing Adam's coat. There's snow in her hair, on the shoulders of the coat. Her cheeks glow red from the cold.

"I hate Ohio," she announces as she stomps snow from her feet. "I swear to God when this is over, I'm moving to Hawaii."

"I take it the snow has begun."

"Coming down like a son of a bitch."

"I didn't realize you'd gone out."

"Left something in my truck."

Turning to her, I raise a brow. "I don't recall seeing anything of importance in your truck."

"This, my friend, transcends mere importance." With great flourish, she pulls a bottle of Gentleman Jack from an inside coat pocket. "The cure for cabin fever and a troubled soul rolled into one."

Despite my efforts, I can't quite keep a straight face. "It has been my experience that Jack Daniels is no gentleman."

"Gentlemen are overrated," she says breezily. "But Jack is smooth and warm with just enough burn to hold my interest."

"I hate to point out the obvious, but we should probably keep our wits about us."

"My wits don't even kick in until that first swallow hits my brain." She strides to the table and sets down the bottle. "No one in their right mind is going to be out on a night like tonight."

I try not to think about the odds of that as I wipe the counters and shove the bread into the bread box. I hear Gina return to the mudroom to remove her boots and hang the coat. I know her too well not to be a tad concerned about the bottle of whiskey. She's responsible to a degree, but I know intimately the part of her that is not. Nestled deep in the heart of all that equanimity resides a wild streak as long as the Ohio River. I've seen her take solace in alcohol. I've seen her use it to escape pain. And I've seen her imbibe for the sheer pleasure of it. With everything that's going on, not the least of which is the fact that we are in an Amish home, I don't want her taking things too far.

She joins me at the kitchen table. Mismatched glasses containing three fingers of whiskey sit on the tabletop in front of us. Too much for me. Not enough for her. The only sounds are the hiss of the propane lamp and the quiet tinkle-tap of snow against the window. It's a thoughtful, comfortable silence. The kind that doesn't need to be filled with meaningless words or chatter, though there is much to be said.

After a moment, she picks up her glass and raises it. "To troubled waters."

I clink my glass against hers. "And ten years gone."

Eyes holding, remembrance flitting between us, we sip. I've drunk more than my share of whiskey over the years, but I've never been a fan. To my credit, it's been a while since I imbibed. Tonight, with the past hovering between us and the road ahead laden with a gauntlet of unknowns, the whiskey goes down with surprising ease.

"I always knew you'd do well for yourself," Gina says after a moment. "You've kept your nose clean. Worked hard. Now, you're a small-town chief of police. You've got a decent man. A future. An unblemished reputation."

"Not quite unblemished," I tell her.

She holds my gaze for the span of several heartbeats, but she doesn't ask the obvious question. She's one of only a handful of people who know what happened when I was fourteen years old. I told her a few months after we met, and to her credit she never brought up the matter again.

"You know what I mean," she says.

Because I do, I look down at the glass in my hands, saying nothing.

"I've always believed the best measure of success isn't where you are at any certain moment, but how far you've come from where you started." She looks at me and nods. "You, my friend, have come a long way."

The old affection stirs in my chest. "Yeah, well, someone gave me some good advice once."

"You would have gotten your GED and found your place even if I hadn't hounded you."

"I wouldn't have gotten into law enforcement."

She grins. "I guess that's one thing I did right." Another short silence and then she says, "It's ironic, though. I was the one who knew what I wanted to be. And yet you were always the better cop."

Once upon a time I would have argued; now, any such argument would be disingenuous. Somewhere along the line she took a wrong turn. While she might be able to find her way back and salvage some trace of her career, she'll never work in law enforcement again.

"I should have stopped you," I tell her.

"Oh, come on. When I have my sights set on fucking up, no one gets in the way."

"If I'd been there," I say, "I never would have let you go down the road you did."

She nods, regret reflecting in her eyes. "You left at exactly the right time. You were smart. Got out or else you might've been sucked into the mess, too."

"No," I say firmly. "I wouldn't have."

"You're right. You wouldn't have." She blows out a sigh. "This is my doing. It's on me. I have to take responsibility." She lowers her gaze to her glass. "For God's sake I never dreamed my career would end like this. Consequences, I guess."

Thoughtful, she reaches for the bottle, pours another finger into our glasses. "What do you think's going to happen?"

I recall my conversation with Tomasetti. I wish I could tell her that there's an ongoing investigation and that she's not the main focus, but because of the sensitivity of the situation, I can't. While the knowledge might help her sleep tonight, I don't trust her enough to share it. The fewer people who know, the better off all of us will be in the long run, so I hold my silence.

"Some of it's going to depend on what we can prove," I tell her. "How helpful you are if this thing moves forward."

"How accommodating the district attorney is feeling," she mutters. "I don't even want to think about what Mercer and Bertrand have put into play."

"You're not the only one who has a credibility problem," I tell her. "Neither of them is squeaky clean."

She thinks about that a moment. "Kate, they're not stupid. They have resources. They're good at covering their tracks. Being cops, they've got their choice of suspects to bring forward for things they themselves have done."

"That is the nature of corruption." The words taste bitter coming out, like a mouthful of bad food. "So much arrogance."

She looks away, swirls the whiskey in her glass. "I don't want to go to jail," she whispers.

"Get a good lawyer. Make yourself valuable. Negotiate for what you want."

"If I have to do time . . ." She shudders, lets the words trail. "If it's the last thing I do, I swear I'm going to nail those sons of bitches."

"Every case they've been involved in over the years is going to get another hard look," I say. "We're talking the affidavits. Warrants. Arrests. Convictions. I would imagine there will be some exonerations coming down."

Movement at the doorway draws my attention. I glance over to see Adam enter the kitchen. Head bent, he's squinting down at a Louis L'Amour paperback novel. He's so engrossed, he doesn't notice us. Gina and I watch as he moves to the propane refrigerator and reaches for the door, likely to sneak a piece of rhubarb pie.

"You are so busted," Gina says.

The Amish man lowers the book, his eyes flicking from Gina to me and back to her. "I didn't realize you were still awake."

"I haven't gone to bed at ten P.M. since I was six years old," Gina tells him.

Adam tugs open the refrigerator door. "You two look like you're up to no good."

"We are," she says, deadpan. "Want to join us?"

His eyes skate away from hers and move to the interior of the fridge. "I thought I might have a glass of milk and some pie."

"Sammy ate the last piece before he went to bed," I tell him.

"I've got something better than pie right here on the table." Gina flicks the bottle of Gentleman Jack with her index finger. "Heaven in a bottle."

I nudge her under the table with my foot, toss her a cut-it-out look.

Adam turns from the refrigerator, his gaze moving to the glasses in front of us and the bottle of Jack Daniel's. Contrary to popular belief, drinking alcohol isn't always forbidden by the *Ordnung,* the unwritten rules set forth by the local church district. It depends on the district leadership. While drinking is generally frowned upon, some Amish—even outside of their *Rumspringa* years—quietly enjoy the occasional cold beer or glass of wine.

Lifting the bottle, Gina wriggles it back and forth. "Plenty to go around," she says.

"Most Amish don't drink," I tell her, hoping to give Adam an easy out.

Noticing my expression, she shrugs. "Hey, no problem. I wouldn't want to be a bad influence."

I laugh. "Too late for that."

As I take another sip, let the smoky taste of it settle on my tongue, I notice that Adam didn't pull the raw milk from the fridge. Instead, he goes to the cabinet above the sink, snags a glass, and brings it to the table.

"A lot of English have the wrong idea about the Amish," he says as he pulls out a chair and sits. "I think you could be one of them."

Grinning, Gina pours two fingers of the amber liquid into the glass. "I'm rethinking all of my preconceived notions as we speak."

"I've drunk whiskey before," he tells her.

A memory tickles the back of my brain. "If I'm not mistaken, it was my whiskey and there were five of us."

He smiles. "The Yoder brothers."

"And Mervin Hershberger," I remind him. "Talk about a bad influence."

"We sneaked down to the covered bridge." He chuckles. "We were what? Sixteen years old?"

"Sixteen going on twenty and looking for trouble."

"Some of us more than others." Adam gives me a pointed look. "Do you remember what Mervin Hershberger did?"

"After one drink of whiskey, he took off his clothes and dove off the bridge into the creek."

"Right about the time his *mamm* and *datt* happened by in the buggy."

Remembering, I nearly choke on my whiskey. "I'll never forget the look on his face."

"I'll never forget the look on his parents' faces."

"We didn't see him again until school started."

All three of us are laughing now. At the time, what Adam and I did that day seemed forbidden and sinful. Looking back, I realize that while what we did was outside of Amish norms, we were good kids, set on breaking the rules. At the time it seemed momentous, but only because we'd led such protected lives.

Gina caps the bottle and raises her glass. "To good memories and good friends."

"And breaking the rules," Adam puts in.

Our glasses clink together and we drink.

He leans back in the chair and stretches his legs out in front of him. "My parents were sad for you when you left, Katie."

I shoot him a smile. "Even though I could play ice hockey better than you."

"You always liked to win," he says, chuckling.

"That's the Kate we know and love," Gina murmurs, and then gives me her full attention. "Do you ever miss being Amish?"

I think about the question for the moment. "I did for a long time after I left. I was confused and afraid I'd made a mistake. I missed my family. The sense of community. I missed spending time out of doors. On the farm." I shrug. "But I was young and looking ahead, too. The longer I was gone, the easier it got, and the more certain I became that I did the right thing."

I feel Adam's eyes on me, but I don't look at him. I'm not sure I want to know that he still disapproves of my decision to leave the fold. A lot of the Amish disapproved. Early on, it hurt, but I got used to it. To this day I still hear the occasional comment. It rolls off me, for the most part. But there are times when an Amish person I respect denigrates the decision I made and the things I've done with my life, and the young Amish girl who still resides inside me flinches.

"*Mer sott em sei eegne net verlosse; Gott verlosst die seine nicht,*" I say. "I heard that a lot when I came back."

"What does it mean?" Gina asks.

Adam replies. "One should not abandon one's own; God does not abandon His own."

"That's harsh," Gina tells him. "Talk about a guilt trip."

"It is the Amish way." Adam looks at me. "I never held it against you, Katie. It didn't matter that you could play hockey better than me."

The sound of snow tapping against the window fills the silence that follows. Gina finishes her whiskey. I try not to notice when she pours another.

"Did you get your problems back in Columbus straightened out?" Adam asks her.

"It's sort of a work in progress," she tells him.

"And your shoulder?"

"Thanks to you and Joe, I could probably beat you in an arm wrestling contest." She looks at Adam and a smile plays at the corners of her mouth. "If you hadn't stopped to help, if you hadn't brought me here, I would have died."

"God always has a plan for us, Gina. For me. For you. For all of us. It wasn't your time and so He sent us to find you."

Smiling, she reaches across the table, rests her hand on his forearm and squeezes. "You opened your home to a stranger. You didn't know what kind of person I was. I didn't exactly make a good impression. You did it anyway."

He looks away, not quite comfortable with her gratitude or her touch, and eases his arm away from her. "Helping those in need is the Amish way."

"Even so, you took a chance on me," she says. "I won't forget it."

I watch the exchange with a combination of fascination and what I can only describe as trepidation. I slant a covert look at Adam and something inside me sinks. I can tell by the way he's looking at Gina that he's not immune to her charms; the last thing on his mind is the possibility that he could be setting himself up for a mistake that will cost him something later on. I want to reach out and stop him, before he does something he'll regret. But I don't. It would be unseemly for me to voice my opinion or intervene.

The rise of protectiveness I feel for him surprises me. I have the utmost respect for the Amish, their beliefs and traditions. But I also know they can be judgmental of mistakes.

Leaning across the table, Gina pours another finger of the amber liquid into his glass. She tries to do the same to mine, but I set my hand over the top.

"Suit yourself," she says.

Finishing the last of my whiskey, I take the glass to the sink, rinse it, and set it to drain. I bid them good night and leave the kitchen.

CHAPTER 23

He'd never seen such endless darkness. For miles, there wasn't a single lit window. No streetlights. No headlights. Not even a porch light. Just a world bathed in the ethereal glow of snow and a low sky making good on its promise of more.

"Fucking Amish," Damon Bertrand growled as he made the turn onto the township road.

It was the second time they'd passed this particular intersection in the last twenty minutes. The first time, he didn't even realize it was a public road. There was no sign. There were no tire marks. Half the back roads in this area weren't on the GPS map. That wasn't to mention the mountains of snow piled ten feet high on both shoulders.

"Welcome to Podunk, USA," Mercer muttered.

The jangle and thunk of the tire chains against the snow-packed road seemed preternaturally loud as they made the turn. Winter-dead trees crowded both shoulders, the branches reaching across the roadway like spindly black hands.

"There's a mailbox," Mercer said, pointing.

"What's the street number of Lengacher's place?" Bertrand asked.

Mercer tapped the screen of his cell, blue light reflecting off his face. "Five zero three."

"That's it." Bertrand punched off the headlights.

They drove past the place slowly, both men craning their necks to take in the details. It was too dark to see much. A long lane clogged with snow and lined with trees. Beyond, he could just make out the roofline of a farmhouse against the horizon. The hulking shadows of pine trees bunched around it. Open pasture in front.

"No sign of Colorosa's truck," Mercer said.

"Could be parked at the rear or tucked away in one of the barns."

Bertrand continued down the road half a mile before finding a place to turn around—not an easy task. The last thing he needed was to get stuck out in the middle of nowhere. The good news was they'd found Lengacher and, ostensibly, Gina Colorosa. They still didn't know if Burkholder was involved. That a second cop might be sniffing around was the most pressing question. There were too many unknowns for him to be comfortable with any of this.

Headlights doused, he drove back to the Lengacher farm and stopped.

"Just so you know," Bertrand said. "I heard from our computer guy. He came through on the bodycam footage. It's done. He said it's flawless."

Mercer's eyes glittered in the light off the dash. "I'll feel a hell of a lot better about this once it's out there."

"He's going to upload it tonight, get it sent. Once the media gets their claws into it, they're going to run with it, and Colorosa becomes enemy number one."

"Going to be damning."

"Let's hope it's enough."

Mercer nodded, his expression a little too thoughtful. "I say we go in tomorrow," he said. "We make it official. Show up with the warrant. Make the arrest." He shrugged. "Take her back and hope to hell no one listens to her."

"We need eyes on Burkholder before we do anything," Bertrand said.

Mercer glanced out the window, at the dark silhouette of the farm beyond. "Look, we're here. It's late. No one around. Why don't I do a quick recon? Check for Burkholder's vehicle and Colorosa's truck."

"Too risky."

"I'm up for it. Snow will take care of any tracks. It's the only way we're going to know for sure if Burkholder's involved."

"Make it quick." Bertrand reached down and turned up the heat. "It's coming down and we cannot afford to get stuck in the snow out here."

"Give me six minutes." With a nod, Mercer opened the door and got out.

Bertrand watched the other man until the darkness and falling snow swallowed him. He stared at the farm, his mind running through options that were quickly dwindling. Early on, he'd entertained the idea of taking his chances and arresting her, hoping the slew of felony charges would prevent her from pointing a finger with any level of credibility. He no longer believed that was the best choice. Even with all the strikes against her, if she had a recording or video or had convinced someone else to turn on them, questions would be raised. As careful as he'd been, he could have overlooked some detail that would come back to haunt him. Other people—maybe even cops—would be coerced or pressured into coming forward, some prosecutor promising immunity in exchange for their cooperation. A shitstorm of investigations would ensue.

He would not spend the rest of his life in prison because of her. He wished he'd been more careful who he'd brought in. Fucking hindsight.

Bertrand was starting to perspire beneath his coat when he spotted the shadow moving toward him. He set his hand on the Glock tucked into the space between the seat and the console when the door swung open. Mercer slid onto the seat next to him with a swirl of wind and snow.

"I was starting to think you got waylaid," Bertrand muttered.

Mercer's expression told him everything he needed to know. "There's a Painters Mill PD Explorer parked in a drift out by the barn. Colorosa's pickup truck is in the barn."

"So Burkholder is here." The garrote around his neck tightened.

"Why the hell hasn't she called this in?" Mercer said. "There's a fucking arrest warrant out for Colorosa."

"She hasn't called it in because Colorosa is talking and that fucking Burkholder is listening. As far as we know, she's already been in touch with another agency and we just haven't heard. That's what you call a worst-case scenario."

Looking worried, Mercer shook his head. "I say we go in first thing in the morning. Do this just like we planned. Reach out to the sheriff's department beforehand. Let them know we're going to execute the warrant. Ask for their assistance. That way we don't get accused of overstepping."

Bertrand let the statement ride for a moment. Then he set his hands on the wheel, stared straight ahead. "You sure that's how you want to play this?"

Mercer hefted a humorless laugh. "What else is there?"

"If we do this by the book, Colorosa is going to put us under the microscope, partner. She's going to name names and she won't stop there. That bitch will drag us through the mud. She will take us apart piece by piece. Destroy our careers and everything we've ever worked for. There go our pensions. Our families will get dragged into it. You want your kids dealing with that? You feel like spending the rest of your life behind bars?"

Mercer stared at him, silent and waiting.

"We can't bring her in, Ken. You know that, right? We do this by the book and this thing is going to blow up in our faces."

Mercer didn't look convinced. In fact, he looked like he was thinking about throwing up. "What the hell are you suggesting, Damon?"

"I'm telling you there's only one way to fix this, and I think you know what that is."

"She's a *cop.* One of us. You can't—"

Bertrand cut him off. "She's never been one of us. Never been a team player. The only person she cares about is herself." Hands on the wheel, he shook his head. "I don't like it, either. In fact, I hate it. But that's the way it is. It's us or her, my friend."

Mercer squirmed in his seat, his breaths elevated, fogging up the passenger-side window enough that he used his hand to wipe away the condensation. "Jesus Christ."

Bertrand didn't give him a respite. "Look, we didn't ask for this. Colorosa turned on us. She made the wrong choice. Whatever happens next is on her." When Mercer said nothing, he pushed. "We got to clean house, buddy. She needs to go away. Permanently. That's the only way we can put this nasty chapter to rest and move on."

The words echoed within the confines of the vehicle. Damning. Final. Terrifying. Not for the first time, Bertrand felt that weird sense of claustrophobia pressing down on him with so much force that he fought the urge to open the window. When Mercer remained silent, he wiped his hands on his trousers, hating it that his palms were wet. "Look, Kenny, if you're not up to it just say the word."

Mercer nodded, but with the enthusiasm of a man agreeing to take part in his own execution. "Lengacher has a bunch of kids in there," he said. "That's not to mention Burkholder."

Bertrand took his time responding, choosing his words with care. "We'll deal with it. No one gets hurt. We're the good guys, remember?"

Blowing out a breath, Mercer leaned back in the seat, scrubbed his hand over his face. "What's the plan?"

"We go in. Execute the warrant. Get Burkholder out of the room. Get the family out. Then we do what we need to do." Bertrand shrugged. "It goes like this: Colorosa is one of us. So we do a cursory pat-down and we miss the pistol she secreted away. In the course of the arrest, she goes for the weapon. She brandishes it. We've no choice but to use deadly force. At that point, we plant the throw-down. Fire it. Make sure there's residue on her hands and clothes. And we are in the clear."

Mercer looked at him, sweat glistening on his forehead. "Jesus, I don't like it."

"No one likes it. But there's no other way. It's Colorosa or us. We didn't sign up for this. That bitch fucked us over."

As convincing as the argument was, Bertrand fought the quiver of fear that ran the length of his body. He knew all too well there were a hundred things that could go wrong. That there were loose ends. Too many people involved. Too many unknowns.

"You know there will be an investigation," Mercer said.

"All we have to do is play it cool, keep our heads, and stick to the script. We'll make it through." Bertrand looked out the window, watched the snow whisper across the frozen surface of the road. "Even if Colorosa *has* talked to someone or she's stashed some so-called evidence somewhere—a video or recording—once that body-cam footage hits, whatever credibility she ever had is gone."

The two men stared at each other for the span of a few seconds.

"What if Burkholder doesn't cooperate?" Mercer asked.

"Then we'll have to convince her."

Without elaborating, Bertrand put the Subaru in gear, but he didn't pull forward. They sat in silence, letting all of the words that had passed between them settle.

Then Bertrand asked. "So are you in or what?"

Ken Mercer looked out the window, blew out a breath. "I'm in."

Bertrand didn't smile, but he felt it pull at the corners of his mouth. Without another word, he took his foot off the brake and started down the road.

CHAPTER 24

I'm dragged from sleep by the sound of pounding. I sit upright, disoriented, realize I'm on the sofa in Adam Lengacher's living room. Crepuscular light slants in through the window coverings. I'm wearing my clothes. A headache hovers at my temples.

I've just swung my legs to the floor when the window on the front door rattles. Cursing Gina and her bottle of Gentleman Jack, I go to the mudroom, grab my .38 off the shelf, and slide it into the waistband of my jeans. Back in the living room, I grab my cell off the coffee table, squint at the display to see that it's not yet six thirty A.M.

Another round of knocking, this time accompanied by a singsong male voice. "*Er hot sich widder verschofe!*" He overslept again, which is the Amish way of poking fun at someone who sleeps too late.

I stride to the door, glance out the window. A middle-aged Amish man, with a full beard and wire-rimmed eyeglasses over small blue eyes, startles at the sight of me. I recognize him from years past, but it takes my sleep-muddled brain a moment to remember his name. I open the door.

His smile falters. "Katie *Burkholder*?" he says, pressing his hand to his chest.

"Hi . . . Mr. Yoder." I stammer his name, keenly aware of how my presence here this early in the morning when I've clearly been wakened from sleep might be perceived—and get the tongues wagging.

His barn coat and muck boots are covered with snow. He looks past me as if expecting an equally disheveled Adam to appear behind me.

Oh boy.

"I'm here to see Adam," Yoder says. "He is home?"

"I believe he is." I look past him, where big, wet flakes are coming down hard. "*Kumma inseid.*" Come inside.

"Katie."

I turn at the sound of Adam's voice to see him emerge from the hall. Not from upstairs where his bedroom is located, I realize, but the hall off the sewing room, where Gina has been staying. Something sinks inside me as I take in the sight of him. He's disheveled, wearing the same clothes he had on last night, hair sticking up on one side, his hat in his hand. For the span of several heartbeats, we stare at each other, unspoken words passing between us. I see discomfort in his eyes. Regret etched into his features. Those same awkward sentiments climb over me, settle onto my shoulders, but I shove them back, keep my mind on the business at hand.

"Amos Yoder is here to see you," I say, a little too stiffly.

Adam's eyes flick toward the front door. He takes a moment to put on his hat, squares his shoulders. "I . . . overslept."

"I think everyone except for Mr. Yoder overslept," I say beneath my breath.

He doesn't so much as crack a smile. Shamefaced, he strides to the front door. "Amos. *Guder mariye.*"

"I thought you'd be up by now." Amos Yoder looks from Adam to me and back to Adam. One side of his mouth twitches, but he covers it with a cough.

"Overslept." Adam clears his throat.

Yoder ducks his head, looks at me from beneath the brim of his hat. "I didn't realize you had non-Amish visitors."

Adam steps back to clear the way for the other man to enter. "*Kumma inseid. Witt du wennich kaffee?*" Come inside. Would you like coffee?

"*Nee, denki.* I still have to feed the hogs." Yoder sobers. "I wanted to let you know . . . there was an English car parked on the road last night in front of your place. Very late."

Adam's brows furrow. "A car?"

Appearances forgotten, I move up beside Adam, open the door the rest of the way. "Mr. Yoder, did you recognize the vehicle? Have you seen it before?"

"No."

"Do you know what kind of vehicle it was?" I ask. "Car? Truck?"

"Well, I'm not sure exactly. Too far away, you know. All we could see were the headlamps. Martha was up sick with a cold. She saw it first and called me over. I thought it was strange for someone to be out here with all the snow, especially so late."

"Could it have been a snowmobile?" I ask. "Someone out for a late-night ride?"

"I don't think so. I've seen the snow machines." He slips his fingers beneath his hat and scratches his head. "What was strange about it is that the driver turned off the headlamps. Sat there in the dark for twenty minutes."

"Any idea what color it was?" I ask.

He shakes his head. "Too dark to see. Too much snow. And you know my eyes aren't as keen as they used to be."

I nod. "Did you see how many people were inside? Anything like that?"

Another shake of his head. "No."

Of course, it's possible someone suffering with cabin fever went out for a drive. Teenagers out in Mom's car for an illicit cigarette or can of beer. Maybe someone who lives nearby got into an argument with their spouse and needed to get out of the house. Things like that happen this time of year when people are snowbound. Still, a thread of worry stirs in my gut. In the back of my mind I wonder if someone is looking for Gina. Law enforcement. Or someone else.

"Do you have any idea who might've been out there that time of night? A neighbor, maybe?" I look from man to man, address both of them. "Do people drive out this way to drink alcohol or park? Anything like that?"

Adam shakes his head. "No one comes out this way, Chief Burkholder. Except for Mr. McKay down on Ithaca Road, all the farms out here belong to the Amish. There's rarely a car on the road."

"With all this snow, I thought it was odd, especially that time of night," Yoder says. "Two A.M. I guess you never know what kind of people are going to be coming down your lane these days."

I've just poured coffee into a mug when Adam enters the kitchen with his coat and boots on. His eyes slide away from mine when I look at him over my shoulder. "No school again today, I think," he says without looking at me.

"Mr. Yoder left?" I ask.

"*Ja*."

He starts toward the mudroom, but I stop him. "Would you like coffee?" I ask.

Shaking his head, he continues on. "I'm late feeding the animals this morning."

His expression is a collage of discomfiture and that Amish shame I experienced myself so many times in my youth.

"Adam. Wait."

He stops in the doorway of the mudroom, sets his hand on the jamb, but he doesn't face me. For a moment, I think he's going to keep going so he doesn't have to deal with me or my questions. All the guilt I see boiling inside him.

"You don't have to . . ." My brain scrambles for the right words. Feel awkward? Guilty? Blame yourself for acquiescing to a weakness that is fundamentally human?

He turns to me, his expression stoic. "I know what you're thinking and—"

"I'm thinking your personal life is none of my business. You don't have to say anything and you sure don't owe me an explanation."

"Nothing happened," he says in a low voice. "I know how all of this might look. When you saw me come out of her room. We . . . didn't . . ."

I shouldn't be surprised. Though I don't know him well, I feel as if I have a pretty good handle on his character. The weight of his responsibilities. The depth of his loneliness. But I understand the Amish mind-set, too. While they suffer with all the same frailties and imperfections as the rest of us mortal souls, they are bound by the rules of the church, the teachings of the Bible, and mores that are instilled at a young age, not only by their parents, but by their peers. Most Amish live their lives beneath the watchful eyes of their brethren and a community that can be judgmental.

"Okay," I say quietly.

"Gina . . . I think she . . ." He lets the sentence trail and sighs. "Last night . . . she wanted someone to talk to. She asked me to stay with her for a bit, so . . . I did. She needed a friend. The rest . . ." He shrugs. "I fell asleep. I . . . we . . . did not. That's all."

We stare at each other a moment. A sense of respect moves through me. A slow rise of admiration. An uncomfortable tinge of embarrassment. "I wasn't going to ask," I tell him. "I just didn't want you to feel awkward this morning."

"I saw the questions," he says. "On your face."

"Thank you for staying with her."

"It was not a hardship. She's . . ." He doesn't complete the sentence. Something unexpected flashes in his eyes.

"A complicated woman," I finish for him. "And she's led a complicated life."

Tilting his head, he approaches me and lowers his voice. "I know she is in trouble. I know she is wanted by the police. Maybe by someone else, too, no? When I asked her about it, she wouldn't say. Wouldn't speak of it. But she's frightened, Katie."

Looking at him, I'm reminded that good men still exist in a world that sorely needs them. "I know."

"Katie, she was shot. She brought a gun into my home. Pointed it at me when I was trying to help her. I need to know if she's brought danger here. I need to know if my children are safe."

They are questions I should have answered by now. That I didn't makes me feel as if I've taken advantage of his kindness and generosity. "I can't get into all the details with you, Adam. What I can tell you is that it's a police matter. Tomasetti is involved. We're trying to work through it."

"What about the people looking for her? Why is she so afraid of them?"

"I think they're dangerous. The rest . . . if it wasn't for this storm, I would have taken Gina somewhere else."

"These men . . . they are police?"

"Yes." When he continues to stare at me, his expression rigid, I reach into my pocket for my cell. "Look, I can call Tomasetti right now. You've already gone above and beyond. I can't ask you to—"

Adam reaches out and lowers my hand. "They are bad men? Who would harm her?"

"Yes. But you are under no obligation."

"Katie, her heart is good."

"Not perfect," I say.

"No one is." He gives a decisive nod. "Where there is darkness, let me bring Your light. Let me not seek as much to be consoled as to console."

Remembering more than is wise, understanding more than I should, I finish the prayer, "For it is in giving that one receives."

"Don't make the call. I can give her refuge. Here."

I stare at him, wondering if his decision is because of all those Amish norms—or if he's a man who's feeling protective of an attractive woman. . . .

"It's just for another day or two," I say. "You're certain?"

He nods. "Where there is despair, let me bring hope."

I look away, take a moment to tuck all of the gnarly emotions coming at me back into their proper place.

"Now, I've got to get to work." He starts toward the mudroom.

I hold up my hand. "Hang on." Quickly, I go to the cabinet, pull out the biggest mug I can find, and fill it with coffee. "Take it with you," I say as I hand it to him. "It's cold out there."

Taking the cup, he starts for the back door.

I find the bottle of Gentleman Jack hidden haphazardly behind a bag of cornmeal in the pantry. I'm in the process of pouring it down the sink when Gina emerges from the living room. Her hair is a wild tangle of black curls, her face pale, eyes warning of a foul mood.

"I see you've decided to do away with the last of my sanity," she mutters as she shuffles to the percolator on the stove and pours.

"Yup." I chuck the empty bottle into the trash. "I hear you had a rough night last night."

"I've had better." She tosses me a sour look, narrows her eyes. "Word travels fast."

"Stay away from Adam."

She rolls her eyes, brings the mug to her lips, and slurps. "For God's sake, Kate, nothing happened. We just—"

"He spent the night with you. That's enough."

She throws her head back and laughs. "We didn't . . . We fell asleep. Although he did kiss me good night. It was sweet. Just a peck on the cheek. I didn't realize men still did sweet."

Her insouciance chafes all of those old Amish sensibilities still scattered about inside me. Her indifference and lack of respect for him and his ways stir my temper. I think about Adam, a young widower for going on two years now, raising a family, and running a farm alone, all of it in a society where the institution of marriage is cherished, encouraged, and expected.

I cross to her and get in her face. "He's not some loser you picked up at a bar."

"Do not go there, my friend," she snaps. "I'm hungover and I already told you nothing happened. So drop it."

It's good advice. Advice a wiser woman might heed. But I know Gina too well to let this go without my driving home my point. "Something *did* happen, Gina. He spent the night with you. That's a big deal. Something that will likely cause him a great deal of guilt and get the tongues wagging."

She laughs. "For God's sake, Kate, this isn't frickin' high school—"

"He's Amish. He's part of a culture you do not understand. He's part of a community that will think less of him if he makes a mistake.

He'll become the focus of gossip that can be cruel and it will matter to him." I jam my finger in her face. "It'll matter to his kids."

She smacks my hand away. "Fine. For God's sake, get off my back."

"Gina, he's a good man. If something had happened between the two of you, it would have . . . meant something to him. You can't play with people's feelings that way. Not here. Not him. Not like that."

She stares at me, blinking, nostrils flaring. For the first time since she walked into the kitchen, I feel as if she's listening, that she heard me, and that I'm getting through to her.

"I got it," she says quietly.

I go to the table, sink into a chair, stuff my temper back into its hole. "A neighbor saw a vehicle parked on the road in front of the house at two o'clock this morning."

Coffee in hand, she joins me at the table, energized now, her eyes sharp on mine. "Did you get a plate? Make? Model?"

"It was too dark and too far away for him to see. He thought it was odd that the driver had turned off the headlights."

"That is odd."

"Maybe." I shrug. "But in rural areas, sometimes people drive out to the back roads to drink or whatever. Teenagers park to make out. I've seen it a hundred times since I've been chief."

"I guess hormones don't give a damn if there's two feet of snow on the ground," she grumbles.

"That said, this road is a ways off the beaten path. I can't see someone braving all the snow and risking getting stuck, especially that time of night."

"Had a plow been by?" she asks.

"I don't know. Maybe once. Even so, there are drifts. You can barely get through with a four-wheel drive and chains."

She thinks about that a moment, but I see the filament of worry take up residence in her expression. "Bertrand owns a four-wheel-drive Subaru Outback."

"I know." At her how-do-you-know-that look, I add, "Tomasetti checked."

"Even so, no one knows where I am."

"Like I said, it's not that much of a stretch for someone to have remembered that you and I were tight once and put two and two together. Cops have resources out the wazoo when it comes to finding someone."

"If they know where I am, why didn't they just knock on the door, whip out their bogus warrant, and arrest me?"

Why, indeed? It's a valid question. One that's been scraping at the back of my brain since I heard about the mysterious vehicle parked in front of the farm. In light of the storm and the road conditions, it's unlikely two detectives would travel all the way from Columbus to execute an arrest warrant and then drive away without making said arrest. Chances are, they'll wait until the roads are open, they'll contact County or me, and then make the trip.

But if that's the case, who was parked on the road in front of Adam's house with the headlights out at two o'clock in the morning?

"Unless they sent someone," Gina whispers.

"What do you mean?" I ask the question, but I already know where she's going, and it adds a distinctly sinister element to an already menacing situation.

She stares at me, her lips parted, the wheels of thought in her eyes working. "They know some very bad people, Kate. Dangerous people who owe them favors. Dregs of the earth who have no compunction about killing a cop."

I rub my hand across the place on the back of my neck where the hairs stand on end, find the skin damp with sweat despite the gooseflesh on my arms. It's bad enough to believe that a police department, an institution I believe in with my whole heart—a department I'd once been part of—runs rampant with corruption. It's inconceivable to believe that sworn police officers could be capable of executing one of their own.

I stare at her, aware that my pulse is up. A question I don't want to speak aloud beats at the back of my brain. "You think they would hire some thug to hunt you down and kill you?" I ask.

"I think they're capable of doing exactly that." She buttresses the words with a hefty dose of bluster. "Remember, I'm the cop who can put them in prison for the rest of their lives. I'd say they're pretty motivated to do whatever it takes to get me out of the picture. They know all the right people, and they don't even have to get their hands dirty."

I look out the window, watch the falling snow, wondering if the bad weather has given us a false sense of security. That we're tucked away and safe when we're anything but.

"We need to keep our eyes open," I tell her.

"That is the understatement of the year," she mutters.

Neither of us laughs.

"I'll see about having one of my officers park in front of the farm. Or at least drive by when they can. Keep an eye on things."

"Then again, we could be wrong about all this," Gina adds with a forced nonchalance. "Come on. There's two feet of snow on the ground. Everyone and their uncle is snowbound. No one knows I'm here. Maybe all this closed-quarters crap has made us paranoid."

That I can see past the faux bravado does nothing to assuage the knot of dread that's taken up residence in the pit of my stomach.

CHAPTER 25

My grandmother lived with us for a while when I was a kid. It was wintertime and I was just young enough that I didn't realize she was sick. In typical Amish fashion, she never complained about the pain; she never let on that her time left on this earth was short. What I remember most about Grossmammi is that she loved to read to us. On those days when it was too cold to work or play outside for long, my siblings, Jacob and Sarah, and I would gather around the woodstove and listen to her singsong voice. Sometimes she read to us from *Martyr's Mirror*. What I really enjoyed were the stories.

I remember vividly a tale about a young Swiss Mennonite woman whose family migrated to America. Her name was Anna and she stayed behind to wait for her husband to return from the city, at which time they would make the trip across the Atlantic to join her family in Pennsylvania. It was a time of horrific persecution for the Anabaptists. Anna survived the long alpine winter in the Bavarian Alps, but by the time her husband arrived in spring she'd gone mad with *Foehnkrankenheit,* a mysterious psychosis caused by the fierce foehn winds.

I never forgot Anna's tragic story or my *grossmammi*'s description of winds strong enough to cause insanity. This morning, troubled and listening to the incessant wind tear at the house, I'm reminded of *Foehnkrankenheit.*

I'm nursing my third cup of coffee when a hard rap on the front door breaks the silence. The .38 is still tucked into the waistband of my jeans, so I head toward the living room. Gina stands at the mouth of the hall.

"Go to the kitchen," I tell her. "Keep your eyes on the back door."

"Yep." Eyeing the front door as she passes it, she heads to the back of the house.

I'm midway to the door when I recognize the silhouette through the glass. I find John Tomasetti standing on the porch, wearing the now-familiar snowsuit, his helmet at his side.

"Where's your cell?" he asks.

"Charging in the Explorer."

"Colorosa?" The tone of his voice, the dark look in his eyes, alerts me that this is not a friendly visit.

"Kitchen." Stepping back, I usher him inside. "What's wrong?"

"Have you checked your cell for news?"

"Not since last night."

He tugs off his gloves, drops them on the floor, and moves past me. "She played us." He heads toward the kitchen without bothering to remove his boots. "She's all over the news this morning."

"What?" I say and follow. "Why?"

Tomasetti isn't some loose-cannon rookie. He's smart and methodical and plenty capable of keeping his emotions in check. But he's human, too, and there's nothing he dislikes more than to learn someone he's trying to help isn't being forthcoming.

Gina stands at the kitchen sink, coffee cup in hand, staring out the window. She turns when he enters the room. Her eyes widen at the sight of him striding toward her, his expression hostile, his mouth set into a hard line. She doesn't give up ground when he reaches her. Sensing confrontation, she slips quickly into cop mode.

"The man knows how to make an entrance," she says.

He stops a few feet away from her, eyes like shards of ice, sharp enough to cut skin. "You have two minutes to explain this."

Yanking down the zipper of his snowsuit, he pulls out his cell phone. Hand perfectly steady, he swipes the screen twice and holds it up for her to see.

Expression amused, she tilts her head, looks at the screen. I move up beside her as the logo of a television station out of Columbus scrolls across the screen. A video, I realize, and something akin to dread stirs in the pit of my stomach. Tomasetti hits the play button with his thumb.

The video rolls. I take in a dozen details at once. It's poor quality. Bodycam footage. Shot at night. The logo of the news station hovers in the upper left-hand corner. The date, the time, and meaningless numbers appear in the upper right-hand corner. Then, voices.

"All you had to do was keep your fucking mouth shut!" Female voice, laced with anger. Gina's?

Dead ahead, front and center, a man in a dark coat, hands up, stepping back, eyes darting and filled with a combination of panic and fear. *"I didn't say nothin'!"* he tells her.

Her right hand appears. She's gripping the black steel of a pistol—a Sig Sauer—the sleeve of her coat visible. *"Do you have any idea what you've done? What the hell do you think is going to happen now?"*

"I don't know!" His head swivels left and right. Eyes big and darting to the pistol. Mouth open. He doesn't trust her, I realize, fears for his safety.

"Piece of shit," she snarls.

"Fuckin' don't!" He raises his hands as if to fend her off. *"Don't!"*

Six shots in rapid-fire succession. The man drops, lies unmoving on the floor. The wearer of the cam moves toward him. An arm extends, a gloved hand tugging off the glove of the other. A female hand touches the side of his neck with an index finger.

"Stupid motherfucker," she whispers.

It's a disturbing, bloody video that shows a complete lack of conscience—and the cold ruthlessness of a killer.

Tomasetti turns off the cell, drops it in his pocket; then his eyes fasten to Gina. "When were you going to tell us about that?"

Gina stares at him, eyes wide, mouth open, and she motions toward his cell. "That did not happen. I don't know where you got it, but it did not happen. Not like that."

"For God's sake." Tomasetti throws up his hands in exasperation. His eyes simmer with fury. "You had better start talking, because I'm an inch away from placing you under arrest. I will transport you to the Holmes County Sheriff's Department, where you will be booked and put in a holding cell until we can figure out what the hell to do with you. Are you getting where I'm coming from?"

She opens her mouth, closes it without speaking, takes a moment to compose herself. "I can't explain something I've never seen. All I can tell you is that it did not happen. Not like that. Not even close. I don't know how they got that video, but that is *not* the way it went down."

"Who's the man in the video?" I ask.

"Eddie Cysco." She snaps the name, but her face has gone pale. "The one they murdered."

"They?" Stepping forward, Tomasetti takes the mug from her hand, spilling coffee in the process, and tosses it into the sink. "Sit down."

"Who the hell do you think you are?" she snarls.

"I'm the dumbass trying to save someone who by all indications isn't worth the effort." He points to the chair. "Sit the fuck down."

Glaring at him, more fight than flight in her eyes, she goes to the chair, hesitates, then sinks into it. "I do not have an explanation for that video. I recognize parts of it. The badge number is mine. But *that* did not happen."

"So you've said," Tomasetti says in a low voice. "Here's a news flash for you, Colorosa. Bodycam footage doesn't lie." He all but snarls the words. "I can't say the same for you."

She starts to stand, but he sets his hand on her shoulder, presses her back into the chair. "Did you shoot Eddie Cysco?" he asks.

"No. He was my CI," she tells him." "I arrested him several times over the years. He never resisted and there was never a shot fired."

"That's you in the video," he says. "Your Sig."

She looks down, her brows furrowing. "I don't know what that is. I can't explain it."

"Maybe you don't want to," he growls.

I watch the exchange, hold my ground at the door, give Tomasetti the room he needs. A knot of tension pulls taut between my shoulders. Is it possible she's been lying to us all along? That she's as corrupt and dishonest as the cops she's accused of the same and simply trying to save herself? Am I so blinded by my past relationship with her that I didn't see it?

Gina leans back in the chair, looks from Tomasetti to me. "That video is doctored."

Tomasetti laughs. "Do you have any idea how impossible it is to alter bodycam footage? Especially when it's from an officer in a large metropolitan police department?"

"I know how it sounds." Tightening her mouth, she shakes her head. "But that's the only explanation that makes sense. I arrested Eddie Cysco. I was there, and I'm telling you that *did not happen*."

"You realize I don't believe a word that comes out of your mouth," he says.

Leaning forward, she puts her elbows on the table, stares down at the tablecloth. "They altered the footage. They leaked it to the media. Dear God, they're going to fry me."

I turn my attention to Gina. "You arrested Cysco at some point?"

"I arrested him half a dozen times. He was small-time, but connected. He knew the big dogs. That particular arrest, the part of it on that video, happened about a year ago," she replies. "It was a simple arrest. Cysco violated his parole. Minor thing that would normally be overlooked. But I needed him. I'd had eyes on him for a while because I wanted him as a CI, and I knew he was just desperate enough to cooperate. So I went after him and made the arrest. When he agreed to cooperate, I went to bat for him. The DA was willing to negotiate—no jail time as long as Cysco told me what I needed to know."

She motions toward Tomasetti's cell phone with her eyes. "Part of that footage is from one of my arrests of Cysco." Her brows knit. "The rest . . . It's like someone used footage from an unrelated arrest I made two years ago."

"Did you fire your weapon?"

"No." She chokes out a sound of frustration. "I don't know where that footage came from. It's like some weird collage."

"So you're saying part of that video shows you arresting Eddie Cysco. What about the rest of it?"

"I think it's an arrest I made of a deadbeat by the name of Lee Kilpatrick."

"That can be verified." He thumbs the name into his cell. "Someone leaked that footage to the media," he tells her. "The department is being accused of keeping it under wraps to protect a bad cop: you."

"Complete bullshit," she snarls.

He's standing a few feet away, his arms crossed at his chest, looking at Gina as if she's a handful of sludge he's pulled out of a clogged gutter. I think about the video, about everything that's been said, and I realize that either she's a master liar or there's a hell of a lot more going on than any of us realized.

"Is it seriously even *possible* to alter bodycam footage?" I ask.

Tomasetti glares at me. "It's damn unlikely," he says with disgust. "Think about it, Kate. Anyone who even *views* the video leaves a digital footprint. There are layers upon layers of security."

Here in Painters Mill, we don't have the budget for bodycams. The subject has arisen in town council meetings on several occasions. While most people believe bodycams protect the officers, the county attorney was quick to point out the drawbacks. For example, the invasion-of-privacy issues for the general public. And for the officers, having to take the time to turn them on—an instant that could distract them during an emergency situation.

I look at Tomasetti. "What's the typical chain of custody on bodycam footage?"

He shakes his head. "Departments differ, but in most cases the officer uploads the footage at the end of his shift. From there it goes to a database that's managed by the city or county's information technology department or else it's contracted out. Anyone who needs to look at the footage—for example, if the officer needs to ensure his or her report is correct—has to sign in." He grimaces. "I've been involved in several cases in which either bodycam or dashcam footage was evidence. In all the years I've been with BCI, I've never heard of or encountered footage being altered in any way. There are too many people involved and a lot of checks and balances."

"That video is a complete fabrication," Gina snaps.

Tomasetti ignores her.

"When you arrested Cysco in the past," I say to Gina, "you were wearing a bodycam?"

She nods. "Every time. It's departmental policy."

"Did you draw your sidearm when you made the arrest?" This from Tomasetti.

Sighing, she gives him a withering look. "Once. But I'd dealt with Eddie before." Another sigh, this time imbued with the sound of regret. "I needed to make an impression on him, so I stepped up the force continuum."

Tomasetti groans. "Of course you did," he mutters.

"I needed his cooperation, and I wanted him to know I was in charge. Cysco might've been small-time, but he was smart. I knew making a good arrest was my ticket, so I came down hard. There was no wrongdoing on my part."

"Is the audio correct as you remember it?" I ask.

"Not even close," she tells me. "That's not my voice."

"Sounds like you." Scowling, Tomasetti pulls out his cell again, scrolls through the menu to the footage. "I want you to take us through every step."

"I can take you through the footage in which I was there," she says.

To entertain the notion of a coordinated effort within the police department of a major metropolitan city to modify bodycam footage in order to frame an officer for murder chills me to the bone.

Holding the cell so that both Gina and I can see the screen, Tomasetti hits the play button. No one speaks as the video unrolls. This time I pay attention to the details. The date and time match the report of Cysco's death. The numbers indicate the division and the officer involved. I look for skips or jumps, anything that doesn't appear intrinsic to the original video.

"That part of the video is from another arrest," Gina murmurs. "Date and time have been altered." She points. "I made contact there. He's cooperating. Nothing in his hands."

"Do you have the report that corresponds with the original footage?" I ask.

"All the corresponding reports are on file. Or should be. Under normal circumstances I'd have access. Now . . ." She shrugs.

The video ends. It's 2:18 minutes in length. Tomasetti hits the play button, backs it up, plays it again.

"Quality is bad," he grumbles. "Dark."

"Especially early on," I say. "Audio is scratchy."

Gina makes a sound of irritation. "A year ago, when that original footage was recorded, the technology wasn't as good as it is now. It's grainy and dark. Whoever altered it tried to match it, but it's not the same."

At 1:17 Gina raises her hand and points. "There," she says. "That's when the original footage ends. Even the voice is different. It's not mine."

Tomasetti stops the video, rolls it back, and hits play again.

I watch, but I don't see anything unusual or suspicious. No skips or bumps. No unnatural movement. The audio is too scratchy for me to tell if the voice is hers or someone else's.

"I can't tell," I say.

"In the original video, my arm is visible from the elbow to hand." She points. "At 1:17, the footage becomes clearer. The voice changes."

"Audio shifts slightly," Tomasetti says. "It's subtle."

But like most bodycam footage, both the audio and visual are poor quality, with a lot of movement, rustling, and background noise that got picked up by the mike.

When the video finishes, Gina straightens, her gaze flicking from me to Tomasetti. "Someone took footage from one of my arrests of Cysco and somehow spliced it with my arrest of Lee Kilpatrick. The rest is . . . added footage that has nothing to do with me."

"Have you ever been involved in a shooting while on duty?" Tomasetti asks.

Gina shakes her head. "I've had to draw my weapon two or three times in all the years I've been a cop, but I've never fired a shot. Not once."

"You upload your bodycam footage after every shift?" I ask.

"Of course I do. It's policy. It's routine. Easy to do. Never had a reason not to comply." As she speaks, despondence and hopelessness leach into her expression. "That footage is damning. I don't see how I can overcome it." She says the words in a monotone, as if suddenly realizing it's the last nail in a coffin that is now sealed. "Bodycam footage is indisputable."

I look at Tomasetti. "Can bodycam footage be authenticated?" I ask. "Forensically?"

"There's an authentication process," he tells me. "BCI is contracted with an image-forensics expert out of Bowling Green. We've used them a dozen times in the last four or five years. They're good." He frowns. "We've never encountered dashcam or bodycam footage that's been altered."

"I guess there's a first time for everything," Gina mutters.

"Especially when it comes to you," he says nastily.

"How do we go about getting it authenticated?" I ask.

"There are procedures in place," he says. "Protections. In some cases, we've had to get court orders. In some jurisdictions, videos fall into the 'personnel records' classification, which means they're private. Some of the unions have gotten involved."

I can tell by the way Tomasetti's looking at me that he's concerned about the ongoing and open investigation. The one his superior refused to discuss and purportedly involves someone in the upper echelon of the Columbus Division of Police. Because of the sensitive nature of it, we didn't tell Gina.

Tomasetti scrubs a hand over his jaw. "Most departments don't keep the original recordings indefinitely."

"If the original has been destroyed or altered, I'm screwed." Gina jabs a finger in the general direction of the cell phone in Tomasetti's pocket. "If I get charged and that video gets to a courtroom, I'm going down for murder." She tosses a defiant look in my direction. "Looks like they found a way to get me out of the picture."

"The media is running with it," Tomasetti tells her. "It's getting a lot of attention. The department is under scrutiny."

"I did not shoot Eddie Cysco," she snaps. "There's got to be a way to prove it."

"I'll see if I can get that authenticated," Tomasetti tells her. "It's going to be tough. That footage is at the center of a media shitstorm and it's probably going to get worse before it gets better."

Gina sinks into a chair at the table, looking defeated. "What the hell am I supposed to do?"

Tomasetti frowns at her. "I suggest you lay low and, if it's not too much trouble, refrain from doing anything stupid."

"I think I've used up my quota of stupid," she mutters.

A moment of silence ensues. Tomasetti makes eye contact with me and then starts toward the door. Knowing there's more, something he didn't want to discuss in front of Gina, I follow. He's quiet, which likely means he's as uneasy about this as I am.

We reach the front door. He turns to me, sets his hands on my shoulders, and squeezes. When his eyes land on mine, they're troubled. I feel that same disquiet pulsing in my gut.

"Denny McNinch told me in no uncertain terms to back off," he says. "Kate, he wouldn't do that if this wasn't . . . important."

"Bigger fish to fry?" I ask.

He nods. "Whatever Colorosa is guilty of, she is not the focus of the investigation."

"You've thought that from the start." I think about that a moment. "How can that level of corruption not be the main focus?"

"They're after someone more valuable."

A quiver of uneasiness goes through me. "Bertrand? Mercer?"

He shrugs. "Someone at the top."

I tell him about the neighbor seeing a vehicle parked on the road in front of the farm last night. "He didn't know the make or model. Just thought it was odd for it to be sitting there with its headlights out, especially in light of all the snow."

"A four-wheel-drive vehicle with chains can probably get around without too much trouble," he says.

"Does anyone have eyes on Bertrand or Mercer?" I ask.

"I'll see what I can find out." His eyes latch on to mine. "Maybe you ought to get one of your guys out here to watch the place."

"Last I heard, everyone was snowed in but Mona and Glock," I tell him. "We're operating on a skeleton crew as is."

He shakes his head, looking worried. "Look, we don't have too much longer. Denny told me this thing is about to break wide open."

"Can't be soon enough," I say. "What do you think's going to happen to Gina?"

"If she's cleared of the shooting. If she's got a decent lawyer who can negotiate immunity in exchange for her testimony." He shrugs. "She might do a year or two. With everything that's going on, it's hard to say."

"A lot of ifs."

"Yeah."

"I think she's ready for this to be over." I sigh. "Me, too."

His expression softens. "Homesick?"

"Sick of snow."

Turning to me, he raises his hand, brushes his knuckles against my cheek. "Think you can handle another day or two here?"

"Well, now that I've dumped the Gentleman Jack, I'm not so sure."

He smiles. "I thought the both of you were looking a little rough around the edges."

"I'll take the fifth on that."

He leans close and presses a kiss to my mouth. "I'm going to try to make another trip to Columbus in the morning. I've got a couple of meetings lined up."

"Keep me posted."

"You know I will," he says. "In the interim, keep your eyes open. Keep your pistol handy. And don't let Colorosa out of your sight."

CHAPTER 26

Live your life with God's goodness and you'll never fear the past.

It was one of my *mamm*'s favorite sayings, and I heard it a hundred times growing up. It basically means if you live your life the right way, you'll never regret something you did in the past. I didn't appreciate the wisdom of those words until I was well into adulthood. In light of the situation with Gina, the things she's done, the people she's hurt, and the uncertainty of her future, the saying has taken on a much more fateful meaning.

I have no idea how all of this is going to be resolved. There's no doubt in my mind that Gina is guilty of serious wrongdoing, that she broke the law. To what degree, I don't know. Even now, I'm not convinced she's being one hundred percent honest with me—or with herself.

I check my cell for the dozenth time, finally tossing it onto the sofa in frustration. Tomasetti left just two hours ago and already I'm anxious for news. Adam and the children harnessed Big Jimmy earlier and took the sleigh to deliver firewood to Mr. Yoder. I've kept myself busy, checking departmental email and returning calls, but I'm restless and antsy. I'm tired of being stuck here, away from my own life and the police station where everything seems to make a little more sense—and I have some semblance of control.

I cruised out to some of the local newspaper and television-station websites on my phone. Sure enough, all the major media outlets are carrying the released bodycam footage that ostensibly shows Gina gunning down an unarmed Eddie Cysco. According to reports, the video was released without the knowledge or consent of the police department. In the hours since, the footage has garnered a great deal of attention—and outrage, from citizens and activist groups alike. The television stations in Columbus are reporting that the Columbus Division of Police chief will be giving a press conference at noon.

Is it possible one or more individuals was able to get their hands on archived bodycam footage? Were they able to modify it or splice it with unrelated footage so that the result shows something completely different from what actually occurred? With so many layers of security and checks-and-balances systems in place, is it even a feasible scenario?

Too restless to sit, I scoop up my cell and go to the kitchen. Gina's not there, so I take the hall to the sewing room. A low rise of alarm goes through me when I find the room vacant, her coat and boots missing. I jog back down the hall and go through the kitchen. In the mudroom, I slip my coat off a hook, jam my feet into my boots, and head out the door.

Cold punches me hard enough to take my breath as I descend the steps. Heavy snow wafts down from a low sky the color of steel. I glance toward the barn to see the big sliding door standing open and footprints leading that way. Flipping up the hood on my parka, I follow them.

The smells of horses and hay, and the lingering redolence of cattle, hover on the cold, still air when I enter the barn. The sleigh is parked against the wall to my left. Down the aisle ahead, the three children surround Big Jimmy, brushing his thick winter coat, running a comb through his mane. Gina's F-150 is parked beneath the stairs to my right. She's kneeling at the front bumper, using a coil of baling wire to secure the damaged hood. Adam stands at the passenger door, his hands in his pockets, watching her.

"What are you doing?" I ask her as I approach.

"Wiring the hood to the bumper so the damn thing stays closed." Frowning, she goes back to the task at hand. "Don't try to stop me."

"Wouldn't dream of it." Of course, that's exactly what I have to do. Not only is it impossible for her to get around without tire chains and four-wheel drive, but with her being part of an ongoing investigation, it's my responsibility to keep her here by whatever means necessary. Still, my gut tells me this will be settled a lot more easily if I let her figure that out on her own.

"I don't think you'll be able to get down the lane," Adam says, not so helpfully.

Giving him an I-got-this look, I go to her and kneel. "Does it even run?"

"I reattached the battery cable," she grumbles. "It runs fine."

She reaches for the other end of the wire, misses. I lean forward and grab it, pull it tight. She takes it from me and, using the fencing pliers, proceeds to twist the two ends together.

"Where are you going, anyway?" I ask.

The fencing pliers in her hand stills, and she gives me a scathing look over her shoulder. "Back to Columbus. To get this handled. Someone has to."

"That sounds like a solid plan," I say dryly.

"I'll figure it out."

"Since there's a warrant for your arrest," I add, "my guess is they'll welcome you with open arms."

"Go ahead, Kate. Make light of it." Using the pliers, grimacing with the difficulty of her task, she twists the wire, securing the hood latch to the bumper, and then snips off the excess. "Someone's got to do something. BCI Boy seems more interested in busting my balls."

"Tomasetti is the best friend you've got right now," I tell her.

"I can't stay here and do nothing." She looks away from her work, meets my gaze, and the underlying implication of the statement isn't lost on me. "Sooner or later they're going to figure out where I am—if they haven't already. They're going to come for me. If something goes down . . . if this goes bad . . ." The words trail, her eyes sliding in the general direction of the children and back to me. "I don't want that on me."

I look at Adam, wondering if he has asked her to leave.

Recognizing my unspoken question, the Amish man nods. "She is welcome to stay for as long as she needs."

"You don't get it." She gives Adam a hard look. "I'm not going to sugarcoat it because you're Amish."

Adam frowns. "I understand more than you realize," he says quietly. "Different doesn't mean dumb, Gina. It doesn't mean I don't understand the ways of the world. You would be a wiser person if you remembered that." It's the first admonition he's given her since she arrived, and it stings even me.

Gina gets to her feet, brushes dust and bits of straw from her coat, and divides her attention between the two of us. "These men are violent. They have no conscience. No heart." She looks past Adam, at the children, unapologetic. "They don't care about collateral damage."

The Amish man starts to say something, but she cuts him off. "My being here could place you and your family in danger. I'm not going to let that happen."

She studies her handiwork, where the wire dangles over the radiator and the truck hood isn't closed quite right, and sighs. "I have to go. I don't have a choice."

This time, Adam doesn't try to stop her.

I think about the viability of taking her to the farm where Tomasetti and I live via snowmobile or even checking her into a motel. While she would be facing the same danger, such a move would at least assure us that the children weren't at risk.

"Gina." I say her name gently. "Even if you could make it to the highway—which you can't—going back to Columbus isn't going to solve anything. In fact, it would likely make things worse. And it could be dangerous for you."

"I can't sit around and do nothing. Not my style. This has to end."

"We'll end it. But we have to do it the right way. At the right time. Not like this. You can't do it alone."

"I'm it, Kate. It's my neck on the chopping block and I plan to do everything in my power to save it."

"You don't even have a plan."

"Before this latest fiasco, I thought I might be able to take what I know to the media. I've gotten to know a couple of journalists over the years. People who know me. People who're interested in the truth." She raps her palm against the hood. "With the leak of the phony video, that option is off the table."

"Gina, let Tomasetti do his job. He's good at what he does."

"Katie is right." Adam's gaze falls on Gina. "You cannot stop these men with guns on your own. Not alone."

"My being here could place you and your family in danger," she hisses, more forcefully this time.

"God will watch over us," he tells her. "That is the one thing I know for certain."

Her face softens and for the first time since she arrived, bleeding and hypothermic, her eyes mist. "I don't have your faith, Adam."

The Amish man looks down at his hands, then raises his gaze

to hers. “Standing your ground is easier when you are grounded in God’s word.”

The three of us fall silent; I’m aware of the chatter of the children and the patter of snow against the tin roof of the barn. After a moment, I cross to the truck, set my hand on the fender. “Gina, the secondary roads are impassable. If we’re unable to get around, everyone else is unable to get around. At the very least that buys us some time. A day or two, at which point we can take you to the farm until this thing comes to a head.”

“For God’s sake.” Throwing up her hand in frustration, Gina flings the pliers to the ground. They thump to the dirt floor a foot or so from the truck and bounce away.

Adam and I watch her stalk away.

Raising his brows, he looks at me. “I think that means we won the argument, no?”

Before I can answer, Gina spins and strides back to us. “Tell BCI Boy to stay the hell off my back.”

“Tell him yourself.” I look at Adam. “He’s bringing pizza for dinner. Pepperoni okay?”

She pops a middle finger at us.

The Amish man grins.

CHAPTER 27

Damon Bertrand had never been much of a drinker. He partook in the occasional draft. A glass of wine with a steak dinner. Unlike many of his law enforcement cohorts, he never fell to hitting the bottle. Tonight, stuck in a dumpy motel with nothing to do but contemplate the advisability of what they were about to do, was enough to make even the most steadfast teetotaler crave the hard stuff.

He and Mercer had devoted the day to making preparations. In light of the weather and poor road conditions, they'd made a trip to the Walmart in Millersburg, an excursion that entailed three hours of creeping along barely passable roads littered with abandoned vehicles and blocked by behemoth piles of snow left by plows. There, they bought two shovels, half a dozen bags of sand, and a couple of heavy-duty tug straps. He'd sprung for a winch that had cost him a week's salary. He figured the peace of mind was worth it. Now, the gas tank was full. The tire chains were in place. He had the warrant in hand. All they had to do was wait.

It was the one thing he'd never been good at, especially when something big was about to go down. He was agitated. On edge. Nervous because he would be risking everything on an operation that, if it didn't go as planned, had the power to destroy his career, everything he'd ever worked for, maybe even his life.

In the last hours, he and Mercer had gone over their strategy a hundred times. They'd anticipated every variable, thinking outside the box, letting each one play out a dozen ways. Bertrand had considered every option, including the idea of scrapping the entire operation. He always went back to the only one he knew would work, because at the end of the day it was him or Colorosa.

It was seven P.M. when the motel room door swung open, ushering in a burst of wind-driven snow. Mercer thrust himself into the room, a cardboard tray of fast food and drinks in hand. "Frickin' snow." It caked his parka and slacks. He stomped ice from his boots as he walked to the desk and set down the tray. His eyes flicked to the TV, which was tuned to cable news.

"Anything new?" he said as he worked the parka from his shoulders and tossed it onto the bed.

"Every TV station in Columbus picked up the story," Bertrand told him. "Colorosa's a star."

"Bad PR for the department."

"It'll blow over. Always does."

The two men dug through the bag, removed burgers and fries. There was a sofa and coffee table in the room, so they set up shop there and began to eat.

"Monaghan has his hands full," Bertrand said, referring to their deputy chief.

"Does he know where we are?" Mercer asked.

"He knows enough not to ask any questions."

"He's on board?"

"He's counting on us to get it done. He got us the warrant. The rest is up to us."

Mercer pulled out his cell, checked the time. "We still set for midnight?"

Bertrand had been thinking about the timing. "Since Burkholder is likely there, and potentially both of them are armed, catching them unaware will be an advantage. I say we go in at one A.M."

Mercer nodded. "All right."

"We leave here at twelve thirty. Take our time. Allow for any problems along the way."

"They're not going to be expecting anyone in this weather."

"Exactly." Bertrand took a bite of burger, chewed thoughtfully, swallowed. "We go in fast and hard. No knock. We secure Colorosa first. We do not cuff her. We get her on the floor. We do, however, cuff Lengacher. We put him and the kids in a bedroom."

Bertrand dragged a fry through ketchup. "I want you with Burkholder. Separate her from Colorosa. While you're checking her ID and getting things straightened out—and I'm in the other room with Colorosa—I'll get it done." He chews, not tasting the food, not looking at Mercer. "Colorosa pulls a gun. Fires it at me. I've no choice but to use deadly force."

"What if Burkholder doesn't cooperate?" Mercer asked.

"Keep in mind, to the best of our knowledge the chief of police is aiding and abetting a fugitive. If she doesn't cooperate, we cuff her. Above everything, we get her out of the room. If the chief is smart, she'll do as she's told." He looked at Mercer. "We do not want problems with Burkholder. Remember, people love small-town cops. They grew up watching Andy Griffith, for God's sake. Something happens to her *and* Colorosa, and we are going to be on the hot seat."

Visualizing the scene, Bertrand took a bite of burger and chewed. "So, we separate them. Put Burkholder in one room. The family in another. I'll take care of Colorosa. I'll plant the throw-down." Now that he'd laid it out, it seemed almost doable.

"Still can't figure why Burkholder didn't call this in or make the arrest," Mercer said. "Especially in light of the bodycam footage."

Burkholder's lack of action had been bothering Bertrand, too. It was one of too many unknowns. He felt marginally better about the whole thing now that they'd "leaked" the video. It established Colorosa as a cold-blooded killer, a dirty cop with no compunction about gunning down an innocent person. It was the impetus that would see them through the endless investigations that would follow her death—and go a long way toward greasing the road to vindication.

"Nothing we can do about it now," he said. "We proceed as planned. Don't take anything for granted."

"Maybe the chief is as dirty as her old friend," Mercer said. "Colorosa shows up out of nowhere with a sob story and the promise of fast money. Maybe the good chief decided she wanted a piece of the pie."

"Good reason for us not to have reached out to her department," Bertrand said. "As far as we know, we've stumbled upon a corrupt small-town cop."

"What about the sheriff's department?" Mercer asked.

"I'll give them a heads-up. But we go in before they arrive on scene. By the time they do, we'll have the situation under control." He shrugged. "It's not a perfect scenario."

"Nothing we can't deal with." Mercer resumed eating.

Bertrand was still thinking about Burkholder. "We're going in blind, Ken. If the good chief causes problems, if she doesn't stand down or she does something stupid, she goes the way of Colorosa."

CHAPTER 28

Supper at an Amish home is a relaxed occasion in which the work of the day is discussed and household decisions are made. A place at the kitchen table symbolizes belonging, being part of the family unit. Adam sits at the head of the table. The three children sit to his left, in order of age, the youngest closest to him. There's no place setting for Leah Lengacher, but the chair to Adam's right is unoccupied, its bareness not acknowledged, but keenly felt.

Tomasetti arrives with pizza at seven P.M. It's late; most Amish generally eat an early supper, around five P.M. or so. But due to the road conditions, the drive from Painters Mill took him longer than he'd intended.

The children are excited by the prospect of pizza. Most Amish meals are homemade, but they are not strangers to contemporary foods. Fast food—or even junk food—is a treat.

The aromas of yeast and onions and pepperoni fill the kitchen when Tomasetti sets two flat cardboard boxes in the center of the table. While the two men engage in a quick haggle over payment, and Adam tries to force a couple of twenty-dollar bills on an uncooperative Tomasetti, Annie and Gina set out paper plates, forks, and folded paper towels. Lizzie and I set to work on the drinks.

Tomasetti sets a six-pack of Pepsi in the center of the table. "Can't have pizza without pop."

"I love pop!" Sammy exclaims as he takes his place.

"*Gebet Vor Dem Essen seahsht,*" Adam says. The Prayer before Meal first.

Tomasetti and I sit to Adam's right, leaving the chair next to him vacant. Once everyone is seated, heads are bowed for a moment of silent prayer and I find myself silently reciting the Lord's Prayer in German, something I haven't done for years. Next comes the Prayer before Meal, which is from a prayer book titled *Christenpflicht,* and is also most often recited silently. But because Tomasetti and I are present, Adam recites the prayer aloud.

"*Oh Herr Gott, himmlischer Vater, Segne uns und Diese Deine Gaben, die wir von Deiner milden Güte zu uns nehmen werden. Speise und tranke auch unsere Seelen zum ewigen Leben, und mach uns theilhaftig Deines himmleschen Tisches durch Jesus Christum. Amen.*"

O Lord God, heavenly Father, bless us and these thy gifts, which we shall accept from thy tender goodness. Give us food and drink also for our souls unto life eternal, and make us partakers of thy heavenly table through Jesus Christ. Amen.

"All right then." Adam rubs his hands together. "Let's see what we have here."

The boxes are opened. I hear the quick intake of breaths as the children lean forward, anxious to see the treasure inside.

"Cheese!" Annie exclaims with the glee that only a five-year-old can manage.

"A girl of my own heart," Gina mutters as she loads two slices onto her plate.

"And it's all bubbly," Lizzie adds, a hint of awe in her voice.

"What are those?" Sammy points at a small plastic cup filled with sliced jalapeños.

"An instant of regret, but worth the pain," Tomasetti tells him.

At Sammy's puzzled look, we adults break into laughter.

It's times like this when I'm reminded that John Tomasetti was the father of two children. He's been through the sleepless nights of having a newborn in the house, the teething, the terrible twos, the first day of kindergarten, and all the trials and tribulations of early childhood. Losing them in such a violent way nearly destroyed him. Healing has been an ongoing process, but he's come a long way since those early days. Watching him with these sweet children, I feel the beat of my own biological clock.

For the next hour, the six of us pile pizza onto our plates and dig in. Adam updates us on the status of the calf that had been abandoned by its cow. "Mama likes him just fine now. He's nursing with no problems."

"He's bigger already!" Sammy tells us.

"Datt says that's because you fed him too much milk," Lizzie says.

"He wouldn't stop eating," Sammy defends.

"Kind of like someone else we know," Adam says, grinning at his son.

Suddenly shy, Sammy looks down at his pizza.

"Mamm always said Sammy would eat his plate, too, if he could get it in his mouth," Lizzie says.

Laughter rings out around the table. It's a good sound that reminds me of simpler times, of years past. My own table growing up was never quite as upbeat; my parents were strict, and oftentimes supper was a somber occasion. But there was laughter, too, and the memory puts an ache just behind my ribs.

"Tomorrow, you and I will cut wood for the stove," Adam says to his son. "It's been cold, so I thought we'd load as much as we can into the sleigh and take it over to the widow Borntrager." He glances at his eldest daughter. "Maybe you girls could make some bread for her. Or cornmeal mush?"

Looking a little too thoughtful for her seven years, Lizzie nods. "How about zucchini bread, Datt? We've over twenty jars of zucchini in the cellar. I counted."

Adam nods. "Zucchini bread it is then." He looks at Tomasetti. "Any idea when the weather's going to break?"

"Snow is supposed to stop sometime tonight."

Taking the final bite of pizza, Gina blots her mouth, and slants a look at Adam. "That means I'll probably be out of your hair tomorrow afternoon."

Adam stares at her for a too-long moment. "What will happen next?"

She meets his gaze and holds it. "I tell my story to the police. Hopefully they'll listen."

"Whatever that story is, peace will find you if you let the truth lead the way." The Amish man shifts his gaze to Tomasetti. "You'll help her, no?"

"I'll do what I can," he replies.

Reaching out, little Annie sets her hand over Gina's. "Me and Lizzie will make a zucchini bread for you, too, Gina. That way, at least you won't get hungry."

When the meal is finished and the two girls are washing dishes, I walk with Tomasetti to the door. He's holding his helmet at his side, already dressed in the snowsuit.

"The pizza was a nice treat." Standing on my tiptoes, I press a kiss to his mouth. "I miss you."

Even before I pull away, I sense the shift of our thoughts, our focus, and I know the situation with Gina is at the forefront of our minds.

Setting his hands on my shoulders, Tomasetti looks down at me. "I'll be here in the morning to take Colorosa to the BCI office in London. Denny McNinch will be there, along with an assistant prosecutor from Franklin County and a special agent with the investigations unit of BCI. She's going to need a lawyer, so if she hasn't taken care of that yet, she needs to make some calls first thing in the morning." He grimaces. "Kate, she needs to cooperate in every way."

"She will." My mind is already jumping ahead. "I suspect at some point, she'll be placed under arrest and taken into custody."

He nods. "She'll be charged. Arraigned. She's going to go to jail, Kate. She needs to be prepared for that."

I'd known it would happen. Of course I did. Still, it doesn't make the reality any easier to swallow. "General population?"

"Because of the nature of the case and that she was a cop, probably not. At least initially." He grimaces. "Kate, this is a large-scale investigation that's only going to get bigger. It's going to be far-reaching and it's going to get ugly. If the feds aren't already involved, they will be. Colorosa can't talk about any of this. Let her know that, too."

"I will," I reply, understanding all too well what the next twenty-four hours will entail.

He continues to stare at me, his expression softening, and I see compassion in his eyes. "Look, I'm not a big fan of Colorosa. She's exactly the kind of cop that makes all of us look bad. But I know you care about her. I'm sorry for that. But there's no other way. She's got to come in. She's got to tell her story."

I nod, not quite trusting my voice to speak.

Raising his hand, he touches the side of my face, leans close and presses a kiss to my mouth. "The meeting isn't until afternoon. Roads should be passable by then. I'll be here late morning to pick her up."

He pulls the helmet on and buckles it at his chin. "Night." He goes through the door and disappears into the lightly falling snow.

I find Gina sitting at the kitchen table, a glass of cola in front of her. She looks up when I enter, tries for bravado, but she's unable to hold my gaze. "I guess tomorrow is D-day, huh?"

I walk to the table, pull out the chair across from her, and sit. "Tomasetti has pulled together a team to meet with you." I tell her the agencies involved. "It's a start. It'll get things rolling."

"He say anything about immunity?"

"No."

She nods, her expression telling me she didn't expect a different answer. "I'll be arrested?"

"Probably."

She nods, having known that, too. "Booked into County?"

"Until they can figure out what to do with you. I don't know about bail. You'll likely have to wait for your arraignment or bail hearing." I look around, not for the first time regretting that I dumped that bottle of Gentleman Jack. "Gina, I wish there was another way."

"I could always hightail it to Mexico." The laugh that follows is cold and rough.

"It's the best we can do. The rest is up to you and the system. The courts."

Finally, she raises her gaze to mine. "I'm sorry for dragging you into this."

"I'm glad we got to reconnect. I wish the circumstances were different."

"I'm ready to be done with this, Kate," she tells me. "Get it over with. Whatever happens, whatever the future holds, good or bad, it's got to be better than this . . . limbo."

Even as she makes the statement, we both know there are no guarantees. She's facing a multitude of serious charges and could possibly spend years behind bars. Her career is finished, her reputation forever tainted. She'll never work in law enforcement in any capacity again.

We fall silent, thoughtful, both of us feeling more than is prudent. The truth of the matter is there's nothing left to say. No comfort to be had.

Rising, I set my hand on her shoulder. "Get some sleep," I tell her, knowing it's the one thing neither of us will do tonight.

And I walk away.

CHAPTER 29

They left the motel at twelve thirty A.M. The snow had stopped at some point. A heavy-lidded moon gazed down at them from an infinite black sky. The wind was nearly calm, and the temperature hovered somewhere in the teens. Bertrand couldn't remember the last time he'd been so edgy. Usually before a raid or the execution of a no-knock warrant, he was pumped up and ready to go.

This was different. This time, there was more risk, more at stake. He didn't have the rest of the team to back him. No SWAT. No cops standing around, hoping for some action. And there were so damn many things that could go wrong. When that was the case, something usually did.

Road conditions were still hazardous. All over town, vehicles were stuck in drifts and abandoned. Piles of snow left by the plows were ten feet high on both sides of the road. At nearly every intersection, they had to break through a foot or so of residual ice and snow left by the blade.

Bertrand cut the headlights as he made the turn onto the township road. Moonlight glinted off the snow, offering just enough light to see the road. He stopped the SUV in front of the Lengacher place, the same spot they'd parked the night before. He could feel his heart beating against the Kevlar vest he'd cinched tight beneath his coat.

"No lights inside," Mercer muttered from the passenger seat.

"Barns are dark," Bertrand said, squinting into the darkness.

They'd put the shotgun in the backseat. Both men carried pistols. Bertrand had the warrant tucked into his shirt pocket beneath his coat. He'd called the Holmes County Sheriff's Department at just before midnight. He'd apprised the deputy of "the situation" and told him they would be serving the warrant "around twelve." The deputy, believing he meant at noon the next day, agreed to have the sheriff call him back "ASAP." Bertrand had also mentioned Kate Burkholder, telling him she would likely be at the scene. He didn't know the whole story there. Seed planted. Everything under control. Time to move.

The lane to the Lengacher farm hadn't been cleared and the snow was too deep for any vehicle to navigate. The neighboring farm was a quarter mile away and there weren't many trees between the homes for cover, so Bertrand idled down the road a ways and parked in the shadows beneath a stand of trees. He shut down the engine.

"You got the throw-down?" he asked.

Mercer unzipped his coat pocket, withdrew a pistol bundled in a hand towel, and unwrapped it. "Picked it up at a bust last year. Serial number is filed off. Never been logged in to Evidence."

Bertrand knew his weapons. Even in the semidark, he recognized it as a Smith & Wesson .380. A common gun. Cheap. Accessible. This one couldn't be traced.

"Give it to me," he said, and dropped it into his coat pocket.

He pulled out his own sidearm, a Glock 22 he'd carried for years. He checked the clip, made sure there was a round in the chamber, and shoved it into his other pocket. Mercer handed him a mini Maglite, a smaller version than the one he kept in his cruiser, which made it easier to carry. The large ones, after all, doubled as a billy club if you needed it.

"Keep your eyes open," Bertrand said, and got out of the vehicle.

The two men stood outside on the road for a minute, looking for anything out of place, listening. Around them, the night was so hushed Bertrand could hear the steady thrum of his heart.

"I guess this is it," Mercer said, his breath puffing out in front of his face.

"Let's get this over with," Bertrand said.

The two men started toward the mouth of the lane.

CHAPTER 30

I'd been a cop for four years the night I found out my best friend wasn't the person I thought she was. That she was keeping secrets. That there was more to her than I'd ever imagined—and not all of it was good. Initially, I wanted to believe she'd taken some bad advice, conceded to impulse, or made a wrong decision somewhere along the way. Or maybe someone had pressured her into doing something she didn't want to do. Hey, maybe she'd simply fallen in with the wrong crowd.

Wishful thinking all.

Everyone knew there were a few rogue cops among us. Patrol officers and detectives who pushed the boundaries of departmental policy, not quite breaking the law but skating the line. The ones who partook in activities that would be frowned upon by the brass—and get you fired if you didn't have the aptitude for a promotion or the solve rate to back you up.

I wanted to believe anything except the truth that had been staring me in the face for months now—and threatened to crush the friendship I'd held dear since the night I wandered into that diner looking for food and walked out with the best friend I'd ever had.

We were working second shift by then and it was the night before my weekend, which happened to fall on Monday and Tuesday.

It was July, and Gina and I had planned a trip to Cleveland and Lake Erie for three unencumbered days of sun and fun on the beach—and whatever else we could get into. It was an hour before quitting time and a slow night to boot. Gina had called earlier to cancel the post-shift dinner we'd planned. She was helping out some task force guys working in an area that abutted my zone. My beat was slow, I had half an hour left on my shift, so I headed that way to pass the time.

I found her at McWhorter Transmission & Parts, a known chop shop, tucked between a salvage yard and an abandoned building near Franklinton. It was a low-slung blue metal building with two big overhead doors in front, a couple of windows, and a smaller personnel door marked OFFICE.

Two Crown Vics and an unmarked vehicle were parked in the alley. The double overhead doors were closed, but I could see lights blazing in the window. Gina's patrol vehicle was parked in a small side lot. It occurred to me that this was a bit of an odd scene. Gina had mentioned some kind of raid and yet no emergency lights flashed on any of the vehicles. I brushed off the thought, assuming the LEOs had been on scene awhile and were finishing up. I parked next to Gina's vehicle and started toward the building.

The door stood open a foot or so. I identified myself as I entered, but there was no one there, which was another oddity. Usually, during and after a raid or bust, the target building was crawling with law enforcement. Puzzled, I took the narrow hall to a front office of sorts with a beat-up desk, a computer and printer, and a fifty-two-inch flat-screen mounted on the wall. An old Lynyrd Skynyrd tune jangled the live version of "Freebird" from a sleek sound system atop the desk.

"Colorosa!" I called out.

No response.

I'd just reached for my cell to call her when I heard voices coming from the garage section of the building at the rear. Male voices. Raised as if in argument. Ahead, another door stood ajar, light bleeding through the gap. I'd just put my hand on the knob when I heard some sort of physical confrontation.

Even as I shoved open the door, I sensed that something wasn't right with the scene. The serving of a warrant, especially if it was a no-knock, required planning. Once entry was made, there were typically a lot of cops present, including SWAT and many times a sergeant or lieutenant. The scene I walked into had none of those things.

I called out Gina's name as I treaded down the hall toward the garage area. I saw overhead work lights. Ahead, the steel shaft of a car lift. The front end of a wrecked Honda Accord. I was keenly aware of my .38 pressing against my hip as I went through the door. I took in a dozen details at once. To my right, two plainclothes cops stood in front of a male subject, his hands cuffed behind his back. The man's face was bloodied, scraggly blond hair, his shirt nearly torn from his body. Ahead, a uniformed patrol officer leaned against a nice-looking Toyota, his arms crossed, toothpick in his mouth, staring at me. I glanced left to see Gina and a young man in grease-stained coveralls standing at the counter. A small, newish cash register stood open in front of them. She looked up, spotted me, and visibly jolted. Surprise. A mishmash of emotions I couldn't quite read flashed across her face.

For the span of several heartbeats, I stood there, knowing in my heart what I'd walked into, my brain scrambling for explanations that suited the narrative I wanted to believe.

Gina started toward me. "Kate . . ."

"What's going on?" I managed.

The two officers who'd been beating the man looked at me, expressions impassive. Unmoved by my presence. Annoyed that I had the gall to interrupt.

The older of the two detectives started toward me, his eyes flicking to my badge. "You're a long way from your subdivision," he said.

I'd seen him around the precinct a few times. A dozen names scrolled through my memory, but I couldn't recall it. He stopped a couple of feet from me, gave me a once-over. "What are you doing here?"

"I'm looking for Colorosa."

"You found her." He motioned toward Gina. "As you can see, she's busy. So get lost."

I'd been a cop long enough to take the insolence in stride. I'd learned early on that most cops don't pull any punches when it comes to driving home a point to some underling. If you can get it done with some badass attitude or humiliate someone in the process, all the better.

I knew first impressions weren't always right. But I'd learned to trust my gut. I knew what I'd walked into, and I was rattled by it.

The garage went silent, save for the tail end of "Freebird" wafting out from the front office. I looked around to find everyone staring at me, their expressions running the gamut from amused to annoyed to downright hostile. When I looked at Gina, her eyes skittered away from mine.

What the hell?

I looked at the man who'd been beaten. He was bent at the hip, a string of bloody drool nearly reaching the floor, immersed in his own misery. I turned my attention back to the cop who'd approached me. "What happened to him?" I asked.

"We executed a warrant." He motioned toward the bloodied man. "Cool Hand Luke there decided he didn't have to cooperate, so we reminded him that he does."

I kept my eyes on the detective, but I was keenly aware of all the other eyes in the room on me. The guy-wire tension running between my shoulder blades. It was the first time in the course of my career that I felt I was being lied to about something important by a fellow cop. I didn't believe this detective. Worse, I didn't trust him. Judging from the length of bloodied air hose in his hand, he was as far outside police protocols as I'd ever seen.

"Looks like you have everything under control." I turned my attention to Gina. "You got a minute?"

The detective's teeth ground. He stepped toward me. "Why don't you be a good little rookie and get the fuck out of my crime scene?"

I held my ground, but my knees had begun to shake. I stared at him, my heart pounding. I didn't know what to say or how to react. This was one scenario the academy didn't prepare me for.

After a moment, he raised his hand and stabbed his index finger into my chest. "Out. Now."

No one said anything. No one moved. Gina held her ground at the cash register.

I backed up a step, made up for the lost ground by swatting his hand away. "See you around."

Taking a final look at Gina, I turned and started for the door.

We never made it to the lake that weekend. When my shift ended, I went home, packed my things, and moved out. It was one of the most painful things I'd ever had to do, but I'd realized she wasn't going to change. A few weeks later, I heard through the grapevine that she'd filed a complaint with Internal Affairs against the detectives on scene that night. I'd almost gone to her to rekindle the friendship that meant so much to me. In the end, I let it go, hoping the incident had set her on the straight and narrow.

I didn't hear anything else about Gina or the things that went down that night, and I never saw her again.

CHAPTER 31

I bolt upright, my breaths coming fast. For an instant, I'm back in that warehouse. The dream scampers back into its hole, but the pain lingers. I'm not sure what woke me. Not the dream. My heart is pounding. The back of my neck is sticky with sweat. My hands aren't quite steady.

Around me, the air is cold and pitch black and for a moment I don't remember where I am. Then I hear the rustle of wind outside the window, the scrape of branches against the glass. The hiss of the woodstove in the corner, and everything that's happened in the last forty-eight hours comes flooding back.

I'm on the sofa in the living room of Adam Lengacher's farmhouse. I relax back into my pillow, staring into the darkness, listening. Whatever sound jerked me awake doesn't come again. I reach for my cell on the coffee table, check the time. Almost one A.M.

"Great," I mutter, knowing sleep will not come again.

Moonlight slants in through the windows, diluted light dancing on the floor, telling me the snow has stopped. I wonder if Gina is awake, too, dreading the day ahead, bothered by the unknowns, and everything she faces in the coming weeks. I'm thinking about checking on her, seeing if she wants some company, when a sound from the front porch gives me pause. Something moving around outside. A raccoon raiding the bird feeder the girls hung on the eave? A deer nibbling the seed strewn about on the ground? Another part of my brain lands on a darker possibility.

I sit up, swivel, set my feet on the floor. I'm reaching for the Maglite I keep next to the sofa when the door explodes inward, swings wide, bangs against the wall. The sound is a thunderclap. Glass shatters, tinkling onto the plank floor. In an instant, I'm on my feet, bringing up the Maglite. Simultaneously, I'm blinded by dual beams.

"Police! We've got a warrant! Get your hands up! Police Department!"

Two men rush inside, shadow figures moving fast, feet heavy on the floor. It's too dark to make out details, but I see the silhouette of a shotgun. Flashlights. I feel a burst of cold air on my feet. One of the men comes at me, reaching.

I step back, bring up the Maglite, tap his hand away with it, and I blind him with the beam. "I'm a police officer!" I shout. "Show me your ID! I'm a cop!"

My mind flits to my .38 in the mudroom. I glance that way, consider making a run for it. The sound of the shotgun being racked stops me cold.

"Police! Do not move." The man keeps coming, swiftly, aggressive, shotgun leveled on my chest. "Get your hands up! Keep them where I can see them."

I raise my hands to shoulder height, train the beam of the Maglite on his face. Recognition jolts me and it's followed by a kick of disbelief. *Ken Mercer*. "What do you want?" I ask, backing up, keeping the coffee table between us. "Why are you here? Show me your IDs."

He raises his hands to shield his eyes. "Cut that fucking light."

"Get that shotgun off me," I snap back.

A thousand thoughts hit my brain at once. Are these men friend or foe? Is this a legitimate raid? Is the warrant official? Sanctioned by a judge? Or is this the scenario Gina warned me about? Is everyone in this house in danger of being gunned down like a herd of deer?

"Where's Colorosa?" comes a gruff male voice.

I glance right, see a second man approach. Large frame. Moving quickly. Pistol in his hand. Pumped up and high on adrenaline.

"Show me the warrant," I say. "Show me your IDs."

They lower their Maglites. I do the same. I can't stop looking at the shotgun, which is still leveled at my chest. For a moment, the only sound is the rise and fall of our breaths, the drumbeat of my heart against my ribs.

"Somebody turn on a fucking light," one of the men growls.

There's no doubt in my mind that Gina heard the commotion. I wonder how she'll handle this. If she'll acquiesce. She doesn't have a firearm; I've kept hers unloaded and locked up in the Explorer. Facing two armed men—one of whom is as of yet unidentified—I wonder if that decision was solid.

"There's a propane lamp in the corner," I tell them.

"Turn it on. Do it slowly. Don't do anything stupid."

The familiarity of the voice clicks, stirs a distant memory. I've heard it before. Damon Bertrand, I realize, and a mushroom cloud of fear erupts in my chest.

I go to the lamp, strike a match. I spot my cell on the table next to the sofa, reach for it.

"Put it down," Bertrand snaps.

"I'm a cop," I say.

"Now."

I do as I'm told. Turning my attention back to the lamp, I twist the key to turn on the gas, and set the match to the mantle. The dim glow of light fills the room. I turn to see Damon Bertrand standing a few feet away. Trooper hat. Heavy parka and boots. Blue polymer Glock steady in his hand. He was a detective back when I'd worked for the Columbus Division of Police. I'd only met him a few times. He's older and heavier, but the same.

Next to him, Ken Mercer stares at me as if I'm some sort of apparition. He was a patrol officer way back when. I went out with him a few times. Slept with him. Looking at him, even now I feel the sharp pang of regret. The shotgun in his hands is trained on me, center mass.

Remembrance glints in his eyes. "It's been a while," he says.

My heart pounds pure adrenaline. Fear crawling beneath my skin. I feel my hands and legs shaking. My breaths coming too fast. Muscles jumping. I can't stop thinking about Adam and the children upstairs. I know he's awake by now. I don't dare look in that direction.

"Get that shotgun off me," I snarl. "What's this about?"

"We've got a warrant for Gina Colorosa," Bertrand tells me. "Where is she?"

"She's in my custody," I tell him.

The two men exchange glances; then Mercer turns away and enters the hall. I hear his booted feet against the floor, heavy stride, opening doors. The bathroom. The sewing room. At any moment, I fear I'm going to hear a gunshot or else he's about to drag Gina out here.

"This would have been a lot easier if you'd just called my office," I say to Bertrand.

"Apparently, there's some question about your loyalties."

"You got your information wrong."

Never taking his eyes from mine, Bertrand steps past me and picks up my cell. He drops it to the floor, watches it bounce once, then crushes it beneath his boot.

I don't react. "You guys are a long way from home."

"So is Colorosa," he says.

"I need to see that warrant," I tell him.

He unzips his coat and retrieves several folded sheets of paper. Stepping closer, he passes them to me.

I scan the document, seeking anything that's amiss. I flip to the second page, my eyes hitting the highlights, the sections I'm familiar with. It's signed by a sitting judge in Franklin County. What the hell?

Mercer emerges from the hall, shotgun at his side. "Window's open," he says. "Either she's upstairs or she booked." He starts toward the stairs.

There's no way I can let him go up there. "This is my arrest," I say forcefully. "Colorosa is my charge. I'm the one who will be transporting her." I pause, struggling for calm, take a moment to shore up my voice. "You didn't get the memo?"

One side of Bertrand's mouth curves. "Warrant trumps your memo." Leaning closer, he plucks it from my hand.

"Where the hell is she?" Mercer snaps.

"She was in the sewing room down the hall," I tell him.

"That bitch ran," he says nastily.

A quick skitter of relief in my gut. Chances are, she heard them coming and went out the window. A silent laugh flares inside me. I hope she gives them a run for their money.

"We need to go get her," Mercer says.

Bertrand looks at me. "Is she armed?"

"Of course she's not armed," I retort. "She's under arrest."

His eyes glitter. "What about you?"

"I'm a cop and you need to back the hell off." I let my eye slide to the stairs. "This is a private residence with children. My sidearm—as well as Colorosa's—are locked in the glove box of my city-issue Explorer—which is stuck in the snow, by the way. The weather is the only reason she hasn't already been booked in." I put some attitude into my voice to cover the lies. While Gina's Sig Sauer is, indeed, locked in the Explorer, my .38 lies on the top shelf of the mudroom cabinet.

"Katie?"

The three of us swivel to see Adam coming down the stairs. Behind him, Sammy and Lizzie crouch at the landing, holding the rails like jail bars, staring down at us, their faces curious and frightened.

"Everything's okay," I tell him, hoping he sees the truth in my eyes. "These men are police. They're going to help me find Gina and then we're going to take her to Columbus. Adam, I need you to go back upstairs. Stay with the children. *Du sinn in kfoah,*" I add quickly. You are in danger.

Bertrand is already across the room, pointing at the Amish man. "Come on down here and talk to us, buddy."

Relief skitters through me when Adam looks back at the children. "*Bleiva,*" he tells them. Stay put. He descends the stairs, his eyes moving from Bertrand to Mercer to me. He approaches us with caution, taking in the broken panes of the front door. The glass on the floor.

His eyes skate to Bertrand. "If you'd knocked, I would have let you in."

"Sorry about the door. We were just following procedure. We'll get it fixed for you." Bertrand hands Adam the warrant. "This is an arrest warrant for Gina Colorosa. We have permission to search your house, outbuildings, and property. It would help if you just told us where she is."

At well over six feet, Adam is taller than both men. He's well-muscled and in good physical condition. Watching Mercer take his measure, I wonder if they realize the Amish man is a pacifist. That even if threatened, he would not defend himself or his home.

I edge closer to Adam, look down at the warrant. The knowledge that it is an official document signed by a sitting judge doesn't alleviate the uneasiness pummeling the back of my brain. I don't trust these men. If my gut is correct, I suspect they're going to take Gina back to Columbus on a trumped-up charge. If something happens to her in the course of the arrest or the trip, all the better.

I look at Bertrand. "You ran off my prisoner," I tell him.

The detective stares back at me, watchdog eyes, weighing my words, my demeanor, judging me. *Trying to figure out how much of a problem I'm going to be.*

"We need to find Colorosa," Mercer says.

"I agree," I say.

Bertrand laser-focuses on me. "You didn't tell anyone you had her in custody. Why is that?"

I meet his gaze, hold it. "I called BCI within ten minutes of taking her into custody. Not my problem that no one called you." I motion with my eyes to Mercer. "We need to find her. She's cuffed," I lie. "She can't have gotten far."

Bertrand looks at Mercer, then motions with his eyes to Adam. "Cuff him. Let's search the house."

I start to protest, but realize I'm more likely to win their trust if I don't. "Mr. Lengacher is not a threat," I say.

Mercer passes the shotgun to Bertrand, then removes zip ties from his belt and approaches Adam. "We're going to detain you, sir. For your safety and ours. Just stay calm and do as I say." A line directly from the procedure playbook.

"*Datt!*" I look toward the stairs to see Sammy fly down them, taking two at a time. The two girls are behind him, nightgowns billowing at their feet as they descend. "Datt!"

The children reach the base of the stairs. Stocking feet sliding on the wood floor, Sammy pivots, runs to his father.

"Samuel." Adam barely has time to brace when the boy flings himself into his father's arms. The Amish man wraps his arms around his son. The girls crowd in next to their brother. Annie has begun to cry, her face pink, her cheeks wet.

"They're not a threat," I tell the two men. "You've no cause to cuff anyone."

Mercer and Bertrand ignore us. The Amish man doesn't resist as Mercer reaches for his arm, turns him around. He places the loop of the zip tie around Adam's right wrist, pulls both arms behind his back, and yanks the plastic taut.

Mercer pats down Adam, finding nothing, then motions toward the sofa. "Sit down and do not move."

Sammy takes in the scene, his expression frightened and confused. "Datt?"

"It's all right," Adam tells his son. But he's watching the men with caution, distrust and trepidation etched into his every feature as he lowers himself onto the sofa.

Bertrand hands the shotgun back to Mercer. "As long as you do as you're told, everything will be fine," he says to the children and Adam. "Just stay calm and be quiet."

Mercer trots to the kitchen, shotgun across his chest, looks around quickly. He ducks into the mudroom, his head swiveling left and right. He then goes to the stairs and takes them two at a time to the top. We fall silent. Tension hums. The ceiling above us creaks, Mercer running from room to room, looking for Gina.

Bertrand studies Adam for a moment, then asks, "Where's Colorosa?"

The Amish man looks back at him. "The sewing room. There is a bed."

"She's not there."

Adam's brows go up. "Then I do not know."

Bertrand takes in the children. "Do any of you know where Gina is?" he asks.

The girls, standing between their *datt*'s knees, shake their heads, not making eye contact. Sammy sits at his father's side, looking at Bertrand as if the detective is some wild animal that's found its way into their home.

Good boy.

"You probably scared her and made her run away," Sammy says in a trembling voice.

Bertrand smiles at the boy. "Where would she go if she wanted to run away?"

Sammy looks from his *datt* to me, not sure what to say.

Before he can answer, I jump in. "We're wasting time," I say. "She gets away or succumbs to the cold, and this is on you."

Mercer clatters down the stairs, looking at us over the banister. "No one there."

"You check the attic?"

"That's affirm."

Grimacing, Bertrand removes zip ties from his pocket. "I hate to do this, Chief Burkholder. For the record, you are not under arrest, but you *are* being detained until we get everything figured out."

My heart begins to pound. "Do not go that route," I snap. "You've no cause."

"You've been aiding and abetting a felon," Bertrand responds. "At the very least, you have some explaining to do. For now, I need to make sure everyone stays safe."

"I'm your best hope of finding her," I tell him. "I know this farm and the surrounding area."

Bertrand reaches for my arm. "Turn around. You know the drill."

I pivot away from him. He makes a grab for me, but I'm faster and he misses. I throw myself into a run toward the mudroom. I envision my .38 in the cabinet. Top shelf. Speed loader next to it. My coat on a hook. Boots against the wall. I've gone two steps when Mercer comes at me from behind. Full-body tackle. He rams his shoulder into the small of my back. His arms go around my hips; he throws his weight against me. I go down fast, hard enough to bruise bone, no time to break my fall. My cheek strikes the floor, dazing me. I try to roll onto my back, get my feet up to kick him. But he's too strong. Too heavy. Fast for his size.

"Get off me!" I scream.

He thrusts a knee into my spine, puts his weight into it. "Stop resisting."

I'm facedown on the floor, unable to move, unable to breathe. Mercer's knee grinding into my back, pain radiating down my spine. I hear the children crying openly now. Then his hands are on my arms. Zip ties looped around my wrists and yanked tight enough to cut off the blood supply. Another layer of dread settles in my gut when strong arms grasp my ankles and secure them together.

The next thing I know I'm yanked to my feet. Mercer turns me around and shoves me onto the sofa. Feet bound, I fall unceremoniously onto the cushions. Breathing hard. Helpless and angry now. Nothing I can do about any of it.

Removing another zip tie from beneath his coat, he kneels at Adam's feet and secures the Amish man's ankles together. When he's finished, he gets to his feet, jabs a finger in Sammy's face. "If you untie them, I'll come back for you. I'll kill your dad. Your sisters. Then I'll kill you." He hefts the shotgun, stopping just short of pointing it at the boy. "You got me, you fucking little pussy?"

Sammy stares at the man, his mouth open and quivering, and he swallows hard. "*Ja.*"

I stare at Mercer, fury humming in my blood. Next to me, Adam sits unmoving, saying nothing, taking it in, but I don't miss the anger simmering in his eyes. Sammy snuggles close to his father. Crying, Annie and Lizzie have climbed onto the sofa on the other side of him, their legs curled, expressions frightened.

"*Fire!*" Bertrand shouts abruptly.

I glance over to see him striding toward the kitchen, eyes on the window. "Bitch set the shed on fire."

From where I'm sitting, I can't see the shed, but a smidgen of hope blooms in my chest.

"Shit." Mercer darts to the kitchen doorway, looks out. "Let's go."

Without another word the two men rush through the kitchen and out the back door.

CHAPTER 32

I wait until the back door slams. "Sammy! Go get a knife! From the kitchen! Quickly! Cut me loose!"

The boy's eyes go wide. "But the man said . . ." He tosses a questioning look at his *datt*.

"It's all right," Adam tells him. "They're gone. Get the wire cutters. In the drawer by the sink. Go on now."

Sammy scrambles off the sofa and darts to the kitchen. I hear drawers being opened and closed.

"By the sink! Samuel, hurry!" Adam turns to me. "Katie, who are those men?"

"Cops," I tell him. "Bad cops."

"What are you going to do?"

"I'm going to stop them." I look at him. "Where's the closest phone?"

"The Freezer. On Ithaca Road."

The community building where the Amish rent freezers to store meat. I've driven by the place dozens of times. "Too far without a vehicle," I tell him.

I'm combing my memory for something closer when he says, "It's less than a mile if you cut through the woods. There's a path."

Sammy rushes back into the room, thrusts a pair of wire cutters at us. "These?"

"*Ja,*" says Adam. "Katie first. Hurry now."

I lift my feet, thrust them at Sammy. The boy falls to his knees so fast he slides across the floor a few inches. Holding the wire cutters in both hands, he snips.

"How do I get to the path?" I ask Adam. In the back of my mind I wonder if Gina was able to get to her cell, which had been charging in the Explorer.

"Go through the pasture. Up the hill. Cut north at the big cottonwood." He seems to struggle with something for a moment. "Katie, those woods are thick. It's dark. I can take you as far as the tree."

I look at him, torn, rushed, afraid. I shake my head. "These men are dangerous. Take the children to the attic. Barricade the door. Don't let anyone in."

The zip tie securing my wrists snaps open. "Your *datt* next," I tell Sammy, and then I'm on my feet, striding toward the kitchen. "*Hurry!*"

I reach the mudroom. Through the window I see the woodshed engulfed, flames leaping thirty feet into the air. No sign of Bertrand or Mercer, but it's too dark to see much. I don't know where Gina is. I yank my coat off the hook. Shove my feet into my boots. I've just grabbed my .38 when the door bursts open.

I catch a glimpse of Bertrand rushing inside, eyes on me, lips peeled back, teeth clenched. Gun leading the way. "Drop it!" he shouts.

Stumbling back, I fire my .38 three times. The angle is bad. My aim is off. Cursing, he lunges back outside, disappears from view. The door slams. Ears ringing, I pivot and sprint to the kitchen. I'm midway through when a gunshot splits the air. The woodwork explodes a foot from my face, slivers of wood gouging my cheek. Turning, I catch a glimpse of Bertrand in the mudroom, and I race into the living room.

Adam and the children are gone. An instant of relief. Then I hear Bertrand behind me. Boots pounding. "Stop!"

Expecting a bullet in my back, I dart to the front door, yank it open. Outside, I spin, raise the .38, fire my final three shots.

Bertrand reels backward, takes cover in the kitchen.

"Katie."

I drop the .38 into my pocket, spin to see Adam emerge from the shadows, expression frightened, a muzzle-loader in his hands.

"Where are the children?" I ask.

"Basement." He places the strap of a leather pouch over my head, thrusts the long gun at me. "God be with you."

Our eyes hold for the span of a heartbeat. A crush of emotion passes between us. "You, too."

He backs away and melts into the darkness.

Hefting the muzzle-loader, I dart across the porch, leap down the steps, and then I'm sprinting across the yard, struggling through deep snow. Out of the corner of my eye, I see the orange glow of flames at the back of the house. No sign of either man.

Where the hell is Gina?

At the edge of the yard, I vault the rail fence, plunge into a drift on the other side. I trudge through, the muzzle-loader heavy in my hands, hampering my progress. Moving as fast as physically possible, I start across the pasture. A glance over my shoulder reveals the flicker of a flashlight beam in the front yard. Bertrand, looking for tracks.

Feeling exposed, I run full out, plow through another drift, nearly lose my footing, right myself just in time. I'm moving too fast for caution. If I fall, I'll lose precious seconds. If he spots me, there's no doubt he'll cut me down. I find my stride, focus on putting one foot in front of the other, doing my best to avoid deep snow.

There's just enough moonlight for me to see. That I'm armed with a muzzle-loader presents a multitude of problems. It's a single-shot weapon that can't be loaded on the fly. But if I can stop for thirty or forty seconds, I can probably get it done.

I trip on something hidden beneath the snow, go down hard. Snow in my mouth. My eyes. Hair. Every sense humming. I scramble to my feet, spitting, keep moving. Blind and exhausted. Fear pushing me. Panic nipping at my heels.

I reach the base of the hill, start up the incline. I reach an area where the wind has scoured away the snow. It's easier going; I should have been able to pick up the pace, but the terrain is steep and within minutes, I'm gasping for breath, the muzzle-loader weighing me down, my quadriceps screaming.

Gunshots ring out. No cover, so I drop to my knees, hunker down. Another shot scorches the air. In the dim moonlight, I see a dark figure silhouetted against the snow, crossing the field I just traversed. Two hundred and fifty yards away. Barely visible. Bertrand found my tracks.

I unloop the leather strap from around my neck, jam my hand inside the bag and feel around. I find three balls. A powder horn. Ticking. The rifle is an old flintlock. I've only fired one a handful of times, never loaded one. But I saw my *datt* and brother do it a hundred times when I was a kid.

Keeping an eye on Bertrand, I jam the butt into the snow, hold it in place between my knees. I yank the powder horn from the bag, set it on the snow. I go back in for a ticking patch and ball.

Another gunshot zings. I duck instinctively, then get to my feet.

Holding the muzzle away from my face, I grab the powder horn, thumb off the lid, and dump powder into the barrel. Too dark to judge the amount. My hands are shaking so violently, I spill more than I get into the muzzle. Next, I lay the ticking over the opening, set the ball on top. Sliding out the ramrod, I jam it into the hole and seat both.

I lift the rifle, place the butt against my shoulder. Finger inside the guard, I set my eye to the sight, catch a glimpse of movement. A shadow against snow. Too dark to see. Pulling in a deep breath, I let it out slowly, try to settle, squeeze the trigger.

The rifle kicks hard. The explosion deafens me. I lower the gun, snatch up the bag, throw the strap over my head. Gripping the rifle with both hands, I launch myself into a dead run. I work my way up the hill, reach the bare-branched cottonwood, lungs on fire, legs screaming. I cut right, approach the tree line at an angle. Thirty yards to go. Twenty. I search for the mouth of a path, but it's too dark to see. At the edge of the forest, I spin, scan the hillside below. Sure enough, I can just make out the dark shape against the snow-covered surface. Bertrand is less than two hundred yards away now. Gaining ground. Too close. If I weren't standing in the shadows of the trees, I'd be in plain sight. I turn and run.

The forest is an obstacle course of bramble and deadfall. Less moonlight reflecting off the snow. For several minutes, the only sound comes from my labored breaths. The squeak and thud of my footfalls. The pound of fear in my brain. Despite the physical activity, I'm cold, my hands and feet aching.

I spot the tracks an instant before I run over them. I stop, fear skittering through me. They lead northeast, deeper into the woods. Same direction I need to go. Whose are they?

"*Burkholder!*" comes a whispered voice.

I startle, my heart slamming against my ribs. Gina stands a few yards away. She's bent at the hip, hand on her knee, breaths puffing out in front of her.

"You hit?" I whisper.

"Spent." Shaking her head, she straightens, struggles to catch her breath. "Everyone okay?"

"Yep," I say. "What happened?"

"Mercer came out of the house with a shotgun. I ran." Still trying to catch her breath. "There's a pay phone through the woods. We have to—"

"I know where it is. Come on."

We break into an awkward, snow-hampered run. Breaths hissing, Gina struggles to keep up. I'm aware of the leather bag flapping against my hip. The muzzle-loader in my arms, unwieldy and heavy. It occurs to me the men will see our tracks. I consider stopping to take another shot, but there's no time. Best to keep going, call for help. Make a stand when we reach the freezer shanty.

We've covered half a mile when Gina goes down. I stop, reach for her. She clambers to her feet. In that instant of silence, I discern the pop and snap of breaking brush behind us. I glance over my shoulder, see the shifting of shadows through the trees. Bertrand. So close I can hear the rustle of clothes, the wheeze of heavy breathing.

For an instant, panic grips me. But I know these woods. I know where I am now. Minutes from Ithaca Road. I make eye contact with Gina, motion left.

We fly down a hill. Dodging trees. Moving fast. At the base, we fight our way through a drift. Holding the muzzle-loader high, I plow through snow that comes up to my hips. Gina cursing behind me. I don't wait for her. Another hundred yards and we burst into a clearing. Ithaca Road dead ahead. I glance left, spot the silhouette of the shanty fifty feet away.

I power through the ditch, hit the snow-packed road, sprint to the structure. I reach the building. Tear around the corner. Yank open the door. Cavelike darkness inside. Transferring the muzzle-loader to my left hand, I slap my free hand against the wall, seeking the switch.

Light rains down. Gina, wild-eyed and pale, enters, slams the door behind her. A dozen freezers line the wall ahead, motors buzzing. A desk and chair to my left. Sink on the right. The place smells of cold air and stale meat.

"Lock the door," I tell her. "Call 911."

Kneeling, I set the butt of the muzzle-loader on the floor, lift the leather bag from around my neck. I reach inside, grapple for the powder horn and ticking.

Gina is midway to the door when it swings open. Ken Mercer rushes inside, Glock in his hand. Eyes wild and seeking. Face red and slicked with sweat.

"Throw down that rifle!" he screams.

Without looking at him, I continue to pour powder into the muzzle-loader. Spilling too much. Hands shaking. Pulse in the red zone.

Grinding his teeth, he strides to me, kicks the flintlock from my grasp. The rifle skitters across the room and strikes the wall. "Get your fucking hands up or I will shoot you dead!" he shouts.

I raise my hands to shoulder height. A fist of fear unfurls in my gut as I get to my feet.

Mercer jabs the Glock at me. "Get against the wall and do not move."

I do as I'm told. Vaguely, I'm aware of Gina on my right, moving toward him. I toss her a don't-do-anything-stupid look, but she doesn't seem to notice and pays me no heed.

Mercer isn't fazed by her closeness. Even though she's as big a threat as me. He doesn't move away from her. Nor does he shift the gun to her. In fact, he barely spares her a glance as she crosses to him. Every ounce of his energy is focused on me. The Glock in his hand steady. Finger on the trigger.

I get an odd quiver in my chest. My heart plummets when Gina sets her hand on his arm. Even before she speaks, I know I've been had. That she lied to me. To Tomasetti. To Adam. To all of us.

"Gina." I don't even realize I'm going to speak until I hear her name. Disbelief echoes in my voice. "What are you doing?" Only after the words are out does the full extent of my naiveté strike me.

Bertrand and Mercer think I took some cash.

The memory of her words rings hard in my ears. The realization that I've been a fool hits me like a rude slap.

"I appreciate everything you did for me, Kate," she says. "I mean that. But this is my only chance. I've got to take it. I'm not going to prison."

"The money," I say. "You've had it the entire time."

"I'm sorry I lied to you." She looks at Mercer, the whisper of a smile on her mouth. "But it'll get us out of the country."

The sense of betrayal crushes me. A dump truck of lead raining down on top of me. I stare at her, trying to get my mind around the breadth and width of it. How could I have been so blind?

"Cuff her." Mercer tugs zip ties from his coat, tosses them to Gina. "Hurry up."

She catches the ties with the hand of her uninjured arm and starts toward me.

"Check her for weapons," Mercer says. "We need to get out of here before Bertrand shows up."

She starts toward me, her eyes level on mine. "Give me the .38."

"It's not too late to end this," I tell her.

"The gun, Kate." She doesn't wait. Leaning close, she reaches around me, slides the .38 from my pocket.

Across the room, Mercer crosses to the pay phone, picks up the handset, and yanks the armored cord from its nest, rendering it useless.

Gina snaps open the cylinder, shakes out the spent cartridges. "Turn around. Hands behind your back." Her gaze flicks from me to Mercer and back to me. "Play it cool and you get to walk away," she says in a low voice. "Marry Tomasetti. Have a bunch of kids. Live happily ever after."

"Does Bertrand know about you two?" I ask.

One side of her mouth curves. "He knows what he's been fed."

She loops the tie around my left wrist, draws it tight, reaches for my right hand. In the next instant, the door explodes inward. In my peripheral vision I see Mercer spin, the stainless-steel phone cord still in his hand. Gina swivels, steps back.

Bertrand enters, boots heavy on the floor. Snow on his coat. The Glock in his hand. Even from twelve feet away, I feel the tension pouring off him.

His eyes sweep from Gina and me, landing on Mercer. I see thoughts ticking in his brain. Suspicion in his eyes. Something niggles at the back of my own mind. Something important I overlooked.

"What the hell is this?" Bertrand says.

"She's going to take us to the cash," Mercer says.

Bertrand doesn't move. He shifts the gun to Gina. "Where is it?"

"Pull that trigger and you won't see a dime," she tells him.

Dark amusement plays at the corners of Bertrand's mouth. The pistol tracks to me. Level with my chest. His finger inside the guard.

I step back, raise my hands to shoulder height, zip tie dangling from my wrist. "She'll take you to it. I owe her. I'll cover for you." It's a stupid thing to say; no one believes a word. But fear is a concrete block dropped into my stomach. My brain is misfiring. There's no way they can let me live.

The tension expands. Like the air an instant before a bomb blast.

"Sheriff's department is on the way," I say.

"Do her," Mercer snaps. "Let's go."

Abruptly, Bertrand swings around to face Mercer.

"Don't!" cries Gina.

Bertrand fires three shots. Mercer staggers sideways, snarls something unintelligible, spittle flying. Blood blooms on the front of his coat. He sways, sinks to his haunches, then falls forward. For a heartbeat span we're in a vacuum. No sound or light or movement. No one breathes. Then Gina chokes out a strangled sound. Out of the corner of my eye, I see her rush to Mercer, fall to her knees.

"Ken!" she screams.

Bertrand swivels to me, raises the Glock, glances over his shoulder at Gina. "She's next," he roars. "Where's the cash?"

A thousand thoughts rush my brain. Run to the door, try to get out before he shoots me in the back. Grab Mercer's weapon. Charge Bertrand and hope he misses. All of it jumbled by fear and the knowledge none of them will work. I'm out of options and at the mercy of a psychopath.

Heart hammering, I jam my hands higher. "I know where the cash is!"

The gunshot pierces the last of my control. I stumble back, expecting pain and blood. Out of the corner of my eye I see Bertrand's head snap back. A spray of blood on the wall behind him. He drops, deadweight.

The next seconds pass in a blur of shock and the horror that comes with the sight of a violent death. The air reeks of blood and spent gunpowder. For an instant, I can't move or speak. Adrenaline sparks, but my thoughts are scattered and disjointed.

Kneeling next to Mercer, Gina lowers the Sig Sauer and shakes her head. "He's gone," she says.

I don't want to see Bertrand. Of course, I'm bound to do just that. Gathering as much of myself as I can, I go to him. The detective is lying on his back, arms sprawled, head tilted severely to one side. His mouth is a gaping black hole. The pale glow of a single remaining tooth. A growing pool of blood glistens on the concrete floor. I don't need to see more to know he's dead.

Gina's eyes meet mine. Slowly, she gets to her feet. Without looking at her weapon, she releases the magazine and crosses to me. Her hand is steady when she passes me the gun.

"You know I don't have the money, right?" she asks.

My hand is far from steady when I take the pistol.

She places the clip in my palm. I reseat the magazine, taking a moment to force my thoughts back into some semblance of order. I don't put the gun away.

Needing air, I cross to the door and open it, the cold be damned. A thousand stars stare down at me, seeing everything. In the distance, I hear the rise and fall of a lone siren.

"I guess I should tell you I'm relieved you found your gun," I say.

"When they broke down the door, I went out the window." She shrugs. "I figured you'd locked it up in your vehicle. So while Bertrand and Mercer were inside, I busted out the Explorer's window, got it out of the console."

I stare at her, struggling to believe her, trying to put everything that happened into some kind of order that makes sense. "Why did they think you'd taken the money?"

"Because I let them." She glances over her shoulder at Mercer's body. "Ken Mercer was in love with me. That made it easier."

"How did they find you?"

"Mercer had my cell number. The burner. I knew he'd use that to find me."

The floor tilts beneath my feet. "You set them up."

"I did what I had to do."

"You could have gotten all of us killed," I tell her. "Adam. The children."

"I didn't." Contempt simmers in her eyes when she looks at Bertrand's body. "They would have come for me regardless of the money. I knew too much; I could put all of them in prison. But without the promise of eighty thousand dollars, they would have killed me on sight, or hired some thug to do it, no questions asked. Their presumption of my knowing the location of the cash kept us alive, my friend."

"Forgive me if I don't thank you."

"Once you've had a chance to think about it, you will." Her mouth twists, but she doesn't quite manage a smile.

CHAPTER 33

It never ceases to amaze me how drastically life can change in a very short period of time. How fragile and yet resilient that life is. How much all of us take for granted.

In the last hour, two Holmes County sheriff's deputies arrived on scene, tire chains jangling, sirens and lights blazing. By all rights, I should have cuffed Gina and taken her into custody. I didn't. The first deputy to arrive is an acquaintance of mine; we've worked together a few times over the years. He didn't question me when I asked him to hold off on taking Gina into custody.

I'm still not sure she's telling the whole truth about Mercer and Bertrand, about the money, about any of it. The one thing I do know is that if she hadn't stopped Bertrand when she did, I wouldn't be here to ponder any of it.

Gina and I are standing on the stoop outside the front door of the freezer shanty when I hear the whine of a snowmobile engine. I watch as Tomasetti slides to a stop behind a Holmes County Sheriff's Department SUV and shuts down the motor. Then he's off the snow machine and striding toward me, working off the helmet and gloves, letting them fall to the snow. I don't remember crossing to him. The next thing I know I'm in his arms. For the first time in what seems like hours, I'm warm and safe. My heart is filled with hope and the knowledge that everything is going to be okay.

I close my eyes, but with Tomasetti close, the darkness is soft and I'm ensconced. "Took you long enough to get here," I whisper.

"You okay?" he whispers.

"I am now."

"Bertrand and Mercer?" he asks.

"Dead." I tell him about the scene inside. "If Gina hadn't stopped him—"

"She's still in a lot of trouble." His eyes flick toward the building, where the woman in question is leaning next to the door, smoking a cigarette she must have bummed from one of the deputies.

"Apparently, that is the theme she's been keeping," I say.

"There are a lot of cops who have a lot of questions for you. BCI, too. Maybe even the feds."

"I figured that would be the case," I tell him. "I can handle it."

"I know you can." He stares at me for what feels like a long time. As if he's looking for something expected that isn't there, and he's surprised by its absence. "Just so you know, Denny and I have your back."

"I appreciate that." It's a pat response. At the moment, it's the only one I can manage. My emotions are too close to the surface. I don't quite trust my voice to betray me.

Tomasetti continues, "BCI took Frank Monaghan into custody twenty minutes ago."

"Top of the food chain."

"There's more to come." He runs his hands down my arms, squeezes my forearms gently. "You did good, Kate." He grimaces. "All the lies aside, Colorosa, too."

Looking at him, I get that unsettling quiver in my chest that eases just short of taking my breath. Surprising me, he reaches out and sets his hand against my cheek. I press my face into his palm, and for the span of several heartbeats, he simply gazes back at me.

"I'm glad you're okay," he whispers. "I'm sorry I left. I should have—"

"You did everything you were supposed to do." Turning my head slightly, I press a kiss to his palm. "No one expected an ambush at the farm."

"Yeah." He looks away, thoughtful, and for the first time I catch a glimpse of his own emotions simmering just beneath the surface. "I think you and I have a few things to talk about," he says quietly.

"We do." I take his hand. "I may have some soul searching to do when it comes to Gina, but I know exactly where I stand with you."

I want to say something about the preciousness of life, the importance of the relationships we forge and how both of those things are intertwined and reliant upon the decisions we make along the way. But my voice fails. Tears heat at the backs of my eyes. The jangle of a harness rigging, the stomp of shod hooves, and the whoosh of steel runners through snow saves me from making a fool of myself.

I glance away from Tomasetti to see a horse and sleigh coming down the road, traveling a little too fast for conditions.

"Looks like Adam Lengacher," Tomasetti says.

I nod, moved by the Amish man's presence. "I need to talk to him."

"You might want to let him know this is a crime scene—"

"I won't let him get too close." I turn away and start toward the road, where Adam has stopped the sleigh.

"Katie, what happened?" Adam climbs down and starts toward me. "I heard gunshots. Are you all right? Gina?"

"Both of us are fine." As I move toward him, I find myself looking for Sammy and the girls, anticipating the soft cuff of pleasure the sight of them brings. "The kids?"

"They are fine. Still in the basement. Sammy stayed behind to look after his sisters."

Of course he did. Sweet, sweet child.

An awkward moment ensues. To embrace Adam would go against propriety. A handshake doesn't seem sufficient. I buck protocol and embrace him. As expected, he stiffens; his arms remain at his sides. Still, when his eyes fall on mine, they're warm with understanding and affection.

I step away from him. "Thank you for coming. For . . . everything."

His gaze travels to the metal building. "The men?"

"We stopped them," I tell him.

He nods, not asking the obvious question. His expression tells me he knows the men met a bad end. That either Gina or I was responsible for it. He lets it go.

"Adam!"

I glance over my shoulder to see Gina striding toward us, moving at a fast clip through ankle-deep snow. Dark hair flying. Mouth pulled into a smile that would have been dazzling had it not been tempered with the stress of the last hours. Her eyes are riveted to Adam and lit with pleasure.

Standing next to me, the Amish man holds his ground and watches her approach. He shoves both hands into the pockets of his coat, looking everywhere except at her. "*Do kumma druvvel,*" he murmurs. Here comes trouble.

I grin. "You've always had a soft spot for it."

"I guess so."

Gina reaches him and, without hesitation, throws her arms around him. It doesn't even cross her mind that it's inappropriate for her to press a kiss to his cheek. But that's Gina for you. She's an "all in" kind of woman. You get what you get.

"Is everyone all right?" she asks, pulling away, holding him at arm's length. "The kids?"

Adam is not unaffected by her embrace. His mouth just a few inches from her ear, he murmurs something I can't quite make out. I don't profess to know what he's thinking or feeling. Likely a combination of attraction and affection, both of which are tempered by the tenets of his culture and the gentility ingrained into his heart from the day of his birth.

"The children are fine," he tells her.

"I'm glad." Her hands slide down his arms, pausing when they meet his, and she grasps both of his in hers. "You know, I never liked little kids. They're weird and they smell bad and ask nosy questions." At his confused expression, her smile augments into a grin. "Sammy sort of changed my perspective."

Adam smiles. "I'm glad he was able to open your heart."

"Will you tell him goodbye for me?" she asks.

"I will." He works his hands from hers and lets them fall to his sides. "Your troubles . . . is everything going to be all right?"

She grins, but this time her eyes are shadowed. She's afraid of the things she's facing. The legal maze that lies ahead. Possible jail time. The end of the only career she's ever known.

Raising her hand, she pokes his chest with her finger. "I'm always all right, Adam Lengacher. Don't you forget that."

Adam isn't sure how to respond and he says nothing.

"Thank you for everything," she says after a moment. "For saving my ass. For letting me stay in your home. For being so kind to me."

He looks away from her. "You are welcome."

She offers a thoughtful smile. “Under different circumstances, I might've—”

“No, you wouldn't,” I cut in, but I keep my voice light.

Adam chuckles, but he doesn't look at me. All of his attention is focused on Gina, as if she's some beautiful and rare animal that isn't quite safe to touch. “Remember, Gina, God is there to give us strength for every hill we have to climb.”

Her bravado falls away. “I've got plenty of hills to climb in the coming weeks.” She looks away, blinking, then raises her gaze to his. “I hope you find a nice girl, Adam, and have a few more kids. I hope she makes you happy.”

Tipping his hat, the Amish man backs away from her, breaking eye contact only when he turns to climb into the sleigh. He raises his hand for a wave, and with a final look over his shoulder, he snaps the lines and drives away.

The area is lit up with emergency lights now. An ambulance and half a dozen vehicles from the Holmes County Sheriff's Department, the Ohio State Highway Patrol, and BCI are parked along Ithaca Road, engines rumbling, clouds of exhaust billowing in the frigid air.

Gina, Tomasetti, and I are standing a few yards from the freezer shanty, looking out at the scene. The Holmes County coroner and crime scene technicians have arrived. We're watching Doc Coblentz lug a suitcase-size case through the snow when I notice the unmarked SUV pull up. No one speaks as the two agents get out of the vehicle and approach.

A middle-aged African American man wearing a navy parka, dark slacks, and a trooper hat emblazed with the Bureau of Criminal Investigation logo stops at the top of the steps. A similarly dressed woman wearing a stocking hat pauses next to him.

Tomasetti extends his hand to both of them. No introductions are made; none are needed. Just a minute or two of weather-related small talk that's stilted and uncomfortable. Neither of them is here to talk about the cold or snow, but to arrest one of their own, a duty no cop relishes.

After a minute, the female agent reaches into a compartment on her belt and removes a pair of handcuffs. Next to me, I hear Gina's intake of breath, the sound of her slowly releasing it as she shores up for what's next.

"Gina Colorosa?" the female agent asks.

Gina squares her shoulders and steps forward, her expression impassive. "I'm Colorosa."

"We've got a warrant for your arrest," the woman tells her. "Turn around and put your hands behind your back."

I'd expected some slightly improper retort from Gina. Something to let us know she'll be doing this on her terms, not theirs. She's the one with the goods, after all, and if we don't like it, the lot of us can go to hell.

Instead, she gives me a single, defiant smile. "See you around, Burkholder."

Lowering her chin nearly to her chest, she turns her back to the woman and offers her wrists. "Let's get this over with."

CHAPTER 34

TWO WEEKS LATER

Life is the greatest teacher of all things wise despite the fact that the vast majority of us are reluctant students. One of the most important lessons time has taught me is that of appreciation. Not just the big moments—those milestones of life—but the small signposts that oftentimes go uncelebrated. Those are the moments I've learned to value. Those snatches of time spent in some mundane but meaningful way that might otherwise be forgotten.

It's been two weeks since the ordeal at The Freezer with Damon Bertrand and Ken Mercer. Both men were pronounced dead at the scene. As Gina Colorosa was being arrested and taken into custody in Painters Mill, a secret task force spearheaded by the Bureau of Criminal Investigation was serving multiple warrants in and around Columbus. Six individuals were arrested that night, including Deputy Chief Frank Monaghan, a Franklin County judge, and four police officers, one of whom was a detective. Charges included witness tampering, obstruction of justice, extortion, bribery, making false statements to investigators, deprivation of rights under color of law, and manslaughter. The following day, the acting chief disbanded the vice unit, terminated seven additional police officers, and reassigned all remaining cops who'd been part of the unit.

I haven't spoken to Gina since her arrest. According to Tomasetti, she was transported to Columbus and booked into the Franklin County jail. During her arraignment, she was formally charged with a multitude of serious charges, including witness tampering, obstruction of justice, making false statements to investigators, and manslaughter. The presiding judge denied bail, citing her as a flight risk and a danger to the community, but I believe that as Gina and her attorney work with investigators and prosecutors, chances are some of the charges will be reduced or dismissed and at some juncture she'll be granted bail. She's a key piece of the state's case against many of the officers who were indicted, after all, and an important witness whose testimony will undoubtedly affect the outcome of what will likely become dozens of cases.

In the two weeks since, I've spent a lot of time thinking about what happened. What I could have done differently. The things I would change if I could, now and ten years ago.

This afternoon, I'm sitting at my desk in my cramped office at the police station, a little too thoughtful, but making a valiant attempt to get caught up on the myriad projects I fell behind on while I was gone. My mind isn't on the task at hand. Since returning to work, I've mostly been going through the motions. I've spent much of my time quietly appreciating the normalcy of this life I've chosen. That I'm alive to live it. That I have people who love me—and that I love them in return.

I hear my officers' voices coming from the reception area down the hall. Glock and Skid are going at it over Sunday's Super Bowl game and a halftime show that didn't quite measure up. Pickles and T.J. are debating the severity of the recent blizzard versus the infamous blizzard of 1978. So far, Pickles is winning. A few feet away, Tomasetti is on his knees next to the printer stand I ordered three months ago and never assembled, using a screwdriver to secure a shelf.

Neither of us will admit it, but he's kept a close eye on me the last couple of weeks. Other than to update me on the happenings of the case, we haven't talked too much about it. We haven't discussed my relationship with Gina, how close we'd once been, and how much influence she had on my life. I suppose I'm still trying to figure some things out. I can't help but wonder: If I'd been a better friend and stayed in Columbus, would I have been able to prevent her from making the mistakes she did? Or is it presumptuous for me to think I ever had any control at all?

"Chief?"

I look up to see Mona come through my office door, ponytail bouncing, a stack of mail in one hand, a large overnight box in the other. "Janine Fourman called to remind us she's still got an abandoned vehicle parked in front of her shop and she would like us to tow it."

"You mean the Prius that's buried in the six feet of snow left behind by the plow?" I take the mail from her, page through it, and toss half into the recycle bin beneath my desk.

"That's the one." She grins. "Want me to ticket it?"

"Is the fire lane clear?"

"Yes, ma'am."

"Who owns the Prius?"

"Tom Skanks."

Tom is the owner of the Butterhorn Bakery, across the street from Janine's shop. He's a good man, an honest merchant, and he makes the best apple fritters in the state. Sometimes, when he has leftover doughnuts at the end of the day, he's been known to deliver them to the police department.

"Tell Tom he has seventy-two hours to move his vehicle. If he needs longer, give it to him. Let him know if he needs a hand digging it out, Tomasetti is pretty decent with a shovel."

Tomasetti looks up from his work. "I heard that."

"What about Janine?" Mona asks.

"If she gives you any lip, ticket her for being an obnoxious fool."

Mona chortles. "Roger that."

"Would you let everyone know there's a staff meeting in twenty minutes?" I ask.

"You got it, Chief."

When she's gone, I pick up the overnight box, shake it, and then pull the tab. Paper crinkles as I pull out the slightly heavy flat object and unwrap it. A tastefully framed photo looms into view. The quick punch of remembrance takes my breath.

It's a photograph of Gina and me taken the evening we graduated from the police academy. I've never seen it before; I have no idea who took it. But I remember the moment with clarity. We're standing in front of the stage where the podium and chairs were set up. We're in full dress uniform—white shirt, tie, and hat—hair pulled back into ponytails at our napes. Gina leans against me, her arm draped comfortably around my shoulders. I've just kissed my badge and I'm holding it up as if to tell the world "Look out! Here I come!" Our heads are thrown back in laughter. Remembering, I smile despite the pang of melancholy in my chest.

Gina and I were opposites from different worlds, but our minds—our hearts—were wide open, to each other, to the world around us, to a future that would be better than the present or the past. She was the girl who had the audacity to poke fun at my Amishness and in the same breath offer me food, a place to stay, and her friendship. She left no doubt in my mind that I would be a fool not to join her. I was the girl life had left behind. The damaged soul on the run from my own identity, a mistake I would never reconcile, and a family that would never love me the way I needed to be loved.

The woman I got to know out at the Lengacher farm isn't the girl I met that night at the diner. The girl I'd loved like a sister and with every fiber of my young heart. But neither is she the corrupt cop she was the night she fled Columbus and wrecked her truck on that snowy township road. I like to think she's somewhere in the middle now, that she'll find her way to a better place.

"Now, there's trouble waiting to happen."

I look up to see Tomasetti approach, his eyes on the picture in my hands.

"It was taken the night we graduated from the police academy," I tell him.

"I think I saw the movie." He comes around behind me.

I elbow him at the mention of the old comedy, but the comment makes me laugh. "Seems like a lifetime ago," I say. "We were so . . . young."

"Not that long ago in the scope of things," he says.

I look down at the photo. "We were so . . . excited. So full of dreams. Plans for the future. No holds barred." I stare at the photo, surprised and embarrassed when I have to blink back tears. "We made a lot of mistakes. Not just Gina."

"Just so you know . . . the two of you don't exactly have the market cornered in that area. Some people refer to that particular weakness as being human."

I nod, my emotions settling. "There was a time when she was a good cop."

"Tough to see someone you care about go down the wrong road."

"She was my best friend. I was closer to her than I was to my own sister."

We fall silent, our thoughts crisscrossing the air between us.

"Do you think she has a shot at getting immunity?" I ask.

"I think if she plays her cards right, the prosecutor will come through in some way." He shrugs. "Ask for a lot, get a little. You know how it works." His mouth twitches. "That's not to mention the force of her personality."

I smile, but I'm still thoughtful. "We take so much for granted. You always think you have time to do the things you want to do, or say the things you want to say to someone. So you put it off, and you never expect fate to intervene. Or old mistakes to come back to haunt you. You never expect to run out of time."

He tilts his head, looks at me with a little too much intensity. "A lot of weighty philosophy coming out of the chief of police's office this afternoon."

"Everything that happened . . . I guess I've been thinking about what's really important."

"And what is that?"

I scoot back my chair, get to my feet, and face him. "Us," I say simply. "Our future." I look around. "This moment. The people around us. The people we love."

"Maybe it's time we did something about it," he says.

I'm keenly aware that the door to my office is open. That my team of officers are just down the hall and it would be unseemly for us to embrace in plain view. Then again, there's no one close enough to see us. When his arms go around me, I don't complain.

"Are you proposing?" I ask.

"For the second or third time now. I've lost count."

"Tomasetti, I think that might be a record."

"I wouldn't have to humiliate myself like this if you'd stop dragging your feet and get with the program."

I can't help it; I laugh. "This is one of those moments," I whisper. "You realize that, right?"

"In that case, what do you say you make short work of this staff meeting and make tracks to the farm so we can discuss this a little more in depth?" he says quietly.

"I think that's the best idea you've had all day."

Turn the page for a sneak peek at Linda Castillo's new novel

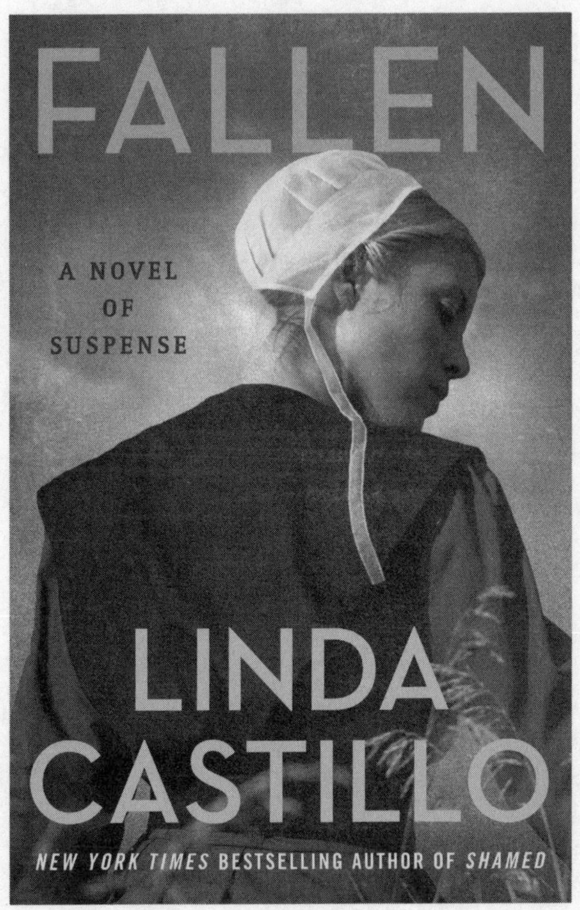

FALLEN
A NOVEL
OF
SUSPENSE
LINDA
CASTILLO
NEW YORK TIMES BESTSELLING AUTHOR OF SHAMED

Available Summer 2021

CHAPTER 1

She knew coming back after so many years would be difficult, especially when she'd left so much hurt behind when she departed. She'd hurt the people she loved, never wasting a moment on the notion of regret. She'd sullied relationships that should have meant the world to her. She'd blamed others when misfortune reared its head, never admitting she might've been wrong. Mistakes had always been the one thing she was good at, and she'd made them in spades.

Once upon a time she'd called Painters Mill home. She'd belonged here, been part of the community, and she'd never looked too far beyond the cornfields, the quaint farmhouses and winding back roads. Once, this little town had been the center of her universe. It was the place where her family still lived—a family she hadn't been part of for twelve years. Like it or not, her connection to this place and its people ran deep—too deep, in her opinion—and it was a link she could no longer deny no matter how hard she tried.

This saccharine little town with its all-American main street and pastoral countryside hadn't always been kind. In the eyes of the seventeen-year-old girl she'd been, Painters Mill was a place of brutal lessons, rules she couldn't abide by, and crushing recriminations by people who, like her, possessed the power to hurt.

It took years for her to realize all the suffering and never-lived-up-to expectations were crap. Like her *mamm* always said: Time is a relevant thing and life is a cruel teacher. It was one of few things her mother had been right about.

Painters Mill hadn't changed a lick. Main Street, with its charming storefronts and Amish tourist shops, still dominated the historic downtown. The bucolic farms and back roads were still dotted with the occasional buggy or hay wagon. Coming back was like entering a time warp. It was as if she'd never been gone, and everything that had happened since was nothing more than a dream. The utter sameness of this place unsettled her in ways she hadn't expected.

The Willowdell Motel sure hadn't changed. Same trashy façade and dusty gravel parking lot. Inside, the room was still dressed in the same god-awful orange carpet. Same bad wall art. Same shoddily concealed cigarette smoke and the vague smell of moldy towels. It was a place she shouldn't have known at the age of seventeen.

If life had taught her one lesson that stood out above the rest, it was to look forward, not back. To focus on goals instead of regrets. It took a lot of years and even more sacrifice, but she'd clawed her way out of the cesspit she'd made of her life. She'd done well—better than she ever imagined possible—and she'd forged a good life for herself. Did any of that matter now? Was it enough?

Tossing her overnight bag onto the bed, Rachael Schwartz figured she'd waited long enough to make things right. The time had come for her to rectify the one wrong that still kept her up nights. The one bad decision she hadn't been able to live down. The one that, for years now, pounded at the back of her brain with increasing intensity. She didn't know how things would turn out or if she'd get what she wanted. The one thing she *did* know was that she had to try. However this turned out, good or bad or somewhere in between, she figured she would simply have to live with it.

The knock on the door came at two A.M. Even as she threw the covers aside and rolled from the bed, she knew who it was. A smile touched her mouth as she crossed to the door. Recognition kicked when she checked the peephole. The quiver of pleasure that followed didn't quite cover the ping of trepidation. She swung open the door.

"Well, it's about damn time," she said.

A faltering smile followed by a flash of remembrance. "I didn't think I'd ever see you again."

She grinned. "No such luck."

"Sorry about the time. Can I come in?"

"I think you'd better. We've a lot to discuss." Stepping back, she motioned her visitor inside. "I'll get the light."

Her heart strummed as she started for the night table next to the bed. All the words she'd practiced saying for months now tumbled in her brain like dice. Something not quite right, but then what had she expected?

"I hope you brought the wine," she said as she bent to turn on the lamp.

The blow came out of nowhere. A sunburst of white light and sound, like a stick of dynamite igniting in her head. A splintering of pain. Her knees hit the floor. Shock and confusion rattled through her.

She reached out, grabbed the night table. A sound escaped her as she struggled to her feet, teetered left. She turned, spotted the bat, saw the other things she'd missed before. Dark intent. Buried rage. Dear God, how could she have been so naive?

The bat came down again. Air whooshed. She staggered right, tried to escape it. Not fast enough. The blow landed hard on her shoulder. Her clavicle snapped. The lightning bolt of pain took her breath. Mewling, she turned, tried to run, fell to her knees.

Footsteps behind her. More to come. She swiveled, raised her hands to protect herself. The bat struck her forearm. An explosion of pain. The shock pulsing like a strobe.

"Don't!" she cried.

Her attacker drew back. Teeth clenched. The dead eyes of a taxidermist's glass. The bat struck her cheekbone, the force snapping her head back. She bit her tongue, tasted blood. Darkness crowded her vision. The sensation of falling into space. The floor rushed up, struck her shoulder. The scrape of carpet against her face. The knowledge that she was injured badly. That it wasn't going to stop. That she'd made a serious miscalculation.

The shuffle of feet on carpet. The hiss of a labored breath. Fighting dizziness, she reached for the bed, fisted the bedsheet, tried to pull herself up. The bat struck the mattress inches from her hand. Still a chance to get away. Terrible sounds tore from her throat as she threw herself onto the bed, scrabbled across. On the other side, she grabbed the lamp, yanked the cord from the wall.

The bat slammed against her back. A sickening wet-meat punch that took her breath. An electric shock ran the length of her spine. Unconsciousness beckoned. She swiveled, tried to swing the lamp, but she was too injured and it clattered to the floor.

"Get away!" she cried.

She rolled off the bed, tried to land on her feet. Her legs buckled and she went down. She looked around. A few feet away, the door stood open. Pale light spilling in. If she could reach it . . . Freedom, she thought. Life. She crawled toward it, pain running like a freight train through her body.

A sound to her left. Shoes against carpet. Legs coming around the bed. Blocking her way. "No!" she screamed, a primal cry of outrage and terror. No time to brace.

The bat struck her ribs with such force she was thrown onto her side. An animalistic sound ripped from her throat. Pain piled atop pain. She opened her mouth, tried to suck in air, swallowed blood.

A wheeze escaped her as she rolled onto her back. The face that stared down at her was a mindless machine. Flat eyes filled with unspeakable purpose. No intellect. No emotion. And in that instant, she knew she was going to die. She knew her life was going to end here in this dirty motel and there wasn't a goddamn thing she could do to help herself.

See you in hell, she thought.

She didn't see the next blow coming.

Pam Lary

LINDA CASTILLO is the *New York Times* bestselling author of the Kate Burkholder novels, including *Sworn to Silence,* which was adapted into a Lifetime Original Movie starring Neve Campbell as Kate Burkholder. She is the recipient of numerous industry awards including a nomination by the International Thriller Writers for Best Hardcover, the Daphne du Maurier Award of Excellence, and a nomination for the RITA. In addition to writing, Castillo's other passion is horses. She lives in Texas with her husband.